ALSO BY ADRIANA TRIGIANI

FICTION

The House of Love

Tony's Wife

Kiss Carlo

All the Stars in the Heavens

The Supreme Macaroni Company

The Shoemaker's Wife

Viola in the Spotlight

Brava, Valentine

Viola in Reel Life

Very Valentine

Home to Big Stone Gap

Rococo

The Queen of the Big Time

Lucia, Lucia

Milk Glass Moon

Big Cherry Holler

Big Stone Gap

NON-FICTION

Don't Sing at the Table: Life Lessons from My Grandmothers

Cooking with My Sisters (co-author)

SCREENPLAYS

Very Valentine

Big Stone Gap

THE
GOOD LEFT
UNDONE

Adriana Trigiani

MICHAEL JOSEPH

PENGUIN MICHAEL JOSEPH

UK | USA | Canada | Ireland | Australia
India | New Zealand | South Africa

Penguin Michael Joseph is part of the Penguin Random House group of companies
whose addresses can be found at global.penguinrandomhouse.com

Penguin
Random House
UK

First published in the United States of America by Dutton,
an imprint of Penguin Random House LLC 2022
First published in Great Britain by Penguin Michael Joseph 2022

001

Printed and bound in Great Britain by Clays Ltd, Elcograf S.p.A.

The authorized representative in the EEA is Penguin Random House Ireland,
Morrison Chambers, 32 Nassau Street, Dublin D02 YH68

A CIP catalogue record for this book is available from the British Library

HARDBACK ISBN: 978–0–241–56584–1
TRADE PAPERBACK ISBN: 978–0–241–56585–8

www.greenpenguin.co.uk

For Lucia

PART ONE

Let whoever longs to attain eternal life
in heaven heed these warnings:

When considering the past, contemplate these things:

The evil done

The good left undone

The time wasted

PROLOGUE

―――――――

𝕶𝖆𝖗𝖚𝖗, 𝕵𝖓𝖉𝖎𝖆

LONG, LONG AGO

The mountain was a tabernacle with one door. Behind that door, beneath cool black caverns chiseled deep into the earth, lay the richest veins of corundum, pyrite, and rubies in all of southern Asia.

Outside the mouth of the mine, the sun blistered the red ground stamped with footprints of all sizes. The scents of cloves and clay hung in a haze so thick, it was impossible to see the road. Gem traders were gathering nearby in the village of Karur to await the haul when they turned toward the mountain. They heard the braying of the elephant, a mournful sound filled with longing, like the low throttle of a trumpet in the dark. When the beast's massive head appeared in the entrance of the mine, her wailing grew louder and echoed through the hills.

The elephant's eyes were clouded with a white film from the cataracts of old age. Burgundy streaks of dried blood where she had been beaten with chains marked her ample coat. Her front and back legs were *harnessed with thick hemp ropes secured with iron clamps that dug into her soft gray skin. She pulled a massive flatbed piled high with rock, speckled with raw rubies.*

The mahout was slight of build, his skin the color of cinnamon. He draped himself over the elephant's back as the iron bit attached to the lead chains swelled in the animal's mouth. The elephant shook her head to loosen the bit. Her master tightened his grip.

The elephant stopped. She was neither inside the mine nor outside of it.

"Jao!" the mahout shouted as the prop timbers across the entrance entrapped him. The elephant ignored his command. The mahout whipped her with the slack of the chain as he lay on top of her. "Jao!"

The animal stood firm.

For the first time in her long life, the elephant did not obey the mahout's command. She did not buckle under the lash of the chain; instead, she lifted her head and raised her trunk to find the way forward.

The elephant remembered the field of sweetgrass on the banks of the Amaravati River. The memory of it gave the beast the strength to pull the flatbed out of the mine and into the light.

CHAPTER 1

Viareggio, Italy

Now

Matelda Roffo closed her eyes and tried to remember what happened next. Something happened to the mahout, that much she knew. Sadly, the details of the bedtime story her grandfather had told her had slipped away with the rest of the nonessential information her mind could no longer retain. Old age was a box of surprises and not the good kind. Why hadn't she written down the story of the elephant? She'd meant to, so many times, but never got around to it. Why was she such a procrastinator? Who would know the ending? Nino! She would call her brother in America! But his mind was shot too. Who would tell the story of the elephant when she was gone? A family was only as strong as their stories.

Matelda's grandfather Pietro Cabrelli, Toscano by birth, had been a gem cutter and a goldsmith. He created chalices, patens, and pyxes for the Vatican using the most precious jewels and metals on earth, but he did not own them. Cabrelli worked on commission set by the buyer. His wife, Netta, was not impressed. "You might as well sweep the streets of Roma because you'd be paid the same for your trouble."

Every day after school, Matelda had joined her grandfather in the workroom of his shop. She sat in the windowsill with her feet resting on the radiator, quietly observing him. Cabrelli worked over an open blue flame, brazing the gold into shapes when he wasn't measuring, cutting, or polishing the stones to be inlaid into their settings. He wore a leather work apron, a magnifying glass around his neck, a pencil tucked behind his ear, and he carried a chisel in his back pocket. The first music Matelda heard was the hum of the bruting wheel, a high-pitched sound similar to a detaché on the violin. Cabrelli would hold a shard of stone no bigger than her fingernail against the coarse surface to polish it. To pass the time, Cabrelli taught his granddaughter to study gems through the loupe. Matelda was delighted every time the light in the facets created a kaleidoscope that played through the colors of the stone. Matelda had fun in the shop, but she also had responsibilities. It was her job to open the windows when Cabrelli soldered the metals, and to close them when he was done.

There was a map of the world on the wall of the workroom where Cabrelli had circled the most productive ruby mines. He showed her places in South America, China, and Africa, but his finger would eventually trace back to India, where he had drawn the most circles. Cabrelli worked with rubies because the Holy Roman Church favored red. He was certain his creations were sparked by the divine. To encrust jewels on a monstrance that held the Blessed Sacrament was to imbue it with the properties of faith and time.

Matelda squeezed her eyes shut and leaned forward as she gripped the church pew, inhaling the scents of beeswax and frankincense, which seemed to jolt her sense memory. Instead of praying in the silence between the distribution of Holy Communion and the final blessing, she scrolled through the hard drive of her brain back to the days when her parents, grandparents, and baby brother lived in the same house and walked together every Sunday to this church.

Bits and pieces of her grandfather's India began to shake loose in

Matelda's mind. The miners chewed on honeycomb to stay awake when working long hours in the dark. Pigeon blood rubies were the color of ripe purple grapes. Pink clouds floated in a lapis sky.

At night, after the family ate dinner together, her parents would go for a walk, leaving her grandfather to tell the children a bedtime story. Pietro Cabrelli stacked pillows on the floor to represent the mountain, and wood blocks to represent the rocks from the mine. He would reach into his pocket for his handkerchief and press it against his face to dramatize the sweltering heat. He performed all the parts, using different voices for the characters, like an actor in a play. Cabrelli even became the elephant. He lurched around the room, swinging his arm back and forth to imitate the trunk of the beast.

"Matelda!" her friend Ida Casciacarro whispered as she gave her a gentle shove.

Matelda opened her eyes.

"You fell asleep."

Matelda whispered back, "I was thinking."

"You fell asleep."

No use arguing with Ida. The pair sat together in the same pew for daily Mass, their routine set in stone like the fleur-de-lis tiles embedded in the granite floor of the church. They stood, bowed their heads, and blessed themselves as the priest cut an imaginary cross through the air. They genuflected together as the morning bells of Chiesa San Paolino pealed the same ancient Kyrie that summoned the women to Lauds when they were girls.

You didn't need a clock to tell time in Viareggio; you lived by the bells and the baker. Umberto Ennico pulled trays of buttery cornetti out of the oven as Don Scarelli began the Mass. By the time the service was over, the puff pastries had cooled and Umberto had brushed them with an apricot glaze so they would be ready for pickup by the devout on their way home.

"Let's stop for pastry and coffee," Ida suggested, pulling her scarf over her head and tying it under her chin as the ladies walked together.

"Not today."

"But it's your birthday."

"I'm sorry, Ida. Anina is coming over."

"Well, another time, then." Ida tilted her head back and examined her friend through her bifocals. "Promise?"

"I promise."

Ida reached into her pocket and handed her friend a small parcel tied with a ribbon.

"Why do you do this?"

"Don't get excited. It's nothing." Ida buried her hands in the sleeves of her wool car coat like the priest buried his hands in the sleeves of his cassock when he delivered a sermon. "Go ahead. Open it."

"What's this?" Matelda shook the white plastic vial of capsules.

"Probiotics. These will change your life."

"I like my life."

"You will like it better on probiotics. Don't take my word for it. Ask your doctor. It's all about gut health these days."

"Why do you spend your money on me?"

"You're impossible to buy for. You have everything."

"Ida, if you don't have everything you want by the time you're eighty-one years old, you're probably not going to get it."

Ida gave her friend a quick kiss on each cheek before turning to hike up the steep cobblestone street to her home. The pink scarf slipped off Ida's head, and her white hair ruffled in the wind. The Metrione/Casciacarros were hard workers, sturdily built people who worked in the silk mill when it was a big operation. Matelda remembered when her friend had black hair and sprinted up the hill after a long shift. *When did we get old?* Matelda wondered.

CHAPTER 2

The village of Viareggio was set on the shores of the Ligurian Sea, on the cusp of Il Tirreno Mare, south of the Gulf of Genoa and north of the Amalfi coast. The candy-colored villas with a view of the sea were shaded by a grove of pine trees with tall, spindly trunks topped by bouffants of green foliage. Viareggio Beach unfurled on the west coast of Italy like a rope of emeralds.

The scents of charred eucalyptus wood and sulfur lingered in the air as Matelda climbed the rickety steps to the boardwalk. Carnevale had officially ended the night before when the fireworks turned to ash in the black sky. The last of the tourists had left the beach before sunrise. The pink Ferris wheel was still. The carousel horses were frozen in midair. The only sound she heard was the flap of the tarps over the empty vendor stands.

Alone on the boardwalk, Matelda leaned against the railing, where she observed curls of smoke from the abandoned firepits on the beach drifting up to the heavens like offerings. The overcast sky blurred into the horizon, where it became one with the silver sea. She heard the blare of a foghorn as a sleek ocean liner appeared in the distance, rippling the surf in streaks of foam. The graceful ship glided past, pulling the banner of daybreak over the water. All her life, Matelda waited for the great ships and considered spotting one good luck. She couldn't remember where she learned it; it was something she always knew.

Come back, Matelda thought as the white ship with a maroon hull and midnight blue trim sailed south. Too late. The ship was on its way to somewhere warm. Matelda was done with winter. It would not be long until the turquoise waves returned under a cloudless sky in springtime. How she looked forward to walks on the beach when the weather was warm.

Matelda typically took a short stroll after church in the morning to shop for the day's meals, and a long walk in the afternoon to think. These rituals had shaped her days in the last chapter of her life, after she retired from her bookkeeping position at Cabrelli Jewelers. Matelda took the time to get her house in order. She didn't want to leave her children with the stacks of paperwork and rooms of furniture her parents had left behind after they died. She wanted to prepare her children for the inevitable as best she could.

Perhaps Matelda felt blessed having dodged the virus that had hobbled Bergamo to the north—after all, a virus that targets the elderly certainly had her number. She was sanguine about the situation because she had no choice. Fate was a wrecking ball. She didn't know when it would swing through to do its damage; she was only certain, from experience, that it would.

The habit of examining her conscience, instilled by the nuns when she was a child, hadn't left her. Matelda reflected on past hurts done to her and took stock of those she had perpetrated on others. Tuscans might live in the moment, but the past lived in them. Even if that weren't true, there were reminders tucked in every corner of her hometown. She knew Viareggio and its people as well as she knew her own body; in a sense, they were one.

The mood turned grim in the village as the revelry of Carnevale ended and Lent began. The next forty days would be a somber time of reflection, fasting, and penance. Lent had felt like it lasted an eternity when she was a girl. Easter Sunday could not come soon enough. The day of relief. "You cannot have the joy of Easter Sunday without the agony of Good Friday," her mother reminded them. "No cross, no crown," she'd say in a dialect only her children understood.

The resurrection of the Lord redeemed the village and set the children free. Black sacks were pulled off the statues of the saints. The bare altar was decorated anew with myrtle and daisies. Plain broth for sustenance during the fast was replaced with sweet bread. The scents of butter, orange zest, and honey as Mama kneaded the dough for Easter bread during Holy Week lifted their spirits. The taste of the soft egg bread, braided into loaves served hot from the oven and drenched in honey, meant the sacrifice was over, at least until next year. Matelda recalled a particular Pranzo di Pasqua with every member from both sides of the family in attendance. Papa constructed one long dining table out of wooden doors so the entire family could sit together at the meal. Mama had covered the table in a yellow cloth and decorated it with baskets of her fresh bread.

"We are one," her father said as he lifted his glass. Soon, the cousins, aunts, uncles, and siblings raised their glasses with him.

There had been many happy moments in Matelda's life, but that particular Easter Sunday after the war was significant. If her memory ever failed her completely, Matelda was certain she would still remember her family in the garden under a glittering sun as they broke the fast together. When Matelda was young, she chased time to get what she wanted. Now she chased time to hold on to it.

The wooden slats of the boardwalk creaked beneath her feet as she walked down the promenade. She turned when she reached the midpoint of the pier and looked back at the wide gray runway. Why had it seemed endless when she was a girl?

Matelda recalled a summer evening on the boardwalk when she was a girl and walked beside her brother's pram during La Passeggiata Mare. Nino was born in 1949. (She retained numbers— bookkeepers usually do.) The war was over. Her mother wore a dress of apricot organza, and her father wore a straw boater with a wide band of raspberry silk. Matelda placed her hand on her heart as the details came together in her mind's eye. Soon the ghosts joined her on the walk, filling the drab boardwalk with color. She imagined men wearing taffy-colored suits and women preening in hats spiked with peacock plumes. Her mother slowly twirled a linen parasol bleached white by the sun. When Matelda stopped to rest on a bench, she closed her eyes and swore she could hear her mother's voice. Domenica Cabrelli had taught her daughter to love the sea by her example. Matelda could feel the warmth of her mother's presence whenever she walked along the water under the coral sun.

Matelda wondered why it was so easy to return to her childhood in particular detail, and yet she struggled to remember what she ate for dinner the night before. Maybe Ida's probiotics would help! She'd have to ask her doctor. When her husband took her to her last appointment, the nurse conducted a memory test. There was not a single question about her past; instead, the doctor and nurse were obsessed with the here and now. *Who is the prime minister of Italy? What day of the week is it? How old are you?* Matelda longed to respond "Who cares?" But she knew better than to get on the wrong side of her doctor. The doctor assured her that her visions and dreams of the past were normal but completely irrelevant when it came to the current assessment of the health of her brain. "The past and the present aren't connected in the human brain," he had explained to her. Matelda wasn't so sure.

She crossed the boulevard and approached the original storefront of her family business, now a dress shop. It gave her a sense of pride to see *Cabrelli Jewelers* still painted on the building, even though the letters were faded. It had been twenty years since her husband moved the shop to Lucca, a bustling small city just a few miles inland from Viareggio.

Matelda shaded her eyes and peered into the shop through the wide storefront window. She could see that the door to the back room was open. The workroom that housed the bruting wheel where her grandfather cut the gems was now filled with racks of clothing.

The shopkeepers on the boulevard were busy taking down the decorations for Carnevale. They lowered the garlands, loosened festoons, and took down strings of lights while another man balanced on a ladder and unhooked red, white, and green bunting along the route where the parade had passed. The grocer swept confetti into the gutter and nodded a silent greeting as she passed.

Matelda cupped her hands and sipped the icy water that flowed down the mountain to ancient cisterns. The spigots were attached to the hands of carved angels whose faces had been worn away by time. The water was loaded with precious minerals that shored up the people who drank it. Matelda thought of her mother as she dried her hands on the handkerchief she kept in her pocket. Not only had Domenica Cabrelli insisted her children drink the water for their health, she also taught Matelda how to count as they passed a series of angel fountains on her way to school. Viareggio had also been her first primer.

Matelda opened her purse to pay the fruit vendor as he selected six unbruised golden apples from his display and gently placed them in a paper sack.

"How's business?" Matelda asked as she paid. "Buona festa?"

"Not like the old days," he complained.

Matelda passed a team of six men on Via Firenze as they folded an enormous blue-striped tent corner to corner like a bedsheet. The Cabrelli cousins had occupied the brightly painted houses that lined the street, stacked one on top of the other, like books on a shelf. Matelda had learned the homes of her relatives by the color of their front doors: rosa for the Mamaci cousins, giallo for the Biagettis, and verde for the Gregorios. Color also signaled retreat. Matelda was not welcome at the house with the porta azzurra because of a long-standing feud between the Cabrelli and the Nichini families, calcified in history long before she was born. The standoff continued after the Nichinis moved to Livorno, leaving the house with the blue door behind. Matelda remembered the summers of her childhood when she stood at the bottom of the hill and whistled to gather her cousins to go to the beach. The front doors would snap open at once, creating a colorful enfilade as the children ran down the street to join her.

For fun, Matelda put two fingers in her mouth and blew. The loud trill got the attention of the tent folders on the street, but not a single door flew open. Sadly, her cousins had migrated to Lucca too. Matelda and Olimpio were now the old timers in the village. The last of the Cabrelli-Roffos of Viareggio.

Matelda's phone buzzed in her pocket. She stopped to read the text.

Happy Birthday Matelda! Thank you for the lovely visit.

She texted her sister-in-law, Thank you. It was fun. Not long enough!

Matelda genuinely liked her sister-in-law, Patrizia. She was a peacemaker and had encouraged Nino to get along with Matelda; after all, they only had each other. Matelda hadn't had a single argument with her brother when he and his wife last visited.

Can you ask Nino if he remembers Nonno Cabrelli's elephant story? Matelda texted.

Patrizia sent back an emoji of a winking face.

Matelda hated emojis. Soon enough, human beings would not need language to communicate, animated small heads with bug eyes would do the talking for them.

Matelda stopped at the gate of the communal garden planted a hundred years earlier by the Boncourso family. Decades later, the lot remained in their name even though the family had died out after the First World War. The fallow garden was carpeted in muck. A few perennial plants were hooded in burlap to protect them against the frost. The white pergola stood alone in the center of the garden like a bridal carriage marooned in mud.

Matelda remembered her first kiss under the pergola. It was summer; she had closed her eyes and inhaled the scent of the grapes that draped over the arch. Rocco Tiburzi took that as a sign and stole the moment to kiss her. Matelda was fourteen years old and thought that nothing more wonderful would ever happen to her again; she practically floated home. When Matelda arrived, her grandmother Netta reprimanded her because she'd forgotten the sack of chestnuts she had been sent to collect. Tenderness and shame would remain closely tied in Matelda's heart until she learned the combination blocked her ability to truly love.

The chestnut trees that lined the back wall of the garden still bore plenty of fruit. Her neighbors continued to collect them in burlap sacks during the harvest, but Matelda chose not to take her share. She had eaten enough chestnuts in pastes, fillings, and dough when there was a scarcity of food after the war; she'd promised herself she would not eat another when she grew up and was in charge of the family kitchen. The current popularity of Italian dishes made with chestnuts befuddled Matelda and reminded her how quickly people forgot hardship and suffering once they'd moved through them.

Matelda and her husband, Olimpio, lived in the attico of Villa Cabrelli angled in the crook of Viale Giosuè Carducci. The Roffos were the third generation to live in the family home. After Matelda's parents died, and her grown children had moved out, she and Olimpio reconfigured the house. They took the penthouse apartment. "We finally made it to the top," Olimpio would joke, "but we had to lose everyone we love to do it."

Matelda had experienced life from every view from Villa Cabrelli. It was too bad that generations no longer lived in one house separated by a few steps between floors. Her own children had moved out as soon as they married. Her daughter lived in nearby Lucca, and her son was farther up the coast. For many years, they were close enough, but not anymore. Matelda wished her entire famiglia had remained under one roof.

The village evolved as the families changed over time. Most of the neighbors who owned homes with a view of the sea had them repurposed into apartments as their owners died and their heirs, intent to hold on to the family homes, found much-needed income in lucrative summer rentals. Villa Cabrelli had been broken into apartments to rent too, but this was more a function of the aging Roffos needing less space to look after than it was financial need. The renovation included the installation of the building's first elevator, which Olimpio insisted they would need one day. He was right. A house renovation at the age of sixty should keep an eye on eighty. It came around quickly.

Once Matelda reached the top of the hill, she fished inside her purse for the key. Arancione meant she was home. The orange door had not changed since she was a girl.

"Signora! I have something for you." Giusto Figliolo, Matelda's white-haired neighbor, waved to her from behind his gate before joining her. "My daughter took a drive to Pietrasanta." He gave Matelda a large triangle of parmesan cheese wrapped in waxed paper. "I have more when you need it."

Matelda lifted the cheese like a barbell. "Are you sure you can spare it?"

"Sì, sì." He chuckled. "She brought me a wheel. It will last us until the next Carnevale."

"Thank you, Signore. Please, take a few apples." Matelda opened the paper sack.

"I'll take one."

"Are you sure? I have plenty."

"One is all I need. Buon compleanno." Figliolo smiled.

It would be like a Figliolo to remember her birthday with a hunk of cheese. They once owned the most popular restaurant in town, where families in the village went to celebrate. The mother had been a good cook, the father a fine manager. All the Figliolo children had worked in the restaurant. They were good-looking people, which helped when you wanted to attract customers. Figliolo's sisters were long gone, but Matelda remembered their black hair, slim figures, and red-polished nails.

"Do you have plans to celebrate your birthday?" Figliolo asked her.

"With great humility. My goal is to be alive this time tomorrow morning. And the one after that, if God is kind."

"May God bless you and give you what you need because what you want will get you in trouble." Figliolo blessed himself. "The Cabrellis have always been fighters. You'll be all right."

Matelda picked up the newspaper. "Here, you take it."

"You sure?"

"There's no news anymore, just obituaries. I don't need any reminders of what's coming."

"You're a kid, Matelda." Giusto was ninety-three years old. "You're just getting started."

The final apple peel fell like a gold ribbon into the sink. Matelda
sliced the meat of the apple into slivers with her paring knife. She
patted the dough on the cookie sheet before artfully placing the
apple slices on top of the dough. She scattered pats of butter on top
of the apple and sprinkled the mixture with sugar. Matelda dusted
cinnamon over the sugar before pulling the four corners of the
dough to the center, making a purse as her mother had taught her.
She slid the strudel di mele into the oven.

Matelda fed the pets. Their mutt, Beppe, ate quickly and fell
asleep under the sofa. "You're just like your master. Eat. Nap. Eat,"
she teased the dog. Argento walked along the top of the bookcase
in the living room, performing her daily circus act. "And you!" She
shook her finger at the cat. "You are crazy! You're too old for
heights." The cat ignored her, but that was nothing new. Argento
acted like the Roffos lived with her, instead of the other way
around.

Matelda pulled off her apron and straightened the living room.

Four gray sofas with low, modern lines formed a square around
the coffee table, enough to accommodate the entire family when
they visited. A vintage Leica camera, a primitive sculpture, and
glass jars filled with seashells collected by their grandchildren were
tucked among Matelda's bookshelves. She brushed a feather duster
over the books.

Satisfied, Matelda pulled a yellowed scrap of paper out of the
Capodimonte vase on the table. She lifted a small painting off its
hook under the stairs, revealing the hidden metal door to a wall
safe. She cocked her good ear against it, followed the sequence of
numbers on the slip of paper, and spun the dial like a seasoned
safecracker. She heard the click of the wheel. The door of the safe
snapped open. She reached inside and removed a velvet jewelry

case. Leaving the safe open, she put the case on the table on her way to the kitchen.

Matelda lifted the strudel out of the oven and placed it on the counter to cool. Steam rose from the golden folds of crust dusted with sugar. Matelda opened her notebook on the counter and wrote the list of ingredients and instructions to make the pastry. Her daughter, Nicolina, was collecting the family recipes. Matelda never used recipes; she made the dishes as her grandmother and mother had taught her: Assemble the best ingredients. No measuring. Use your instincts.

Matelda unscrewed the top off the moka pot. She lifted out the strainer and measured freshly ground espresso beans into the strainer cup. She filled the bottom chamber with water. Using the blunt end of the spoon, she patted the grounds across the top of the rim to make them level before gently twisting the top onto the pot. She placed it on the stove and lit the burner.

The kitchen filled with the earthy scent of morning when Matelda realized she had spilled coffee onto the scatter rug under the sink. Matelda bent over, cursed, and rolled the rug like a cigar. She carried the rug out to the terrace and shook it over the side. She hung it on the railing.

Matelda shivered in the cold, pulled her sweater tightly around herself without buttoning it, and crossed her arms over her chest. The surf had begun to churn along the coastline. The brisk winds that blew over the peaks of the Alpi Apuane and whistled through the Pania della Croce practically guaranteed there would be at least one more storm before spring. Matelda could not recall a Toscano winter more severe than the one they had just endured. She gave the rug one more shake before folding it.

She turned to go back inside when she heard a screeching sound from the sky. She looked up and saw a fat seagull dive through the fog. "Shoo!" she shouted, unfurling the rug toward the bird. But instead of flying off, the bird veered toward her, so close the sharp tip of its hooked yellow beak nipped her cheek.

"Beppe!" Matelda shouted for the dog. The dog leapt through the open glass door and barked at the bird. The cat slunk out onto the terrace, curious about the fuss. The seagull swooped down to taunt the cat, who arched his back and hissed.

"Argento! Inside!" She scooped the cat up in the rug. "Beppe! Andiamo!" The dog bounded back into the apartment. Matelda snapped the sliding glass door shut. She placed the cat on the chair, pulling the rug away, while the dog jumped up on her legs, tongue wagging.

Matelda reached inside her blouse for the handkerchief she kept tucked under the strap of her brassiere. She gently dabbed the perspiration on her forehead and rested her hand on her racing heart. She peered out the glass door, searched the sky, but the seagull was gone. She had a funny feeling as she sat down to catch her breath.

Too much excitement for an old lady, she said to herself. "And for you too," she mumbled to the dog and the cat.

CHAPTER 3

Nonna?" The sound of her granddaughter Anina's voice on the intercom startled her as it echoed through the apartment. "It's me. I've got my key."

Anina was talking on her cell phone when she stepped off the elevator and into the apartment. She mouthed *Ciao, Nonna*, pursed her lips in an air-kiss, handed her grandmother a sack of fresh fruit, and motioned that she needed to finish the call. She pulled off her coat and threw it over a chair before sinking down onto the sofa and continuing her conversation.

Anina Tizzi at twenty-five years old was a dazzler. She had the Cabrelli mouth, straight nose, tawny complexion, and trim figure. Her hair was thick and brown, like Matelda's used to be, and while Anina's eyes were wide-set like her grandmother's, they weren't brown but green, favoring her father Giorgio's side, the Tizzis from Sestri Levante.

Anina wore white denim jeans that had a series of small rips in the fabric from the tops of the thighs to the ankles. The pants showed so much leg, her grandmother wondered why Anina bothered to wear pants at all. Anina's navel was also on display. The cropped pale blue sweater barely grazed her waist. Matelda wondered how Anina hadn't frozen to death.

Anina twisted her hair into a topknot as she carried on the conversation on the phone. Her engagement ring, a simple emerald-cut diamond on a platinum band, sparkled in the light. From Matelda's perspective, the ring was the only note of refinement on a young woman who should have been nothing but elegant—after all, Anina had been exposed to the best; the Cabrellis were the town artisans.

Matelda brought the fruit into the kitchen. Her cell phone buzzed on the counter. She put it on speaker. "Pronto," she greeted her husband.

"What did Anina choose?" Olimpio wanted to know.

"Nothing. Yet. She's on the phone. When a young person visits an old person, they assume that the old person has nothing to do all day but sit around watching the clock, waiting to die."

Olimpio laughed. "Tell her to get off the phone. Take a breath. Relax."

"It's not easy for me to do."

"I know. I haven't seen you take a breath in fifty-three years. Not a deep one anyway."

"What time will you be home?"

"The usual. Say a prayer. I'm going into a meeting with the bankers."

"Persuade them with your charm."

"Sì. Sì. I will make them feel special. You do the same for Anina."

Matelda prepared a tray with dishes, silver, and linen napkins. She placed the strudel di mele in the center, sliding a serving knife under it.

"You're still on the phone?" Matelda complained as she placed the tray on the table. She ran her hand across the marble top.

When her parents died five months apart, twenty years earlier, they had left four floors of furniture and stuff behind. The marble-top dining table had a history. There had been talk of selling it when money was needed after the war and the shop struggled to remain open. But no one wanted to buy it because the last thing people purchased during hard times was antique furniture.

Matelda had no idea what to do with her parents' possessions when Signora Ciliberti, a wisewoman who lived on Via Castagna, advised Matelda that she only needed to keep one special object to remind her of her mother. *Everything else could go*, she told her. Free of the guilt, Matelda unloaded her mother's gilt without any help from her brother. Nino attended their mother's funeral, mourned her with the village, and left soon after, leaving his sister to do everything else, including the dishes after the sympathy lunch. When it came to the home, Italian women handled all matters of importance between birth and death.

Matelda positioned the box of jewelry at the place she had set for her granddaughter. "Anina."

Anina turned and smiled. She held up her finger, pleading for another minute, and kept talking.

"Anina. Hang up the phone," Matelda commanded.

"Ciao. Ciao. I must go." Anina got off the call. "I'm sorry, Nonna. When Paolo wants to talk, I have to drop whatever I'm doing." Anina joined her grandmother at the table. "Lately, all he wants to do is talk."

"I made your favorite—" Matelda began.

Anina's cell phone rang. "Sorry." Anina reached to answer it.

"Give me your phone." Matelda extended an open hand.

Anina handed her grandmother the phone as it buzzed. Matelda walked to the safe. She threw the phone into the safe and closed the door, locking it inside. "It's rude to visit your grandmother and spend the entire time talking on the phone."

"May I please have my phone back?" Anina was bewildered.

"Later."

"You're just going to leave it in there?"

"Sì." Matelda poured the coffee. "You can call them back later."

"Nonna, what happened?" Anina squinted at Matelda's face. "There's blood on your cheek."

"Where?" Matelda got up and looked at her face in the mirror. Anina was right. There was a faint streak of burgundy on her face. "Have I been bleeding this whole time?"

"You must have cut yourself. Didn't you feel it when it happened?"

"No, I did not. Well, wait. It might have come from a little scuffle I had with a seagull before you got here."

"What do you mean?"

"I was on the balcony waiting for you to arrive. A seagull swooped down out of nowhere. I didn't think it got me."

"It got you."

"Maybe it wasn't the bird. Maybe I scratched myself."

"And you didn't feel that either?"

Anina worried about her grandmother, though her mother assured her that Matelda would outlive all of them. It might be true, because it seemed Matelda had not aged like other grandmothers. Like volcanized rubber, her grandmother seemed to get stronger over time. If she fell, she bounced. Matelda was the only nonna Anina knew who didn't slump. Her upright posture was something out of a military exercise. Her style was classic. Matelda dressed in classic wool skirts and cashmere sweater sets. There was always a tasteful brooch and a string of pearls. Matelda dressed like a woman of means who worked in a city, even though she was now, in retirement, a housewife who lived by the sea.

"Stop staring." Matelda put her hand to her face and found the cut with the tips of her fingers. It was no thicker than a thread and went from the top of her cheekbone to her ear.

"If a bird attacked you, all those germs got into the cut. They carry disease; plus, it's bad luck."

"I wouldn't worry. It's my bad luck, not yours."

Anina opened the jewelry case. The contents glistened like ribbon candy. "I remember this case. When I was little, you'd let me play with the jewelry."

"That doesn't sound like me."

"Well, you let me help you polish the pieces. Remember?"

"That sounds more like me. Putting idle children to work to keep them out of mischief."

"You took a chore that needed to be done and made it fun."

"I was fun?" Matelda chuckled to herself.

"Here and there." Anina closed the jewelry case and looked at Matelda.

"What's the matter?"

"Do you have ointment or a bandage or something? I won't enjoy our time together until you put something on that wound."

"*Madonne.*" Matelda pushed her chair from the table and went to the powder room. "It's just a scratch."

"It's a *wound*," Anina called after her. "I'd google it, but you stole my phone."

Matelda opened the first aid kit she kept under the sink. She washed her hands before applying a thin line of antiseptic to the cut on her face. She pressed a gauze pad against it to let the ointment soak in. "All right, I am cured." Matelda returned to the table.

"Grazie mille." Anina lifted the compartments out of the case, placing them on the table. "How did the incident with the bird happen exactly?"

"What difference does it make? We can't file a police report."

"Was the bird alone, or was there a flock of them?"

"Only one. I see what you're getting at. There's some meaning in all this. I'm afraid I don't know what that would be. My mother knew Italian folklore. She was the expert. She used to say if a bird perched in the window looking into the house, it meant someone in the house would die."

"What would she say about a bird that attacks an innocent woman unprovoked in broad daylight?"

"I have no idea."

"We could call a strega," Anina suggested.

"All the stregas I knew in the village are dead," Matelda admitted.

"Mama might know someone in Lucca."

"We are not calling around Lucca to find a witch."

"It's just a thought." Anina pulled a ring from the box and tried it on. "I'm just trying to help."

"It's nothing," Matelda assured her. But she wasn't entirely certain. This was the worst aspect of being old: There was no one left to call when Matelda needed answers. "Your coffee is going to get cold. How about the strudel di mele?"

"I can't."

"It's your favorite."

Anina patted her taut midsection. "I have to wriggle into a wedding gown."

"You're wearing one of those?" Matelda couldn't hide her disappointment.

"I'm not wearing a big skirt. I don't want to look like a bombolone on my wedding day."

"Instead you'll wear a tight gown like a television game show hostess with everything spilling out."

"I won't have spillage. There are alterations to take care of that." Anina examined a platinum brooch with a bow of tiny blue sapphires, holding it up to the light.

"The priest will have something to say about it."

"He did. I've been going for instruction with Paolo. I showed Don Vincenzo a picture of the gown. He thought it was lovely."

"There are rules. A bride is required to have her head and arms covered in church. No bosoms."

"But I have bosoms."

"Modesty. It's a sign of self-respect to stay covered. It's keeping something just for you and your husband."

"I don't know what you mean."

"And it's too late to teach you."

"Does it matter?"

"Probably not." Matelda smiled. Most of the things that mattered to her didn't matter to anyone anymore. Matelda didn't have a right to complain, but she remembered a time when an elder could. "Anina, wear whatever makes you happy."

At least Anina was getting married in a church. Plenty of Matelda's friends had grandchildren who were married in public parks or on the beach without a mention of God. All they got was a barefoot bride, a sunburn, and warm prosecco in a paper cup. "Do you know what today is?"

"The day you asked me to come over and choose a piece of jewelry for my wedding." Anina placed the brooch back in its velvet envelope. "Cabrelli family tradition. Your grandmother gave you a piece of jewelry to wear on your wedding day, your mother gave jewelry to my mother, and now it's your turn to give it to me."

"It's also my birthday."

"No." Anina placed her hands on the table and thought for a moment. "It is! I am so sorry! Buon Compleanno!" She got up and gave Matelda a kiss on her cheek, the side without the cut. "I didn't forget altogether. I remembered it yesterday; I just forgot this morning. I should have brought you a present!"

"You did. You brought me fruit, a gift that has to be used immediately. It's the perfect gift for a woman of eighty-one if I don't die before it spoils."

"I'm sorry, Nonna. I can't do anything right when it comes to you."

"That's not true. I'd just like to see more of you, and that's not a criticism."

"Whenever someone says, 'That's not a criticism,' it's always a criticism."

"Is that why you don't come and visit more often? Am I too critical?"

"Yes." Anina tried not to smile. "Truthfully? I'm busy."

"Doing what?"

"I'm planning a wedding." Anina waved her hands in frustration over the jewelry case.

"At your age, I was already keeping the books for my father."

"I'm taking over for Orsola when she goes on maternity leave."

"Excellent. When you're not out front with the customers, try to spend time with your grandfather in the back. That's where the real work is done. Learn the trade from a master. It might spark your creativity."

"Let's see how I do filling in for Orsola, and then we can talk about my creativity."

"Seize this opportunity and make something of it. You should think about a career."

"First I want to make a home for Paolo and me. You know, make strudel and paint the walls. Grow a garden."

"You need an enterprise beyond growing arugula. Sometimes things happen in life and you will have to carry your family. You'll need money to do it."

"I don't care about money," Anina shot back. "Can we talk about something else? I thought we were going to have fun today."

A wave of shame washed over Anina. Her grandmother was trying. Nonna had prepared for this special visit and planned how it all would go. She reached for Matelda's hand and patted it gently. "Thank you for doing all this for me. I don't know what to pick. Will you help me?" Anina held up a small gold religious medal.

"That's a miraculous medal."

"Is it yours?"

"It belonged to my mother. I used to know the significance. I can't remember now. But it will come back to me. By then, we won't care. Old age is terrible."

"There has to be something good about getting old."

Matelda thought about it. "Sleeves."

Anina laughed.

Matelda held up the medal of Santa Lucia. "There's a story to go with this one. It also belonged to my mother."

"I want to hear it."

Anina lifted a small envelope out of the box. A one-carat Peruzzi-cut ruby fell out of the envelope and into the palm of her hand like a tiny red gumdrop. "Whoa."

"That is the Speranza ruby. My grandfather insisted his friend from Venezia was the best gem cutter in Italy. You could have something made with the stone if you like."

Anina put the ruby back into the envelope. "I had enough trouble coming up with a design for my engagement ring. Let's leave this for someone with an imagination."

Matelda removed a dowel with three rings from the box. She lifted a thick gold band off the dowel. "This band belonged to my mother's mother, Netta Cabrelli. This was her wedding ring."

Anina tried the ring on. "I can't get it past my knuckle!"

"Nonno will size it for you if you want it. There's plenty of gold there. She was smaller than you, but to me, she was a giant, and not always a gentle one. There's a photograph of her on my night-stand."

"I've seen it. It's scary. People photographed in sepia always look miserable."

"Because they couldn't move. They had to hold still in order for the photographer to get the picture. But that's only part of the story. Netta Cabrelli was stern for other reasons."

"What's this?" Anina held up a vintage timepiece set in a carved rectangle of green aventurine stone.

"Where did you find that?"

"It was at the bottom of the case."

The pale blue oyster-shell face of the watch dangled from an embossed gold bar pin. The *12*, *3*, *6*, and *9* on the face were set with a jewel baguette.

"I thought I left it in the safety deposit box at the bank."

"Is it valuable?"

"Only to me."

"The filigree on the pin would make a great ankle tattoo."

"You have a tattoo?" Matelda groaned.

"Mama told me not to tell you."

"Where?"

"I have a heart on my hip."

"You already have one in your chest."

"But the one on my hip is cute." Anina held up the aventurine watch fob. "Nonna, I want this. May I have it?"

"Pick something else."

"You said I could have anything in the case."

Matelda handed Anina a dainty ring, a cluster made of briolette rubies set in yellow gold. "It will look lovely with your diamond. Your grandfather made it for me for my fortieth birthday."

Anina slipped the ring onto the middle finger of her right hand.

"It's stunning, but it's too much, Nonna." She returned the ring to the case and picked up the watch fob again. "Why is the face on the watch upside down?"

"So my mother could read the time."

"Why would she have to read the time upside down?"

"Because she was often using both hands to do her work. She wore this on her uniform. She was a nurse."

"Did I know this? I don't believe I did. You don't talk about your mother. Why?"

"I talk about her." Matelda folded her hands in her lap. "You don't listen when I tell stories. You kids are too busy on your phones."

"Are you all right? You look pale. Do you want to reschedule? We could do this another day."

"It's too late."

"For what?" Anina looked around. "Do you have somewhere to go?"

Matelda wished she did. Her heart was racing. Frustration, the jet fuel of anxiety, welled within her. She could see the future. She would die; the children would gather around this table. Her daughter, Nicolina, would sort through the contents. Her son, Matteo, would sit back; when his sister was done, he would rummage through the case. Her children would have, at best, a sketchy knowledge of the history behind the pieces. Without facts, there was no meaning behind them; without meaning, there would be no value. They would have no recourse except to sell the collection to the highest bidder. The stones would be plucked from their settings; the gold would be weighed, parceled, and melted down to be repurposed. The pieces that remained intact would be salvaged to sell as vintage collectibles on one of those websites that wealthy people peruse because they have nothing better to do than acquire more stuff. Matelda's stomach churned.

"Nonna, are you all right? Seriously. You look terrible." Anina went into the kitchen.

Matelda took a moment to collect herself. When a housewife grew old, her final task was to imagine what would endure of her life's work after she was gone. The mother shaped the mission of the family, and if she failed, the family failed with her. Matelda had a hunch she wouldn't like what her children would do once she was gone, but she had no one to blame but herself. She had given up too easily. She had not shared the truth and made her family history a priority. Matelda had not taken her children to the place she was born and shared the story of her father. A vacation in Montenegro was more important than a trip to Scotland. But Matelda had her reasons. There were limits to what she knew about her father, but that was no excuse. Her children and grandchildren needed to know certain facts before Matelda forgot them entirely or died suddenly. A bird didn't have to drop out of the sky to deliver that message.

Anina returned with a glass of water. "Nonna. Drink this."

Matelda slowly sipped the water. "Grazie."

Anina picked up her great grandmother Domenica Cabrelli's watch and held it to her ear.

"It hasn't been wound in years," Matelda admitted.

Anina studied the watch. The aventurine was different from the other gems in the case; it was not warm like the magenta rubies from India set in the birthday band. It was not soft, like the swirls of gold in the Capri coral. It did not catch light like a diamond. It was not Italian. The stone was dark green and brooding, mined in a country far from Italy, in a place where the dense roots of tall trees absorbed a steady season of monsoons followed by months of hot sun. The filigree and embossing were not Italianate in design either. The watch was the awkward beauty of the collection, the foreigner.

"I think it was an antique long before Bisnonna owned it," Anina said. "It's nineteenth-century for sure."

"How do you know?"

"Nonno taught me how to read the markings." Anina turned it over in her hand and showed Matelda. "The gold is stamped. There are other clues. The timepiece is not Swiss, not its face or its gears, typically used in Italian construction. It's not German or French either. Where did it come from?"

Matelda did not answer her.

"Look. It's engraved. There's the *D*, then there's an engraved ampersand and then the *J*. Who is the *J*?"

"I'm not ready to part with it."

Anina placed the watch back into the case. "I always want what I can't have."

Matelda rested her face in her hand, as she often did when she needed to think. Her fingers grazed the cut on her cheek. The faint wound stung just enough to remind her that she was hurting.

Outside, the late-winter day split open with a drumroll of thunder followed by flashes of lightning.

"Uh-oh." Anina turned to the terrace doors. "Squall moving in!"

A heavy, cold rain began to fall, pummeling the terrazzo floor on the terrace like silver arrows.

"The bedroom windows!" Matelda cried.

"I've got them!" Anina jumped up and ran up the steps to her grandparents' bedroom.

Matelda pulled the electrical plugs of the appliances in the living room in case the storm caused a power surge. Beppe barked and ran around in a circle in the excitement as Matelda pulled the emergency lamp off the shelf.

"You're all set." Anina sat down, breathless. "Closed them all. You're the only person I know who keeps their windows open in the winter."

"My mother taught me to open the windows in the morning to let out the bad spirits. I forget to close them."

"Was your mother a strega?"

"I don't think so."

"So how did she know all that stuff?"

"Domenica Cabrelli was one of those wisewomen. She had common sense, but she acknowledged the spirit world. She also respected science. The neighbors called her before they called the doctor." Beppe jumped up and sat on Matelda's lap.

"I'd like to know about her."

"My mother was born in this house; ninety-three years later she died in it. She lived in Viareggio all her life except when she was a young nurse and had to leave her family for a while."

"Why did she leave?"

"Look. The sea is wild. This is the big storm they promised us."

"Nonna, I want to know why my great-grandmother left the village. I'm getting married. I want my children to know about their ancestors."

A stripe of orange light rested on the horizon, illuminating the churn of the surf as the storm took hold. The Ligurian Sea had a story too. Anina would soon find out where the sea had taken Domenica Cabrelli before it swept her away, along with her true love and their secret.

CHAPTER 4

Viareggio

1920

Domenica Cabrelli cupped her hands, turned toward the dunes, and belted out, "Sill-vee-oh!" The eleven-year-old girl had the lung capacity of a great soprano. The beach belonged to her, not a soul in sight. The sky was Tiepolo blue with tufts of flamingo clouds floating on the horizon, a sure sign that it would rain later in the day. Under the noonday sun, the sea rippled peacefully as the tide rolled to the shore. The girl rubbed her stomach. She was hungry. Domenica grew impatient and called Silvio's name again. There was work to be done. Where was he?

The girl's intense black eyes surveyed the ridge of the dunes like a general before battle. She folded her arms across her clean, pressed work apron, which had been mended, then patched by her mother with an overlay of odd squares of burlap from a sandbag and remnants of fabric from the slag floor of the silk mill. Most girls in the village wore a similar style. The apron had a square neckline with two wide straps over the shoulder that fastened with two buttons in the back. Utility pockets were sewn on the front, deep enough to hold a straight edge, small scissors, a coil of thread with a needle, and wide enough to accommodate an embroidery hoop and any extras. Signorina Cabrelli saved room in her pockets for seashells and small stones, which she would find a purpose for later.

Domenica was barefoot, as all Italian children were during the summer. The soles of her feet were thick from carrying pails of fresh water up and down the wooden planks of the promenade. The white sand beneath her feet was as soft as a Persian carpet. Her dark brown hair was braided neatly and twisted into a crown on top of her head, though a few curls had escaped the plaits. She brushed away the loose strands when the sea breezes caught them. The cotton slip and pantaloons she wore underneath the linen jumper were hand-me-downs from a cousin, but that was where the charity ended. Gold hoop earrings, made by her father, the jeweler's apprentice, twinkled in her earlobes. The earrings were made of gold mesh so delicate, you had to be close enough to whisper in her ear to see them.

Silvio Birtolini appeared at the top of the hill. The black-haired boy was exactly her age but a couple inches shorter than she, as were most of the boys in school. She waved to him. "Hurry!"

Silvio slid down the dune and ran to Domenica as fast as he could, kicking up sand as he went.

"Did you get it?"

Silvio pulled a slim cylinder of paper tied with a ribbon from the back of his pants. He gave it to her, keeping his eyes on her, eager to please, hopeful for a positive reaction. Domenica untied the ribbon and unrolled the paper. Her eyes darted around the map of Viareggio proper as she consumed the information.

"Did anyone see you?" she asked without taking her gaze off the grid drawn in black ink on a field of beige.

"No."

"Good." She nodded. "If we are to find the treasure, no one must know we are looking for it."

"I understand." Silvio never knew which part of the time he spent with Domenica Cabrelli was make-believe and which part was actual fact. Was there a treasure? Who were the "no ones" exactly? Silvio had no idea.

Domenica rolled up the map and, using it to point, picked a spot on a dune at the far end of the beach. "Follow me." She began to trudge up the long beach in the direction of Pineta di Ponente. "The fate of all things rests upon us."

"How could that be true?" Silvio walked beside her.

"Because it does."

"But the fate of *all* things? You're not the Creator." They had studied God's will in catechism in preparation for the sacrament of confirmation. Silvio noticed that Domenica was often inspired to act in real life in direct opposition to whatever dogma they had been learning in school.

"Didn't Don Fernando tell us that we were authorized to baptize someone who needed the sacrament if no priest were available?"

"Yes, but that doesn't make you a priest."

"He gave us permission to baptize the unchristened. We are holy enough to do it! A sacrament is an outward sign of inward grace. Everyone has inward grace. Even me. Even you."

"I wouldn't baptize anyone. I would run for the priest. The nuns taught us to get a priest. You have to do it over again if there's no priest."

"Listen to the good nuns of San Paolino, but don't believe everything they tell you."

"Says who?"

"Papa. I wasn't supposed to be listening, but I heard him say it to my mother, so it must be true."

Silvio didn't have a father, so he was at a disadvantage to counter the point. There were times he wished he could say, *My papa said,* just to challenge her.

"When my parents whisper, I make sure I'm close enough to hear what they're saying. I watch them when they divide the purse and pay attention when they discuss the priest. I stay inside when they have company and stay close to Papa when he talks to customers in the shop. When we have company, the guests always bring lemons or tomatoes, but they also bring stories from Lucca. You cannot believe what goes on there. There's the man who brings pigs' feet from Lazio. He knows where the money in the poor box at San Sebastiano goes. And there's Signora Vanucci, who gives my mother sugar when she has extra, but she is also looking for business. Signora has so many stories."

"The matchmaker?"

"That's her! She marries off nice men with clubfeet to women who are past the age of courting and won't get asked for their hand in marriage otherwise. But I wouldn't know *that* if I didn't listen to her long stories. She told Mama if she were young, she would not be a matchmaker. She would seek her fortune and make it her life's work to hunt for buried treasure. That's how I found out about the loot from Capri." Domenica made a circle in the air with the map. "Signora Vanucci found the story had some truth to it. That's good enough for me."

"What if we don't find it?"

"We'll find it."

"Don't you worry someone else got to it first?"

"Anyone who finds treasure brags about it."

Silvio wondered how Domenica knew things for certain. "I haven't heard a word about the treasure, so maybe—" he reasoned aloud.

"Because it hasn't been found! There's your proof!" Domenica was impatient and couldn't get the words out fast enough to explain the urgency of this mission to her friend. "When the pearls and the diamonds were stolen on Capri by pirates before the Great War, first they went to Sardinia to hide them. Then Ischia. Then Elba. They stopped in Ustica. Corsica. Finally they came ashore right here, on this beach. They hid the jewels *here*. It's for certain. Many people in Viareggio saw the pirates come and go. When they left, the pirates got back on their ship to sail to Greece to steal more, but they were all killed off the coast of Malta in a bloody battle unlike any the people there had ever seen! Throats were slashed! Brains were bludgeoned! The priest lost both arms!"

"All right, all right." Silvio wiped the sweat from his face on his sleeve.

"But the treasure survived! Because it's *here*. Hidden in Viareggio, the best place to hide what must not be found except by the people doing the hiding because we have the dunes, the forests, the canals, the marble mountains! Trails and paths and secret roads that lead to grottoes! Don't forget. Napoleon himself put his sister here and no one knew!"

"Princess Borghese of Tuscany. My great-grandfather groomed her horse."

"Okay, so the locals knew. It doesn't matter," Domenica assured him. "The law says, if the missing treasure is not claimed by the owners within three years, whomever finds the lost treasure on Italian soil owns it outright. That could be us. It will be us!"

"But this beach goes on for miles. There are hundreds of coves," Silvio complained. "The dunes have two sides, like the mountains. They could have buried it anywhere. And what if they escaped into the forest or up into the Alpi Apuane? What if they left it up there somewhere? How will we know where to dig? It's impossible."

Domenica stopped to consider their options. Her feet sank into the soft sand by the water's edge. She allowed the gentle lapping of the incoming tide to fill in the impressions around her feet. She sank ankle deep into the cool sand until she was eye to eye with Silvio. His curly hair was thick from the ocean mist, making him seem taller than her at last. Domenica stood up straight so he wouldn't be. "Do you want to find the buried treasure or not? Because if you don't, I can do this by myself. And if I am alone when I find it, I don't have to share it with you."

"I don't want to miss the festival at Chiesa della Santissima Annunziata," Silvio lamented. "This is the day of the bomboloni."

"Is that all? A doughnut is more important to you than a lifetime of riches?" Domenica tried to balance herself by putting her hand on his shoulder, but her feet were stuck like two rubber stoppers in the wet sand. Silvio gave her a good yank to release her, but instead they tumbled onto the beach laughing.

"The map!" Domenica held the parchment cylinder high in the air to keep it dry.

Silvio snatched it and stood. "I've got it."

"Thief!" A voice bellowed from the peak of the dune behind them. The children looked back to see Signore Aniballi, the town librarian, looming over them wearing his rumpled waistcoat and wool pants. "Bring that map back to me! *Subito!*"

Domenica grabbed the map from Silvio and began to run down the beach.

Silvio ran after Domenica.

"I thought no one saw you!" Domenica panted as Silvio caught up with her. A pack of boys appeared on the peak and formed a line like a row of black crows on a wire.

Aniballi pointed. "There he is! The Birtolini boy! Get him!"

Aniballi's army scattered down the dunes. When the boys reached the beach, they began to chase Domenica and Silvio along the water's edge. Aniballi slid down the sandy hill in his work oxfords, until his feet got tangled in seaweed. He fell forward and tumbled down to the beach. He stood, cursed, dusted off his trousers, checked the pocket of his waistcoat for his watch, making certain it had not been damaged in the fall, and followed the boys.

Domenica and Silvio ran down the beach; the mob followed them. Domenica's heart pounded in her chest. It felt as though it might burst through her skin, yet she relished the feeling of danger from the thrill of being chased. She heard her name called but ignored it and ran faster. She pretended the map was a baton in a foot race. She held it high in the air, kicked back her heels, and pumped her arms. Her jumper, which her mother had noticed was too short and needed the hem let out, was the right length for a chase. She had speed.

The boys' taunts carried over the sound of the surf. Domenica ignored the insults, but Silvio heard them and was afraid. His heart was pounding for a different reason from hers. The mob had chased Silvio before. When he was alone, he had only himself to worry about. He could calculate exactly how long it took for the bullies to lose interest in the chase, and knew where he could hide to wait it out. Domenica was slowing him down, but he would not leave her. He kept pace with his friend to protect her.

"This way!" Domenica pivoted. She scanned the beach and scrambled across the sand to the dunes in the direction of the steps that led up to the boardwalk.

Silvio stopped. "No, this way!" He pointed to the dune that would take them into the pine woods, where he knew of places to hide.

"Follow me!" She ran.

Silvio followed behind her. The boys, who were bigger and faster, soon gained on them.

"Papa's shop! Come on!" Domenica panted as Silvio joined her at the bottom of the steps. Together they had turned to climb the steps when Domenica heard a loud thump.

A spray of blood exploded in the air like red pearls.

The rock, aimed at Silvio, had hit him in the face and torn open his skin.

"My eye!" Silvio cried as he fell to the ground. Domenica knelt next to him. The gang chanted "Il bastardo!" as they surrounded them.

Domenica felt claustrophobic; the pungent scent of the breath and sweat of the mob mixed with seaweed sickened her.

"Enough!" Domenica shouted.

Guido Mironi, the tallest boy with the thickest neck, grabbed the map from Domenica.

"Step aside, boys!" Signore Aniballi panted, pushing the boys out of his way. Mironi handed the librarian the map.

"Grazie, Guido, grazie," Aniballi gushed. "Good boy."

Domenica was on the ground next to Silvio, shielding him with her body. The boy was in agony. He had curled up tightly in the shape of a snail's shell, his hand covering his eye, protecting it as blood streamed through his fingers.

Domenica stood up. She grabbed the rock that had done the damage. "Move away so I can see what you did!"

"We're not done with him," the Pullo boy hissed from behind the librarian. He was the smallest boy in Domenica's class, who found his courage only when backed by a mob.

"That's enough, boys." Aniballi raised his voice. "On your way. I will handle this."

The mob dispersed slowly.

Domenica heard their slurs and laughter, which meant Silvio could hear them too.

Domenica looked up at Aniballi. "He needs to see Dottore Pretucci."

"I can't carry him." He brushed the sand off his trousers.

Domenica spoke softly to Silvio. "Let me see."

Silvio shook his head. If it were even possible, he had contracted even more tightly into a coil, like an animal whose instinct was to camouflage when in danger.

"I won't touch it. I just need to see where the rock hit you," she whispered.

Domenica took Silvio's bloody hand and gently lifted it away from his face. The skin was torn away on his forehead, revealing the wound, a ruby-red gash over his left eyebrow. Silvio squeezed his eye shut, protecting it, but blood poured out of the wound and down his face. Domenica wiped the blood off the lid of his eye with her thumb.

Aniballi shuddered at the sight of the blood on Domenica's hand.

"Open your eye." Domenica used her hands to shade Silvio's face from the sun. "You can do it."

Silvio's eyelid fluttered open, but the sun was too bright even in the shade she had created, so he squeezed it shut.

"They missed your eye." Domenica slipped off her apron and stuffed the contents of the pockets into the bodice of her dress, leaving the pink shells on the sand. She folded the apron into a square. "Here. Hold this over the wound and press down hard on it. We have to stop the bleeding." She helped Silvio stand. "We have to get the cut sewn up."

"No!" Silvio cried.

"It's deep. You have to. I'll take you."

Signore Aniballi observed Domenica as she helped Silvio climb the steps and disappear behind the crest of the dune. Aniballi removed a monocle from the breast pocket of his jacket, placing the glass over his right eye. He unscrolled the map, which appeared to be in no worse condition than it had been when the boy took it from the levered glass case in the library. Princess Pauline

Bonaparte Borghese commissioned the map when her brother Napoleon crowned their sister Elisa the Grand Duchess of Tuscany. The librarian would lock all the cases from now on.

As Aniballi rolled the map into a cylinder, he spied one flaw. There was a maroon dot, no larger than the period at the end of a sentence, on the parchment. Il bastardo had left his mark on the official map of Viareggio after all.

CHAPTER 5

The young doctor rolled the blotter over the wet ink, sealing 15 July 1920 in his ledger. The physician was around thirty, but his receding hairline and thick eyeglasses made him appear middle-aged. Luckily, Dottore Armando Pretucci was in his office on Via Sant'Andrea and not at the hospital in Pietrasanta when Domenica Cabrelli pushed his office door open with her elbow and helped Silvio Birtolini inside. The boy had begun to shake at the sight of his own blood, which had saturated his shirt and Domenica's apron.

"Don't look at it. The head bleeds the most. It doesn't mean anything," Domenica assured the boy. "Dottore, my friend is bleeding badly. He needs to be sewn up."

Pretucci sprinted into action. He helped Silvio to the examining table to lie down. He applied pressure to the wound with a thick, clean square of gauze and placed a pad of flannel over the boy's eyes before pulling the overhead work lamp close to Silvio's face to examine the injury. Domenica climbed on the stool next to the doctor to observe.

Pretucci concurred with the little girl. "You're right about the head."

"That it bleeds the most? I know." Domenica peered at Silvio's wound.

"What happened?" Pretucci asked as he gently dabbed the blood to get a better look at the depth of the wound.

"He was hit by a rock," Domenica explained.

"Did you throw it?"

"No. He's my friend."

"So, the rock was thrown by an enemy?"

"We don't know which one."

The doctor addressed Silvio: "You have more than one enemy?"

"Many," Silvio whispered.

"The patient speaks at last. What's your name?"

"Silvio Birtolini, Dottore." The boy trembled.

"Where does your father work?"

Domenica answered before Silvio could: "His father is dead. His mother works at the church."

Pretucci could tell from the boy's clothing that his mother did the kind of work that paid a pittance. "Do you have brothers and sisters?"

"No."

"He's alone. Except for me, of course. I have been his friend since we were five," Domenica explained.

"That's a lifelong friendship," Pretucci said.

"So far, Dottore. Can I help you? Shall I get fresh water?" Domenica looked around. "And cotton rags? Do you have some?"

"The bandages in the cabinet are clean." Pretucci had scrubbed the bandages himself and set them in the sun to dry. He could not afford a nurse. He kept the clinic in Viareggio to tend to the local shipbuilders, sailors, and the employees of the silk mill. Most of his time was spent in general practice caring for the sick with private home visits. Pretucci had not solicited a single patient in Pietrasanta or Viareggio since he returned from his studies at the Università di Pisa. He didn't have to; the patients in need always found him.

Pretucci's clinic was spare and clean and smelled like rubbing alcohol. Two wooden chairs, a stool, and a desk with a chair were lit by a single lamp covered by a white enamel shade hung over the examining table. A portable glass cabinet filled with small bottles, tinctures, cotton bandages, and medical instruments was propped open on the desk. They were the most modern instruments available.

By the time Domenica had collected the fresh water from the fountain in the street, gathered the gauze, and found a tin cup to give Silvio a drink, the doctor had assembled the instruments to close the wound with stitches. The boy lay still on the table with his eyes closed and his hands folded across his waist. He appeared brave, but a steady flow of tears fell silently from the corners of his eyes, cutting clean rivulets through the sand and blood caked on his face.

"Don't cry, Silvio."

"It's better if he cries. It flushes out any debris. Cry all you want, son." Pretucci patted the boy on the shoulder.

Domenica dipped a strip of cotton in the cool water and gently removed the dirt from Silvio's face, starting with his jawline, the area farthest from the gash, and working her way toward his eye. Pretucci monitored her technique. Domenica stippled the dampened cotton strip against Silvio's skin, pulling the sand out of the wound. She rinsed the cotton in the bowl of water and repeated the procedure until the area was clean. Silvio winced when she dabbed near his eye.

"Does that hurt?" Domenica asked him.

"A little," Silvio whispered.

"I'll try not to hurt you. They really got you."

"Use more water on the gauze to flush the wound," Pretucci advised her. He measured the surgical thread against the light and snipped off a long piece of it. He threaded the needle with a small loop, knotting it. He placed the flannel over Silvio's eyes and pulled the lamp close. "Good job, Signorina."

"Grazie, Dottore. Do you mind if I give the patient a drink? Fear makes a boy thirsty."

"They didn't teach me that in medical school."

"My mother told me that." Domenica knelt on the stool. "She's strict but kind too." Domenica placed one hand behind Silvio's neck and lifted it slightly so he might take a drink. She held the cup to his mouth. He sipped the cool water slowly.

"Grazie," Silvio whispered when he had enough.

"You may want to hold your friend's hand. Sometimes this part stings a bit."

Domenica hadn't held Silvio's hand since they were little. They were eleven, that strange hammock of time stretched between child and teenager when they knew the world was about to change but did not have the words for it. Domenica took Silvio's hand. He gripped it hard.

The doctor leaned over the patient and gently pressed the open wound together at the farthest point of the gash. Silvio's smooth skin was the texture of gold velvet.

"Do you want me to do it?" Domenica offered.

Pretucci was amused. With a steady hand, he began to sew the wound closed with stitches so small the thread was barely visible. "You know how to sew surgical stitches?"

"Yes, Dottore."

"Who taught you?"

"I sewed my father's hand in the shop when he cut it on a blade. The injury was on his right hand, so he couldn't sew it himself, so I had to do it. I do needlepoint too."

"That's excellent practice."

"I know. Papa was brave and that made it easy. It's a lot like sewing a hem. The stitches have to be tight and straight," she explained. "I'm really good at it."

"No, Domenica," Silvio roared. "I want the doctor to do it." It was the only demand the boy had made since he arrived. The doctor smiled.

"So I will finish the job."

Domenica was not pleased.

"You already helped me a great deal," Pretucci assured her.

The compliment did not make up for not being allowed to close the wound. "Grazie," Domenica grumbled, remembering her manners.

The work light swayed on its wire. Outside, a crackle of lightning was followed by thunder. A hard rain soon danced off the windowpane. Domenica kept her eyes on the doctor as he worked.

Pietro Cabrelli was slim and moved quickly through the world, as though time wasted were a sin. He wore a fashionable thin mustache and a three-piece brown serge suit, the only one he owned. He escaped from the rain into the doctor's office, followed by his twelve-year-old son, Aldo.

Cabrelli removed his hat and set it on the chair. The boy tossed his wet head, shaking off the rain, which flew in every direction. Domenica glared at him. Her brother had terrible manners.

"Why did you bring him, Papa? He doesn't know how to behave."

"Don't bother with your brother. This is about you. Domenica, I warned you. Not another fight." Cabrelli was weary of meeting with the nuns, who begged him to get control of his daughter, who roamed through the school seeking justice for those children unable to defend themselves.

"It wasn't a fight this time, Papa. We were chased."

Cabrelli pointed to the floor, which meant she was in for it. It was almost impossible to make her father angry, but somehow she managed to do it. Domenica slid off the stool and went to her father. She stood before him like a defendant before a judge. "I'm sorry, but there has been a misunderstanding," Domenica said diplomatically. "Let me explain." She dusted a few raindrops off the lapel of her father's suit.

"There is always a misunderstanding. There is always an excuse. I told you, no more fighting."

Aldo smiled wickedly as he poked his fingers between the ribs of the model of a skeleton hanging on the wall. "Are you going to beat her?"

"No!" Silvio tried to sit up on the table.

"Lie down and don't move again," the doctor ordered. Without looking up, he directed a comment to Cabrelli. "I have work to do here, Signore."

"Forgive me, Dottore. I'm here to take my daughter home."

"Forgive me too, Signore, but I need her to stay," Pretucci countered.

"I don't understand."

"Of all people, you should understand. She sewed up your hand, didn't she?"

Cabrelli was confused.

"They got him good." Aldo had wandered over to the examining table and was watching the doctor as he sewed the stitches.

"You were on the beach this afternoon." Domenica's eyes narrowed suspiciously. "You were chasing us with the rest of them!"

"Your brother followed the boys to try to protect you. He tried to outrun the others to help you."

"Is that what you told Papa? That's a joke. I don't need his help." Domenica put her hands on her hips with authority. "Besides, I can run faster than Aldo any day."

"No, you can't!" Aldo's face turned red with fury.

"When I'm done here, I'll prove it."

"You're skinny," Aldo charged.

"You're fat."

"Children."

"Papa, you see how she is. She is mean."

A woman, small and dark, with a black cotton kerchief tied over her hair, soaked from the downpour, pushed through the door and looked around the room furtively.

"Signora Vietro!" Domenica motioned to her. "Silvio is over here."

The doctor stepped aside to reveal her son on the examining table. Signora Vietro moved toward Silvio swiftly without a sound, finding a spot on the far side of the examining table. She squeezed between the table and the wall into a space barely wide enough to fit a broom. Signora surveyed her son's face. As she took in the severity of the wound, her expression shattered from one of concern to one of despair. Her eyes filled with silent tears, but not one fell down her face. She slid her hand under her son's shoulder, placing the other on his chest, where she could feel his heart pounding in fear.

"I'm here, Silvio," she said softly.

Pretucci continued his work.

"I am his mother. His eye?"

Pretucci continued to sew. "His eye was spared. He's a lucky boy."

Her son was anything but lucky. Signora Vietro surveyed Silvio for further injuries. He lay obedient and still as the doctor worked on the wound. Silvio's eyes were masked in flannel, so she could not see the terror in them, but she knew her son. Silvio's hands were formed in tight fists. His forehead was slick with sweat. She covered his hands with her own. They were ice cold. "You're brave. It's almost over."

"Signora, the rock hit him just above his eyebrow. It will leave a scar."

His mother whispered in Silvio's ear, "I'm sorry."

Silvio squeezed her hand.

"Signora, it's my fault." Domenica made a fist and tapped her chest as the nuns had instructed when seeking forgiveness. "My grievous fault. Forgive me. I asked Silvio to borrow the map for me. Signore Aniballi sent a mob to get it back. They chased us down Viareggio Beach."

"No. Tell the truth," Aldo said, interrupting his sister. "He stole the map!"

"He did not steal it. He borrowed it."

"We will talk about this later," Signora Vietro said quietly to her son.

"Signora, I needed the map. I asked Silvio to bring it to me. I wanted to find the pirate treasure from Capri."

"I can't believe this." Cabrelli threw his hands in the air.

"Papa, I heard tell of it in our home. Mama had a visitor, and she told the story. Anyone who finds the treasure gets to keep it. It's been years since they hid it. A pirate treasure would do a lot of good around here. We need it. I wouldn't give any of it to the church either."

"Domenica," her father warned.

"They have enough. We could use a horse and carriage. We have to walk wherever we go. Do you have one, Dottore?"

"I don't."

"See? You could borrow it too."

Netta Cabrelli peered inside the doctor's office through the window. The storm was getting worse as charcoal clouds moved in from the sea. She held on to her straw hat as she pushed through the door. "Mama!" Aldo ran to her.

"I came as soon as I heard," Netta said to her husband. Signora Cabrelli's deep blue eyes were red from weeping. Domenica felt bad that she had made her mother cry again. Netta possessed a simple, unadorned beauty, like the statue of the Madonna at San Paolino, but her expression was one of an angry mother.

"Mama. Believe me." Aldo pointed at the examining table. "Silvio stole the map!"

The sight of the boy on the table made Netta shudder. "Quiet, Aldo. Domenica, I want you to take your brother home. Now."

"Yes, Mama."

When it came to punishments, Domenica was more afraid of her mother than she was of her father. Mama knew how to top any assigned penance levied by the priest after confession with the kind of deprivation that could make a young girl change her bad ways for good. A few Hail Marys weren't enough for Netta Cabrelli. She made a punishment sting. No supper. No reading. No playing on the beach or hiking the trails in the woods. And the worst: Domenica's chores would increase. She would be fetching water for the neighbors until her arms fell off. Her mother would make her bundle kindling and deliver it until there were no more trees left in the forest. The punishment could end up being far worse than Lent. Yet, despite her daughter's behavior, Netta embraced her.

"Where's your apron?" her mother asked.

Domenica patted her dress. She forgot about the apron.

"There it is!" Aldo squealed, pointing to the corner near the cabinet.

The clean apron Domenica had put on that morning was ruined. It was balled up on the floor, saturated with Silvio's blood, which had dried to the color of a brick. "I just mended that apron. Now you'll go the rest of the year without one."

"I'm sorry, Mama."

"And you." Netta smacked Aldo on the back of his head. "What were you doing with the older boys on the beach?"

"Signore Aniballi sent us after the thief." Aldo rubbed the back of his head.

"Silvio. Did. *Not.* Steal." Domenica spoke to her brother as though his ears were full of sand. "Silvio *borrowed* the map for me. Libraries loan books and maps and ledgers and blueprints. We were going to return it."

"We were making sure you would return the *borrowed* map," Aldo mocked her.

"You wouldn't know how to read a map," Domenica shot back. "You have the brains of an artichoke."

Pietro Cabrelli was exhausted. "Enough."

Domenica studied Pretucci's technique as he knotted the thread on Silvio's stitches. "Mama, it was my idea, not Silvio's. I should be punished," she said, not taking her eyes off the doctor's technique.

"Oh, you will be punished."

Silvio tried to sit up. "Signora Cabrelli—"

Pretucci gently touched his shoulder. "Lie down. Signorina, show your mother and father your skills. Trim the thread and finish with the astringent, please."

"Sì, Dottore." Domenica washed her hands in the basin before she climbed onto the stool. She trimmed the surgical thread carefully with Pretucci's scissors. She sprinkled a square of gauze with astringent, carefully dabbing around the stitches.

Vera Vietro did not take her eyes off her son.

"What is going on here?" Netta Cabrelli asked her husband before she turned to Pretucci. "Why is my daughter helping you, Dottore?

"Because she's able." Pretucci washed his hands in the basin of fresh water. "Your daughter assisted me. She prepared this basin, the bandages, and she cleansed the wound. She even volunteered to sew the stitches."

"I'm sure she did." Netta Cabrelli sighed. "Va bene, Dottore. Domenica, come home as soon as you're done here."

"Thank you, Mama."

"Your father will stay with you until the doctor releases you." Netta grabbed her son by the scruff of his neck and led him out the door without saying a proper goodbye to Signora Vietro.

As Domenica dabbed the fresh stitches, the skin around Silvio's wound turned bright pink. "Signora Vietro, see the pink skin? That means it is healing."

Domenica studied the doctor's artful stitchwork. The surgical thread had been sewn in a row of small stitches so tight, a series of black dots followed the arch of Silvio's thick black eyebrows. "Well done, Dottore." Domenica was impressed. She turned to Silvio's mother. "If you put olive oil on the stitches before Silvio goes to sleep, there won't be a bad scar," Domenica said.

There was still a good chance that Silvio would not have a permanent reminder of this awful day. But Domenica would. It wasn't Aniballi's charge to the bullies, or the sound the rock made when it hit Silvio's face, or the taunts of the mob that she would remember; it was her parents' shameful behavior in the doctor's office. They had failed to greet Signora Vietro, who was, as far as Domenica could tell, a fine person besides being the mother of her best friend. Domenica was treated well by Signora, and for that reason, her parents should have reciprocated, but they ignored her completely.

Perhaps Mama had forgotten that Signora Vietro had made their family a pot of potato soup with bits of smoked ham the previous winter and mended their wool stockings when the moths had gotten to them. Had Mama forgotten that Signora had given pastels and paper to the children so they might trace the frescoes in San Paolino while she worked inside, polishing the pews with lemon oil for Holy Week? Maybe if her parents remembered how kind Signora Vietro had been to their family, they would treat her with the same respect they gave to the other families in the village, the families with two parents. And even though Signora Montaquila was a widow, her sons were treated with respect at school. They were invited to picnics and parties. Her parents welcomed the Greco, DeRea, Nerino, and Tiburzi families into the Cabrelli home. Their children were allowed to play in Boncourso's garden without an invitation; why not Silvio? Domenica couldn't think of one good reason to justify her parents' behavior. Maybe they had failed to greet Signora Vietro properly because she was not wearing a hat. Her mother could be a stickler about silly things like gloves and hats.

Poor Silvio. He spent his days trying to be invisible to avoid trouble, while his mother moved through Viareggio as though she were.

CHAPTER 6

Netta Cabrelli dipped the rag into the slick black paste and buffed the toe of her husband's work shoe. She rubbed the leather back and forth in small strokes, applying pressure. The scuffs soon disappeared. The wax filled in the cracks where the leather had worn thin. She held the oxford up to the lamp and examined the repairs Massimo the shoemaker had made. He had installed an extra layer of black pebbled rubber between the upper and sole.

Massimo explained that the rubber had come from the finest lot out of the Congo. It had been mixed in vats with hearty black ash to thicken the sap made from the hemp. The goo was poured into sheets, dried in the sun, and cut into boards before being shipped to Italy. The shoemakers customized the rubber and sewed it into shoes and boots. The layer of rubber prevented the shoe from leaking through the rains of the long winter, while helping to preserve the leather and extend the long life of the handmade shoe. Netta wanted her husband, the apprentice, to look like a master craftsman as he worked hard to become one, so she took special care with his appearance, down to his shoes. *La bella figura* also applied to men, especially breadwinners.

Pietro closed the bedroom door.

Netta held up the shoe. "Look. Massimo repaired your shoes."

"Va bene."

"They're heavy now. You won't feel the cold in these when winter comes." Netta buffed the shoe with vigor.

"Aldo is supposed to polish my shoes. We had an agreement."

"He was tired."

"All that running on the beach. He's not used to moving fast."

"At least you can catch him." Netta sighed. "Even if we had a head start, we'd never catch Domenica. She's a fox."

"I don't know. She's more intelligent than cunning."

"Too intelligent"—Netta smiled—"for her own good."

"No such thing."

"The children at school are afraid of her."

"She's a leader."

"Who does she lead? She has no friends. The girls don't invite her over to play. So I said, invite them to the garden. She wouldn't. Domenica said the girls her age are silly. 'They giggle too much,' she told me."

"Because they do."

"That's just how young girls are."

"If she doesn't like them, she doesn't like them. She's capable of making friends."

"The wrong ones! I should have forbidden her to spend time with Silvio Birtolini from the start."

"It wouldn't have made any difference. She would have found a way to be his friend."

"She only became his friend because he has none. She pities him."

"That makes her kind."

"No good will come of him. Anyone that associates with him will eventually be marked too. Now he steals."

"At our daughter's request."

"I understand that. But do the women at the church? I don't think so."

"It's up to us to explain what happened. They're children. Our daughter heard a story, and she was intrigued by the idea of a buried treasure. It's all quite innocent when the truth is told."

"How will we pay for the map they destroyed? Aniballi insisted the map was ruined and covered in blood."

"I agreed to make it right. The library is in need of repairs. It will take me months to complete the work."

"You make sure the Birtolini boy helps you."

"Aniballi won't allow him near the library."

"It will be a miracle if they let him back in school. So, you see what I mean. Domenica should not be around him anymore. Look at his background."

"It's not his fault."

"They don't ask whose fault it is when the rock is thrown."

"And they should, Netta. But they don't. They bully the boy without a father."

"He has a father! But his father has a wife and a family in Orvieto. He would not take the boy. I imagine the wife had something to say about that."

"Gossip. Just gossip."

"Gossip that affects our daughter and her reputation."

"The Vietro family are good people. Her father was a blacksmith in Pietrasanta. The mother's side was from Abruzzo. Honest farmers. One mistake erased generations of pious living," Cabrelli lamented.

"It was more than a mistake. Don't feel sorry. It was a mortal sin."

"A sin that is not ours to atone. All this talk about Vera and Silvio is just that. I don't want my wife participating in it. Ignore it."

"I have enough to worry about. I am failing with my own children."

"Children get into mischief," Pietro said wearily. "I am not going to beat my children."

"You're the only father who doesn't, and it shows! Domenica fears nothing. I send her to church. She takes her sacraments. But the fear of God is not in her; it floats over her like a vapor and disappears into the clouds like smoke. It does not get in. She challenges the Sisters. They say she is polite when she asks questions, but who is she to ask questions? And if she doesn't like the answer, look out! She's wild. She will argue until the school bell rings."

"There's nothing wrong with having your own mind. It should be encouraged, especially in an intelligent girl."

"We have to punish her for her role in the theft because if we don't"—Netta wiped her tears on a handkerchief—"how will she ever grow up to be a respectable woman? To be a wife? A mother? She believes Viareggio is her kingdom and she makes the rules. She should have been born a Bonaparte. She is arrogant like them."

Cabrelli sat next to his wife. "You took away her supper and the library. That's all she has. Domenica does her chores, doesn't she?"

Netta nodded.

"She studies hard. She says her prayers. She is obedient."

Netta cut her husband a look.

"She has a problem with obedience," he admitted. "But she always has a good reason to start a ruckus. She is moral."

"In her fashion. But this incident shows she lacks judgment." Netta was bereft.

"I'll talk to her."

"Tonight."

"Why the urgency, Netta?"

"That rock was not meant for the Birtolini boy."

CHAPTER 7

Behind Chiesa San Paolino, down a stone path, before the new barn was built and next to the garden shed, was the stable, used to keep the priest's carriage and horse. Once the new priest acquired the first motorcar in Viareggio, the horse and carriage were sold, and the stable was left vacant.

Signora Vera Vietro was the church and rectory housekeeper. She exchanged half her wages for rent of the stable. She moved in before Silvio was born and, with the help of the gardener, made it habitable. The stable had a rustic charm. Trumpet vines, with orange blossoms shaped like horns set among thick green leaves, climbed up the side wall and over the tile roof, drenching the weathered wood in color. The windows were wooden shutters with hooks and no slats. The floor was notched pine, left over from the wood used when new floors were installed in the rectory.

The tack wall had iron hooks that once held the reins, headpieces, nosebands, and saddles of the parish horses. Signora Vietro used those same hooks to hold watering cans, garden tools, and buckets. The gardener installed leftover materials from the church renovation, including tiles and wood planks, to shore up the structure. The walls of the stable were painted the same butter yellow as the sacristy of San Paolino, because there were a few cans of leftover paint when the church renovation was completed. It was an eclectic room, but it was warm and dry, the only home the Birtolini boy ever knew.

The stable doors were propped open, letting the clean scent of the earth after the rain waft through the room. His mother had done the laundry. Silvio's pants and shirt, along with his mother's work dress, were pinned to a rope, hooked between two beams.

Silvio swept the floor, knowing his mother would appreciate his efforts. He also felt guilty for taking her away from her work at the church that afternoon. The priest didn't like it when she was called to the school on Silvio's behalf, or when she stayed home to care for him when he was sick. His mother never made him feel like a bother, but no matter her intention, he felt like one.

Silvio always needed an escape route and a place to hide. He had managed to keep the place where he and his mother lived a secret, which did not keep the children from school from inventing wild tales about them.

Some children gossiped that Silvio lived in the woods with the wild boars; others spread a story that he lived in the sepulcher of the church, sleeping upright next to the tombs. Silvio had heard Beatrice Bibba tell a group of girls at school that his mother was forced to clean the church because she carried a mortal stain that could only be diminished by servitude. In truth, his mother cleaned the church because she needed to put food on the table and a roof over their heads. There was no man to rely upon, no father to protect them. The children made up stories that were the stuff of serial adventure stories in the newspapers. The stories were an effective way to keep Silvio Birtolini in his place as il bastardo.

"Don't sweep, Silvio. Rest," his mother said when she arrived home carrying a small parcel. "Here." She opened the cloth wrapper and placed a hot bomboloni on a small plate. She gave it to her son. "Your favorite."

"I'm not hungry, Mama."

"Eat, Silvio. They're fresh. I got them at the festa."

"I know. But it's not the same when you bring them home. They taste better at the stand after I play games."

His mother placed the bombolone back into the cloth and wrapped them tightly. "It won't taste sweet as long as you have bitter thoughts."

"Most of my thoughts are bitter, Mama. It's a miracle I can taste anything sweet at all."

"I don't blame you." She pressed her palm to his forehead and gently touched the bandage over his eye. "How do you feel?"

Silvio waved her hand away. "It's sore."

"It will heal. You'll see. Tomorrow morning, it will feel better. In a few days, you'll forget about it."

"I don't forget."

"We must forgive."

"I can't."

"Even if I promise you it won't happen again?"

"It will happen until I'm old enough to make it stop. And then I'll have to build my own army. Right now, I have nobody. There's only me." He tried to smile, but it pulled the stitches.

"Shame on them for chasing you and the Cabrelli girl like animals. They should be punished for what they did."

"They won't be." Silvio patted the bandage.

"Domenica told me to put olive oil on the stitches and you won't have a scar."

Silvio rolled his eyes. "She thinks she's a doctor."

"She's a good friend."

Silvio didn't want to say it aloud because he knew it would hurt his mother, but Domenica was, in fact, his only friend.

"It will be so hard to leave here," his mother said quietly, looking around the room.

"Does the priest want the stable back?"

"You know the church, they always need more space."

"Mama, do you ever notice that the village priest lives in a big house all alone? Why does one man need so many rooms?"

"Because he's important."

"I like our home. I want to stay."

"What we want doesn't matter. I've made a decision. We have to leave Viareggio."

"Why?"

"Because you still have both your eyes. They won't rest until they hurt you so badly you cannot recover. I know how this goes. It just gets worse until they drive you out entirely. Then they find another child to pick on. It's always the way."

"Where will we go?"

"Zia Leonora will take us in."

"No, Mama."

"She's not that bad. We just have to listen to her carp about her aches and pains and make her rum balls. She's all right."

"When?"

"Tomorrow, before the sun is up. Don Xavier arranged a driver to take us to the train to Parma. He provided the fare and a letter for me to secure a position at Chiesa di Sant'Agostino."

Silvio wanted to argue to stay, but he felt so bad for his mother, he dropped the cause. "There are lots of things I will miss about Viareggio."

"After all this? You are a good boy." Vera embraced her son and held him for as long as he would allow. "Let's get some rest. We have a big day tomorrow."

His mother finished her chores. She pressed their clothes, sprinkling them with lavender and lemon before pressing the hot iron onto the fabric. She packed their meager belongings, which fit into one cloth satchel. Vera got down on her knees and loosed a stone from the hearth. She removed their savings hidden in the hole underneath it. Silvio's eyes widened as he watched his mother sit at the table and count the lire. She placed it in her purse, a small leather clutch Zia Leonora had given her when she no longer had use for it. His mother placed the purse on top of the satchel. She looked around the room, making sure she left the stable as she had found it.

His mother lay down and fell asleep so quickly—it was a joke between them. Across the room, on his cot, Silvio lay awake. It took him hours to go to sleep because he worked in the dark, plotting the life he would someday lead when he was old enough to claim it. He imagined different scenarios depending upon his mood. Sometimes he was a soldier in a mythical kingdom from the Zella cartoon series, other times a sailor on the high seas navigating storms and pirates, or he imagined a life where he wore a brown suit, black shoes, and a hat to an office somewhere. His favorite fantasy: He schemed how to get a government job that provided a uniform and a motor scooter. He would park it outside his apartment with a terrace overhead and terra-cotta flowerpots on the stairs. He dreamt of an ordinary life when he was tired, the kind of life where people were nice to him. The more fantastical options required his concentration.

It was not the worst thing to leave Viareggio, he reasoned. His mother needed a fresh start even more than he did. It hurt him when his mother was ignored by the people who attended church, even though she was the one who cleaned the pews, buffed the floors, and washed the stained glass windows. Did the parishioners ever wonder who rolled the beeswax candles and refilled the offering trays so their precious prayers might be answered before the wick gave out? Vera Vietro was treated shabbily, but she endured it because their home on the church grounds came with the pittance of pay she received. The disdain for his mother didn't seem to faze her, but it bothered her son. Vera Vietro was so busy holding their lives together, she didn't notice how she was treated, and if she did, she ignored it for the good of her son.

Silvio had observed his mother fill with false hope whenever a child besides the steadfast and loyal Domenica Cabrelli befriended him. When a boy invited her son to play a street game, she hoped that it meant that Silvio was finally accepted by his peers. She would fortify any fledgling friendship with acts of kindness. She would send a cake or a pot of soup home with the new friend as a gesture of gratitude, in hopes her largesse might gently encourage the friendship to take root. In those moments, when it appeared that things had changed for her boy, Signora Vietro believed that the worst was over. But of course, it wasn't. The parents of the children would sever any new ties when they learned of the circumstances of Silvio's birth. They made a point of ostracizing the Birtolini boy from their proper families.

As Silvio grew older, the bullying deepened to contempt, the portal to violence. There was no way to change their perception of Silvio, especially one that was deeply ingrained in the people who perpetuated the pain. There was only one person in the world who could change people's minds about Silvio, and he wouldn't do it. Silvio was unwanted by his father, which made him unwanted in the world. Despite all of it, Silvio kept trying to fit in.

Every day of his life, Silvio Birtolini started over. He left his mother's home with high hopes each morning, believing that this would be the day that would erase the sin, or at least leave it in the past to be forgotten. He tried his best to fit in, to be a good pal, but Silvio accrued no loyalty, even when he gave it. No kindness was returned when he offered it. No one thought to include him, even when he spent sleepless nights considering how to make friends and find camaraderie in simple connections that came so naturally to other children. If that weren't enough pain to endure, he saw what it did to his mother. The rejection of Silvio by his teachers and fellow students was an open wound for his mother. It broke his tender heart to live a helpless life.

The only respite he had was the library, and now even that had been taken from him. Before the incident, if Silvio was quiet and followed the rules, he was allowed to stay as long as he wished, a privilege for a boy who wasn't welcome anywhere. Silvio and Domenica spent hours in the library together poring over books that delighted them no matter how many times they read them. Domenica was encouraged to be bold as she read *The Three Musketeers*. The boy learned to cope by reading Charles Dickens, who wrote of Silvio's circumstances like no other writer. The stories of the travails of others helped him make sense of his own; the only difference was, the fictional characters who endured hardship were safe inside of books. Silvio was not. He had to live in a village where he had no protection.

Silvio would turn twelve in a few days, and he was eager to become a man. Manhood meant he could finally seize control of his own life. There were signs that it was coming, so he was in preparation for the new role. He approached it in the same fashion he had studied for his sacraments. Silvio knew that his mother could not guide him in this regard, only a father could do so for his son. He would figure it out on his own by reading about it.

Before Silvio had taken the map from the library, he had lost track of the time in the stacks reading about the changes in his body in *The Doctor's Guide to the Adolescent Male*. He read things that disturbed and thrilled him, so much so he almost forgot entirely about taking the map and meeting Domenica. But he would not let his friend down. If only he had kept reading and stayed in the library, he would have avoided the worst of this terrible day.

He wished that he would have had time to finish the book about puberty. He had read enough to discern that by the time he turned fourteen, he would physically be a man, well on his way to a strength, height, and weight that would make it impossible for anyone to cross him. At that point, he could leave school, apprentice at a trade, and get a job to earn a wage to care for his mother and himself. Silvio thought it was funny that his glands in puberty were in control of his fate and would be the catalyst to help him leave the pain of his childhood behind. According to the book, it would be so. Manhood would change his life. He would shed his boyhood on the road to Parma. He no longer wanted to explain himself, endure the daily taunts, and be forced to hide when he was chased in the dark. Beyond Domenica's loyalty, there was nothing for him in this village by the sea. No matter what good he could do, or what he might attempt to achieve or become, in Viareggio, he would remain il bastardo.

CHAPTER 8

Domenica lay in her bed under the window in the kitchen and looked out at the night sky. She was attempting to examine her conscience, but the process was tedious. She disliked the spiritual exercise almost as much as her least favorite chore, the arduous task of pulling the tiny bones from the baccala to cure it for the winter. There were always more fish bones, no matter how many she removed. So it went with sin. She picked apart her actions to prepare for confession, but there were invariably more sins she could report. What good could come from going over and over events that had already happened, whose outcomes could not be changed, and whose residual effects could not be stopped? It all seemed pointless.

It had been a day of shame for the Cabrelli family. Her brother wiggled out of any punishment and made himself out to be some sort of hero for the town library by joining the ruffians on the beach. Aniballi promised the boys lemonade and cookies to celebrate the return of the map. It was disgusting. And just as she expected, her mother's punishments were severe. No dinner until Sunday. She had been banned from the library for one month. The latter was practically a death sentence, but she would live with it. At least she had seven books under her cot waiting to be read. Silvio probably wouldn't ever be able to go back to the library, so she would share her stash with him. That was the least she could do. After all, he would have a scar because of her. She felt guilty about that and had already asked God's forgiveness. And yet, in spite of the fracas, this had been the best day of her life. She had worked for Dottore Pretucci and done a good job. Domenica had found her purpose. She would be a nurse. The happiest moment in a person's life was when they found the thing they were born to do. Domenica was giddy in the moonlight.

"Domenica, are you asleep?" her father whispered from the archway.

"No, Papa, I am praying."

"Continue to pray. We can speak in the morning."

"I'm done." Domenica quickly blessed herself and sat up in the cot. "Is Mama ever going to speak to me again?"

"I hope so." Pietro sat down in the straight-backed chair next to the fireplace.

"When I'm a mother, I will always talk to my children no matter what they do."

"You will do your best when the time comes, just like your mother."

"Why is everyone angry with me?"

"You're a strong person, and you pushed a weak one to do a bad thing."

"Silvio is not weak. He's a good partner. He's the only boy I know that can keep up with me on the trails. He's strong."

"It doesn't matter what he is. It was *your* scheme. You put this in his head! Domenica, there are only two blows to a reputation you cannot recover from in the village. Once you are known as a beggar or a thief, you will always be known as one or the other."

"We *borrowed* the map from the library."

"That's not what Signore Aniballi told me. Silvio stole the map. He went into the geography room and pulled it from a display case without asking."

"We are allowed to look at the maps."

"With permission."

"We were going to return it. Half the time Aniballi is asleep at his desk. He doesn't even notice who goes in and out of the library. He has it in for Silvio."

"That may be true, but it doesn't matter. Aniballi was alert enough to see Silvio steal the map. The man that steals a loaf of bread and eats it can never return the stolen bread. And even if he pays for it later, he still is a thief."

"Papa, this is a map, not bread. Signore Aniballi got his map back."

"And it was ruined."

"It was not ruined. I know. I held it."

"That's not what Aniballi told me."

"Aniballi." Domenica clucked. "I won't say what he is because I'm about to be confirmed and I don't want the Holy Ghost to send down a blazing fireball to punish me."

"Then don't."

"Tell me this: What is Signore Aniballi's punishment? For lying about the destruction of the map? For turning the boys in the village into a pack of dogs?"

"You can't blame him for that," Cabrelli countered.

"Why not?" Domenica closed her eyes and tapped her chest. "It is my grievous fault. Silvio was following my orders. Forgive me, Blessed Mother, Holy Communion of Saints, Baby Gesù, and God

Himself, for praying for justice. Aniballi should taste bitterness in his mouth until he learns to tell the truth. Amen."

"That's not fair. Aniballi has a job. He has to protect the books and maps in the library. Don't blame him for your mistake. Listen to me. You are the instigator. When the forest burns, it is *you* we find holding the box of matches. You and your choices. Your crazy scheme led to all of this. You can't go around telling the other children what to do. You aren't their mother or father. You are not the carabinieri. You don't make the rules and you aren't the law to enforce them."

"I wish we were rich. Don't you want to be rich, Papa?"

Cabrelli sighed. "Working with priceless gems cures you of wanting to own them."

"I want to own them. When you're rich, no one can tell you what to do. The mayor and the bishop? No one tells them what to do."

"Your conscience tells you what's right, rich or poor. And that's what has your mother and me worried. You didn't show good judgment."

"If we borrow books from the library, why can't we borrow a map? Doesn't the library belong to all of us?"

"The map belongs to the state. You could have been badly hurt today. Silvio will have a scar."

"Like a pirate."

"Pirates are not saints. They are thieves. I forbid you from hunting for that buried treasure. It doesn't exist. It's a fable that resurrects itself in the village and makes the rounds whenever people believe that money will save them. I am sorry my own daughter believes that nonsense. Your friend could have lost his eye. And you could have lost yours. The boy who threw the rock didn't care who got hurt—he was just trying to stop you."

"Where's his punishment?"

"Aniballi doesn't know which boy threw the rock."

"Aniballi was on the dunes. He could see the whole beach. Only Saint Michael on his blue cloud saw more. It doesn't matter. I know who threw it."

"You saw the boy?"

"No. But Guido Mironi got to me first and took the map from me. So it was him."

"You can't accuse him unless you're certain."

"The wound on Silvio's brow was long and deep and the rock was heavy, which means the boy who threw it was close. The angle of the cut on his forehead meant the rock came from overhead, so it was thrown hard by someone taller than we are. It was the Mironi boy. He taunts Silvio at school. He takes his book and his bread. Half the time Silvio doesn't eat because they steal his food."

"And you share yours with him."

"Yes, Papa. But don't tell Mama."

"You will not be punished in this house for being kind. But it doesn't make up for stealing the map. You had the angels on your side today, Domenica. I don't know if you will the next time you take something that doesn't belong to you."

"The angels know the difference between stealing and borrowing. They're on my side. Trust me on that."

Cabrelli sighed. "Say your prayers."

"I did."

"Say a few more." Pietro walked to the door.

"Papa, why doesn't Silvio have the same name as his mother? She is Signora Vietro and he is a Birtolini."

"Signora Vietro could not marry Silvio's father because the man already had a wife."

Domenica thought about that. "Is Birtolini his father's name?"

"No. The way Italian law works, there's a letter for each month, and the mother without a husband chooses a name, any name, using the letter. Silvio was born in a month where *B* was the designated letter. His mother chose his name from a list."

"Poor Silvio. Il bastardo," Domenica said softly. "Papa, I thought you said that in Viareggio the only two things you cannot be are a beggar or a thief."

"That's right."

"But that's not true. You can't be il bastardo either."

"Domenica."

"It's not Silvio's fault. How can he be blamed for something he didn't do? Why is he marked?"

"We have to pray for him."

"That's not going to get him a father."

Domenica was right, and her father knew it. *Il bastardo* was not simply a taunt. It was an indictment of his future. Silvio would inherit nothing and was barred from getting an education beyond primary school.

Aldo's snores could be heard from the alcove in the next room. Prepuberty had turned him into a hulking, burping, flatulent bear of a boy. He was even offensive when he slept. Domenica couldn't wait to grow up and get as far away from Aldo as she could.

"Are you hungry?"

"No, Papa," Domenica lied.

"Mama will make a frittata for you in the morning."

"How do you know?"

"She arranged for the eggs."

"She did?" Domenica settled under the covers with the confidence that her mother hadn't blamed her for the events that day after all.

Cabrelli blew out the flame inside the hurricane lamp, and sweet almond oil filled the air. "The sooner you sleep, the sooner you eat."

Domenica turned over in her bed. When she heard the gentle click of her parents' bedroom door as it closed, she flipped onto her back, put her hands behind her head, and looked up at the ceiling. She said a quick prayer of thanksgiving for the eggs. Her mother loved her. She prayed for her father because he loved her no matter what she did. She also prayed for Aldo because she was obligated to do so.

Her eyes were fluttering closed when a face appeared in the window like a tintype, backlit by the moon. Too stunned to scream, she rolled off her cot and onto the floor. She jumped to her feet to run out of the room when she turned back to look. The shape of the head was familiar, round like a hazelnut, with a point to the chin. The black curls on his head blended into the scrollwork of the Figliolos' wrought iron fence across the street, making it hard to see. The boy stepped into a shaft of light.

Domenica knelt on her cot and opened the window.

"Did you have any supper?" Silvio whispered.

"I am not allowed any supper until Sunday. They're trying to starve me to death."

"Here."

Domenica unwrapped a cloth. The sweet fragrance of vanilla and butter filled the air. The puffy pastry was drenched in sugar. "How did you get these?"

"Mama went to the feast."

Domenica took a bite. She chewed slowly, savoring the buttery sweetness of the dough and the sugar as it melted on her tongue. "Have one." She held the pastry out to Silvio.

"I can't."

"Why not?"

"My stitches hurt when I chew. Pretucci must've tightened something up." Silvio demonstrated by baring his teeth like an orangutan and attempted to move his bared teeth up and down. Domenica laughed.

Aldo snored loudly and turned over in the next room.

Domenica climbed out the window. She sat down next to Silvio on the stairs.

"Go back inside. You'll get in more trouble," Silvio warned her.

"Once you're in trouble, it's too late to get in more trouble."

"Is that true?"

"It's common sense." Domenica finished the first bombolone. She carefully picked the sugar sprinkles off the cloth and licked her finger. "That is the most delicious treat I ever ate. Ever. Thank you."

"Prego." As hungry as Silvio was, it made him happier to see his friend enjoy the pastry.

Fortified by a full stomach, Domenica presented a new scheme to her friend. "We don't need that stupid map. Aniballi can keep it in his dusty library. We can find the treasure without it. We will work our way through the pine forest. I have a hunch the pirates left it close to the canals."

"Are you certain?"

"That would make the most sense. They would have to make a fast getaway. We'll go tomorrow! When the sun comes up. After I've fetched the water."

"I won't be able to help you find the treasure."

"Well, perhaps not right away. We have to let Aniballi's curse wear off. He has it in for us."

"No, I mean I won't be here. We have to leave Viareggio tomorrow."

"Where will you go?"

"We are going to my aunt's in Parma."

"Not her!" Domenica remembered Zia Leonora, who had airs. She had the unlined brow and high hair of an aristocrat. Zia visited the seashore in August. Signora Vietro had to wait on her like a maid. They called her Zia Regina behind her back. "She's awful!"

"I know. But I have no choice. I'll have to do my chores and behave myself. That's what Mama says."

"How are you supposed to do anything when boys throw rocks at you?"

"Maybe they don't have rocks in Parma." Silvio tried to smile, but it hurt his face.

"Who will protect you? I don't like the idea of Parma at all. But I don't like this town either. I don't have anything nice to say about Viareggio. You almost lost your eye."

"I shouldn't have turned. If I had listened to you, I wouldn't have been hit."

"There are always more rocks and there are always more boys to throw them." Domenica patted his hand. She and Silvio sat on the step for a long time as the white moon flickered in and out behind the clouds. "Silvio, listen to me. When you get to Parma, don't tell them about your name."

"They find out anyway."

"Not if you have a better story," Domenica offered.

"What do you mean?"

"You have to talk about your father before they assume you don't have one. Something like this: Signore Birtolini was a great man, a sea captain who battled pirates. He saved a treasure belonging to the Holy Roman Church, on a ship that was burned at sea."

"But that's not true."

"It doesn't matter! It's your story. You make it up! Say this: Your father jumped off the ship with the precious relics, into a small fishing boat. He held on to the relics through hurricanes and blight and starvation and delivered them back into the hands of the pope himself, who went to anoint him in front of all the cardinals when Signore Birtolini . . ."

"Was hit with a rock."

"No! Your father suddenly died, having been bit by a poisonous fish off the coast of Napoli *while saving the relics*. That's the important part. Signore died while returning the loot! The pope dropped to his knees and kissed your dying father as he gave him the last rites. Extreme unction. Your papa was now whole in this world and the next. The cardinals stood in a red circle and wept. The pope wept. Together, they prayed as the angels came to take your father's soul back to God."

"You don't need to go to the library. You don't need to read books. You are a book."

"Have a story ready, or people will make up one for you. You have to do it before they can. Promise?"

"Promise."

"At least you listen to me. Nobody around here cares what I think."

"I think you're the most intelligent person I know. I'll never make another friend like you."

"Sure you will," Domenica assured him.

"I don't think so. You're strange, Domenica. But there's strength in what makes you different. Coraggio."

Domenica opened the cloth. She gave Silvio the remaining bombolone. He accepted it and split it in two to share with her.

"Take small bites so it doesn't pull the stitches," she said.

Silvio ate most of the second bombolone in tiny bites. She ate the rest. They left not a single granule of sugar on the cloth.

Domenica folded the cloth into a neat square and gave it back to Silvio. "I was really hungry," she said as she climbed back into the house. She poked her head out of the open window. "Thank you."

"Domenica?"

She leaned against the windowsill. Her face—the only face he looked for in school, or at church, or anywhere for that matter, ever—was so close to his that for the first time in his life, the boy felt lucky. "Before I took the map, I found something that I thought might help you."

"A weapon?"

He smiled, but the stitches hurt. "No. There's a book called *The Log of Captain Nicola Forzamenta* in the map room. Pirates often hid treasure in churches."

"Interesting."

"It is." Silvio went down two steps on the stairs.

He stopped at the bottom of the steps before turning around and bounding back up the stairs two at a time to face her. "Domenica?"

Domenica leaned on the window sash. "What is it?" she whispered.

He did not answer her; instead, Silvio took Domenica's face in his hands and kissed her.

Silvio's lips were softer than the bomboloni, which surprised her.

"Ciao, Domenica." Silvio, having expressed himself so intimately to his best friend, was overwhelmed by what he had done. "I must go." He climbed down the steps; when he reached the street, he looked up at her and smiled, holding the side of his face where the rock had landed because it still hurt. "I will return for you someday," he said, so softly only the moon heard him.

Domenica waved goodbye before she pulled the shutters closed, lowered the window, and secured the latch. Through the slats, she watched Silvio Birtolini walk away.

It would be so much easier to fall asleep now that her belly was full. What would she ever do without Silvio Birtolini's friendship? The old people said that every person was replaceable, but in her young life, that wasn't true. There was no replacing Silvio Birtolini, because if there were, she would have already done it. He was the only friend she had whom she trusted with her secrets and her dreams. Silvio had the cunning to hunt for the buried treasure, and he was the only friend she liked enough to share the loot with once they found it. A true friend would steal for you.

There was a chance Silvio was right, that the pirates didn't bury the riches in the dunes as she imagined, but instead hid the jewels in one of the churches. It was also possible the pirates had buried the treasure in the pine groves or found a spot up on Pania della Croce. She thought about this long enough to eliminate some localities that carried ancient lore. The pirates couldn't have gotten as far as Monte Tambura, because they made it back to the ship docked in Viareggio in the same day. It was possible that they hiked up to Rifugio Rossi, left their things in the hut, and went farther up the trail to bury the valuables, retrieving their essentials on the way back down to the ship. There were so many options, so many places the pirates might have hidden the treasure. She doubted she could find it without Silvio.

Domenica had lost her partner, and when it came to finding buried treasure, she knew she needed one. The obvious choice for a replacement was her brother, but Aldo wasn't bright, and he was lousy at following instructions, especially when they came from her, so it was unlikely she could bring him in on her plan.

The thought of going up the mountain alone made her uneasy. Domenica had heard the stories of Uomo Morto, the rock formation on the crest of the ridge on the mountaintop that looked like the face of a dead man. Only God could see his expression, she'd heard the boys in the village say. It was a massive image, one that was so startling, travelers had fallen off the edge of a nearby mountain when they came upon it. It must be a horrible thing! It must be avoided. If she ever had to travel north to Milano or Bergamo or Cremona, she would not go over the mountain; instead, she would stay close to the water, following the sea all the way north. She would not climb the marble hills, because she did not want to see the face of death.

Domenica turned over onto her side to sleep. She couldn't hold her eyes open any longer to think. She licked her lips. Lingering there was the sugar from the bomboloni. She licked them again as her head nestled into the pillow. She was drifting off to sleep when she realized it wasn't the sugar from the pastry that remained on her lips; it was something else entirely. It was the sweet taste of Silvio Birtolini's kiss.

"Domenica!" her mother, Netta, called down to the street from the window. "Take two pails. One for Signora Pascarelli and one for me."

Domenica looked up and waved to her mother. "Yes, Mama." Domenica was glad her mother was speaking to her after the trouble with Aniballi, even if it was just to send her down the promenade for fresh water.

"I'll make the eggs when you get back," her mother promised before closing the shutters.

Instead of grabbing the pails, Domenica darted back into the house and up the stairs at a clip. Domenica found her mother in the kitchen, ran to her, and embraced her. "I'm sorry, Mama."

Netta held her daughter close and kissed her on her head. "Now go," she told her.

Domenica flew back down the stairs. Outside the gate, Domenica unhooked the wooden pails from the post. She had turned to take the empty pails down the promenade when she saw a bundle on the step.

She placed the pails on the ground and picked up the bundle. It was addressed to her! *Signorina Cabrelli*. She opened the accompanying envelope carefully.

Cara Domenica,

You are a good friend. Thank you. The regalo was blessed by Don Carini.

Signora Vietro and Silvio

She untied the bundle, wrapped in clean burlap. Domenica lifted her apron out of the cloth. A small regalo wrapped in a bit of cloth was tied to the bundle with a ribbon. She untied the ribbon, setting the gift off to the side.

Domenica unfurled her apron. It was as white as the sun and the pristine clouds that covered it. There was no trace of Silvio's blood anywhere on the garment! Even the patches were clean! She pulled the apron on over her head and fastened the button behind her neck. She buried her hands in the pockets. The pressed fabric held the scent of lemon and starch. Domenica realized how much she had missed her apron and its pockets when she no longer had one to wear.

Domenica sat down on the steps and opened the package. A small gold medal tumbled out. She examined it closely. Santa Lucia, the patron saint of vision, glittered in the morning light. She carefully wrapped the note and the medal in the cloth and placed it in her apron pocket. She picked up the empty pails and set off to the promenade to fill them with fresh water.

She felt the outside of the deep apron pocket to make sure the medal was safe inside it. She would not share the note or the medal with her mother, father, or brother. She would not even share it with the LeDonne girl, even though Amelia was known for keeping secrets better than any girl in Viareggio.

Domenica didn't know a single person in the village who would be happy that the Birtolini boy had given her a gift. Domenica believed Silvio and his mother were good and kind, even if the people of Viareggio did not agree. Besides, only the most devout remembered to get a medal blessed before they gave it to someone. Signora Vietro and Silvio Birtolini had faith despite their circumstances; therefore, the girl accepted their talisman with humility. Domenica Cabrelli had the protection of a saint, and at eleven years old, she knew she would need it.

CHAPTER 9

Viareggio

Now

Olimpio Roffo parked his car on the street in front of Boncour-so's garden. Olimpio was an amiable husband who looked forward to a hot meal and conversation with his wife after a long day of dealing with artisans and customers. The rain and traffic had been heavy on the autostrada. He took the back road that snaked over the hills in curves that followed the streams that led to the sea. The fog was heavy on the road, which made him overly cautious, so he drove slowly, which caused him to be late. He had a good reason to take his time. Olimpio had news for his wife and wanted to make it home safely to deliver it. Wouldn't it be like fate to ruin a run of good luck before he had a chance to enjoy it? He turned off the engine. The rain was so heavy, he could barely see out the windows of the car.

He checked the sleeve of paperwork from Banca d'Italia by the light of his phone. He had signed the banknote for Cabrelli Jewelers' new venture, which, he was certain, would be the last major move of his career. It was also, most likely, the last major move of his life.

Thursday, March 3, would be a day to remember in a life calendar full of important dates to celebrate. He closed the folder, placed it into a large envelope, fastened the brads shut, and placed it in his briefcase for Matelda's co-signature. He lifted the bakery box from the back seat. He got out of the car and made a dash for his front door as quickly as a fit man of eighty-one could move, which in his case was impressive.

"Nonno!" Anina embraced her grandfather as he came off the elevator. She helped her grandfather out of his soaked raincoat.

"My perfect day just got better." Olimpio kissed his granddaughter.

"Perfect? You're soaked!" Matelda observed from the kitchen doorway before returning to the stove.

"And I didn't melt!" Olimpio turned to Anina. "Have you been here all day?"

"*All* day. I chose an old watch for my wedding and Nonna doesn't want to give it to me."

"I will talk to her," Olimpio said quietly. Anina brought her grandfather's wet coat and briefcase to the powder room to dry.

When Anina returned, Olimpio smiled. "So you know the story."

Anina nodded. "Nonna opened up the family vault in more ways than one."

"Don't make it sound like a prison sentence, Anina," Matelda called out cheerily.

"It wasn't at all, Nonna. Your food is better." Anina followed her grandfather into the kitchen. "Although they take your phone in jail and Nonna took mine."

"I gave it back, didn't I?" Matelda said sweetly.

"I don't want to know why you were punished," Olimpio said to his granddaughter as he handed Matelda the bakery box—"Buon Compleanno"—before kissing her.

"Grazie." Matelda smiled as she opened the box filled with her favorite sfogliatelle, pastries made from paper-thin layers of dough filled with sweet ricotta, in the shape of a seashell, sprinkled with sugar and drizzled in honey.

"Nice. Biagetti's?" Anina looked in the box.

"Who else? They're family." Matelda placed the box on the counter.

"What happened to your face?"

"A seagull attacked her," Anina answered before her grandmother could.

"Those birds can be vicious when they're hungry." Olimpio examined the scratch on Matelda's cheek. "Especially after the tourists have fed them during Carnevale."

"She wouldn't put on ointment, but I made her, and she refused to go to the doctor."

"Sounds like you."

"It's nothing."

"Mama?" Nicolina Tizzi's voice blared through the intercom speaker, startling them. "I'm here."

"Is that how I sound when I call up?" Anina laughed. "It's like the loudspeaker on the beach."

"Olimpio. Please fix that thing. It scares me."

"All right. I'll take care of it. Remind me later." Olimpio sighed.

"Come up, Mama," Anina said into the intercom.

Matelda put her arms around her husband. No matter the time of day or night, Olimpio's neck smelled like peppermint. His beard was always trimmed and the thick white hair on his head was neatly cropped. His dress shirt was as crisp as it had been that morning when he took it off the hanger, even after a full day of work, even after the downpour. "Thank you."

"What did you make for dinner?" He pulled his wife closer still.

"Orecchiette. Fresh peas. Mint."

"My favorite dish on your birthday?"

"She wouldn't let me make dinner, Nonno."

"Nothing to it." Matelda drained the pasta and peas into a colander. The steam fogged her eyeglasses. Olimpio removed them for her so she could proceed with her task. "All went well with your meeting?"

"I have the paperwork with me."

"Congratulations. You worked hard."

"*We* worked hard," Olimpio corrected her. "Your signature is as important as mine."

Anina marveled at her grandparents' partnership, as Matelda sprinkled olive oil on the orecchiette. She crushed mint leaves over the oil before she gave the bowl to her husband. Olimpio grated cheese over the pasta.

"Happy birthday, Mama." Nicolina kissed her mother.

"You're wet."

"It's still raining." Nicolina kissed her father and daughter. Nicolina's black hair was damp and streaked with silver. She had her father's delicate features and her mother's upright posture. She was a policeman's wife, which meant she hoped for the best but was practical about dealing with the worst. Their son, Giacomo, had just joined the carabinieri, so her anxiety had doubled. Anina took her mother's coat and hung it in the powder room.

"Where's Giorgio?" Matelda asked.

"When it storms, they need him on the autostrada. Giacomo is working the desk at the precinct. Sometimes they're assigned the same duty. Not tonight."

"It was rough out there," Olimpio confirmed as he placed the bowl of pasta on the table. "I got off the autostrada and took the back road. With the fog, it might have been worse."

"This bad weather is far from over. Giorgio is not pleased. Long hours for the carabinieri. Excuse me." Nicolina went to the powder room.

Anina checked her phone. "Paolo can't make it."

"What happened?" Matelda was disappointed.

"He's meeting with a friend to get some advice about a job he applied for."

"He has to eat, doesn't he?"

"They're meeting at a café. He sends his apologies."

"Take away his place setting, please."

Anina removed Paolo's plate. "I could call him one more time to remind him."

"People make the time to do what's important to them," Matelda said curtly.

"Nonna, he's busy and it's hard to get him to go to dinner. Don't take it personally."

Nicolina returned from the powder room and fluffed the ribbon on her mother's birthday gift. She placed a box wrapped in fancy paper on the table. "Happy birthday, Mama."

"It's too pretty to open."

"I hope you like it. You're hard to buy a gift for, you know."

"So I've heard. Ask Ida Casciacarro. She gave me a bottle of capsules." Matelda unwrapped the present. "I didn't even know my gut had health." She lifted a framed photograph out of the box.

"Do you know who this is?" Nicolina asked.

"I've never seen this photograph."

The black-and-white photograph of Matelda and her mother on Viareggio Beach was proof that her dreams of late weren't made up, but based in truth. Domenica wore a linen shift. Her black braids were plaited neatly and wrapped into a chignon. Matelda was a little girl, wearing a straw hat and lace dress. She could feel the warm sand under her feet, as her eyes filled with tears.

"I'm sorry, Mama. I thought this would make you happy."

"No, no, it's a beautiful gift. It makes me happy. It helps me remember her. To see her again." Matelda shared the photograph with Olimpio. "I miss my mother." She dried her tears on her handkerchief. "You never get over the loss. The best I can do is to go to daily Mass to pray that I see her again."

Nicolina stood back from the table as though the gift had been a mistake. The last thing she'd wanted to do was upset her mother. Anina nudged her mother to comfort Matelda. Nicolina went to Matelda and put her hands on her shoulders.

"I'm all right, Nicolina."

"But I'm not, Mama." Nicolina embraced her mother. "I know what it means to love my mother too."

"It's a sin how much I love Biagetti's sfogliatelle." Matelda savored another bite followed by a sip of hot espresso.

"I'm glad you love them. There's eight more in the box and I'm not a fan," Olimpio joked. He picked up the photograph. "It's enchanting. And it's not scary like the pictures you have on your nightstand. Where did you find it?" Olimpio asked his daughter.

"At the newspaper sale. The *Stella di Lucca* sold their archives to pay off debts. This is a photograph they never used in the newspaper. There are boxes of them. Luckily, the photographer catalogued the photos by year, so I went over there several times and went through the boxes. I found this and they sold it to me. It's sad to see the paper go out of business."

"We subscribe."

"Not for long, Mama."

"It's a shame. It's a good newspaper. That's how the Fascisti got in. The first sign. Mussolini shut down the newspapers," Olimpio said. "People never learn, not even in Italy when we've lived through it and we know better."

"Let's hope that's not the case this time around," Nicolina offered. "I was told they can't compete with the internet and free news."

"I wish I had lived back then." Anina rested her face in her hands as she studied the photograph of her great-grandmother and grandmother. "You look just like your mother," Anina observed.

"She was talented. She made my clothes. Mama said that hand-stitching my hems helped her skills as a nurse. My grandmother Netta made my hats. They were artistic."

"What year was this taken?" Olimpio asked.

"Nineteen fifty." Anina showed her grandfather the inscription on the back of the frame. "Right across the boulevard on Viareggio Beach."

"I was nine years old," Matelda confirmed.

"I thought your parents married in 1947. The priest showed us the great book with their names in it. Paolo and I will sign the same book on our wedding day."

"You are correct. My parents were married in 1947."

"You were born before they got married?" Anina looked at her grandmother. "You were born out of wedlock?"

"No!" Matelda and Nicolina said in unison.

"Nonno?"

"Don't look at me. I don't prune the family tree; I only married into this tribe. I didn't set any dates other than my wedding to your grandmother."

"My mother was married twice. Her first husband was my father."

"Did you know this?" Anina asked Nicolina.

"I did. But there wasn't a lot of information about him."

"Most families in Toscana have a story like this, or a version of it. War displaces people and things happen," Olimpio reasoned.

"What was his name?" Anina wanted to know.

"John Lawrie McVicars."

"An American?"

"He was a Scot."

"We're Scottish? This would have been nice to know. Do you have a picture of him?" Anina asked.

Matelda shook her head no.

"All your grandmother has of him is the watch he gave your great-grandmother Domenica. That's why she couldn't give it to you," Olimpio explained.

"Papa, what watch are you talking about?" Nicolina asked.

"The green one," Anina said impatiently. "The upside-down watch."

"Have I seen this watch?" Nicolina asked her mother.

"It's in the case. I thought I kept it at the bank, but I was mistaken."

"You asked me to get the watch for you, honey. About a year ago. You wanted it close. Remember?" Olimpio said gently.

"Bisnonna Domenica was a nurse," Anina said to her mother. "You didn't tell me that either."

"She wasn't a nurse when I knew her," Nicolina said defensively. "She was a grandmother with white hair. Like Nonna here."

"Hey."

"You're in better shape, Mama. When Nonna Domenica was your age, she had a hard time walking."

"Either your body or your mind goes when you get to my stage of life, and you are not offered a choice," Matelda said.

"That's why we need to know about our ancestors. We can prepare for the bad stuff if we know it's coming," Anina insisted.

"I should've been told the story of Bisnonna Domenica before now."

"What difference would it have made?" Nicolina wondered.

"Maybe I would've thought about becoming a nurse," Anina said.

Her grandparents and mother laughed.

"Okay, maybe not. I can't stand anything messy or anything sad. But it doesn't matter. There might be something else in her story that would inform my life now. One person in a family impacts the whole group. Dad went to have his family roots traced at the Università di Milano. I found out the Tizzi family was partly French."

"I looked John McVicars up and couldn't find him," Matelda admitted. "He was on a list of the merchant navy, but that was it."

Nicolina was surprised. "You didn't tell me that."

"Now you know how I feel." Anina sat back. "Pull up a chair in the dark."

"Maybe I didn't look hard enough. My mother had died, and when I mourned her, I found myself mourning the loss of my father, John McVicars."

"Are there any other family secrets I should know?"

"Well, there was that great-great-grandfather of mine who spent a summer in Romania with an opera singer. I should follow up on that one," Olimpio teased Anina.

"Maybe you should. No one should have a family of their own until they know their history."

"Sensible girl," Olimpio complimented Anina.

"*Sensible* is not a word I would choose to describe Anina."

"Mama." Nicolina put down her fork.

"Anina, forgive me. You're a clever girl. You're a beauty. Sensible? Well, work on it," Matelda said.

"I don't care about being sensible. Sensible is the cardigan sweater of character."

"Thank you." Matelda straightened the cardigan sweater she was wearing, sat back in her chair, and buried her hands in the pockets.

"You know what I mean!" Anina said impatiently. "Sensible is frumpy. I'm too young for frumpy."

"And I'm too old for frumpy," Olimpio joked.

"You will never be old, Nonno. Neither will you, Nonna. I can't see you wearing a black wool dress and knee socks in the summer like the widows in the village."

"We'll have to see. I'm not a widow. Yet."

"I won't let you die first, Matelda. I'm going first. So pick out your black woolens now."

"Whatever you say."

"I couldn't live without you. There. I said it." Olimpio joined his hands in prayer. "Are you listening, God?"

Matelda laughed. Olimpio couldn't live without her, and she couldn't imagine living without him. He took care of the family business as if he were born a Cabrelli. He understood her pain despite her best efforts to hide it. When she was unsure where her impatience or anger came from, he gently guided her to the source. Matelda refused to believe the father she never met was the cause of her anxiety. She did not want to blame the dead—neither her father, nor her mother, nor her stepfather—for her problems at the age of eighty-one, but her problems were also Olimpio's. He had spent their marriage attempting to convince her that the loss of her Scottish father was something she needed to face in order to heal her heart. Finally, Matelda was getting around to the task.

CHAPTER 10

𝔏𝔲𝔠𝔠𝔞, 𝔍𝔱𝔞𝔩𝔶

Now

Anina stood in the kitchenette in the small apartment she shared with Paolo as he lay on the couch in the living room. The television volume was on full blast as he texted on his phone, oblivious to the football game on the screen. Anina arranged the leftovers from Nonna's birthday dinner on the plate. Even though she was annoyed with him, whenever she was near her fiancé, she forgot why she was irritated with him. She knew what she had. Paolo was a catch, and there were plenty of girls in Lucca who pursued him, but he chose Anina. Anina grabbed a napkin and utensils and joined Paolo in the living room.

Paolo had taken off his shirt and shoes. His black curls were in need of a cut, and his beard was coming in, even though he had shaved that morning. There was a glass of wine on the coffee table.

"Nonna made your favorite pasta." She placed the leftovers on the table.

"I'm starving. Thanks, babe."

"I knew you wouldn't eat at the café. I wish you would've come to celebrate Nonna's birthday."

"I couldn't get out of the meeting."

"I know. They like to see you once in a while, that's all."

"I'll drop by and say hello when I'm in the village."

"That would be nice." Anina doubted Paolo would make a special trip to see her grandmother. Viareggio was out of the way. Anina turned to go.

"Where are you going?" Paolo took her hand and pulled her onto his lap. "Is there something wrong?"

"You're watching a game."

Paolo turned off the television set. "What can I do?"

"I don't know." Anina rested her head on his shoulder.

"Are we okay?"

"Yes."

"So why the weird mood?"

"I don't know."

"Your mother?" Paolo made a face.

Anina laughed. "We're getting along great."

"That's because we're getting married. Your mother doesn't like that we live together."

"I don't think that's it."

"It's me then. They're worried. Once I get a job, they'll all be happy."

"You might be right. How's it going?"

"Getting close." Paolo grinned. "We might have to move to Roma. What do you think?"

"Wherever you get a job, we will live," she assured him. "Papa said you can always put in your application for civil service. Giacomo is happy working for the carabinieri."

"I don't want to work with my future father-in-law and brother-in-law. I don't want to be a cop."

"Giacomo wasn't sure about it either, and now he likes it."

"Good for him."

"Okay, let's drop it." Anina reached out and stabbed a few ore-cchiette onto the fork. She fed Paolo the bite of pasta. "Good?"

"Your grandmother might be mean, but she can cook." Paolo kissed her.

"She's not mean. She has high standards. That's all."

Paolo had told his parents when he moved into Anina's apartment. She had not told her parents, not at first. Anina had not wanted to put her mother in an awkward position with Matelda. When she finally told her parents, Nicolina said, "Don't say anything to your grandmother. It would kill her."

Paolo had taken temporary positions since he graduated from college. He wanted to work with a sports agency, but those jobs were scarce. Now that he was engaged, he took the permanent job hunt seriously. There were so many things Anina loved about Paolo. He made her laugh. They came from similar backgrounds. Maybe he wasn't as ambitious as some young men, but Anina appreciated that he put living a happy life above a material one. After all, he had volunteered at an animal rescue in Viareggio when there was an oil spill off the coast. Paolo had a good heart.

"Sometimes you look at me as though you have no idea who I am," he said.

"Do I?"

"Like you're sizing me up."

"I've already done that. You passed."

Paolo scooped Anina up in his arms. He carried her down the narrow hallway to their bedroom in the back of the apartment, covering her with kisses as they went. For Paolo, the small room with the bed that hugged the walls on either side of it was as vast as a field of sunflowers. He would stay there with Anina forever, if it were up to him. He gently placed her on the bed. He kissed her hands, her neck, and her lips. His body covered hers as she pulled the coverlet over him. When they made love, they solved all their problems without saying a word.

Paolo fell asleep wrapped around her. Anina lay awake, her fingers laced through his. She found the tiny bedroom confining. The poster of a beach in Montenegro did not make the room seem larger, as promised in a magazine article. The only way out of the claustrophobic feeling was to dream. She pictured a house by the sea. Their bedroom would be large and white, with a deep feather bed and many windows, which she would leave open. The sound of the surf would lull them to sleep at night, and in the morning, the reflection of the sun on the water would wake them. Somehow she had to make Paolo see her dream. She loved him but had to find the key to his ambition. Paolo pulled her closer as he slept. No one lived on love, and plenty survived without it, but she did not want to be one of them.

VIAREGGIO

Matelda sat on her bed with her earbuds in her ears. She removed one and looked over at Olimpio, who was in bed scrolling through the emails on his phone.

"You won't believe this. Nino recorded what he could remember of the elephant story."

"You're kidding. He knew how? I had to show him how to clear his voice messages when he was here."

"Patrizia helped him record it. Do you want to listen?"

"You go ahead and tell me later."

Matelda put the bud back in her ear. She listened to her brother's voice.

Hey, sis.

Pat told me you wanted the elephant story. I remember Nonno running around the room like a wild man acting it out. He wanted us to understand where the gems he cut came from, and how there were people who risked their lives to mine them. That was his point, I believe. I remember that he'd change things here and there just to keep it interesting.

Now about Nonno's story. Okay, here goes. Here's what I remember. It started with an elephant trapped inside a mine in India. Somehow she gets out. It was a she—her coat had been painted with red lines for a parade or something. I remember the part about what happened inside the mine because I imagined the layers of workers in the layers of earth like an ant farm with tunnels and curves stacked one upon the other.

Nonno described the great fire that collapsed the mine. Men tried to climb out. I can't believe he told a couple of kids such a gruesome story, but what the hell? He did. We were different from the kids today. It's all kitten stories now. Anyway, the elephant broke free. That was the happy part of the story. But I don't remember where the elephant went. And I don't know if the elephant died. The terrible part was the father and son who could not get out of the mine. Whoever dug the mine did not dig an adit, and the workers were trapped. The dangerous work they did provided beauty and value to the world, but they risked their lives to extract the stones. Was it worth it? How could it be? They died in the mine. I remember Nonno saying that a father will do anything to feed his family, and that always stuck with me.

Yeah, sis. That's the part that always got me. It was dangerous, but it was worth risking their lives for food. I wish I remembered what happened to the elephant. Sorry about that. Oh yeah, I remember one more thing. Nonno said the miners were barefoot.

That's right. They didn't have shoes or work boots. I can only imagine what it was like to walk over the sharp stones and rock walls in that mine where the tunnels went deep and on for miles. All for a ruby. Or rubies. The treasure they needed to eat. That's all I got. I'm signing off. I hope this is what you're looking for. Thanks for a nice visit. Who knows if we'll ever get back there again? We're getting up in years, Matelda. Sad, but this is the way of life. It ends as promised. Anyhow, it's always good to come home and practice my Italian. It was good to see you and Olimpio and the kids.

"Nino doesn't remember what happened to the elephant either." Matelda took the buds out of her ears and placed them into the case. "He doesn't sound like us at all anymore."

"He sounds like an Italian American from New Jersey because that's what he is. He's lived there for fifty years. You are what you eat, where you live, and what you drive."

"That's a sad observation." Matelda placed her phone on the nightstand. "That was disappointing."

"At least he called you back. He was never going to write it down."

"No, but he tried. He did *something* for me. That's a first for my brother. I asked him to do something for me, and he did it."

"You've let go of the old grudges. You two are getting along now."

"We are, aren't we?" Matelda had worked hard at releasing any resentment she had for Nino. He had pulled many stunts over the years. Nino hadn't taken responsibility for his role in the tumult; instead, he blamed Matelda. Nino accused his sister of stealing his father's fortune. He sued her for the profits from the sale of the storefront in Viareggio. She gave Nino half of the money, even though it was she and Olimpio who worked in the business. Nino claimed he wasn't consulted and therefore the building should not have been sold. Nino asked for the original drawings of their grand-father's designs; she sent them when he assured her there was a university that had inquired about them, only for him to turn around and sell them to a fine jewelry outfit in New Jersey. Matelda had to buy the drawings back to keep them in the family when Nino refused to do so. He didn't care about family history, though he moved to America with a loan from Cabrelli Jewelers. He made a killing manufacturing crystal embellishments used on handbags and shoes. He never repaid the loan. There were years when brother and sister did not speak to each other. Matelda and Olimpio were not invited to his daughter Anna's wedding because Nino was furious at his sister over something she could no longer remember. Patrizia could not convince Nino to come to Nicolina's wedding, because she and Olimpio had not attended *their* daughter's wed-ding. Finally, Olimpio and Patrizia called a truce between the brother and sister. Fingers crossed it would last until the end of their lives.

"Nino is a tit-for-tat person. He always has been. It's only lately that his primary emotion is not anger. Maybe he is on some kind of medication."

"Maybe he's tired of fighting." Olimpio offered.

"I don't think our problems were about Papa. Nino might have resented how close I was to my mother. Maybe he had a problem with us living in this house with my parents. Maybe he wanted the house."

"We paid him for his portion."

"He has plenty of money. There's a hole in my brother that nothing can fill. Unfortunately, he thinks I dug it."

"You know, Matelda? Maybe he just didn't like your face."

"That's it!" Matelda laughed. "That only took you fifty years." Olimpio laughed.

Matelda lifted a nightgown out of her dresser drawer. "I'm

going to do my routine." She closed the bathroom door behind her.

"Are we going to be talking about your family for the rest of our
lives?" Olimpio called out to her.

Matelda opened the door. "Is that a problem?"

"That's a yes," Olimpio grumbled.

Matelda stood at the sink brushing her teeth when her eye
caught a layer of bright blue bubbles at the bottom of her drinking
glass. She spit out the toothpaste and felt around her neck for her
reading glasses. She turned the glass over into the palm of her
hand. A bracelet of shimmering blue aquamarine stones set in pavé
diamonds slid out of the glass.

"Olimpio!" She dabbed her mouth and went into the bedroom.
"What is this?" She held out the bracelet.

"Happy birthday."

"You put an expensive bracelet in a glass in the bathroom? On
the sink? Are you crazy?"

"I wanted to surprise you." He grinned.

"It could have gone down the drain."

"But it didn't."

"But it could have." She felt her face flush with anger.

"Oh, for God's sake, Matelda. It's a surprise. I made it for you
myself. You said you wanted a bracelet to go with your earrings.
Don't ruin the fun. Just enjoy the gift for once."

Matelda went back into the bathroom. She sat on the edge of
tub and cried. There was a soft rap on the bathroom door. She
grabbed a towel and dried her tears.

Olimpio opened the door and peeked inside. "Matelda."

She looked up at her husband in despair.

"Give it to me."

Matelda handed him the bracelet. "I'm sorry." She extended
her wrist.

"I'm sorry too. It was silly of me to surprise you." Olimpio placed the bracelet on her wrist, snapping the gold hinge. "I just felt like having fun like the old days."

"This coming from the man who hid my engagement ring in a sfogliatella." Matelda gently turned the glittering stones over her wrist in a full circle. "It's magnificent. Thank you."

"Happy birthday, bella." He kissed her and took her hand. They returned to the bedroom.

She turned away from him as she sat on the side of the bed. "I can't be happy."

"You've been happy."

"Have I?"

"Lie down. Let me hold you. You're tired."

"I mean it. I can't enjoy anything. Who is given a beautiful gift and before she's even tried it on imagines it lost?"

"Someone who doesn't want to lose anything."

"You always have an answer."

"Stop being so hard on yourself. When you're in pain, it's like observing someone being tortured during the Crusades. Forget the past. You can't change it."

"What if it's the only thing I can remember anymore?"

"Then hold on to the good memories. I'm just the lucky man who fell in love with a girl in a white two-piece bathing suit fifty-six years ago on Viareggio Beach." Olimpio helped Matelda into bed.

"I'm blessed. The terrible things that happened to me came with a gift to be opened once the difficulty passed. I lost my father, but then I had my stepfather, who was kind to me. He grew up without a father, so he had empathy for any child who knew that kind of abandonment. You know how that goes. Whatever disease you have is the one you want to find a cure for."

"All this happened a long time ago."

"You got that right. And I've the bones to prove it." Matelda shifted under the covers to find a comfortable spot. "It's here. The day I dreaded has arrived. I'm old."

"So am I."

"I'm breaking down like a used car." She sighed.

"As long as it still runs and gets you where you want to go, who cares?" Olimpio kissed his wife good night. "Even when we're broken, we're beautiful."

CHAPTER 11

Viareggio

1929

Early-morning sunlight bathed Pretucci's office with such intensity, there was no need to turn on the work lamp over the examining table.

Pretucci perched on a stool on one side as Domenica Cabrelli, nurse in training, stood on the other. Her hair was tied up neatly under a cap. She wore the navy apron of the apprentice. Her pockets were filled with nursing essentials: scissors, gauze, thread, and a tincture of iodine.

"Are you ready? Let's make fast work of this. The mayor of Pietrasanta has the gout." Pretucci checked his watch.

"Again?"

"Again, Signorina."

At twenty years old, Domenica was earning her practical hours as a student nurse under Pretucci. He had arranged for her to study with the Sisters of the Sorrowful Mother, a Franciscan order of nuns in Roma.

Pretucci folded his arms, sat back, and observed his student.

Domenica placed a ripe orange on the table. The outer skin was loose enough to pinch. She opened the kit with the equipment used for inoculations. She removed a syringe.

"Ten cc's," Pretucci instructed.

Domenica cleansed a small area of the outer skin of the fruit with a small gauze square soaked in alcohol. She raised the vial of practice serum up to the light. She flipped it over to check the amount inside. She held the syringe to the light. She assessed the vial and filled it to the line of measurement. She aspirated the syringe by tapping on it, removing any bubbles. She squeezed the pump with her thumb. A droplet of the liquid appeared on the syringe. She held the orb steady on the table with one hand and held the syringe in the other.

"You want to inject at a forty-five-degree angle. Find the fat," Pretucci reminded her. "You don't want to pierce the muscle. Well, if you do, the patient will let you know it."

Domenica pinched the skin, creating a small fold. She eased the syringe into the skin of the orange, releasing the pump until the serum was gone. She gently removed the needle, placed it on the work tray, and swabbed the area again with gauze soaked in alcohol. She looked up at her boss.

"Good. Now, when it's a patient, will you have that confidence?"

"I hope so, Dottore."

"When you return to Roma for your final exams, the practicals are given by the Sisters. If the needles don't scare you, the nuns will."

"My mother always says, 'A good seamstress is not afraid of needles.'"

"A yard of satin doesn't scream when you puncture it."

"I can handle the patients. The more chaos, the louder the screaming and yelling, the calmer I get."

"Why is that?"

"I don't question it, Dottore. I just do the job that must be done."

"Sister Eugenia asked me your weaknesses on the job, and I couldn't think of any. You have an affinity for the work. You have the talent to be an excellent nurse."

"Thank you."

"Be careful. The nuns are persistent. They trained you well in medicine, and they expect something in return. They will appeal to you to join the order."

Domenica smiled. "Most of my prayers have gone unanswered, which makes me wonder if He listens. Why would He send out the call to someone like me to join the blue army?"

"I wouldn't share those feelings with Sister Eugenia"—the doctor picked up his hat and case—"until you've completed your exams."

"Yes, Dottore."

"It's completely selfish on my part. I want the nuns to pass you and send you back to Viareggio to work for me. I need a good nurse. If you fail, I imagine I will have to offer the job to Signora Maccio, who is a fine nurse but never stops talking. I'll be driven mad if you don't get your license and return to the village as soon as possible."

Pretucci left, leaving Domenica to prepare the clinic to open the next morning. She straightened the tinctures, cleaned the instruments, and swept the floor.

The ripe orange she had used to practice inoculations lay on the instrument tray. She sewed a thick thread through the skin, and knotted it into a loop before taking it outside.

Domenica stood on her toes, pulled a branch on the barberry tree close, and hung the orange on it. She let go of the branch, which snapped back into place overhead.

Soon the birds would peck at the orange until there was nothing left but the string. Domenica went back into the office, stood at the window, and watched as the finches made their descent.

CHAPTER 12

Viareggio

Now

M ama?" Nicolina called out as she stepped off the elevator into her parents' apartment. "Mama, it's me. I got the anchovy paste you wanted. And I picked up a few—"

The door to the terrace was open; the sheers billowed into the room. Nicolina placed the grocery bags on the table. She stepped out onto the terrace.

Concerned, she went back into the apartment and looked around. She went up the steps to the bedroom, calling for her mother. The bed was neatly made. She quickly went down the steps and into the kitchen. She found her mother lying on the floor.

"Mama!" Nicolina knelt beside her mother.

"I'm all right," she murmured.

"You're on the floor."

"I got dizzy."

"Who am I?" Nicolina asked as she helped her mother sit up.

"You're my daughter, Nicolina. You weighed nine pounds, seven ounces when you were born, and I can still feel it fifty years later."

"You scared me to death." Nicolina poured her mother a glass of water. "Stay there. Don't get up. I'm calling the ambulance."

"You will not!"

"I'm calling your doctor."

Matelda did not object. She sipped the water.

Nicolina called her mother's doctor. She helped her mother stand and grabbed her mother's coat and purse. They walked slowly to the elevator. Once outside, Nicolina helped Matelda into the car before snapping her seat belt into place.

"You're treating me like a child," Matelda said.

"The moment has come, Mama. Do you remember what you said to me?"

Matelda nodded. She had cared for her mother, Domenica, until she died; it didn't seem possible that she was now the elderly person who needed Nicolina to care for her.

Nicolina got in the driver's seat, put on her seat belt, and started the car. She drove onto the main boulevard slowly and stopped at the light. She opened a small bottle of water and handed it to Matelda. "Drink this, please."

"I'm fine."

"Drink it. Anything bad that happens to older people happens because they don't drink enough water."

Matelda sipped the water. "It's probably the sfogliatella. I ate the whole thing. I guess I can't eat what I love anymore."

"A pastry won't make you faint."

"I was barely out."

"We don't know how long you were out. Papa went to work at seven, and I came over at nine."

"It was just a couple of seconds."

"How do you know?"

"I was thinking of my mother when she was a young nurse in the clinic. What does that mean?"

"You needed to see a doctor?"

"I take care of myself." Matelda was defensive.

"Let's have the doctor decide."

Ida Casciacarro was at the market when she saw Matelda in Nicolina's car as they passed by. She thought to wave until she noticed that Matelda and her daughter were bickering. "The Cabrellis. Always fighting," she said under her breath.

Olimpio stepped outside the shop and called Nicolina.

"What did the doctor say?"

"He said her heart was weak. It may be causing her mood swings. That's why the crying all of a sudden. It's also why she's having issues with her memory. She told him she's having vivid dreams. She's dreaming of her childhood. She believes that her mother is calling her to be with her. She can see them." Nicolina's voice broke.

"Did the doctor say anything else? What can we do?"

"He said that Mama was in the first stages of whatever this is."

"Dementia?"

"The doctor doesn't think so. It's not Alzheimer's either."

"Thank God."

"The doctor said nothing had changed since you brought her in for tests."

"Good."

"He said her heart issue is causing a lack of oxygen to her brain. He wants Mama to take oxygen at night when she sleeps. He says that will help. I'm going over there with the machine now to show her how to use it."

"I'm on my way home."

"No, Papa, stay. I can handle this. The doctor said to stick to our routines but keep an eye on her. It will agitate her if we start acting differently."

"I understand. I will call your brother."

Olimpio stood on the sidewalk. He had to expect this; after all, they were octogenarians and something was bound to go wrong with one or the other, or even both of them. But the time had come too quickly. There were still memories to make.

Nicolina drove down the boulevard with her mother in the passenger seat. "Mama, are you all right over there?"

"Va bene."

"I'm sorry you had to go through this today."

"Going to doctors is my new career. With bookkeeping, I had the weekends off. Being old and going to doctors is a seven-day-a-week grind."

Nicolina stopped at the light.

"You see the gelato shop?" Matelda pointed. "That used to be Dottore Pretucci's clinic. My mother used to work there. She was the first woman in this village with an education."

"That makes me proud."

"Me too. She paid for the achievement, believe me."

Nicolina noticed that her mother's memory was best when they were walking or driving. It was as if motion itself triggered details and encouraged Matelda to share them.

"What happened to your mother?" Nicolina asked. "Do you remember?"

CHAPTER 13

𝔙𝔦𝔞𝔯𝔢𝔤𝔤𝔦𝔬

FEBRUARY 1939

The village was quiet as Domenica Cabrelli walked to work on the eve of the finale of Carnevale. Only a few locals were out, conducting the business of early morning. The fishermen were setting up their haul at market, and two nuns were haggling with the local farmer over fresh bunches of broccoli rabe to make Lenten broth. The food stands along the boardwalk were covered with tarps. The bunting that crisscrossed over the promenade fluttered in triangles of red, white, and green. The only sound she heard was metal against metal as a vendor scraped the grill of the sausage-and-pepper stand, preparing for his biggest night of sales.

The pink sky was dappled with streaks of gold light like feldspar. The light broke through, illuminating the crests of green waves. The tourists would not notice the necks of the periscopes on the submarines of the Italian regimen as they ran practice formations in the middle distance, but she did. Italy was preparing for a war no one wanted.

When she unlocked the door of the clinic, she opened the windows and propped open the door to let the fresh air into the room.

The smells of the alcohol-based tinctures, ammonia, and formaldehyde intensified inside when the clinic was sealed shut.

Domenica went about her chores to prepare the clinic for the day ahead. She swept the sidewalk, then went inside and swept the floor. She dusted the surfaces with a rag spritzed with alcohol. She even swabbed Dr. Pretucci's fountain pen. She put on her apron and cap and washed her hands. She put out the gauze, tongue depressors, and thermometer on the worktable before taking a seat at the desk. She was looking over the patient list when Monica Mironi entered the clinic with her three small children.

The young mother carried her sleeping newborn in a cestino, and her one-year-old balanced on her hip, while her three-year-old son walked dutifully behind her. The children's cheeks were bright pink on the chilly February morning. Their mother had a similar blush to her cheeks, with the delicate features and expression of a sad doll.

"How can I be of service, Signora?" Domenica pulled out a chair. She gave the boy an apple and took the infant in the basket and placed her on the table. "I'm sorry there's no heat. Dottore Pretucci keeps the clinic cold."

"Say 'Grazie,' Leonardo."

"Grazie, Signorina."

"Prego." Domenica ruffled the boy's hair. "Good manners."

"I hope so."

"Dottore Pretucci won't be back until tomorrow morning."

"I don't need to speak with him. I wanted to talk to you."

Domenica sat down. "How can I help you?"

Monica lowered her voice. "I want you to teach me how not to have a baby."

"You don't want any more children?"

"I would have more children, but I shouldn't. The midwife

from Pietrasanta told me that I have bad blood. She birthed my daughter three months ago. She told me if I have another baby, it will endanger my life. I worry that if I become ill, or something happens to me, there will be no one to take care of my children."

"Do you live with your family?"

"My in-laws. That's why I'm worried."

"I understand."

Monica nodded sadly. "My husband wants lots of children."

"Did you tell your husband what the midwife said?"

"He thinks it's a lie."

"Why would a midwife lie? She's in the business of birthing babies. It would not be in her best interest to curtail the activity, would it?"

"True." Monica smiled.

"We can have Dottore Pretucci examine you when he's in the office and issue a report. Maybe then your husband would believe the severity of your condition. You know, if he saw it on paper."

Domenica knew Guido Mironi would never take the word of a nurse as fact, but he might listen to Pretucci. She made notes about her conversation with Monica in her logbook. "I will make a note that the doctor should expect a visit from your husband." Domenica put her pencil down and leaned forward in her chair. She wasn't supposed to advise patients, but in this instance, she felt it was important. "Signora, do you understand the science behind how a woman conceives a baby?"

"I know some things."

"It's possible to prevent a pregnancy with a barrier method. Do you know what I am talking about?"

She nodded.

"Dr. Pretucci can provide them to your husband."

"He won't use them."

"What if the doctor recommended it?"

"Is there something I can do?"

"Without telling your husband?"

She nodded.

"It would be helpful for your husband to participate in planning your family."

"Guido won't hear of it." Monica lowered her voice. "I have a friend who told me about a device. She showed it to me."

"I would have to speak to Dr. Pretucci about it."

"Would you? Would he tell my husband?"

"Your visits in this office are confidential."

Monica exhaled.

"Let's make another appointment for you to come in. I can ask your midwife to join us if that makes you more comfortable."

"She sent me to talk to you, so I'm sure she won't mind. She's a Catholic and told me that the priest would give me absolution."

"I hope so. You have a serious condition and you must listen to the doctor." Domenica made an appointment in the log.

"Signorina, you went to school with my husband, didn't you?"

"Yes." Domenica forced a smile.

"What kind of a young man was my husband?"

"Guido was high-spirited," Domenica said diplomatically. Guido Mironi had been held back twice. During school, he was either in trouble or in close vicinity of it. There had been the incident with the rock and many more like it. But it was not her place to tell Monica about him. She scribbled *Silvio Birtolini* in the margin of the report and closed her notebook. "Guido was full of pep."

For Monica's sake, Domenica hoped Mironi had changed. Monica's parents, who came from another village, could not have known the truth when they agreed to a match. "What kind of man is he now?"

"Il Duce."

Domenica laughed with her patient. "Oh no. I'm sorry to hear it."

"He had to go to Lucca today, so I had the morning. I can't thank you enough for taking the time to talk to me."

"I'm sure he wants what is best for you. For your health."

"I hope so." Monica gathered up her children to go.

Domenica went to Pretucci's desk and opened the drawer. She removed a pamphlet and gave it to Monica. "Here's a pamphlet about birth control. Look it over before your appointment and you can discuss it with Dottore Pretucci."

Domenica found herself watching the family walk to the end of the street until they turned the corner and were out of sight. A feeling of dread pressed on her heart. Domenica was grateful Pretucci was working in Pietrasanta and was not present to witness her emotions. She brushed her tears away quickly and went back to her paperwork.

Domenica pushed the gate of Boncourso's garden open and picked up a burlap sack full of chestnuts, one of several stacked under the pergola. The garden had changed since Domenica was a girl. The trunks of the chestnut trees had grown so thick over time, Domenica could no longer wrap her arms around them.

In summer, the garden was a hodgepodge of beauty and sustenance; red beach roses and yellow sunflowers grew among neat rows of summer endive, scallions, tomatoes, arugula, and peppers. Vines thick with grapes created a canopy over the pergola that provided shade when the gardeners took their lunch. In winter, the same pergola became a spot to sort dry beans and take in the faraway sun through the open roof of bramble.

Domenica hurried home with the sack of chestnuts. A few fell out onto the cobblestone streets, hitting the stones with a clatter. She didn't stop to pick them up. She could see the fractured beams of the stage lights pull on through the trees.

Domenica called for her mother and father once she was inside the house, then remembered they were already at Carnevale. She hiked up the stairs quickly, dropped the chestnuts in the kitchen before taking the steps up to her bedroom two at a time. She ran a hot bath. She brushed her teeth as the tub filled. Soon steam rose from the surface of the water, fogging the mirror. Domenica sprinkled lavender oil into the bath before she slipped off her work clothes and eased into the water.

Her body ached. Her shoulders and hands were sore from a long week at the clinic. Her legs were tired from assisting the midwife during a long labor. Slowly Domenica revived as she scrubbed down with goat-milk soap. She rinsed with cold water and stepped out of the tub. She wrapped a towel around herself and went into her bedroom, where her mother had laid out her dance costume on the bed. She began to hum as she dressed, and soon she was singing. She pulled on her stockings, slipped into her dance shoes, and skipped down the stairs.

The village was packed with tourists. The revelers came from up and down the Ligurian coast and from as far north as the Dolomites to be entertained by jugglers, magicians, and music acts. Vendors from Firenze and Milano peddled their silk, straw, and leather goods in stands along the canals. Each Sunday during the month of February, the boulevard was cleared for the parade that featured a flotilla of gigantic papier-mâché puppets with the garish faces of politicians, movie stars, and saints. The exaggerated depictions of the famous and notorious, with their googly eyes and oversized red mouths with teeth shaped like enormous piano keys, wearing the candy-color harlequin and stripes of the stock players of la commedia dell'arte, loomed over the crowds like a squall of monsters from a bad dream.

Domenica quickened her pace to make it to the dance floor on time. A large crowd had formed around the lip of the stage to watch. They wore painted masks decorated with crystals and pearls, a Carnevale tradition. The older folks wore simple velvet masks tied with a satin ribbon, leaving the sparkle to the young.

Domenica tightened the laces on her bodice as she joined the dancers. Her petite figure was shown off to its best advantage in the white blouse with full sleeves and the traditional red skirt cinched tight at the waist.

The Cincotto brothers pulled Domenica into their circle. The whisk of the drums, the lilt of the violin, and the jubilant trills of the horns scurried the dancers into formation. Domenica lifted the sides of her full skirts, and with a simple chassé, she beckoned the Cincottos to follow her in the box step.

"Get ready to fly, Domenica," the elder Cincotto promised.

Domenica laughed. "Don't drop me, Mauro."

A group of men stood on the edge of the dance floor. One of the men was only half listening to the conversation in the group when his eyes fell upon Domenica Cabrelli. The man loosened the ribbons on the back of his mask and let it fall around his neck to get a better look.

Domenica stood center stage. She raised her arms, forming a wedding-ring stance, and spun in a pirouette. The layers of her skirt twirled in a full circle, revealing her shapely legs. Mauro lifted Domenica off the ground. The lone plait of her brown hair snapped like a whip.

The stranger pushed his mask up over his eyes and watched the dancer as she sailed through the night air.

"Your parents are at the gelato stand," Amelia LeDonne said as she passed Domenica. "The band is going on break. Next up, Bergamasca. Twenty minutes." She tapped her wristwatch.

Domenica made her way through the crowd. She had forgotten how hungry she was as she inhaled the scents of sausage, peppers, and onions on the grill.

The line was too long for a sandwich, so Domenica stopped at the fig stand. The operator spun the figs on sticks over the fire. The special treats served during the festival almost made the forty days of deprivation that followed worth the sacrifice. Fichi su un bastone, figs stuffed with prosciutto and cheese, were roasted on a stick over a hot coal fire until the skin of the fruit caramelized into a sugary crust. Children savored them because they were sweet, and parents encouraged the children to eat them because there would be no meat consumed until the fast was broken on Easter Sunday. Domenica took a bite of the savory and sweet, closed her eyes, and chewed.

Customers formed a line at the bomboloni stand on the first day of February that did not end until the last day of Carnevale. Enormous tubs of dough were whipped by hand with large wooden spatulas from a combination of flour, yeast, and eggs, and artfully spooned into bubbling vats of hot oil until the globs exploded into weightless puffs of gold. The fried dough was lifted from the vats with open-mesh paddles, dredged in sugar, and served hot.

Down the boardwalk, two stout men pedaled the contraption that mixed the fresh ice cream. Their pedaling powered large metal beaters in a rotund barrel lined with rock salt. The cold custard was made with fresh cream, eggs, and a handful of crushed vanilla beans. Once the gelato was thick, it was ladled into a warm pizzelle cup and drizzled with melted chocolate that froze into delectable spikes as it hit the ice-cold mixture.

Domenica found her parents sitting with their house guests at a café table outside the gelato stand. She greeted the Speranzas da Venezia, Agnese and Romeo, her parents' lifelong friends. The couple joined their family annually for Carnevale. Cabrelli and Speranza were expert gem cutters who forged a friendship years earlier on a trip to India when they were young apprentices learning their trade.

"Your daughter is beautiful," Agnese said to Netta. Agnese was a trim redhead who wore a chic navy dress and a red straw hat.

Domenica wished she were wearing the latest fashion and not the village costume. "Thank you, Signora. I love your dress and hat," she said as she gave Agnese a kiss on each cheek.

"Don't forget me." Speranza extended his cheek.

"Who is going to forget you?" Cabrelli joked. "They put your picture in the Vatican newspaper. They called you the greatest gem cutter in Italy."

"Thanks to you." Speranza smiled.

"I would never forget you, Signore, whether you were famous or not." Domenica kissed Speranza on both cheeks.

Netta scooped the gelato with the chocolate that served as a spoon. "Taste," she said to her daughter.

Domenica took a bite.

"We can't wait to see you dance," Agnese said.

"Come see the Bergamasca after I've warmed up. Hopefully Mauro Cincotto still has the strength to lift me." Domenica fluffed her skirts. "Don't want to waste all your hard work on this costume, Mama. Ciao."

Domenica loosened her braid as she walked through the crowd

back to the stage. Her hair cascaded over her shoulders in waves. She had thought about bobbing her hair, as was the fashion, but hadn't gotten around to it.

"This is how I remember you," a voice said from behind her.

Carnevale was a magnet for riffraff, parlor snakes, and worse. Domenica quickened her pace to lose the man in the crowd, but he circled in front of her wearing a mask.

He was tall and slim with a head full of black curls. He loosened the ribbons, removed his mask, and revealed his face. "Do you remember me?"

Domenica may not have recognized his nose, his regal forehead, and the planes of his face, but it was his smile that she would know anywhere. "Silvio Birtolini!" She threw her arms around him.

"I didn't think you'd know me."

"What happened to you? I was the tall one. By about a foot."

"You're not much taller now than you were when I left the village."

"When you left, I stopped growing," she joked.

"It was a devastation to lose me, wasn't it?"

"You'll never know."

They laughed.

"Nineteen years. Can you believe it?" Silvio sighed. "I thought for sure you had forgotten me."

"I would never forget my best friend."

The cherub face of Silvio's youth was gone. No longer did he have the round features of the carved putti that decorated the altar of San Paolino; instead, he had the height and athletic build of the statue of Saint Michael, who could hardly be contained in the arch of his shrine. Every girl who ever prayed at San Paolino was in love with Saint Michael, and now Silvio Birtolini had become him.

Silvio's face was angular, his nose strong; the only remnant of the little boy she knew was his eyes. They were the same soft dark brown velvet color, with the same tinge of sadness. Domenica was certain only she could see what his eyes revealed because she knew the source of his pain. "How did you find me?"

"I was looking all over for you."

"You know where I live."

"Is there still an orange door?"

"You remember! Papa painted it for Carnevale. Freshened up the whole place."

"Are there still chestnuts in the garden?"

"There was a big harvest this year."

"That was going to be my next stop."

"You only want to see the things that haven't changed."

"But everything has. You and I and the stable behind the church. They've made our home into a garage for automobiles. Not a horse to be found."

"They sent the horses to live up on the mountain. At least that's the word in the village."

"When we were children, most families had a horse and no one had a motorcar. Automobiles were too expensive. And rare. Soon every family will have a motorcar and no one will be able to afford a horse," Silvio said.

"You sound like Papa. How long are you here?"

"Just tonight."

"That's too bad."

"Before I leave town, I'd like to meet your husband."

"So would my mother."

"I don't understand."

"I'm not married."

"Signora Zanella said you—"

"You don't know? Signora Zanella, poor thing. She makes up stories. She believes she's a countess that owns the Banca d'Italia."

"She doesn't?"

"She doesn't even have an account."

"You're not married?" Silvio took a step back and looked at her.

"I have a profession. I'm a nurse. I work for Dottore Pretucci."

"Is he still alive?"

"He was close to our age when he sewed you up. He helped me become a nurse."

"But that doesn't explain why you're not married. Are you a nun?"

"Does this look like a habit?"

"You could be a Sister of the Tarantella."

Domenica laughed. "How about you? Are you married?"

"Betrothed."

Domenica looked around the pier, happy to have something to do to hide her disappointment. "Where is she? I'd like to meet her."

"She's in Parma."

"When are you getting married?"

"This summer."

"Congratulations. You deserve happiness."

"You're the only person that thought so. Well, that's not exactly true. You and my mother."

The bandleader blew the whistle to summon the dancers to the stage.

"I have to go. Will you wait for me?"

"I'm sorry. I have to meet my friends for the drive back to Parma."

Domenica couldn't hide her disappointment. "That's too bad. So much more to talk about." She bit her lip. "All this time I've been praying for you. Take care of yourself."

Domenica turned to the stage to join the dancers when Silvio took her hand. "Before you go"—he leaned down and whispered in her ear—"did you ever find the buried treasure?"

The band began to play. The dancers moved across the floor without Domenica.

"I never found it."

"That's too bad. I have a reminder every morning when I look in the mirror." Silvio moved the lock of hair that had fallen across his face, revealing the scar over his eyebrow. The black arch was staccatoed with tiny pink dots where the stitches had been.

Domenica leaned closely to Silvio's face to examine the scar. She touched the outline of the arch gently with her finger. She was close to his mouth, her finger tracing the outline of his face to his lips.

"Domenica," he whispered. His lips grazed her cheek.

"You can barely see the scar. It healed beautifully. You made a wise choice. I wanted to sew you up and you wouldn't let me."

Silvio laughed. "But I took your advice about the olive oil. Looks less like a gash, thanks to you."

"Now that I don't remember."

"That's all right, because I do." Silvio took her hand. "I remember everything."

"Remember your fiancée in Parma." She let go of his hand. "Where do you work?"

"I'm an apprentice to Leo DeNunzio, a master gem cutter in Torino. I was lucky he took me on."

"Papa will be pleased that you took up the trade."

"How is your father?"

"He works hard and my mother pushes him to work harder."

"Your father has a fine reputation throughout Toscana."

"Grazie. And how is your mother?"

"She married a nice man from Firenze. A stonemason. After so long, she found happiness."

"She deserved it too. Was he a good father to you?"

"He was gentle and fair."

"I'm glad," Domenica said sincerely. "Your mother is one of the finest ladies I've ever known."

"I'll tell her you said so. How is your brother?"

"The same."

Silvio laughed. "Aldo hasn't changed?"

"Not at all."

"Where is he?"

"He joined the army. Maybe that will help."

"It might make him worse."

"That's what Mama said!"

Mauro Cincotto came to the edge of the stage. He motioned to her. "Domenica. Box formation. We need you." He lowered his voice. "I can't lift Stella Spadoni."

"Yes, you can." Stella, tall and broad shouldered, yanked Cincotto back into formation. "And you will."

"I lost my partner." Domenica turned to Silvio. "Would you like to dance?"

"I'm not a good dancer."

"Don't let that stop you!" Ignoring his pleas to let him go, Domenica pulled Silvio onto the dance floor. "Come on. You're a native! Follow me," she commanded. She took Silvio's hands in hers and placed them on her hips. She put her hands on his shoulders. "Now count." She patiently taught him the box step until he was comfortable with the footwork. "We add the skip." Silvio skipped in time to the music. "Well done. Now, move!" Domenica instructed.

"I thought we were."

"Like this." Domenica led Silvio until he took the lead and reversed their movements. She laughed while he concentrated on his feet.

Silvio and Domenica took a skipping tour around the dance floor until they reached the edge of the stage. Instead of pivoting, Silvio lifted Domenica and swung her around before placing her on the ground. A smattering of appreciative applause was heard from the tables where the old people sat with a view of the stage.

"Do it again," Domenica said. Silvio lifted her into the air, this time twirling her aloft above the other couples.

The Cabrelli girl always makes the Birtolini boy do things that he shouldn't do. Silvio remembered what the nuns had told his mother when she went to school to tell them that they were leaving the village.

Silvio placed her on the ground gently.

"Excellent! You did a good job and you deserve a prize," she said as she bowed to him. "They have bomboloni."

"Are they as good as they used to be at the feast?"

"We'll have to see." She took his hand and led him off the dance floor.

Silvio followed Domenica through the crowd. He felt lucky to take his place anywhere near the light of her. Silvio Birtolini hadn't realized how much he missed Domenica Cabrelli until he danced with her.

Silvio bought Domenica a bombolone. "You don't want me to go, do you?"

"But you have to. You have a lovely girl waiting for you."

"How do you know she's lovely?"

"Anyone you chose would be."

"You think highly of me."

"Is that allowed?"

"Yes, and it's appreciated. Would you like to know what I think of you?"

"I already know." Domenica fed him a bite of the doughnut.

"You do?"

"Bossy."

"It's true." He laughed.

"Who else could get you to dance at Carnevale? Filomena Fortunata? You liked her for six days when we were ten."

Silvio did not take another bite of the pastry because he was too busy talking to Domenica. When Silvio's friends found him, it was time to go. Domenica walked them to the car.

"Just like the old days, you have to make sure I get home safely," Silvio joked.

"Be careful." She embraced her old friend.

She watched them drive away and wondered how long it would be before the four young men would be called into military service. She said a prayer and kissed the medal of Santa Lucia around her neck for their safety. Domenica wished she had remembered to show the medal to the boy who had given it to her so long ago. There hadn't been enough time.

Domenica walked home from Carnevale barefoot, carrying her dancing shoes, one in each hand, swinging them like the two pails of water she used to fetch for her mother when she was a girl. It was almost hard to remember what life was like before the pipes brought the fresh water down the mountain and into their home. She did not mind the feeling of the smooth, cold cobblestones beneath her aching feet. Her feet must have been hurting all night, but she didn't feel them in the company of Silvio Birtolini.

The stairwell of Villa Cabrelli was dense with the scents of cinnamon and anise. She joined her parents and the Speranzas in the kitchen.

Speranza was in the middle of a story as her mother stirred the pot with chestnuts on the stove. The kitchen table was covered with pristine muslin. A mound of sugar sparkled in the center of the table. Agnese dredged the chestnuts in sugar and arranged them on the pan to cool. Close by, a tray of the blanched, tender chestnuts rolled in the sugar were being stacked in a tin by her father. They looked like they had been dusted in snow.

"That's plenty," Agnese said to Cabrelli.

"When you work, you eat," Cabrelli said.

"See how useless I am," Speranza said to Domenica. "I let your papa and mama do all the work."

"That's all right, Romeo. You're doing the driving tonight."

"You're going back to Venezia?" Domenica asked.

"Romeo has a lot of work," Agnese explained. "He is creating a monstrance for the cathedral at Castel Gandolfo."

Cabrelli snapped the lid on the tin of chestnuts. Domenica went up the stairs to the guest room and picked up their suitcase. She brought it down to the kitchen where the Cabrellis and the Speranzas were saying their goodbyes. Cabrelli took the suitcase from Domenica and followed the Speranzas down the stairs.

"Try one," Netta offered.

"I had a bombolone."

"One chestnut won't hurt you."

"All you do is feed me." Domenica tasted the buttery, sugarglazed candy. "Mama, why so many tins of chestnuts?"

"We will need them. Have you noticed? I'm filling the pantry. There's a lot of talk in the village. Did you know the old Stampone palazzo is full of Blackshirts? That's half a mile up the beach. They get closer and closer."

"Maybe it will all blow over."

"I pray about it. You should pray too." Netta dredged the chestnuts in sugar. "You were out late."

"I caught up with a few old friends. Do you remember Silvio Birtolini?"

Her mother had to think. "That awful boy. Let me guess. Someone murdered him."

"Mama!"

"That's the fate of petty thieves. They start young, and over time they get worse and eventually they have a horrible end."

One of Domenica's favorite things about her mother was that she never forgot anything, but it was also one of her worst attributes, as she held grudges until they became mythical. "He's grown up to be quite handsome."

"A good-looking thief. Big deal. You can find cell after cell of them in the prison at Lucca."

"I danced with him tonight."

"Ugh! He's in Viareggio?"

"Just tonight."

"Did he behave himself?"

"He's betrothed to a nice girl. A schoolteacher."

"What does he do?"

"Diamond cutter apprentice."

Her mother rolled her eyes. "Another one. Diamonds and pearls for the pope, while the wife gets pasta e fagioli and a thimble of homemade wine if she's lucky."

"Shh, Mama. Papa will hear you."

"He's heard it all for thirty years. And if God is kind, he'll hear it for thirty more. The jewelry business is only good for the people that buy the jewelry. Never for the one that makes it. The artisan is always chiseled in the end. Commission! They can keep it."

"Silvio is proud of his trade."

"He's done better than anyone thought he would, I will give him that."

"I never believed the gossip."

Mama sat down at the table across from her daughter. "Domenica, whatever he stirred up in you, leave it on the boardwalk. You've gone to school. You're educated. You're a nurse. I want you to marry a doctor, not a troublemaker."

"Pretucci is already married."

"Not him. A young doctor. From Milano. Or Firenze. Roma is fine too. Wherever there are doctors in great supply."

"I may never find a nice fellow. I don't want you to be disappointed if I don't have luck. I'm happy the way I am."

"You say that, but I don't believe you. You work too hard. Sometimes seven days a week."

"People get sick on weekends too."

"Let them wait until Monday."

"Maybe I love my work too much. It fills me up. But I wouldn't mind a nice man to court. I'd like that."

"You deserve the cream. Don't settle for il bastardo or his type. Better to be a woman alone with a profession than marry beneath your standing."

"Mama, who are you talking about?"

"Carnival snakes. You know, they hang around the stands at the festa looking for pretty girls. Don't forget the story of Giovanna Bellanca. Lovely girl. Sang like a bird! A life of good behavior and high morals shattered like glass one night after one spin on the carousel. Carnevale ended and she took off with a juggler. Her parents were bereft! That beautiful family ruined by a circus actor. You make me worry. You have the eyes of a fish when it comes to Birtolini. Wide open, seeing nothing but him!"

"I hadn't thought about him in years," Domenica lied. She had thought about Silvio from time to time, wondering what had become of him. Now she knew, and sadly, he belonged to someone else. "Maybe Aldo will come home with a princess and your dream will come true after all."

"Aldo? We'll be lucky if he finds his way back to Viareggio with a guide and a map, much less a princess."

"Don't worry about me, Mama."

"You'll see how many hours a day can be eaten up by worry when you become a mother."

"I've always felt lucky."

"Luck runs out. So does a woman's beauty. You're old enough to see what's true in the world. Pay attention."

Domenica kissed her mother good night.

"You aren't going to see the Birtolini boy again, are you?"

"He went back to Parma. It was luck that I saw him at all."

"Bad luck. Well, since he's marrying someone else, whatever he wishes for us, I wish him double."

Domenica rolled her eyes. "Mama, you are so kind."

"I finished your new dress. It's hanging on the back of your door."

"I have a good dress."

"And I only have one daughter. And she is going to be dressed better than Principessa Borghese on the finale of Carnevale. You need to stand out in the crowd."

"Whatever makes you happy, Mama."

"I'm looking for your future happiness. Believe me. You won't get a husband wearing the old linen."

CHAPTER 14

The last night of Carnevale was a fashion show; ladies wore their best dresses on the promenade while the men turned out in ties and vests. The sideshows of singers, musical combos, jugglers, and gymnasts provided spectacle while the food tents provided the final bites of sustenance. The lines at the food tents doubled as the clock ticked toward midnight and the start of Lent. The prices dropped on souvenirs and leather goods as the night wore on. The vendors cleared the last items of their inventory before packing up to return to their cities to the north.

The weather was cool and clear. The full moon was a pearl button in the blue velvet sky. The round firepits on the beach blazed in the dark, as the revelers fed the flames with the last of the pine logs. The air was sweet with anisette, cocoa, and earthy tobacco. The boardwalk was so crowded that by the time Domenica ate a sausage-and-pepper sandwich and threaded through the throng down the pier to the gelato stand, she was hungry again. The lights blurred in streaks of pink as the carousel spun to the organ music.

Gilda Griffo, the village chanteuse, was now close to seventy years old. She had sung at most weddings and ribbon cuttings since the Great War. She typically gave an a capella concert on the last night of Carnevale. Since the stage at the end of the pier was occupied, Griffo was sent to sing aloft on the wine barrels, filled with sand, that anchored the boardwalk and kept seawater from spilling onto the street during high tide. The previous evening, the same barrel perch had featured a magician who enjoyed quite a turnout.

Griffo remained in fine voice, but her contralto was hard to hear over the buzz of the crowd, the carousel music, and the churning of the gelato contraption, which was louder than a cement mixer. Domenica pushed through the crowd to listen to Griffo's program. She felt bad for the singer as the barge loaded with fireworks rubbed against the pilings and squeaked loudly as it was guided slowly out to sea during her aria.

Soon the sky would be filled with sparklets of candy colors and scribbled with smoke. Griffo concluded her program and bowed. Domenica applauded the singer along with a small coterie of her local fans. Griffo sang in a style that few appreciated. She was a classical singer—her presentation was like calligraphy in the air, her phrasing full of curlicues. The young Italians preferred effortless American swing and jazz. Gilda Griffo was out of style. She bowed, jumped off the barrel, and landed on the dune. She shook the sand off the hem of her skirt.

"You're in fine voice, Signora," Domenica complimented her.

"Who can sing on a wine barrel? I need a proper amphitheater, but it's booked. They're playing frog hop on the stage. Carnevale has gone to the weeds. The old days were better. There was respect for craft." Griffo walked off.

Monica Mironi waved at Domenica from the middle distance.

She carried her infant in a basket and the one-year-old on her hip. Her oldest son walked ahead of them.

"La bella famiglia!" Domenica greeted the Mironi children.

"They should be home asleep, but Leonardo didn't want to miss the fireworks."

"Tonight will be the twenty-ninth finale of fireworks I've attended." Domenica knelt and spoke to the little boy: "I understand why you don't want to miss them."

"What a beautiful dress!" Monica took in Domenica's drop-waist dress with a ruffle on the hem. "Emerald green is my favorite color."

"How have you been?" Domenica asked.

"I will come and see you again."

"You have an appointment, remember?"

Domenica watched Monica walk to the carousel with her children. She needed help, but where was her husband? There were some men in the village who provided for their families but spent little time with their children. She was grateful her father had not been one of them.

Domenica walked along the pier. The merchandise that was exotic and new at the start of the festival had now been picked over. She heard the gelato maker shout that he was almost out of sugar. The bomboloni stand had enough dough for a final batch, and there wouldn't be more until the next festival. It seemed the tourists had left and taken the best food and fun with them.

"Cabrelli. I need to talk to you," Guido Mironi yelled as he jumped onto the boardwalk and cut her off. He was soon joined by a few faces she recognized. They were men who worked with Mironi at the marble mine. They had been drinking. They had loosened their ties and unbuttoned their vests. Domenica kept walking.

"Cabrelli, are you deaf?" Mironi shouted.

The men laughed.

Domenica turned and walked back to face him. "Signore Mironi."

The men in his company began to taunt their friend. "Signore! Signore!"

"I went to school with her." Mironi toasted her with a bottle.

"When you bothered to show up," she said. "Excuse me."

Mironi blocked her from moving past him. "I want to talk to you," he said.

Domenica looked down the boardwalk, searching the crowd for Monica and the children. They were gone. "Signore." Domenica folded her arms across her chest and planted her feet firmly on the boardwalk. As a small woman, she had learned how to take up space and fill it with confidence. Her stance and Mironi's tone of voice caused a crowd to form around them in anticipation of an argument. Domenica searched the circle for a friendly face but did not find one.

"Stay out of my business," he sneered. He handed the bottle of grappa to one of his pals in order to fish into his pockets. He reeked of wine but remained sober enough to stand, though his ample weight shifted from one foot to the other.

"What is this?" He waved a pamphlet in the air.

Domenica realized it was the booklet explaining family planning that she had given to Monica. She snatched it from him. "This is not the time or place to discuss private matters. Come to Dottore Pretucci's office if you have questions."

"I tell her what to do. Not you. Not Pretucci. *Me*."

"She's well aware that you're the padrone."

"I am the padrone!" Mironi roared.

"And now the entire village knows you're the boss."

The crowd laughed, enraging Mironi. He lunged for Domenica.

He was big and lumbering, but she was quick and stepped out of his way. She folded the pamphlet and tucked it inside the sleeve of her dress.

"Stay away from my wife!" Mironi warned her.

The crowd split into two sides: men and women. Domenica felt the tension of the two camps as she became the voice of the women. She stood firm as Mironi turned back toward the beach, but instead of leaving, he spun around and spit at Domenica's feet.

Domenica looked down at the ground and up at Mironi. "Aren't you a big man in every way but the important one?"

A ripple of nervous laughter went through the crowd. The fight was lopsided, a bear and a mouse. The people were riveted by the sight of the young woman standing up to the giant.

"Guido Mironi, you have been a brute all your life," Domenica said evenly. "You pulled your nonsense in the shadows so as not to get caught. But you and I know what you've done. You grew up to be a drunk: the fate of all cowards who cannot face themselves."

"You told my wife to leave our bed. You go against the natural law. Against the Church. Stay out of my business, Cabrelli."

The opening fireworks shot into the sky with a loud whistle until they found their highest peak and exploded in a shower of hot blossoms in the night sky. The whistle, boom, and shatter sounds of the fireworks drowned out anything further Mironi had to say.

Mironi's gang pulled him off the boardwalk back onto the beach. Domenica turned her back on the spectacle. She walked home under the showers of light, whereas in years past, she had stood on the beach and reveled in their beauty. She did not show it, but she was afraid. Whenever there was a fight at school, at the bottom of the pile was a hot-tempered Mironi. That had not changed since they were children. But something had shifted for Domenica during the altercation. For the first time in her life,

Viareggio did not feel like home. The locals had lost respect for Domenica somehow or were angry that she had the temerity to take a stand, or perhaps it was something worse: they sided with Mironi and wanted the young nurse to know her place in the long shadow of the Holy Roman Church.

CHAPTER 15

Domenica had never seen Pretucci angry. She had made mistakes for sure, but he was usually patient as she found a solution.

The shades in the office were pulled so far down over the sash, no light came in. The lamp over the examination table made a ring of light on the marble that looked like the moon. Domenica stood on one side of the table. Pretucci paced on the other. The doctor raised his voice for the first time to her: "You cannot give medical advice that goes against the Church."

"I was not speaking out against the Church, I was trying to help Signora Mironi. She cannot keep having babies; she has weak blood."

"That's not your concern."

"She came to me for help. The Church doesn't seem concerned about the three children who are already born. Who will take care of them when their mother dies in childbirth? I've yet to see Don Giuseppe pushing a pram."

"Signorina!"

"It's the truth. Why does Monica's fathead husband make the decisions when it comes to the children? Isn't holding the purse, the property, the rights to the children, and any inheritance enough? Why does he also have a say over her health?"

"I made it clear she should not have another child. To Mironi, the priest, and the mayor."

"Il sindaco? What business is it of his?"

"The law."

"Bassini is a buffoon."

"It doesn't matter. He holds the law of this village in his tiny hands."

"Three men against one woman? Her weak blood is a medical concern, is it not?"

Pretucci remained frustrated. "Yes, it is."

"So tell them. Tell them the situation. Explain it to those dunces. Give them the pamphlets!"

"The pamphlets are for the sailors who dock here. We don't want them spreading disease up and down the shore. I don't give those pamphlets out to married couples."

"You should! Those pamphlets can help women take care of themselves."

"You humiliated Guido Mironi in a public forum."

"Carnevale is not a forum, it's an amusement. He was drunk."

"It doesn't matter! He is the head of his family!"

"He shouldn't be."

"But he is! His wife is his business."

"She was afraid to tell him about the birth control. I could tell."

"The solution to their family issues was not to teach the woman birth control. That falls outside your role as a nurse."

"How? If I have learned something in school, am I not to apply it?"

"You can apply it, but you need to understand the scope of what you are saying to a patient."

"I shouldn't tell the truth?"

"You could leave that to me."

"But you leave the women to me. I recommended, with your approval, a tincture of black cohosh to Signora Luccizi, who is going through the change of life. How is giving a mother of three a pamphlet going to hurt her?"

"In this instance, and you must listen to me, it's because your honesty has become a problem. Signore Mironi went to the priest, who came to me. He demands your license."

"He has no right in the matter."

"The priest supports Mironi's position. And so does the law. We have to be careful in the area of reproduction."

Domenica felt a rage rise within her. "I have to be careful because I'm a woman." She sat down on the stool next to the examining table and tried to think.

Pretucci leaned on the table. "I'm afraid they're serious."

"I will go and see the priest myself and explain."

"Don't. He's angry. I can protect you if you leave Viareggio. I will be able to argue that I sent you away to teach you a lesson. There's a hospital in Marseille."

"France? My mother needs me here."

"You must be practical, Signorina. You don't want the priest to decide where to send you. You'll end up at the bottom of the world somewhere. If you go, in time, they will forget this happened. Listen to your boss. Your friend." Pretucci pulled his handkerchief from his pocket and cleaned his eyeglasses. Dottore did this whenever he needed to think. "If you go to Marseille for a few months, in time, I'm sure this will blow over and you can return to your home and this position."

Tears stung Domenica's eyes. She wiped them away quickly.

"Guido Mironi was a mean child and he's grown up to be a cruel brute. I'm not sorry I told him off."

Pretucci tried not to smile. He had heard, in a matter of hours, as gossip wended its way through the small village, the story of Domenica Cabrelli and Guido Mironi at Carnevale. The details had gone around more than once, each time embellished with more, but always with a narrative of begrudging respect for his nurse's determination to stand up to a bully. "You said what you had to say."

"It might not have been the best idea, but I had no choice. The people of the village need to understand that they can come to the clinic when they need help."

"There's only one thing you need to know. You may be right, and your position has merit. But that's all it has. You will not win this point in Viareggio, not ever, even if the entire town agrees with you. The priest always has the last word."

Domenica lit the stove with a match. She placed the moka pot on the blue flames. The small lamp on the table flickered in the dark. She sat down and waited for the espresso to percolate.

The leather suitcase she had packed the night before belonged to her father. When Pietro Cabrelli was young, he had apprenticed with a goldsmith in Barcelona to learn soldering and filigree. His father, Michele, had given Pietro a suitcase for his first trip abroad. Eventually Pietro took the bag to India and Africa. Now it was filled with Domenica's clothes, though she wouldn't need them. She would wear the white uniform provided by the nuns of the Sisters of Saint Joseph of the Apparition.

"Did you sleep?" her mother asked from the doorway.

"Not at all."

"Maybe you will sleep on the train?" Signora Cabrelli wrapped her arms around her daughter. "You must."

"Have you ever been to France, Mama?"

"Once. In the south. I was young. I went with my cousins. We learned how to make soap."

"I never wanted to leave you," Domenica said softly.

"It won't be for long."

"That's the only way I will survive. If I know it's short in duration, I can get through it."

"I want you to go to Mass. And say your rosary. Even if you have doubts, pray for me."

"I will."

"And I will pray for you. Your papa will be fine. He has the shop and his problems, which will never be solved, but it doesn't matter. They keep his mind occupied."

"I know you wanted to help, Mama, but why did you go to the priest?"

"You are my child and I am your advocate. I will fight anyone, any army, any cleric, even the pope himself, on your behalf. I was so angry when the priest punished you I wanted to take the cathedral down to its studs with an ax. That is *my* church. *My* faith. I have never missed a Sunday Mass or a holy day of obligation. Your father and I tithe. The Church has not survived for centuries because of the priests. The gold robes don't scare me. The cardinals and bishops and the monsignors can talk to me and I will set their heads straight. I went to the priest because I believed I could change his mind. But he was impossible. He said if he allowed you to stay, every woman in the village would hear of your medical knowledge and come to you for a pamphlet, and soon there would be no babies in Viareggio! Imagine the stupidity of such a statement. I almost told him what he could do with his immortal soul, but your papa makes the chalices for Roma, and we can't afford to lose the business."

"Mama, it would be the first time in your life you held your tongue."

"Well, there's the greater good, isn't there? I know how it works. And it's not worth it. Do your penance and come home, and we'll never speak of it again."

Domenica swallowed hard. She thought her mother was naïve, and for that matter, she thought Pretucci was too. She knew what it meant to be marked in a small village. Silvio Birtolini was almost stoned to death for being born in illegitimacy. She remembered how they treated Vera Vietro. Locals treated Domenica like Vera. They looked past her in public, as though Domenica did not exist. Any good Domenica had done was forgotten. Even if you were well liked, even if you served them, there was no defense against the powerful. They could discard you on a whim.

Mama made the coffee just as her daughter liked it. Netta set the espresso pot off to the side, flipped the hatch on the icebox in the floor, removing a tin canister of fresh cream. She heated the cream in a small pot on the blue flames until it foamed, pouring the espresso and cream into a small bowl. Netta measured a teaspoon of sugar on a spoon and placed it in the bowl before handing it to her daughter.

Domenica drank the sweet coffee and cream slowly, savoring it. She didn't know if they made caffè in Marseille the way her mother made it in Viareggio. For most of her life, this had been her breakfast. She couldn't imagine the morning without it. She placed the bowl on the table. "I don't want to go, Mama."

"Domenica, don't say it. You have to be strong. You must not cry. You must not let them break you."

"I'm being punished for doing my job."

"You're the only educated woman in this town. The village is not big enough for your mind."

Domenica worried about her mother's blunt tongue. "Mama, you have to be careful of what you say to powerful people. I counted more periscopes. They're here."

"The Germans?"

"Not yet. The Italians. Regia Marina. Il Duce's Royal Navy."

"Your father and I will work hard whatever comes."

"Trust no one, Mama. I mean that."

Netta sat down at the table with her daughter. "If they come for us, I won't fight it."

"You should go now. Don't wait." Domenica fretted. "We have our cousins on the mountain. They will take you in."

"I'll talk to your father."

"And don't worry about me. I'll do my work and come home as soon as I can."

"Stay close to the nuns." Netta embraced Domenica.

"Stay away from them. No daughter of mine is going to be a nun," Cabrelli said as he joined them in the kitchen.

"They don't want me, Papa."

"I don't care if they do. They can't have you. You would rely on charity for your clothes and food and a pair of new shoes. You would be nothing more than a chaste beggar. No daughter of mine will ever accept charity. Besides, the shoes are ugly."

"Don't worry, Papa. I can provide my own shoes. And they'll be pretty. See?" Domenica showed her father the black leather dress shoes the local cobbler had made for her.

"Remember, the nuns are crafty. Don't let them talk you into their way of life. They make a lot of noise about how wonderful the cloistered life can be when they come through with their missions. When they traveled through, I hid you. They let the families believe that in offering their daughters for service, they would be taken care of too." Her father placed his gold pocket watch in her hand. "You take this."

"Papa. You need your watch."

"I want you to have it."

"It should go to Aldo."

"I decide who gets my watch."

"Thank you, Papa." Domenica placed the watch in her pocket.

"When you own something of value, people assume you are worth something too. Wear the watch so they know your worth." Papa kissed her on the cheek and went to the front door. He picked up her suitcase.

"It's time." Mama stood. She put her arm around her daughter. They walked together in silence to the front door.

Papa opened the front door. It was dark, but the first glow of sunrise peeked over the village with its waxy fingers on the horizon. A crowd had gathered on the street in front of their home. Domenica could make out the faces of her cousins from Via Firenze and some of her old friends from school. Even her boss, Pretucci, on his way to work, stood with them and held his medical bag as if he, too, were going on a trip.

A cheer went up in the crowd as Domenica greeted them. Signora Griffo presented Domenica with a bouquet of flowers. "What has been done to you is wrong," she said as her warm breath made a small cloud in the cold air, "and we know it."

Pretucci and Griffo led the group to the train station on foot. Soon the street was bathed in morning light; each door, window, stucco wall, and rooftop appeared gilded as they passed. Perhaps Domenica was being punished for taking her village for granted. She had not been grateful enough. The group walked in silence. The only sounds were their soft footfalls on the cobblestones punctuated by the occasional squeak Domenica's new shoes made as she walked. Why had her mother insisted on new shoes? The same reason her father made her take his gold watch. If Domenica Cabrelli looked like she was a young woman of means, she would be treated as one.

Domenica had only traveled as far north as Sestri Levante on the Gulf of Genoa and as far south as the outskirts of Roma. She had never left her country, or navigated a strange new place alone. "I've never changed trains, Papa. What if something goes wrong?"

"You will be fine," her father reassured her, as if he read her mind. "Look up, read the schedule, find the platform number, and go to the platform." She nodded. She would take the seven a.m. train to Genoa, where she would board a French train that would take her to Nice and on to her final destination to Marseille by the sea. Maybe it would be warm there too; maybe it would feel familiar. Maybe she would be all right.

As Domenica stepped onto the platform, the crowd murmured their goodbyes. She turned and waved to them, thinking it would not be long until she saw them again. That thought would keep her from crying. She climbed the steps to enter the train car. Through the window, Domenica saw her mother wave a handkerchief and smile, but Domenica could see the tears streaking her face. Her father removed his hat and held it over his chest so his daughter would not see his heart break.

Domenica clutched the sleeve of train tickets in one hand and the bouquet of flowers in the other. The porter took her suitcase and guided her to her seat. There was a straight pin that fastened the velvet ribbon that held the bouquet together. The sharp end of the pin pierced her hand, but she did not feel it. Domenica Cabrelli felt nothing as she lost everything.

The train crisscrossed over the rhubarb fields, taking her farther from home with each turn of the wheels. If she hoped to return to Viareggio someday, she must stay alert. She would pay attention to the route. She would study the geography and count the local stops. As the train rolled north, Domenica would mark the tracks in her memory with points of interest as she looked out the window. A gray barn. A cement factory. A zoo. She would observe the trains running in the opposite direction, just to reassure herself that the Italian line ran both ways.

PART TWO

LET WHOEVER LONGS TO ATTAIN ETERNAL LIFE
IN HEAVEN HEED THESE WARNINGS:

When considering the present, contemplate these things:

The shortness of life

The difficulty of saving your soul

The few who will be saved

CHAPTER 16

Marseille, France

MARCH 1939

The South of France did not remind Domenica Cabrelli of the pearl beaches and quiet bliss of the Ligurian coast, yet at first sight, it had its charms. The squat, white stucco homes built by the Greeks centuries earlier were tucked between new Art Deco buildings shaped like cigarettes, with spirals that punctured the low clouds. Beyond the city, the cliffs of the Calanques massif formed a jagged green hem on the skyline.

The evening Domenica arrived in Marseille, Sister Marie Bernard of the order of Saint Joseph of the Apparition met her at the train station. The nun had been easy to spot in the crowd in her black habit and white bonnet. Her bright red cheeks, cheerful smile, and clear blue eyes indicated a happy disposition. Domenica would soon learn that they also were a sign of the nun's constitution.

"Signorina Cabrelli," Sister Marie Bernard greeted Domenica in Italian. "Ciao."

The nun took Domenica's suitcase before leading her new charge through the streets of Marseille. The nun was built like a panettone and rolled like a wheel in perpetual motion. Domenica skipped to keep up with her, all the while trying to take in her new home. Domenica wanted to ask Sister Marie Bernard some questions about her job. Domenica was anxious about the language and her skill set, but the nun was in a hurry. Sister cut through alleys and strode across a plaza staggered with gurgling fountains and young couples. The nun and Domenica ducked under wet laundry hanging on clotheslines that crisscrossed overhead in an alley. The scent of pine tar soap would be Domenica's first memory of France. They passed the waterfront, whose docks were cluttered with jittery boats that bobbed up and down at the whims of the waves.

Marseille was nestled on the rocky shore of the Mediterranean Sea. There were narrow channels and wide waterways carved into the coastline, with enough slips to dock ships of all sizes. An industrial pier reached out into the sea, accommodating the ocean liners. Cruisers from Monte Carlo carried gamblers, yachts brought the wealthy, while the local skiffs brought nets overflowing with fresh fish. This was not a city of trains and automobiles; it was a city of boats.

Fatima House, the official dormitory of the nurses of Saint Joseph, was on the end of rue de Calais with a view of the harbor and the sea beyond it. Hôpital Saint Joseph was next door to the dormitory. The nuns lived on the upper floor of the hospital, close to the action. The complex, which included a large outdoor garden, fenced in by a nine-foot stone wall, gave the nuns a private sanctuary.

"Benvenuta alla tua nuova casa," Sister Marie Bernard said cheerfully. "Breakfast at five a.m. Sister Juliette makes fresh croissants on Wednesdays and eclairs on Saturdays. During Lent, no eclairs." Sister frowned.

Domenica followed the nun up the stairs. "Three to four nurses to a room," Sister Marie Bernard huffed as she climbed. "You'll find the living spaces nice enough. I don't know what you're used to. We provide your soap and shampoo. I make it myself. I grow the lavender and keep the bees, so I know it's the best. Some of the girls don't want to leave Saint Joseph's because of the soap."

Domenica laughed. "I'll let you know if it's reason enough to stay, Sister."

"The secret is the frankincense. Flowers and honey together can be awfully sweet, so I cut the crème with a smidge of frankincense." Sister Marie Bernard rapped on the door of 307. "Girls must be out. Sorry. No roommates to welcome you." Sister Marie Bernard reached under her cassock and found the door key on a ring loaded with them. She unlocked the door and flipped on the light. The room had three beds. The nightstands of two were cluttered with hairbrushes, books, and ashtrays. A single bed was made in the alcove with a white coverlet and pillow. The nightstand was clear. The breeze from the open window fluttered the sheers. "You're over here, Cabrelli." Sister placed the suitcase on the bench at the end of the bed. "Lucky you. You're in a triple."

"Thank you, Sister." Domenica exhaled. The accommodations weren't a prison after all.

Sister Marie Bernard gave Domenica the once-over. "I'll send up your uniforms—we provide two. Standard white jumper and apron with regulation blouse and stockings." She looked down at Domenica's feet. "You look to be a thirty-one?"

"Exactly."

"Don't ruin your nice shoes. I'll also send your undergarments and cap. The nurses do their own laundry in the convent. The girls will show you."

The nun left Domenica to unpack. Domenica removed her hat. She knelt on the bed and leaned out the window. She could see the ships in the harbor, their deck lights glimmering on the surface of the teal water. She inhaled the fresh ocean breeze and closed her eyes. No matter where she went in the world, the sea was her soul and salvation.

*   *   *

Domenica was determined not to be overwhelmed by the scope of the work at Saint Joseph's. She had never staffed in a hospital, but she was a quick learner. Domenica wondered if she would ever learn the names of all the nuns and nurses, a daunting task in addition to the ten-hour shifts the nurses were required to work.

The Sisters were devoted to the healing power of the saints and angels with the same fervor they held for modern medical science. A statue of the Blessed Mother greeted patients as they entered the lobby. There was a chapel on the ground floor.

The design of the hospital resembled a church. The wide corridors had vaulted ceilings and polished terrazzo floors reminiscent of a Gothic cathedral. Lancet windows with amber glass bathed the hallways and rooms in golden light. Life-size plaster statues of the saints had been tucked into the alcoves like sentry guards. A crucifix hung over each hospital bed, and a holy water font hung next to every door.

However, there was little religion inside the nurses' dormitory. The only shrine in Fatima was a paper one, to Robert Taylor, the handsome American actor known for his thick, black French eyebrows. The girls relaxed, smoked, and gossiped after their shifts as their radios blasted swing music. They plastered eight-by-ten glossy photographs of Ronald Colman, Spencer Tracy, and Clark Gable on their mirrors, and more than one of the matinee idols had a smear of lipstick on his black-and-white cheek. The nurses came to work at Saint Joseph's from all over the world—the Philippines,

Cuba, the United States, Jamaica, Ireland, Liberia, and Italy—having been recruited by the nuns through their network of schools. No matter where in the world they came from, the young nurses were devoted to American movie stars.

There were two sisterhoods in full operation at Saint Joseph's: One group wore habits and had taken vows, while the other had sewn their own version of fashionable dresses, knew the latest dances, taught one another passable French and English, and set one another's hair.

On Saturday night, out of their uniforms and sprung from work obligations, the nurses became carefree young women. They took off their white uniforms and replaced them with their best party dresses. Marseille pulsated with jazz music and silly chatter until the sun came up, replacing the drone of machines from the factories with laughter. The nurses lost themselves on the dance floors up and down the beach. Sailors, infantrymen, and even well-dressed men in Savile Row suits became their partners. The nurses called the Americans "Burmas," because they smelled of cedarwood and vanilla, the scent of the American shaving cream.

Off duty, Domenica and her new friends also took long walks through the city. They sat by the rococo fountain at Palais Longchamp, rode the transport ferry to Vieux Port, and ended a day off on rue du Panier under a tent sipping ice-cold Chablis and eating delicate snails baked in garlic and butter.

"Domenica, come with us. There's a dance on the pier. A new band." Stephanie Arlette, an American nurse from Chicago, never missed an opportunity to have fun. "Club Mistare."

Domenica put down the newspaper. "Sounds like fun, but I'm going to stay in tonight."

"Again?" Stephanie dropped onto the bed next to Domenica. "You're not going to spend your day off writing to your mother, are you?"

"I thought I'd write to Dottore Pretucci for a change."

"Is he handsome?"

"He's old. He's not for you."

"You never know." Stephanie removed the strips of fabric from her hair where she had tied it up in sections so it would curl as it dried. She shook out her blond ringlets. "I'm marrying for money."

"That's as good a reason as any," Josephine Brodeur, a lean twenty-four-year-old Jamaican, said as she filed her nails.

Stephanie stepped into her blue organza party dress. She crouched as Domenica zipped up the back. "Are you sure you don't want to come with us?"

Josephine coaxed her silk stocking up her leg. "You will never meet a handsome man and fall in love as long as you stay in this room and scribble."

"Maybe Domenica doesn't want to fall in love."

"I don't believe it." Josephine pulled on the second stocking. "I've been in love three times. It goes like this: Imagine you're on the highest mountain in the world and you're pushed off the cliff. Falling in love is the feeling you have between the time you are pushed and the moment you hit the ground."

"I've been in love once," Stephanie admitted. "And I hope I never see him again."

"I'm not ready to be thrown off a mountain. I'd rather sleep on my day off." Domenica smiled at her roommates.

"I didn't mean to ruin it for you." Josephine sat down and snapped her stockings into their garters. "Everyone is different. Maybe when you fall in love it will feel like a warm bath."

"I didn't make it sound as wonderful as it can be." Stephanie spritzed on perfume. "It's only awful when it ends." She loaded her evening bag. "The crash is as terrible as the feeling was wonderful. But it's always worth it."

Domenica scanned the newspaper. "The *Arandora Star* is docking tonight. They say there's a Vanderbilt on board. And maybe the movie star William Powell. Tomorrow, the *Avila* arrives—all five of the Blue Star Line are coming to Marseille."

"When they send Clark Gable, lemme know." Stephanie ran the brush through her hair. "They can keep their lousy ships."

"I hope they don't ruin the trains. I want to go home someday," Domenica said quietly.

Josephine shot Stephanie a look. "You'll make it home. But you should enjoy your life now. Stephanie and I are worried about you. You should have fun. Don't use that silly punishment from your priest as an excuse to stay cooped up in the dorm. Sister Marie Bernard said you were free to come and go as you please. The Italian rules don't apply in France," Josephine said kindly.

"You could use some fresh air. And that doesn't mean sitting in the window staring at the sea." Stephanie pulled the sheers across the open window.

"She's right. Take a walk. Go see the passengers on the promenade. And let us know what the fancy girls are wearing."

Domenica waved them off cheerfully. "Va bene, girls."

"Save me a Vanderbilt," Stephanie joked.

The ladies left a languid trail of My Sin and Joy perfume in the air. Someday, long after she left it, the scent of gardenias and roses would remind Domenica of France. The Italian nurse had made true friends in Marseille. Maybe their mutual love of nursing bonded them, or the experience of living and working together encouraged them to rely on one another, but whatever the reason, Domenica had found friends she could trust. She kept their secrets and they kept hers. Only Sister Marie Bernard and her roommates knew why she had come to Saint Joseph's, and they didn't care. Domenica Cabrelli was far from home, but she was not alone.

21 March 1939

Dear Mama,

I am not homesick any longer. The Sisters keep us so busy. We have to attend Mass—the girls from Africa give Sister Marie Bernard a hard time about it. They are not Catholic, so they don't see the point. I tell them, go to Mass, put your head down, and think about whatever makes you happy. They've come up with some funny scenes! One of the girls spends Vespers making coconut milk in her imagination. You remember Josephine? She almost has enough money saved to go to New York City. She plans on working at Saint Vincent's Hospital there. The Sisters write letters to place us. Whenever they ask me if I need a letter, I say, Send me home to Viareggio! Stephanie is so funny. She is a good nurse, but when the shift ends, she has to go dancing or else. I am training for emergencies now. Sister Marie Bernard is teaching us about how to care for injuries inflicted in battle, though there is little talk of war in Marseille. She said war or no war, we need to know how to handle emergencies. How is Papa? Please write. Aldo is still training in Calabria. Mama, he sent me a letter. He sounded so grown up! Hope!

Ti voglio bene,

Domenica

The guard was asleep in his chair at his post at the entrance of the dormitory when Domenica dropped the letter to her mother in the out-box on his desk. She tied the ribbons on her straw hat under her chin before going outside.

The music coming from the pier was underscored by the moan of an occasional foghorn and the shimmy of the boats as they rubbed against the pilings. The weather-beaten pier creaked as she walked over it. The railing was crumbling, and planks were missing. Domenica could see through the holes as shallow seawater sloshed over the rocks underneath it. One sure sign of eventual war was obvious: Repairs on public property had ceased. Manpower was officially needed elsewhere; besides, there was no point in fixing the structures that might be destroyed. Better to let the weak fall and shore up where the infrastructure was strong.

Domenica joined the crowd that had gathered on the long pier to welcome the *Arandora* docked in the harbor. The great ship was so massive, she blocked the night sky with the curves of her hull. The shell of the *Arandora* was bright white; she was trimmed in lipstick red and navy blue. Two bright blue stars on her smokestacks marked the ship as one of the five most exclusive ocean liners to ever sail the seas. Domenica stepped back and went up on her toes to take in the grandeur. The polished brass bindings twinkled as they caught the light of the flames from the torches that lit the pier. The upper decks began to fill with passengers dressed in their finery as they formed an orderly line to disembark. The gangplank was lowered on clanking chains that hit the ground with a thud.

"Here they come!" a young French girl shouted. A woodwind quartet began to play an airy tune. The parade of stylish ladies floated down the gangway one by one wearing satin drop-waist dresses in ice cream colors with matching wide-brimmed hats embellished with mounds of tulle that resembled tufts of cotton candy.

A group of photographers from the French newspapers gathered around a particular young woman wearing a white lace chemise with flutter-cut sleeves. *She must be a famous performer*, Domenica thought as the flashbulbs popped, turning everything bright white. Domenica stood on her toes to catch a glimpse of the young woman as she sashayed past. Domenica was disappointed when it was revealed that she was not Janet Gaynor or Myrna Loy but just another pretty girl who had sailed around the world on a luxury yacht. There had not been a movie star or a Vanderbilt or a Russian ballerina from the Ballet Russe disembark the *Arandora Star*.

Domenica decided to walk the length of the pier before returning to Fatima House. A crowd had gathered outside a popular club where the band had moved outdoors to play. Soon the patrons spilled out onto the pier from inside and began to dance. Domenica was lost in the music when she felt hands clamp around her waist, only to be scooped up off her feet and lifted into the air. She ordered the stranger to place her safely back on the ground.

"Next time ask me before you throw me in the air," Domenica snapped.

"Forgive me. I saw you moving to the music."

The young man went off in search of a willing dance partner. It wasn't like Domenica to chastise anyone caught up in the moment, especially when music was involved, but the last time Domenica's feet had left the ground was at Carnevale, when she danced with Silvio.

When the girls asked her if she had been in love, Domenica had claimed she hadn't been, but truthfully, she couldn't be absolutely certain one way or the other. The only love she had known for another in that regard had not been impetuous or dramatic. There had been no falling off a mountain, no breathless moments in midair, because her first love began in friendship. She loved

Silvio Birtolini first as a friend, with a love that was practical, sturdy, and, in her heart, everlasting. And even though he did not belong to her, she loved him anyway. Wasn't that the nature of true love? To hope for his happiness more than your own? Or did that make her a *sap*, as the Americans called those who had no will of their own? *He's marrying someone else, Domenica*, she reminded herself. *He doesn't belong to you.* That settled *that*.

CHAPTER 17

The bucket that Sister Marie Honoré had placed under the leak in the roof over the corridor on the first floor of the hospital was about half full of rain. Domenica emptied it and returned it to the spot and waited until she heard the first ping of water through the hole in the roof.

Domenica placed the clipboard with her notes from the night rounds on a hook by the door before returning to her station in the lobby. The only sound was the ticking of the big clock on the wall. She slipped out of her shoes. It was 2:05 in the morning. Whenever she worked the overnight shift, Domenica managed to catch the clock as it read 2:05, the day and month of her mother's birth. She yawned and thought about going down the hallway to the nurses' station and making herself a cup of tea. One of the girls had made macarons. Instead she leaned back in the chair and stretched.

Olivier Desplierre, fifteen, was on duty with Domenica on the shift. The night watchman/janitor fought nodding off to sleep in his chair. Domenica felt compassion for the boy—he reminded her of Aldo. She placed her hand gently on his shoulder.

"I'm sorry, Nurse Cabrelli." Olivier sat up.

"You're going to get a stiff neck sleeping like that. There's a cot in Room 13. Go."

Domenica pulled a basket of freshly laundered cloth bandages from underneath the desk. She had begun to fold the fabric into tight squares when her eye caught a beam of light spilling out from the closed door of the chapel. Maybe a vagrant had snuck into the chapel while she made her rounds. The nuns warned the nurses about locals who used the hospital like the public park.

Domenica opened the chapel door wide and said, "Bonjour," loudly before peering inside. The pews were empty. She exhaled. The light had come from the sanctuary lamp that flickered on the altar near the tabernacle. She blessed herself with holy water from the door-side font and was pulling the chapel door closed behind her when the entrance doors of the hospital flew open.

A raucous group of men, reeking of motor oil and smoke, their skin covered in soot, piled into the lobby. Domenica assumed they were firemen, but upon closer inspection, their uniforms, what was left of them, were once navy and white. Some of the men were shirtless; a few were barefoot. They made such a racket, Domenica could not sort out what they were saying in English because they spoke so fast. The tallest of the lot entered carrying an injured man in his arms. The men parted in deference to let them through.

The tall man's face was covered in black soot like the others'. She wouldn't have been able to provide a single detail about the man because something came over her as she looked up at him. The lights flickered. Her stomach fluttered. Her pulse raced. The sound in the room went away. Domenica looked at the clock; the second hand swept around its face as usual. She looked up at the ceiling, certain the bulbs had blown in the chandelier, changing the chemistry of light and dark in the lobby, but the bulbs blazed bright white.

"There's been a fire. This fellow took the brunt of it. He needs a doctor," the man said to her.

Olivier, roused by the ruckus in the lobby, pushed through the throng to get to Domenica.

"Call Dr. Chalfant. Ring the bell at Fatima and go get Sister Marie Bernard in the convent," Domenica told him.

"Right away."

"Follow me." Domenica led the man carrying the injured sailor to the closest examining room. "You can put him down here. I've sent for the doctor. You may wash up in the sink." Domenica turned to go.

The stranger grabbed her arm. "Stay with him. Please."

"I have to admit the injured," she said calmly. "Hospital protocol."

"Please, give him a look. He was in the boiler room," the man explained. "He hasn't woken up since the explosion."

"He's in shock. He needs to see the doctor."

"Please. Won't you give him a look?"

Domenica placed her hands on the young man. She observed his injuries. When she put her hands on his face, his eyes fluttered open. "You're going to be all right," she assured him. She lifted his head and placed a pillow under it.

Sister Marie Bernard barreled through the door, tying a nurse's apron over her habit. "What have we got, Cabrelli?" She washed her hands at the basin.

"He passed out. Abrasions on his chest, and a bad burn on his left arm, and a deep gash on his leg. That's at first glance."

"I'll fix him up. Clear the lobby. Assign the patients in descending order of the severity of their wounds to the examination rooms."

"Yes, Sister."

Stephanie, her hair tied up in curling rags, joined them in the room. "Reporting for assignment, Sister."

Sister took a quick look at the nurse and issued instructions. "Arlette. Take over for me here. Clean the wound on his arm and dress it. The doctor will have to examine his leg."

The stranger followed Sister Marie Bernard and Domenica out of the room. He tried to eavesdrop on their conversation as they walked down the corridor, but Sister Marie Bernard had lowered her voice so only Domenica could hear her. "Have Nurse Arlette remove her curling rags when she's done."

"Yes, Sister."

"And what kind of a nurse is woken out of a deep sleep in the middle of the night wearing lipstick?"

"One that wasn't asleep, Sister," Domenica answered quietly.

Sister Marie Bernard turned around to face the stranger. "Who are you?"

"I'm Captain John Lawrie McVicars of the *Boidoin*." He saluted the nun. "These are my men. My crew."

"I will need your manifest. We have to document the injured. Accurately," she said to the captain. "Take care of the paperwork, Cabrelli. And take a look at the captain. I don't like the look of his neck."

"Yes, Sister." Domenica leaned close to the nun. "Is this an act of war?"

"Who knows anything anymore?" Sister Marie Bernard moved to the ward to check the beds.

The captain followed Domenica down the corridor. "That nun is mean."

"You'll be glad she's direct when she fights for your men." Domenica opened the door to an empty examination room.

"Bernard is an odd name for a woman."

"For the saint. Saint Bernard of Clairvaux. French. Founded the Abbey of Clairvaux and expanded the order of the Cistercians."

"Oh yes, the famous Cistercians."

"I need to take a look at you."

"Why?"

"To make note of your injuries for Dr. Chalfant." Domenica lifted the clipboard off the ring and grabbed a pencil. "Can you spell your name for me, Captain?"

McVicars spelled his name.

"How old are you?"

"How old are *you*?" he shot back.

"Younger than you, evidently." She placed the clipboard on the table and leaned in to examine his neck. "How did this happen?"

"Sunterland had a grip on me."

"Sunterland is the patient in Room 1?"

"Yeah. That's him."

McVicars had the face of a swashbuckler on the cover of one of those American dime-store novels that were passed around the dormitory by the girls like a fresh pack of cigarettes or a new box of chocolates. The captain had a Florentine profile. His strong nose and chin reminded her of her people, though he spoke English. Familiarity bred compassion in this situation. His hair was thick and brown. He appeared to tower over his men, but his build was not of the reedy type, but of the substantial-build-with-broad-shoulders variety. The captain's teeth were straight with a glint of gold in the back of his mouth; his eyes were blue-green like the surface of Il Tirreno Mare in summer. How could a man so far from her home remind her of it? She felt the warm waves of the surf wash over her when she looked at him. She had no idea where these feelings came from, so she had no idea how to stop them. In her training, she had learned how to care for her patients while keeping an emotional distance. The man who came crashing through the front door carrying one of his crew had taken that wall down with him.

"Are you all right, miss?" McVicars wanted to know.

Domenica blushed. "I'm hungry, that's all."

Domenica reached into her apron pocket to make notes on the chart when she dropped the pencil. It rolled under the examining table. She knelt and reached under the table, trying to find it.

"Is that the last pencil in Marseille?"

"We're always losing them around here. Sister gets annoyed when we do. With the war coming, there's already a shortage of lead."

"I am certain your pencil will move us one step closer to victory."

"You never know, Captain." Domenica tried not to smile. She reached into the cabinet and handed a set of gray pajamas to McVicars. "Go behind the screen and change into these. Leave your uniform and underclothes in the bin, and we will wash and press them for you."

"I don't need to change my clothes."

"Hospital policy. You must. If you don't, Sister will get you into these pajamas herself. Don't test her. I've seen her do it."

McVicars grunted and went behind the screen.

"Melanie. Is that what the nun called you?"

"*Cabrelli.* Sister calls us by our surnames."

McVicars emerged in the pajamas and sat on the examining table. Domenica gently swabbed the wound on his neck. He was close enough to her face to count the sprinkle of freckles on the bridge of her nose. He pulled away. "I want to wait for the doctor. He may find something," McVicars growled.

"I have an idea what he'll find." Domenica wrapped the wound in gauze.

"A laceration so deep it requires surgery?"

"No. A difficult patient."

"Cabrelli. An Italian in Marseille, France. Why? Don't tell me. It's a sad story, isn't it? No family. No friends. No home. The nuns took you in because you had no place to go. They taught you nursing in exchange for free labor, but you knew that the education they provided was worth so much more, so you decided to work off your debt to the good Sisters in this rundown hospital."

"I'm from a fine family. The nuns didn't take me in. I earned my nursing credits in Roma before I came here. This hospital isn't rundown, it's busy. And nobody pays, so the nuns have no money to fix the place. Keep that in mind when you're on your way out. Throw something in the poor box in the lobby."

Domenica excused herself. McVicars lay down on the examining table to wait for the doctor and promptly fell asleep.

Dr. Chalfant moved through the ward. He was around forty, with a slight build and a shock of red hair. From a distance, wearing his white lab coat, he looked like a lit match. He observed Nurse Cabrelli ease a patient into an ice bath.

"Docteur, I'll take you to the examination rooms in a moment."

"Cabrelli, I need to talk to you," Sister Marie Bernard said.

"I've got him," Josephine said, taking over for Domenica.

Domenica followed the nun outside into the corridor.

"Sister, I ordered the baths because I didn't know how else to treat the severity of the burns. I knew from my training that an ice bath is the first step in alleviating their pain. Forgive me if I overstepped my—"

"You did an excellent job, Cabrelli. I don't know how you rallied the nurses, but they took orders from you better than they've ever taken them from me."

Domenica wiped her face on the edge of her apron. She leaned against the wall and closed her eyes.

McVicars spotted Domenica from the end of the corridor. He joined her, leaning against the wall beside her. "I've visited most of my men. Well done. You're a better captain than me."

"I'm just a nurse."

"Let's be friends, Cabrelli. I was teasing you before."

"Were you? Did your men fill out the forms?"

"Everyone but Donnelly. He can't read or write."

"Where did you get that robe?"

"Sister Aloysius or something or the other." McVicars tied the sash around his waist. "Like it?"

"The doctor is making the rounds to the examination rooms," Domenica said as she walked down the corridor. "You need to be on your table waiting for him."

"I'd like to follow you and learn my way around the hospital, if you would oblige me. I will need to check on my men."

"It's simple. There are two floors and thirty rooms." Domenica pointed in the direction of the rooms as she moved down the hall-way. "We're not a fancy hospital, but we're a good one." Domenica commandeered an overflowing laundry bin down the corridor. McVicars followed her.

"Any sailors in your family?" McVicars wanted to know.

"Not one. We do love the sea. We live on the water. Does that count?"

"Depends. What sea are we talking about?"

"Il Tirreno Mare."

"The Tyrrhenian Sea! I know it well. I have also sailed the Ligurian Sea and the Mediterranean. The Gulf of Genoa to the north is as blue as a broken heart. Fond memories of that port."

"I'm sure. Do you know Viareggio?"

"No, I don't. We dropped anchor at Gioia Tauro. Do you know it?"

"On the Tyrrhenian coast." Domenica leaned down to retrieve a bundle of dirty sheets on the floor and threw them into the bin.

"You aren't just a French girl faking that Italian accent, are you?"

"The English think every accent is fake but their own."

"I'm not English! I am a Scot. Couldn't you tell?"

"How do you tell the difference?"

"In every conceivable way! Have you been to Scotland?"

"I have not. I know my village and I know Marseille. I've been in exactly two countries in my lifetime. France is the second one." Domenica pushed the bin into the laundry room. McVicars followed her inside. The room was sweltering hot. The machines made a loud racket. A nun in a kerchief and apron pushed a bedsheet through the wringer washer. Another nun in the same work habit operated the industrial iron that chuffed clouds of steam when she pressed the fabric. They looked up at McVicars, and then at each other.

"He's a patient," Domenica explained as she emptied the bin and sorted the hospital pajamas from the towels for the laundress.

McVicars shouted over the din, "Do you like the rain and cold?"

Domenica shook her head no.

"You'll get past it. There is much to recommend it. The green pastures. The lakes. Me."

"I just met you, Captain. But I won't hold that against your people. You're blunt."

McVicars laughed. "I am, aren't I?"

"But it doesn't bother me." Domenica lifted a stack of fresh sheets off the shelf from the supply closet in the laundry. "You're just scared."

"Whatever do you mean?" McVicars pretended not to hear her as he followed her out the laundry room door and back into the corridor. "I will have you know that I am known for my courage."

"You did lead your men to the hospital tonight. Some are worse off than others, but all of them will heal. You had good luck."

"You won't say that when you see the *Boidoin*."

McVicars followed Domenica into the examining room. He stood by while she made up the examining table with a fresh sheet. "Do you think we could be friends?" he asked.

Domenica helped the captain onto the examining table. "It takes time to make a friend."

"Well, obviously you're a quick thinker. What are your thoughts? Do you think you can be my friend? Like? Not like? Ruminating? Indifferent? Undecided?"

"You talk too fast." She swung McVicars's legs onto the examining table.

"How did you do that? I'm three times your size."

"Hot towels." Josephine opened the door with her hip and smiled at McVicars.

McVicars took a towel and wiped his face. "How's this, Nurse?"

"Better," Josephine said.

"How about you, Cabrelli, what do you think?"

"I don't see an enormous difference. Josephine, how are we doing on the floor?"

"We've got the boys cleaned up. Dr. Chalfant is overseeing the binding. Sister Marie Honoré has already put three men to sleep reading Scripture aloud."

"Forgive them." McVicars shook his head sadly. "Tell the good sister to read the racing forms. They'll stay awake for that."

"I must go." Domenica turned to leave.

McVicars grabbed her hand. "The nurse said the situation is under control."

Domenica pulled her hand away gently. "She's not the boss. It's my shift and I'm in charge. That's why I can ask you a question."

"What is it?"

"Would you like a cup of tea, Captain McVicars?"

Stephanie poked her head in the door. "Domenica, you're needed on the floor."

"Excuse me, Captain. The tea and macarons are at the nurses' station at the end of the hall. Help yourself."

CHAPTER 18

As the sun rose over Marseille, the lobby of Hôpital Saint Joseph was drenched in light. Olivier, exhausted, slowly pushed the mop back and forth across the floor.

"Why are you still here?" Domenica took the mop from Olivier.

"Sister Marie Bernard said I couldn't leave until I got the smoke smell out of the lobby."

"It may take a while. I'll throw some cologne around."

Olivier smiled and took the mop back from her to finish his chore. "Why are *you* still here, mademoiselle?"

"Because I'm the boss until the next shift begins."

The hospital was quiet as Domenica made the rounds. The sailors of the *Boidoin* had been examined and treated. They slept quietly in their beds on the main floor. The nurses on the morning shift had already gathered in the hospital kitchen to prepare breakfast for the patients. The scent of freshly brewed coffee and hot croissants drifted through the corridor. As hungry as Domenica was, the thought of her bed was more appealing than food. She signed out of her shift and picked up the work log. She stopped to bless herself with holy water from the font outside the chapel when she remembered a final task she had promised to complete. She entered the chapel, closing the door behind her. She genuflected at the altar in the cool darkness. The scent of carnations filled the air. She placed the Holy Book on the lectern and placed the cruets, bells, and linens on the side table for Mass.

"I couldn't find the light." A man's voice cut through the silence.

She squinted into the darkness. "Captain McVicars?"

"I'm not praying."

"It's not an accusation."

"What are *you* doing?" the captain asked innocently.

"Sister Claudette asked me to prepare the chapel for Mass."

"Is it Sunday?"

"We have daily Mass. What are you doing?"

"The laundress is pressing my uniform. I don't know how she got the oil stains out of it, but she did. I offered to kiss her."

"Did she accept?"

"That's between Madame Esther DeGuisa Wing and me."

Domenica turned to go.

"Stay," he said.

"Mother Superior is waiting for the paperwork."

"Any person with *Superior* in her name should be kept waiting, if only to teach her humility. Come sit with me."

He slid into the middle of the pew to make room for her. He spread his arms across the back of the pew like wings.

Domenica sat at the end of the pew, as far away from him as possible. "Are you Catholic?"

"No. No. No. No."

"One *no* would do."

"The great tunes sound better in four-part harmony. Miss Cabrelli, you may not know this, but there aren't many Catholics in Scotland. They were drummed out."

"I know the story."

"Then why did you ask?"

"Knowing the history, the last place a good Protestant would want to be is in a Catholic chapel. So I thought maybe you were Catholic."

"Am I allowed to laugh in here?"

"You're the captain. You can do whatever you want."

"Who is that fellow?" McVicars pointed to a statue.

"That's Saint Bernard of Clairvaux. The saint I told you about."

"Right. That one. He looks ill."

"He's French. Saint Bernard was known as the doctor of the church."

"Seems to me a saint should have vigor so that the devout have something to aspire to, something to emulate. Makes a better statue too, don't you think? The Catholic church should go to Scotland and find a champion pole tosser with thick legs to pose for their statues. Saint Bernard was not worth the bronze. I wouldn't trust my soul to a puny bloke with sloped shoulders and a weak chin, would you?"

"Too late. I have prayed to him."

"You have exactly seven freckles on your nose."

"And you have a slight chip on your front tooth. The left one," Domenica countered.

"I fell off a horse."

"How's the horse?"

"Long gone, I'm afraid. I was ten."

"The Sisters invited you to breakfast. When I didn't find you in the bed you were assigned to, I assumed you left the hospital. You must be starving. I can take you to the dining room on my way out."

"If those holy women kept a biscuit in the drawer, I wouldn't be hungry."

"I should have served you your tea and a macaron."

"Falling down on the job, Cabrelli. That's all right. Truth be told, I had a macaron with a lovely blonde."

"So you figured your way around the hospital after all."

"I did. And then I had a bicarbonate with Sister Marie Honoré. Are you a nun?"

"No."

"Good. They scare me."

"They shouldn't."

"But they do. They run in packs. They move in formation like a swarm of bees."

"You're the second man in a month to ask me if I'm a nun. Should I take that as a sign to become one?"

"That depends. How do you feel about bees?"

The nuns' dining room was bright and cheerful. A deep stone fireplace on the far wall crackled with orange flames over an open grill that held three teakettles. A large mirror over the fireplace reflected the Sisters at breakfast at one long table in the center of the room.

"The Mother Superior would like to meet you," Domenica whispered. "You go."

"Which one is she?"

"The one wearing the biggest cross. At the head of the table."

Domenica watched as McVicars, in his pajamas and robe, gingerly approached the Mother Superior. Domenica tried to hide her amusement.

"Thank you, Mother Mum, for your attention and care for my men." McVicars motioned to Cabrelli to join him. "Nurse, forgive me, what's your name?"

"Cabrelli."

He snapped his fingers. "Nurse, what's your first name again?"

"Domenica."

"Nurse Domenica Cabrelli did a wonderful job."

"She's one of our talented novices."

"A novice lacks experience. Miss Cabrelli ran the ward like a general last night."

"*Novice* in her case means that she is in the first phase of becoming a Sister of Saint Joseph of the Apparition."

McVicars looked at Domenica. "You said you weren't a nun."

"I'm not. I'm praying about it."

Mother Superior looked the captain up and down. "Captain, may I see your hands?"

McVicars's hands were ruddy and had mild surface burns from the fire.

"Captain, I insist you have Nurse Cabrelli dress those wounds. You don't want an infection. Your blood would turn." The Mother Superior turned to Domenica. "Bring him back for breakfast when you've taken care of him."

The examining room was pristine. The tile floor was as spotless as the windows, which were washed so clear and clean, they appeared to have no glass in the frames.

McVicars refused to look as Domenica gently swabbed the burned surface of the skin on his hands to cleanse the abrasions. She placed his hands in a pan filled with ice and fresh water. "I'm sorry, but if I bandage your burns without cleansing them thoroughly, you'll scar. You have beautiful hands—that wouldn't be right."

"I'm not going to thank you for the pain. But I will thank you for the compliment. You speak English quite well, Miss Cabrelli."

"It's better than my French. I'm on shifts with Mary Gay Mahoney a lot. She's one of the nurses. She's from Scotland, too. She has the most exquisite wool blanket on her bed. She said it was made there."

"How are you going to give up nice things when you take your vows?"

"A nun doesn't have to give up beauty. That's one of God's greatest gifts to the world, isn't it? Here's your wedding ring." Domenica placed it safely in the hospital shirt. She buttoned the flap.

"It's an insignia ring. I earned it in the Great War."

"But you were just a boy."

"Sixteen. That's why I wear it on the small finger. My hands grew larger than my feet, it seems, in the intervening years. I keep meaning to have it sized."

"My father could size it for you. He's a goldsmith. And a gem cutter."

"Oh, so you're like Saint Catherine—she was a rich society girl, a flapper, if you will, of her day, who gave up all the fun to go into the convent. Forgive the obvious, but that's what we Scots call fire insurance. You give your life to good works, and it buys you a chit to stay out of hell when your hour of death comes."

"For a Protestant, you know a lot about my canon of saints."

"I read."

"Then you know that not all jewelers are wealthy. My father makes a living, and like any artisan, he waits to be paid. While Papa waits for his commission, our family goes without while my mother stews."

"More famine than feast."

"Italians never starve. We eat with cunning. We live by the sea, so we fish. We eat chestnuts and dandelion greens and eggs. Tomatoes. We make bread. You know. You've been to Italy."

"My mother boiled meat and made porridge, but we always had a bottle of good whiskey in the house so we might chase down all the bad victuals."

"That's a fine diet for a cold-weather climate."

"I've never eaten a chestnut."

"They're delicious." The thought of her mother at the stove stirring the chestnuts saddened Domenica.

"I've upset you." McVicars lifted his hands out of the water. "Don't cry."

"Keep your hands in the ice bath." Domenica wiped away a tear with her sleeve.

"I will behave if you tell me why you had a weep." He placed his hands back into the ice bath.

"I was thinking of my mother."

Domenica lifted one of McVicars's hands out of the ice bath. She gently dried his hand and brushed a thick antiseptic goo onto the abrasions.

"What is that?"

"Honey."

"As in tea?"

"As in medicine. The nuns have their own beehives in the garden. They make their own antiseptic out of honey. People come from all over France for a jar, I'm told." Domenica gently wrapped his hand in fresh cotton. "I took a small jar and use it for face cream."

"They should bottle the goo and sell it so women who use it turn out as beautiful as you."

Domenica turned away from McVicars and stifled a laugh. She had served many male patients in the hospital. Most of them were so full of gratitude that they called her their beautiful angel. It turned out the grateful patients said the same to all the nurses.

Domenica wrapped his other hand. "How does that feel?"

"I don't have any pain."

"Sister will make you eat. Once you're fed and your uniform is pressed, you can go back to the ship and sail on to wherever it is you're going."

"Miss Cabrelli? I love you."

Domenica laughed.

"No, I mean it sincerely. My hands were on fire, and now they are wrapped like a newborn babe." McVicars held up his hands. "I know a little bit about your line of work. I once pulled a bullet out of a man's gut on a battlefield—well, it wasn't a battlefield, it was the barroom floor at my favorite haunt, a pub called Tuck's in Glasgow—but I saved his life. But I don't believe I've ever actually taken away another person's pain. And you did."

McVicars followed Domenica back to the dining room. The captain was dizzy from hunger, but he had no appetite. His body ached, but he didn't feel the pain. He wasn't himself, and he didn't understand why.

Mother Superior approved of the bandages on the captain's hands. She thanked Domenica and invited her to have breakfast in the dining room with the captain. This was a rare invitation, and Domenica humbly accepted. The captain sat by the fire with Domenica as she entertained him with stories of home. He took in every word as he consumed the best meal of his life. The strawberry jam on the croissant exploded in his mouth like a sweet summer day. The fluffy omelette was seasoned with fresh herbs and melted in his mouth. The coffee was the hottest he had drunk since the *Boidoin* docked in Colombia, in South America. This was no ordinary hunger satiated by a good meal; the captain's soul was being fed too. He wondered if the brown-eyed nurse from Italy had something to do with it.

McVicars stood by as the nurses filed into the chapel. Cabrelli nodded in his direction. He also received his share of winks and smiles
from her co-workers. The Sisters followed the nurses inside. Sister
Marie Honoré smiled at him as she stooped down to remove the
wooden wedge from under the chapel door before closing it. He
could hear the murmur of the priest's opening prayers. McVicars
turned to leave Hôpital Saint Joseph through the door he had entered the night before when he came eye to eye with the statue of
Mary on a pedestal. He stood for a moment and looked up at her.
He patted the breast pocket on his uniform, retrieving his gold
signet ring. He picked up paper and pencil from the front desk and
scrawled.

23 March 1939

Dear Mother Superior,

  Thank you. The men of the Boidoin are eternally in your debt.

  For now, please accept this ring as payment for your superior
service.

Truly yours,

Captain John Lawrie McVicars

  He wrapped the note around the ring and deposited both in the
donation box by the front door. The captain had followed Nurse
Cabrelli's order. He left the hospital and walked back to the docks,
where he understood how the world worked.

CHAPTER 19

APRIL 1939

Stephanie switched off her bedside table lamp. Josephine slipped out of her house slippers before sliding under the coverlet on her bed.

"The nuns need to turn the heat up at night," Josephine complained.

"It will soon be so hot you'll forget how cold the winter was." Stephanie unfolded the extra blanket on the end of her bed and covered herself with it.

Domenica reached up from under the covers and shut her window tight.

"That's where the cold air was coming from."

"I'm sorry, girls."

"Any mail today?"

"I put it on your desk," Domenica answered.

"Not for me," Stephanie said. "For you."

"No mail," Domenica said.

"I thought for sure that was not the last we'd see of your captain," Josephine said.

"He's not *my* captain." Domenica was defensive.

"Some men are slow." Josephine punched her pillow and turned on her side.

"Ladies. It's only been a week," Stephanie reminded them. "He's in the fighting stage."

"With whom?"

"Himself. He's fighting his feelings."

"Why would he do that?" Domenica sat up in bed.

"They don't really want us, you know. Men wish we didn't exist so that they wouldn't have to surrender. It suits them to wander the world with no ties. Why else would a man choose to live at sea?" Stephanie applied her face cream without a mirror.

"You have an encyclopedic knowledge of the male species." Josephine was in awe.

"I don't care if he writes to me. I don't want to be involved with a sailor," Domenica insisted.

"You *are* involved. Plus, he's got a rank," Josephine noted.

"Never marry a sailor," Stephanie began. "They do more shipping out than shipping in. Domenica would have a brood of kids to raise on her own, and the captain would be nowhere to be found."

Domenica rolled over in her bed. At least she knew how her closest friends felt about the captain. It had been a long day. As she said her prayers, the convent life took on a patina in her imagination that she found comforting. She thought again, as she went off to sleep, about becoming a nun. With the world outside in turmoil, was it such a sacrifice? Domenica craved serenity and the peace that came from knowing her own heart. She was soon to find out whether it belonged to the Sisters of Saint Joseph or the captain.

The bell rang three times on the fourth floor of Fatima House, indicating there was a guest in the lobby. The attendant called up to the fourth-floor house phone and summoned Domenica to the front desk. She had been cleaning the room on her day off, wearing faded dungarees and a cotton blouse. Stephanie had put Domenica's hair up in rags to curl it, so her head was covered in the mismatched bows. "You have a visitor, mademoiselle," the attendant said.

Captain McVicars stood up. "Good morning, Miss Cabrelli." He was out of uniform. He wore a somber gray suit and blue tie.

"Is there a funeral?"

"No, this is my good suit."

"You look well," she offered.

"I've been in Marseille for the past week."

"Eleven days," she corrected him.

"Has it been that long? Been working right here in the harbor. Around the clock, of course. Trying to get the old *Boidoin* seaworthy again."

"Is she?"

"Quite."

Domenica processed his litany of excuses carefully. When she'd left him after breakfast eleven days earlier, she was hopeful she would see him again, and soon. But patients who got well and were discharged rarely, if ever, returned to the hospital.

McVicars offered another excuse. "This is a strange time for merchant seamen. Some of our routes are shut down or compromised—"

"I understand."

"I took leave and remembered you had a day off on Saturdays. Clearly you're not on duty."

Domenica patted the rag bows in her hair. "This is the only day I have to do my hair," she said sheepishly.

"I see." McVicars went on: "I thought you looked a little pale when we were last together, and I wondered if you'd like to go for a drive? I borrowed a car. A convertible. It won't go more than thirty miles an hour, but we're not going thirty miles so we should be fine."

"All right."

"All right that I borrowed a car or that you'll come for a drive?"

"Both. Let me get my hat."

Domenica went upstairs to her room. She stood inside the door of her room and froze.

"What's wrong?" Josephine looked up from the book she was reading.

"The captain is here. And I accepted an invitation to go for a drive."

"Stephanie!" Josephine called out.

Stephanie entered their room with her laundry basket resting on her hip. "What?"

"Domenica has a date with the captain."

Josephine pushed Domenica into a chair. Stephanie dropped the laundry basket. She and Josephine went to work. Josephine untied the rags in Domenica's hair and brushed out the curls, while Stephanie went through Domenica's closet and pulled a madras sundress and sandals. The girls helped her into the dress. She slipped into her sandals while Stephanie knelt and buckled the ankle straps. Domenica leaned into the mirror and applied her lipstick.

"Here's your purse." Josephine placed it into Domenica's hands. "There's cash in the side pocket. You may need it. Go."

"Wait!" Stephanie said, reaching for her bottle of Joy perfume. She gave Domenica a spritz on the neck. "Scram."

Domenica returned to the lobby, leaving a trail of vanilla and roses on the staircase. The captain stood and took her in.

"Am I all right?" She touched her hair.

"A vision."

"Thank you."

"But you forgot the hat."

The Route de la Gineste unspooled like a silver ribbon laced between green hills on one side and a free fall of white rocks on the other. Whenever the road bent into a hairpin curve, a patch of the blue Mediterranean peeked through the vale beyond the rocks.

McVicars passed an ornate castle before continuing up the mountain road. "Napoleon stayed there."

"Napoleon came to my village too, so the legend goes. His sister Pauline lived on the beach in a villa with her Italian prince. Napoleon made another sister, Elisa, the grand duchess of Tuscany."

"Generous brother. Took care of his own."

"Despots are known to take good care of their own families. The rest of us don't fare as well."

"You didn't come to Marseille because you wanted to, did you?"

"I am working off a punishment."

"What did you do?" McVicars smiled.

"It's not funny, Captain."

"You're not a spy, are you?"

"No. There's little intrigue in my situation. I went against the teachings of my church on the job. My boss, Dottore Pretucci, had me sent here to keep up my nursing. He thinks the priest will eventually forget about my transgression. But I don't think the doctor understands my priest."

"What was your terrible sin?"

"I advised a young mother how to plan her family."

McVicars whistled. "In a Catholic country?"

"They're the only countries I know."

The captain shifted gears in the old jalopy. He took the opportunity to reach for her hand. She did not take it; instead, she turned to him.

"Captain McVicars, are you married?"

McVicars returned his hand to the steering wheel. "Miss Cabrelli! How indecent of you. Would I ask you to go for a joyride if I were a married man?"

"I hope not."

"You have nothing to fear. I am not married now and have no plans to marry in the future. The promise comes with my personal guarantee. Besides, I gave the good Sisters of Saint Joseph my ring as payment for services rendered to my crew."

"You're the talk of the convent and Fatima House."

"Am I?"

"You have your choice of young ladies. They find you fascinating. Handsome and generous, they say."

"Thank you. I am all those things."

"And yet, you've managed to remain a bachelor. I suppose if you were to marry, you would have already."

"What do you mean?" McVicars took his eyes off the road and looked at her.

"A man is set by the time he is forty."

"Who told you that bit of chum about men?"

"My mother."

"I suppose you have to listen to your mother."

"I hope you don't think this is a rude question. Why haven't you married?"

"The women that marry sailors make sure their husbands give up the sea. That was reason enough for me to avoid the institution. I like my freedom."

"So do I." Domenica took the captain's hand. "Did you know

when you hold someone's hand, it's good for their heart? Their blood pressure goes down."

"I didn't know I had a problem."

"And now you won't."

The Café Normande on a hill above Cassis was an old farmhouse with a kitchen garden surrounded by fields of lavender. Domenica heard the low hum of the bees at work on the purple buds as she walked the grounds. She found the highest point on the cliff and looked out over the French countryside. From her perch, she could see the rooftops of Cassis and beyond, where the mountains met the sea. The hot sun felt good on her skin. She finally found in France what she had left behind in Italy: heat. McVicars called to her. She joined him at a garden table where he had set out their lunch.

"Here you go. I hope you like it." McVicars served her.

"Looks delicious."

McVicars took the seat across from her. "Go ahead, try it." She took a bite of the buttered brioche filled with thin slices of ham.

"Do you like it?"

She nodded. He poured a glass of wine for her and one for himself. He held up his glass. "They make the wine here on the farm. To you." He sipped the wine.

Domenica also took a sip. "We make our own wine too, you know."

"Is this as good?"

"Yes, it is."

"It's risky to present a table wine to an Italian."

"I was four years old when I had my first taste. Naturally, it was cut with a lot of water. Wine, the harvesting then mashing of the grapes, and the sleeping barrels that ferment it, is part of life for us."

"They don't give us liquor in Scotland until we are old enough to sneak it. And then some of us sneak it for the rest of our lives. The Italians and the French have it right. Drink from the start and kill the craving."

"And now the Italians are sworn enemies of the French. How did that happen?"

"The enemy next door is always the most dangerous," he said. "I wish I could stop them."

"You'll get your chance."

"Am I overdressed?" He took a bite of his sandwich.

"I don't think so. I had to change when I saw you in the suit."

"You didn't go upstairs to spiffy up to please me? If you did, you were too late. I was already pleased."

John McVicars leaned across the table and kissed her. The kiss was a surprise. She tasted the wine on his lips. He kissed her again with tenderness. When she opened her eyes, she felt the warm sun on her skin, while the breeze that washed over them was cool. The temperature of the world was just right for them.

"I should have asked for that kiss," he said. "Forgive me."

Domenica leaned over and kissed him. "You're forgiven."

"Come with me," he said as he stood. He took her hand.

Domenica followed the captain down a narrow path into the woods behind the farmhouse. The forest was dark. The trees were gigantic on either side of the path, the sun barely peeked through the foliage. She heard a rush of water and turned to the source. She looked over the ravine for a river, but there was none.

The captain led Domenica to the sound. A glacial waterfall began at the top of the mountain and crested over a cliff, where it cascaded in clear ribbons of water past them to the depths below.

"Here's a thought," he said over the sound. "They should bring every general of every country here before they drop their bombs."

The waterfall was a wonder. Domenica stood behind the captain, placed her arms around him, and rested her head on his back. He pulled her arms tightly around him and wove his fingers through hers. They stayed there until the sun was the color of a ripe peach.

Domenica Cabrelli had spent many hours of her life in prayer. The rituals of her faith had brought her comfort, but none of them compared to the serenity of this moment. Even home, where she had found solace, did not come close to the peace she found in his arms. Maybe John McVicars would show her the world in ways that would help her forget all she had lost. Maybe he was the compass who would show her the way forward.

McVicars wanted to make Domenica happy, a desire that had eluded him in the past romantic entanglements whereby he slipped the knot and escaped so graciously, a young lady barely knew he had left before he was gone for good. But Mademoiselle Cabrelli was different. He, too, wanted to forget the past and wondered if the Italian nurse could give him his highest dream: a happy life that seemed to come so easily to other men.

CHAPTER 20

Domenica looked down at her white work shoes. She had been too tired the night before to polish them, but they needed it. She shook the bottle of white polish, poured a bit onto a cloth, and dabbed over the scuff marks on her shoes.

"Hey. Cabrelli. Mail." Mary Gay Mahoney handed Domenica a package. "Looks like you have a sweetie in Scotland."

"Grazie."

"Prego. One month in a cloister in Bologna and this Scottish lass can speak Italian."

"I'd like to learn more about your people."

"Ask me anything. I was born and raised in Drimsynie. We were the only Catholic family in the village. That's how the nuns found me. Next to a loch. They look for the marooned."

"How do you tell if a man fancies you in Scotland?"

"The only proof of a man's love is how he cares for the family cow."

"What if he doesn't have a cow?"

"You're out of luck."

Domenica opened the package and read the letter.

9 April 1939

Dear Signorina Cabrelli,

I wish you a glorious Easter Sunday. I am most grateful for your bandages and care. My own mum marveled at my hands, as she was the first to hold the wee ham fists when I was born. Your honey salve spared me the scars of the burn—my manual extremities no longer look like boiled pig knuckles, but the fine fingers of a duke, just as they were before the trauma. I have shared the vat of honey serum you gifted me with the men of the Boidoin. They have nothing but compliments for the Sisters and their pageant of fine nurses, "each a perfect rose"—their words, not mine.

Our shared ham brioche in Cassis is now my favorite meal and memory. Your kisses by the waterfall will make any kisses that come my way for the rest of my life uneventful by comparison. You are delightful company. Enclosed please find a wee gift from the looms at Dundee.

Captain John L. McVicars

The Boidoin Star

She lifted out a paper sleeve tied with a ribbon from inside the box. When she loosened the bow, a cashmere scarf in woven shades of lilac and purple tumbled out. The colors reminded her of the shades of lavender on the hillsides above Cassis. She wondered if the captain chose this scarf because he remembered too.

The Feast Day of Saint Bernadette of Lourdes

"Sister Marie Bernard rang the bell," Josephine said as she slipped into her good dress.

"We heard it." Stephanie pinned a chapel veil to her hair. "You ready?" She turned to Domenica. "Andiamo. See? The Italian you taught me stuck."

Domenica draped the scarf from McVicars over her shoulders. The nurses walked to the convent garden together.

"That scarf is so chic," Josephine complimented her.

"I finally have someplace to wear it."

"Mademoiselle Cabrelli. Finally you like a fella!" Stephanie teased her. "We've been waiting. We were afraid you might take the veil."

"Don't," said Darlene Heck, a surgical nurse who greeted them as they entered the garden. "Never make any major decisions when you're exhausted. These nuns are experts at running a girl ragged." Darlene handed each of the nurses a velvet bag containing rosary beads. "A gift from the Sisters."

"Do you think Saint Bernadette would approve of a fuss on her feast day?" Stephanie whispered. "She seemed humble."

Josephine looped the rosary around her wrist and through her fingers. "It's a good excuse for Sister Marie Honoré to get her mitts on the vintage champagne stored in the convent basement."

"Thank God she doesn't like to drink alone." Stephanie blessed herself.

The pale green buds of spring twizzled on the branches of the lemon trees. The nuns knelt on the soft grass, followed by the nurses. As the women bowed their heads to pray, the buzz of the bees in their hives along the wall underscored Sister Marie Bernard as she led the group in reciting the rosary. Soon their incantations were louder than the hum of the bees.

No matter their country of origin, nurses were French on the feast day of Saint Bernadette of Lourdes, the patron saint of healing. As the priest asked the nuns and nurses to pray in silence for their intentions, Domenica looked around the garden and prayed for the small army of fellow nurses and nuns that protected her at Saint Joseph's, remembering, too, one sailor she hoped was thinking of her.

John Lawrie McVicars walked through Kelvingrove Park in Glasgow carrying a book. The title was of no importance to him because he had no intention of reading it. Its purpose was strictly utilitarian. He stored sheets of clean onionskin paper between the pages, and the blue envelopes between the endpapers. McVicars could sit in the middle of Glasgow, balance the book on his lap, and, with the fountain pen he kept in his jacket pocket, compose a letter whenever he pleased.

A sailor learns to take up little space on a ship, so it becomes a habit on land. Most tools in McVicars's possession had multiple purposes. McVicars was shaped by his life in the military. He joined the merchant navy when he was eighteen; he had spent more of his life in service than he had as a civilian. He took out his pocketknife and gently opened a letter stamped *Marseille, France*. He smiled in anticipation as he opened the first letter he had received from Domenica Cabrelli.

17 April 1939

Dear Captain,

I hope your hands have continued to heal nicely. I purchased a small vial of holy water from Lourdes on the feast day of Saint Bernadette. Mary Gay thinks the holy water might have come from the faucet at Saint Joseph's Church, but even if it isn't officially from Lourdes, it has been blessed.

You are popular here at Saint Joseph's. When you feel blue, remember the nuns of Saint Joseph are praying for you. They are also praying for my family.

My brother, Aldo, in the Italian army, has been assigned to a field operation in Tunisia. He wrote simply "I am here" on the postcard he sent to me. I don't know if this has any meaning beyond my brother's inability to write a letter. I have heard from my mother. There is talk in the village that an announcement was forthcoming. The old saying goes, if you want to know what the king is up to, ask the farmer, or in my situation, ask my mother.

Mama wrote that the Villa Borghese in Viareggio has been taken over by the Fascisti. The Blackshirts chose to occupy the most opulent residence in our village for their own use. Mama was also told the Fascisti were establishing field operations all along the coast of Italy. Lucca, the city closest to my village, is changing rapidly. The silk mills have been seized to make military uniforms. I pray it's all just the typical pageantry.

Thank you for the scarf you sent, which reminds me of you and the way things used to be.

With a big kiss,

Domenica

McVicars was worried. An Italian émigré working in France in a Catholic hospital would soon be without a job and a country. He knew how these situations could go. The nuns would not be able to protect their nurses, so they would be discharged. Domenica would not be safe in France or Italy.

McVicars predicted his next assignment would most likely take him to the grid of the southern hemisphere. The *Boidoin* had been requisitioned by the British government, and he would be reassigned to a new ship. Like Domenica, he would be forced to transition out of his current position into the unknown. At his level and rank, they would likely send him as far away from home and Domenica Cabrelli as a ship could take him.

CHAPTER 21

Glasgow, Scotland

MAY 1939

The first Italian immigrants to arrive in Scotland at the end of the nineteenth century went into business as soon as they unpacked. They made gelato, opened pizzerias, and mastered deep-frying fish and chips, a local delicacy. Their dark eyes and hair and olive skin stood out in contrast to the robust, pale, blue-eyed Scots. The Italian women matched their hardworking men in ambition, as they worked side by side in the bistros and pubs. The Italians married and had children. In three generations, the Britalians had become part of the fabric of Scotland, giving the native silk wool a new heft, strength, and color.

Arcangelo Antica was part of the first wave to arrive in Scotland from Italy to peddle ice cream in Glasgow. His brother, Francesco, the smarter Antica, according to Arcangelo, became weary of the life of a peddler and borrowed money to put up a factory to make gelato. The factory did well enough to take care of his family in Scotland, with extra money left over to send home to Bardi, Italy. Arcangelo was happy to peddle his brother's product.

Antica maintained a route through the streets of Glasgow that began on the west side and ended at the pier. At seventy years old, he wondered how much longer he could do the job. He had loyal customers, but there was more competition for their business now. The current Italian immigrants had brought an array of new offerings to cart service: peanut brittle, candy floss, and hot waffles and cream. When it came to selling, Antica remained faithful to the past. He burst into song along the route, usually an Italian folk song, and the old schtick attracted customers. He knew that children chose his cart not because his gelato was the best, but because it was an excuse to see the three-fingered man. When Antica was a young man, he had lost two fingers on his right hand in a quarry accident. He even turned that loss into a sales tool.

"General Antica!" McVicars saluted from across the street before crossing it to join the peddler.

"Where have you been, Captain?"

"Oh, you know. On the high seas. Port side, we were in Marseille for a spell."

"Good for you, McVicars. France. Beautiful women."

"My eyes hurt from the sight of them." McVicars reached into his pocket. "How about a gelato?"

"How about it?" Antica scooped the vanilla ice cream into a cup and handed it to McVicars. "Keep your money today. I want our sailors strong."

"You think we're in?"

"Soon. And not just me. That's what they're saying in the pub. More accurate than the paper."

"I don't know if your friend Il Duce has the guts."

"He's not my friend. He's an embarrassment to my people. My mother had an expression: 'Just because they're Italian doesn't mean they're good.' There are good and bad people everywhere. How's your mother? I haven't seen her in a long while."

"Signora McVicars is holed up in the old house with the

shutters closed. She lived through the Great War, so she has decided to hide until England takes a proper stand. If we go to war against Germany, she'll head down to the basement and stay there for the duration."

"I am sorry to hear that."

"This is all too much for her."

"She should leave Glasgow and go to the country. Can your brother take care of her while you're gone?"

"That would be difficult. Reverend McVicars is in New Zealand on another mission to convert the pagans."

"He should stay there until the trouble blows over."

"If you knew my brother, you would know that he has a way of staying as far from trouble as trouble allows."

"The opposite of you."

McVicars laughed. "True enough. I met one of your own in France. An Italian nurse."

"What's the name?"

"Domenica."

"Means '*Sunday*.'"

"Cabrelli."

"Cabrelli. Hmm. She's Toscana."

"Viareggio on the sea. Do you know it?"

"Bella! The beach goes on for miles."

"I've sailed the Ligurian Sea."

"That's why you have the eye of the fish. Someone waits for you on the shore."

"I'm not so sure about that. I haven't received a letter in weeks. Of course, you never know, the nuns may have her digging trenches in the South of France and she hasn't time to write."

"You make a joke, but you don't find it funny," Antica said. "You like this young lady."

McVicars took a moment to think. "Very much, my friend."

"The one you want is usually the one you can't get."

"Is that true, Antica? I do not accept your treatise. Do you know how many ports there are on the coast? Too many to count. Do you know how many women live in those port cities? Too many to count. I stand before you, one man. One man in a sea of women looking to drown him."

"Va bene! Hundreds. Thousands. But the girl you want is only one girl. And only one girl can save you." Antica rang the bell on the cart and pushed it toward the pier. "The Cabrelli girl. Her name sounds like a bell." Antica pulled the string attached to the bell on his cart. "Bellissima!"

CHAPTER 22

𝔐𝔞𝔯𝔰𝔢𝔦𝔩𝔩𝔢

JULY 1939

The Garden of the Angels at Hôpital Saint Joseph was a haven for the Sisters and a source of additional income for the order's purse. Inside the walls, the nuns grew vegetables and lavender, prayed the rosary at the shrine of the Blessed Mother, and cultivated beehives for honey. The bee colonies were housed in black wooden boxes set in a row along the back wall, where graceful orange trumpet vines crawled up the bricks behind them.

"Nurse Cabrelli, over here!" Sister Marie Bernard called to Domenica before lighting the smoker.

Domenica shielded her eyes from the sun as she walked through rows of lettuce, cucumbers, and yellow peppers. She saw a flurry of black snow in midair; on closer look, it was a swarm of bees hovering over their hive. Sister fanned the hives with the smoker, a rusty can with a spout. When lit, the smoker burned cedar chips, producing a clean white smoke that forced the bees back into the hive like soldiers into a foxhole.

"Don't you love the scent?" Sister said as she closed the trap on the can. "Reminds me of my dear father who smoked cigars. Cedar burns like tobacco, you know. Quick and clean. Is your father a smoker?"

"No. He takes snuff once in a while."

"So he enjoys the occasional tobacco. Which is what God intended. Here and there, it does no harm, but a daily habit of it, no good."

"I don't smoke, Sister."

She smiled. "Good for you. I wish you would convince your fellow nurses to drop the habit. But a day off, a pub crawl, and cigarettes seem to go together. Nurses need their diversions too."

"Smoking keeps them slender. Or so they say." Domenica chuckled. "Mother Superior asked me to meet with you."

"I'm sorry to report that the Sisters of Saint Joseph won't be running this hospital any longer. The Mother Abbess has requested we move our hospital back to the motherhouse outside of Tours. I wish I could take you with me, but that's not possible. There's a position at the convent in Dumbarton, Scotland, where you can work off the remainder of your punishment."

"Please, Sister. I don't want to work in Scotland. Send me anywhere else."

"It's the only position we can offer you. The Sisters run a school called Notre Dame de Namur. They need a school nurse. Mother Superior has made the arrangements."

Domenica Cabrelli was not in control of her own life as long as she had to work off a debt to the Holy Roman Church. Fate was toying with her. Scotland was the last place on Earth she wanted to go. She had written faithfully to McVicars and received nothing in return, not one letter. Clearly, he had changed his mind about her. She felt foolish having fallen for him. Any thoughts of McVicars triggered a spiral of regret, which made her feel worse about the emotional letters she had sent to him.

"We'll give you a proper habit for travel, with the Red Cross insignia. We will purchase the tickets you need, including the ferry across the channel. We plan to move you out on Bastille Day."

"Thank you, Sister." But Domenica wasn't grateful; she felt manipulated. In her mind, the position in Scotland was another punishment. Perhaps the order banished her once more because she had told the Mother Superior that she would not become a postulant, the step before taking final vows. But now that the captain had abandoned her too, she wondered if she had made the right decision.

Domenica walked back to the hospital in a fog. She didn't hear the birds in the garden, or the horns of the automobiles, or the music that swelled as a convertible sped past the hospital. She would soon be uprooted again, without her consent.

It would take a few more weeks for the nuns to close the hospital and return to the motherhouse. There were patients to transfer, packing to be done, and paperwork to complete.

The nurses of Fatima House would also depart, returning home or, like Domenica, reassigned to another city. One by one, like pearls off a broken string, the young women scattered in all directions. Domenica said goodbye to Josephine and Stephanie, who took positions in London. They promised to stay in touch. The Sisters arranged official letters and passports, sought permission, and made arrangements for each of their nurses. Domenica wished she could have convinced just one of the girls to go with her to Scotland. The heartache of losing her friends was as devastating to her as having been ignored by the captain. She believed she could get over a failed romance but wasn't so sure she would ever heal from the loss of her friends.

As Domenica Cabrelli boarded the train in Marseille for the

first leg of the journey to Scotland, she wore her nurse's cap and a red cross on her uniform. A train took her to Paris, and another to Calais, where she would board a ferry across the English Channel to Dover. She would take another train from Dover to London, and finally north to Glasgow. It would take fifteen hours from Marseille to Glasgow. With every turn of the wheels on the train, she was farther away from home. Italy was just a dream now.

Heavy rainstorms along the route caused delays as tracks flooded, and the cars were rocked by gale-force winds. It was so hot she could not sleep. Her appetite left her. When the storm subsided, she stood between the train cars and took in the cool breeze after the rain. When the train pulled into the London station, Domenica Cabrelli was the loneliest she had ever been in her life.

LONDON

Domenica made the connection that would take her north to Scotland. After she took her seat and the porter punched her ticket for Glasgow, she wept. She felt relief, having navigated the complicated steps of the journey through the terrible weather. She allowed herself a cup of hot coffee and a soft roll from the sweet trolley. Her stomach had been too upset to take any food, but now that she was close to her final destination, she became ravenously hungry.

The train was packed with men in uniform, which made her wonder about the state of the world. But Liverpool was an industrial city, where ships were built and soldiers were trained. In peace time, the train full of troops was a sign that the English were industrious. The mood was upbeat; occasionally she would hear laughter and conversation around their card games. Most of the soldiers disembarked in Liverpool. Domenica was relieved to depart the

Liverpool station. The port was a gray steel wall of battleships so massive she could not see the sky or sea. The claustrophobia she felt in the port melted away as the train chugged north to Scotland, where the hillsides were green and the sky had no edges.

Serious matters weighed on Domenica's mind. She agonized about her parents, and hoped they were getting on without her. She had seen the submarine drills off the coast of Viareggio with her own eyes. If they ran drills on Il Tirreno Mare, and sidled up the Ligurian coast like snakes, surely the Italians were preparing to go to war. Her father wasn't a fighter, and her mother talked too much. The Fascisti were cruel to older people; she had witnessed their contempt—they were like Guido Mironi: relentless.

Domenica opened the paper sack from Sister Marie Bernard. Inside, she found a pot of raspberry jam, a sleeve of crackers, a chocolate bar, a small bottle of whiskey, and a jar of the miraculous bee ointment. She snapped off a square of chocolate and savored it as it melted on her tongue. Domenica said a quick prayer of gratitude for the treats, and another prayer so her luck might hold. If she needed a sign that all would be well, she found it; at the bottom of the sack, Sister had placed a set of rosary beads.

MARSEILLE

August 1939

The peal of the bells at the entrance of Hôpital Saint Joseph reminded Mary Gay that she had promised the Sisters she would unbolt the wheel and chimes and pack them to be taken with the final round of boxes to the motherhouse. As a postulant of the order, she was assigned chores that required youth and stamina.

Mary Gay quickly made her way down the stairs to the entrance to answer the bells. She wove through the boxes stacked in the lobby and unbolted the front door. An attractive young seminarian wearing a long black cassock and a wide-brimmed Saturno hat fished a stack of mail out of a worn leather sleeve and gave it to Mary Gay.

"Are you being punished, brother?" she joked.

"They thought it wise to send a religious instead of a layman. There are people who fear the hat." He tapped the brim. "It's getting more difficult to move mail through France."

Mary Gay thanked him and went inside. She bolted the front door, sat down on a packing box, and shuffled through the mail. She whistled when she came upon a blue onionskin envelope addressed to Mademoiselle Domenica Cabrelli. She remembered when the Italian nurse arrived at Fatima House. Mary Gay had hoped that Domenica would join the order with her, but it soon became clear that Domenica would not become a nun. And now, the mail confirmed it. The return address on the envelope was Glasgow, Scotland, with the seal of Captain John L. McVicars. It was postmarked 10 August 1939. Mary Gay slashed a line through the hospital address and rerouted the letter to Dumbarton, Scotland. Before placing it on the stack, she drew a small Sacred Heart on the back for luck.

CHAPTER 23

Viareggio

Now

Anina waited for her grandfather near the entrance of the hospital.

Olimpio pushed through the doors. "Where is she?"

"The doctor is with her. Follow me." Anina held the elevator doors open for her grandfather. She followed him inside. When the doors closed, Anina pressed three.

"What happened?"

"She was teaching me how to make the strudel, and she had to sit down. Then she fainted."

"Did you give her a pill?"

"What pill? She didn't mention a pill. I brought her here as fast as I could."

"Thank God."

They stepped off the elevator together.

"This way, Nonno."

Olimpio quickened his pace; when he saw his wife's name on the door of her room, he bolted inside. Anina followed behind him.

"Matelda!" Olimpio was out of breath.

"Why are you panting?" Matelda said calmly as she sat upright in the hospital bed.

"You scared me to death." He kissed her.

"I had a little spell. It was nothing. Anina insisted I come to the hospital, but there was no reason to—"

"You fainted, Nonna."

"I hadn't eaten."

"We just had lunch."

"Well, I hadn't eaten much."

"You ate a chicken breast, a bowl of soup, and a salad of tomatoes and mozzarella. Oh, and two slices of bread."

"Well, then maybe I overindulged."

"Did you take your pill this morning?" Olimpio asked her.

"I didn't need it."

"Evidently you did." Olimpio kissed her forehead. "You're going to kill me."

"Before I do, get me out of here. You know that hospitals aren't a good place for healthy people."

Anina and Olimpio looked at each other.

"I know you think it's funny," Matelda said, "but I'm serious. There are more germs here than there are in the train station."

The nurse entered with a rolling cart of machines to check Matelda's vitals. "I'm sorry; if you'll step outside, I will check Signora."

"I'll stay," Anina offered.

"Get out," Matelda ordered. "Allow the nurse to gather her numbers. The sooner you leave and she can poke and prod, the sooner I can go home where I belong."

Olimpio and Anina stepped out into the hallway.

"She's going to be fine," Anina said nervously.

Olimpio nodded in agreement, but he wasn't confident his

granddaughter was right. This wasn't the first time Matelda's heart problem had brought her to the hospital, but it was the first time anyone else in the family besides Olimpio knew about it.

Nicolina jumped into the car on the passenger side as Giorgio started the engine. She yanked the seat belt across her chest for the ride from Lucca to Viareggio.

"Take it easy, Nic."

"I'm going to kill both of them."

Giorgio took his wife by the hand. "Stop it."

"How can they do this to me? They call me for every little thing except when it's life-or-death." Nicolina yanked her hand away from her husband's like a petulant child. "Thank God Anina was with her or I would know nothing. My father is secretive and my mother thinks she's immortal. Those two are in their own little world, the devoted lovebirds. Leaving the rest of us out until there's a crisis."

"Maybe they didn't want to upset you," Giorgio offered.

"If they told me things as they unfold, I wouldn't be upset. I could prepare. I hear things after the fact. It's rude. My mother had a ministroke last year and my father never told me. I heard in the street. Ida Casciacarro stopped me at Ennico's."

"There was no permanent damage."

"That's not an excuse to withhold information. Besides, how would they know if she didn't suffer from permanent damage? Who did the tests? Where are the results?"

"I'm not a doctor. I'm telling you what your father told me."

"So nobody knows anything."

"She has a weak heart. That's the diagnosis."

"There were decisions made, and I was left out of the mix entirely. I should have known about this. I should know what's going on," Nicolina cried. "I'm her only daughter."

"Nic, your family has a problem. When people get sick, they have no compassion. They get angry—as if someone gets sick to irritate them."

"You mean *me*. Just say it. I can't handle my mother being sick."

"You're angry. That's all I'm saying."

"Of course I'm angry. I jump whenever they need me. My brother comes for dinner and he's treated like a prince. I get all the bad and none of the good."

"Matteo and Rosa have called and asked us how they can help."

"They don't mean it. They offer and cross their fingers hoping you won't take them up on it. My brother, the golden boy. It's been this way all our lives. No matter what Matteo does, he is revered. No matter what I do, I'm judged. Can you imagine what my mother would have done had I divorced you and remarried? Well, it wouldn't have happened. I wouldn't have put my parents through it. Am I the only person who sees what is actually going on here?"

"They like your brother more."

Nicolina Tizzi barked her name at the attendant as she passed her and went to the elevator, leaving Giorgio to sign in. She squeezed onto the crowded elevator. She disembarked and barreled down the hallway until she found her mother's room.

Matelda was alone, asleep in the hospital bed. Everything in the room had a tinge of green to it, including her mother. Nobody ever looked well in hospital light, and perhaps that was the point. Nicolina took in the features of her mother's face.

Matelda's left eyebrow, though perfectly arched, had a space where a few hairs were missing. Usually her mother drew them in with a light brown pencil, but not today. Matelda wore lipstick but only a stain of pale pink remained. Her nose, one any Italian would envy, was straight as a pin and defined her mother's noble profile. The cut on her cheek left by the seagull had faded.

Matelda slept in a nearly angelic state. Nicolina began to miss her mother even though she wasn't gone. The gnaw of guilt at all she would lose when Matelda died replaced her anger and gave way to an unmoored shame. *What was I thinking?*

Nicolina began to weep like a lost child in the fairytale who suddenly found herself alone in the woods as night fell. The sun was sinking fast. The forest would soon be too dark to find a way out, and without the light, there was no hope that the child would find her way home. Nicolina fell to her knees and buried her face in the loose square of the untucked bedsheet that draped over the side of the hospital bed.

Anina pushed the hospital door open and found Nicolina in tears. "Mama!" Anina rushed to her.

Olimpio followed Anina into the room. "Nicolina, what are you doing?"

Matelda woke, startled. "What is this?"

Giorgio entered the room, followed by his brother-in-law, Matteo, and his wife, Rosa.

"Nic!" Giorgio, in his police uniform, went to his wife's side and removed his hat.

"Nicolina, why are you crying?" Matteo was frustrated. He removed his sunglasses and folded them into his jacket pocket.

"Matteo!" Matelda beamed.

Rosa, a tall Neapolitan, comforted Nicolina.

"Mama." Matteo gave his mother a kiss and took her hand.

Matelda smiled up at her son as though she were looking into the face of God. "You're here." She exhaled a serene sigh of relief.

"Yes, Mama, I'm here. Now tell me. What did you say to upset Nicolina?"

"I said nothing." Matelda folded her hands across her waist outside the blanket. "I finally got to sleep. I was trying to get some rest, and I woke up to find Nicolina kneeling and hysterical next to my bed."

"She's worried about you," Anina said softly.

"It's all right, Nicolina. Don't cry." Matelda waved her hand in the direction of her daughter. "I am going to be fine."

"See, Nic? Mama is going to be fine," Matteo said without taking his eyes off his mother.

Anina brought her grandmother a cup of broth. "I'm going to get coffee. Would anyone like a cup?" Everyone raised their hand. "I'll be back," Anina promised.

When she stepped out into the hallway, her father and Aunt Rosa were sitting in the waiting room. Anina texted Paolo.

I brought Nonna to the hospital.

Is she all right?

DK.

Love you.

Love you.

Olimpio, Nicolina, and Matteo sat around Matelda's hospital bed as she sipped broth. "You're staring at me," Matelda said. "You're all staring."

"It's just the four of us, like the old days," Matteo said. "I like it."

"I'm sorry, Nicolina," Olimpio said softly to his daughter. "I don't like to see you get upset."

"You didn't do anything wrong, Papa. You just follow orders."

"What orders?" Matelda asked.

"Let's not get into that," Matteo said quietly.

"I don't understand. I want to understand." Matelda wiped her mouth daintily with a paper napkin. "Evidently I'm difficult."

Olimpio sat on the bed and took his wife's hand. "I know you love Nicolina—"

"Olimpio, please don't condescend to me." Matelda pulled her hand away. "I love my daughter and my son. My children are my life. Get to the point."

"What Papa is trying to say is we need to be kind to one another," Matteo offered. "Especially now, Mama. We want peace. No arguments. It's better for your health."

"I did *not* make her cry." Matelda was resolute.

"It's all right, Mama." Nicolina leaned back in the chair. Her face was puffy from weeping. She had tied up her long black hair in a topknot. "Papa, it's fine. Matteo, it's fine. I'm fine." She turned to her mother. "Let's get you well," she said, as the red splotches on her face deepened to burgundy.

The flurry of clicks from the machines connected to Matelda filled the silence of the small room like the beating wings of a swarm of butterflies. "You're not *fine*, Nicolina. You have a problem with me."

"Because you treat Matteo better than you treat me."

"That's not my fault," Matteo said.

"And how exactly do I treat him better?" Matelda asked.

"We have different rules for the women in this family. As a son, he's allowed the luxury of failure. A daughter is not allowed to fail. Daughters must be virtuous and hardworking, beautiful and slim, la bella figura! Perfetto! The son can do whatever he wants. Matteo has the cheerful demeanor and smooth brow of a prince who has only ever lived in an era of good times. I'm three years younger and look twenty years older because I live under the stress of being judged. I am tired of it. I surrender." Nicolina, clutching tissues, put her hands in the air.

"Nicolina."

"Let her talk, Olimpio. Obviously, she needs to unburden herself. Go ahead, Nicolina." Matelda opened her hands as if to bless the proceedings. "What else would you like to say?"

"If I'm not good enough, why am I expected to do all the heavy lifting? I know you love me, but your love came with conditions. And it still does."

"How else can a person love?" Matelda asked. "You love because you are compelled to love. It's not like I have a say in the matter."

"But, Mama, you do," Nicolina argued.

"Nicolina, stop this right now." Olimpio was weary of the long ride on this merry-go-round of pain. "Dammit. This is your mother. This is who she is. You cannot expect her to change at this late date. Out of all the mothers in the world, this is the one you got. And as far as I can tell, despite her flaws, you are blessed. There's no time left to change anything. It's finished. That part of your life is over. You're a mother yourself. A generation has passed. You have Anina and Giacomo. Matteo, you have Arturo and Serena. You will soon realize where life leads. Your mother and I know what is ahead for you because we have already lived it. We are redundant as parents, and you will be too. Our work is done. If your mother was lacking, or I was lacking, then do better than she did—by all means, do better than me! But stop this nonsense. It's not good for you or for her. It will not change a single thing. And it hurts your brother and me too. We want peace."

Nicolina stood and moved to the door. "Excuse me."

Matteo stopped his sister and whispered something in her ear. Nicolina turned and went back to the bed. She leaned down and kissed her mother on the cheek. "I'm sorry, Mama."

Nicolina left the room, closing the door behind her.

CHAPTER 24

Lucca

Anina put on her best silk nightgown. The flimsy straps fell off her shoulders as she brushed her teeth. She spritzed on her perfume before dabbing some lip gloss on her lower lip. She went into the living room and had picked up a book to read when she heard the key in the lock.

Paolo took off his jacket, which stunk of stale smoke, as he entered the apartment. Anina waved her hand in front of her face.

"Hang it out the window."

"I wasn't smoking. Everybody else was though." He threw the jacket on a chair.

"Where were you?"

"Pazzo's."

"You met your friends."

"No. I was alone."

"Tonight. But last night?"

"I was with friends. Why the questions?"

"I don't care if you go out. But you're going out every night."

"I get bored here by myself." Paolo sat down on the sofa.

"My grandmother is in the hospital. It cheers her up to have me around."

"I wish you were concerned about what might make me happy too."

"Seriously? I have a sick grandmother. You know you make me happy. I don't know why you are making this difficult."

"I didn't get the job."

"I'm sorry." She went and sat next to him. "It's okay, Paolo. It would have been hard to make it in Roma. It's an expensive city. We'd be far from family."

"You don't think I can get a job and make a decent living and take care of us, do you?"

"Of course you can. The right position will come along." As soon as the words left her mouth, she realized that she had said these words before, many times. Paolo didn't believe them any more than she did. Anina picked up his jacket.

"I'll do it," Paolo groused, and made a half move to hang the jacket out the window.

"I've got it." Anina pulled a hanger from the closet, opened the window, hung the jacket, and hooked it over the curtain rod to let it air out. "Smoke ruins fabric."

"I kissed a girl at the bar tonight."

Anina's mouth went dry as her heart pounded. "Why did you do that?"

"I just did it." Paolo placed his head in his hands. "I don't know."

"Why are you telling me this?"

"Because I tell you everything."

Paolo went into the bathroom.

Anina felt her legs give out. She sat down.

A few moments later Paolo returned and sat in the chair across from her. "I'm sorry."

"Were you drunk?"

"A little."

"Sober enough to know what you were doing." She crossed her arms over her chest.

"I was horsing around. The moment I did it, I felt sick. I love you and you're everything to me."

"*Everything.* What does that mean?"

"What it's always meant. I want to spend my life with you."

Anina became angry. "What kind of a kiss was it?"

"What do you mean?"

"What kind of a kiss?"

"It wasn't good. We were talking."

"About what?"

"She had broken off with her boyfriend, and she decided to challenge herself and kiss one man a day until she found a man she could be with again."

"What's her name?"

"I don't know."

"You had a conversation with a woman and you kissed her and you don't know her name?"

"I didn't ask."

She glared at him.

"What do you want from me? I made a mistake. I wasn't going to tell you. I shouldn't have."

"So the alternative is keeping secrets? What you shouldn't have done is kiss another woman and disrespect me, whether you tell me about it or not. This is more about you than it is about me."

Anina went into the bedroom. She returned with a blanket and pillow. "Sleep out here tonight."

He reached for her hand. "I'm sorry."

"Are you?"

Paolo had tears in his eyes. Anina had never seen him cry. He looked ugly. "You can't kiss some random girl in a bar because you're angry at me," she said quietly.

Anina went into their small bedroom and closed the door. She ripped the large poster of the romantic beach in Montenegro off the wall. There would be no honeymoon where catamarans floated on still waters lit by the moon. She sat down on the edge of the bed as their future plans slipped through her fingers like sand. Paolo's tears were one thing, but where were hers? Having a good weep always made her feel better, cleansed in some way. But Anina could not cry, which meant the real pain would come later.

Matelda sat up in the chair by her hospital bed. She took a small bite of a biscotto before dunking it into her weak tea. "Did you make these?" she asked Nicolina.

"Rosa made them. No good?" Nicolina remade her mother's hospital bed with sheets from home.

Matelda took another bite. "A little too much baking powder."

"She's a better cook than baker." Nicolina shoved the pillow into a satin pillowcase. "It doesn't matter to Matteo. He thinks she is Venus."

"He does." Matelda nodded. "They say love is better the second time around. I will never know."

"Neither will I, Mama."

"Your brother and you are a lot like Nino and me."

"Are we?"

"Don't you think so?"

"We don't bicker as much, Mama."

"I don't fight with Nino at all anymore."

"Is that true?"

Matelda nodded again her head. "He helped me remember a story my grandfather used to tell us about India."

"The elephant story?"

"Don't tell me you know it." Matelda put aside her tea.

"Sure. Nonno Silvio used to act it out for Matteo and me. He learned it from Bisnonno."

"When?"

"When we stayed overnight with them. When you and Papa took your trips. We loved the story because it was scary, but it also had a moral. Like all good stories."

"I remembered the beginning, and Nino filled in the story through the mine collapse. But neither of us can remember the ending. Do you know it?"

"Let me think." Nicolina sat on the edge of the bed. "There was a fire. The elephant was pulling a flatbed of rubies. When she got outside the mine, the load was so big, it ripped away the roof, and it triggered a rock slide, which sealed the entrance."

"Is that when the mahout died?" Matelda asked.

"He hung on, but then the smoke got him and he slid off the elephant and died."

"Was he run over? I think he was run over by the flatbed."

"I don't remember, Mama. The elephant was free of the mahout and the chains and the beating. She began to run. She got to the town—"

"Karur!"

"That's right. All the people in the town came out of their homes to cheer the elephant. The rubies were priceless, and the elephant saved the town. They took her to the river. She dipped her trunk into the depths and filled it with fresh water. She showered herself with the cold water, bathing herself. She slurped up more water and let it run off her back. I loved that part. Nonno Silvio was so funny when he did the snout."

"My grandfather was funny too." Matelda smiled.

"I'm sure he taught Nonno Silvio. He would watch Bisnonno Pietro act out the story sometimes."

"That's the beauty of all the generations in a family living in one house," Matelda said wistfully. "Everybody shares the same stories. Go on."

"There was the sad part. The elephant remembered her babies, and how she bathed them in the river. She remembered the faces of her children even though they were long gone. That was depressing enough, but then the story took a turn. The elephant laid down on the riverbank. Her head was resting on the ground when she heard the mountain collapse from within from the fire. The elephant understood what happened and she wept."

"The elephant didn't die at the end?"

"Not in the version I heard. Why, Mama? Are you disappointed?"

"Not at all. I remember the point of it was that you had one life to live and it was important to live it in service to others, no matter the cost. The noble elephant gave her life for the town."

"That's what you got out of it? I heard it differently. It was the story of how women, represented by the female elephant, are abused and lose their children just because they are more valuable hauling rock than they are free."

"Nicolina, bedtime stories aren't political statements. They weren't to your grandfather, who told them—I promise you. He wanted you children to understand where these gems we cut came from. There was a great deal of sacrifice involved."

"It made me want to visit India."

Anina entered the hospital room, closed the door behind herself, and began to cry.

"What is it about this room?" Matelda looked at Nicolina. "I need to change my room."

"It's not the room! Pain follows us wherever we go." Nicolina went to her daughter. "What happened?"

"I've been busy and I haven't seen much of Paolo and he went out and kissed a girl in a bar."

"That's not right. I'm sorry, honey." Nicolina held Anina close.

"Has he been pursuing other women besides you on a regular basis?" Matelda asked.

"Yes. No. Only one, he says. He just met her. He says he doesn't remember her name."

Nicolina looked at Matelda, who winked at her daughter. Matelda patted the bed. "Come and sit. If the story of the elephant in India is old, ancient is the tale of the Italian man who kisses women in bars whenever he pleases." Matelda took Anina's hand.

"It sounds like nothing," Nicolina said to Anina.

"Not to me. I trusted him."

"He has to make it right," Matelda said.

"There are some things that are unforgivable. I can't marry someone who forgets me so easily."

"Did he confess?" Nicolina asked.

"Right away."

"He made a mistake. You really want to break it off over one mistake?" Nicolina said diplomatically.

"Do I break it off after the eighth time he does it? Do I break it off when we have a baby and he goes out at night and doesn't tell me where he's going? Where is the line exactly?" Anina looked to her mother and then to her grandmother.

"You draw it," Matelda said. "But it's a line, not a barbed wire fence. You can't police your fiancé. You shouldn't make decisions in haste, and you don't make a final decision until you've seen a priest."

Nicolina put her arms around Anina. "Mama's solution to most problems."

"Because they've heard it all in the confessional," Matelda explained. "If there's a sin out there, someone has knelt in the dark to confess it. The priest will put this transgression in perspective for you. You'll see."

Don Vincenzo was the parish priest in Lucca. He had come from the north, somewhere in the Lombardia region in the Italian Alps, where year-round the snow glazed the mountain peaks like spun sugar. Occasionally, he made an inside joke about polenta in his homilies that the older parishioners who had family in the north appreciated. Though the priest wasn't yet fifty, he seemed old to Anina. Whenever her grandmother referred to anyone as *robusto*, it usually meant they weren't young but they were in good shape for their age. Don Vincenzo was definitely robusto. He resembled an Alpine bear, tall and broad with a big head.

Paolo had more interest in the priest and his premarital instruction than Anina did. He was, in fact, more religious than she. Paolo kissed the medal around his neck before bed and first thing when he woke in the morning. He was devoted to Our Lady of Fatima. He walked in the holy procession and said the rosary on her feast day.

"Let's begin with a prayer," Don Vincenzo said from behind his desk. Anina and Paolo bowed their heads. "You may join hands."

Paolo reached for Anina's hand. He placed his hand over hers, which remained on the handle of her chair.

"Tender heart of Jesus, teach us to pray, help us to think, and lead us to love."

Paolo and Anina murmured, "Amen."

"I'm confused." The priest swung his feet onto the desk and leaned back in his chair. "You completed your instruction. We posted the banns of marriage in the church bulletin. I've got your wedding date in the calendar. As you may know, I have a line of young lovers around the block waiting to get married and go through instruction. Anina called and said there was a problem. How can I help?"

"It's been a stressful time," Anina began.

"As sacraments go, weddings are the worst when it comes to stress. I've officiated, I don't know, about a hundred of them, and they are generally tense situations. Two families—one side wears tuxedos and holds a gas can, the other wears a frilly gown and holds a match."

"I used to believe weddings were magical," Anina said quietly.

"They can be, or they serve as a low point in the couple's relationship and the only way is up. I'm speaking of the stress, va bene? It does dissipate eventually. So, have you pinpointed the source of your anxiety?"

Neither Paolo nor Anina answered the priest.

"What is going on with you two?"

"Anina is angry with me. I did something wrong."

"Unforgivable," she corrected Paolo.

"No such thing." Don Vincenzo swung his legs off the desk and leaned toward the couple. "We're taught that, you know. You own the sin; you unburden it with the grace of God and seek true forgiveness for yourself from the person you hurt. The short version: Forgive. Forget. Repeat."

"We have not gotten through step one. She refuses to forgive me."

"Is this true, Anina?"

"I'm hurt, and I'm furious."

"I could tell by the way you white-knuckled the arm of the chair when Paolo tried to take your hand."

"Paolo was unfaithful."

"One kiss! One kiss in a bar." Paolo threw his hands in the air. "I don't even know her name."

"You're a weak individual," Anina countered.

"I'm trying to do better. The only person I can change is myself."

"I wish you'd hurry," Anina sniped.

Don Vincenzo raised his voice firmly, interrupting the argument. "Is this an ongoing situation? With the young lady with no name?"

"No, Don Vincenzo, it is not. But that doesn't matter to Anina. She wants to crucify me for one mistake."

"Are you truly sorry, Paolo?" the priest asked.

"You know I am. I went to confession. You absolved me of the sin last Saturday. I have begged her forgiveness repeatedly. How many times and in how many ways can I say it? Yes, I'm sorry. And I'm ashamed. The entire family knows about it, hers and mine, and I'm getting it from all sides."

"Paolo, I absolve you of all sin, evidently for the second time. Anina, I encourage you to forgive Paolo."

Anina was stunned. "Don't you want to know the specifics?"

"Don't need them."

"But you need to understand him—his father, the men in his family. The Ulianas. They have trouble being faithful."

"One uncle! One uncle has a mistress in Foggia." Paolo threw his hands in the air again.

"I would appreciate it if you would be upset on my behalf, Don Vincenzo, and defend me," Anina insisted.

"What good would that do?"

Anina gasped. "I would feel supported."

"I support you. But my job is also to support love. Your love for each other."

"I've asked for forgiveness. I've not returned to the bar. I've not looked for the woman. I don't care about her. I love Anina."

"Ask him why it happened." Anina kept her eyes on the priest.

"I think he knows. He's trying to change."

"I have changed!" Paolo turned to Anina. "You just want me to suffer. You want to control me. You have to be right."

"I am entitled to my hurt feelings."

"Entitlement is for kings. We got rid of the king of Italy seventy-five years ago. Besides, we're all royal in God's eyes. What do you think God wants in this situation? Paolo? You go first," the priest said.

"He wants me to be better."

"Pretty good answer. Anina?"

"He wants me to do what's right."

"What if I told you He also wants *you* to be better?"

"I would be confused," Anina admitted. "I didn't do anything wrong."

"That doesn't help your case. Righteousness may make you stand taller, but you'll be standing alone. I believe Paolo is truly sorry for having hurt you."

"I didn't sleep with her," Paolo whined.

The priest took a deep breath. "Paolo, go get a drink of water. And please, stay in the foyer until I come to get you."

Paolo did as he was told.

Don Vincenzo got up from his desk and sat beside Anina in Paolo's chair. "Men will never understand that saying stupid things like 'I didn't sleep with her' does not help the situation. In fact, that is not the point at all, is it?"

"It's not. It's the betrayal."

"Anina, I don't care if you marry Paolo Uliana."

"You don't?"

"Who is he to me? Another parishioner I have to love. I have to look past his faults and forgive him when he comes to me in confession. My investment in all this is the salvation of his eternal soul. And yours. So tell me about Paolo. Why did you agree to marry him?"

"He can be loving and compassionate."

"But I can see he's difficult."

"I'm so glad! Sometimes I think I'm crazy. My friends only see the good."

"Why are you still with him?"

"I love him."

"Do you? What if I told you that most couples that show up here aren't able to be honest with each other? They bat around the truth like a cat with a tinfoil ball, sometimes for years. The *truth* is what makes the difference between them and you and Paolo. He came straight home and told you what he had done."

"What difference does it make that he told me about it instead of catching him?"

"A lot. He knew he did wrong. Paolo examined his conscience. He begged forgiveness and promises to change. That's about the best you can expect from another human being in any situation. Ever."

"How about he doesn't do stupid things in the first place?"

"That wouldn't work for me. It would put me out of business."

Anina laughed. "You're the worst, Don Vincenzo."

"I know. That's why I don't get the fancy assignments. I'm the quick-fix priest, the bubble gum they stuff in the holes of a boat about to capsize, hoping it won't sink."

"I'm sorry, Don Vincenzo. You have a lot of pressure on you."

"And so do you. And so does every person who tries to love. That's my point. But that's also the job. You want to be a wife? Get ready to work like a farmer. When you've solved one dilemma, here comes a new set of problems. When you're serious about love, you've got to be just as serious in your commitment to work at it. No running away. No moving out. No disappearing. It wouldn't help anyway. You can't outrun your pain because it can be as stubborn as love."

"Should I marry Paolo?"

"Only if you expect the worst. A wise woman once said that the bride should wear black and the widow white. The bride mourns the loss of hope and the widow is finally free of the pain."

"I can't get the picture of what he did out of my mind."

"The memory is often the monster, not the transgression itself. Being unfaithful is not a part of love or a rejection of it—it's a lack of will. I'm sure you have experienced a lack of will in your own life."

"I have."

"So then you know what he did was a failure of his will, but not of his love." Don Vincenzo got up and went to his desk drawer, where he punched a tablet of Nicorette gum off the sleeve and popped it into his mouth. He chewed. "What do you want out of life, Anina?"

"I wanted to get married and have a family with the man I love."

"It's a job."

"I guess it is, Padre."

"It's a tough job if you don't know who you are. A mother is not just a loving presence in a family who cooks and cleans up and comforts the children. She sets the example and teaches the family, including her husband, how to love. She has to know herself. If she doesn't, she's going to look to the people she loves to fill her up. That's a terrible burden to put on your husband and children. A job, on the other hand, can soak up a lot of the ambition and ego we have so we are free to love once we get home. Look at it like the heel of the bread that soaks up the sauce at the end of the meal. You take the last bite and the plate is clean. Has Paolo gotten a job?"

"Not yet."

"And you?"

"I'm going to fill in at Cabrelli's for the manager when she goes on maternity leave."

"Hmm." The priest folded his arms across his chest.

"Did Paolo cheat on me because he doesn't have a job?"

"I don't know." Don Vincenzo looked at her. "Do you think he kissed another woman because *you* don't have job?"

"I don't know." Anina was confused. "What does my job have to do with anything?"

"When you find your purpose in life, it changes you. You see things differently. More clearly. You love more and better. You solve problems and are able to help others solve theirs because you stand in strength. You live in the whole world, not in your small corner of it. You serve."

Don Vincenzo moved to the door to bring Paolo back into his office. Anina, who hoped to leave Don Vincenzo's office with an answer, had found it. No one would be more surprised than Anina when she decided to follow her heart.

CHAPTER 25

As Anina unlocked the entrance door of Cabrelli Jewelers promptly at eight a.m., her grandfather was bent over the bruting wheel in the back room. The high-pitched hum of the wheel was the sound of her childhood. She and her brother came to the shop every day after school and waited for Nicolina to pick them up. Anina called out to Olimpio, locked the door behind her, and hung her purse on a hook behind the desk before flipping on the lights in the empty showcases.

Anina unlocked the safe and pulled the jewelry inventory out, lining up the storage trays on the glass counter. She counted the diamond rings and cross-checked them against the manager's inventory list. She arranged gold hoop earrings on their stands and positioned them in the case. She placed the pin light directly on the platinum hoops studded with sapphires.

She moved the brooches around like chess pieces, until each one was displayed to its ultimate advantage. Most shoppers had no idea what they were looking for. It was up to the salesperson to present the possibilities, Olimpio had taught her. The customer was buying a piece of jewelry and a story. Anina observed that women bought pieces that reminded them of happy times. When men bought jewelry for someone they cared about, they wanted it to be the best.

"All set, Nonno. The cases are done."

Olimpio took off his work goggles, went into the showroom, and checked Anina's work. "You've got an eye."

Anina began to cry. "I haven't been paid a compliment in a long time. I'm sorry."

"Paolo doesn't pay you compliments?"

"We're fighting a lot. Things were better after we went to Don Vincenzo, and now they're bad again. He says I don't pay enough attention to him. I think it's because I'm worried about Nonna. I'd like to come and stay with you. I could help you and help her get better."

"The day may come when we need you, but not now. I'll take care of my Matelda, and you need to take care of your Paolo."

Anina raised the shades and unlocked the front door. A customer waited on the sidewalk. Anina opened the door and smiled. "Welcome to Cabrelli's." The bells jingled as Anina went behind the counter to serve her.

Anina pulled a sheet of tinfoil off the roll. She peered into the oven. The chicken thigh, wing, and breast were browned and cooking on a bed of rice, seasoned with fresh garlic and mushrooms. She opened the oven and tucked the tinfoil over the top of the chicken and rice. She lowered the heat on the oven. She set the fresh greens off to the side and set the small table outside the kitchenette for one. Anina returned to the kitchen and dressed the salad. Anina heard the key in the lock; her stomach fluttered from nerves.

"You cooked?" Paolo stood in the doorway. He took in Anina, who looked lovely.

She nodded. "I made you dinner."

Paolo looked at the table set for one. "Are you going out?"

"No."

"You're dressed to go out."

"I'm leaving you." Anina walked to the bedroom and opened the door. He could see her suitcases on the bed. "I put my engagement ring in the box on the dresser. I was going to write you a note, but I thought that was cowardly, so I waited."

"You're serious." Paolo sat down as though he had been shoved into the chair.

"I think it's important to say what you mean in person," she said softly.

"Okay."

"We have control over nothing except the way we want to live. And I don't choose to live like this anymore."

"We're going through a rough patch, Nina. It's all getting real." Paolo looked down at his hands.

"Isn't it?" Anina thought to say, *It's been real for me all along,* but she resisted the urge to start another fight. She was tired of arguing with him. Instead she went into the bedroom and picked up her suitcases. She dragged them to the front door. She slipped into her boots.

"It's raining," he said.

"I know."

Anina pulled on her raincoat. Paolo went to her. "Don't do this. Please. Stay with me."

"This is about me." She smiled. "I know this is what other people say when they're breaking up, but in this instance, it happens to be entirely true."

"You can't forgive me."

"I have forgiven you. Once I did, I found out the job wasn't done."

Paolo was confused. Anina was calm.

"I had to forgive myself. And when I did, I found the guts to try and make something out of myself outside of the person I am with you. I was wrong to try and make you my purpose in life. That wasn't fair."

"I know we fight too much, but we love each other." Paolo took her hands into his own.

Anina loved Paolo, but she couldn't stay, because there was someone who needed her more. "Forgive me," she said as she opened the door, picked up her suitcases, and walked out into the storm.

The hospital elevator was filled with young residents in scrubs when the doors opened to reveal Anina carrying two cups of tea and a carton of soup for her grandmother. "I'll wait for the next one," Anina said cheerfully.

A handsome resident looked at her appreciatively and said, "We'll make room."

Anina squeezed onto the elevator. The resident held the door open as she disembarked moments later. She smiled to herself as she walked down the corridor to her grandmother's room.

Anina placed her purse on the chair and kissed Matelda.

"You don't have to come to the hospital every day."

"I want to."

"Nonno said you're watering my plants. How's the hibiscus tree?"

"It blooms big red blossoms when the sun is out."

"It's supposed to."

"It's peaceful in your home."

"Stay as long as you want. Sometimes you need a little distance," Matelda said. "And then you get it, and with it comes perspective, and you can find a way to work things out."

"Maybe," Anina said. "I'm just happy that I have a chance to spend more time with you."

Anina pulled the chair close to her grandmother's bed. "I want to hear what happened when your mother went to Scotland."

"You need to hear a story about a woman who survives losing the man she loves?"

"I guess I do, Nonna." Anina handed her grandmother a cup of tea. She took the lid off the other cup and settled into the chair.

Matelda raised the headboard on her bed to a sitting position. She smoothed the top blanket over the sheet. She closed her eyes and conjured the first home she ever knew in a place that lived in her dreams.

CHAPTER 26

Dumbarton, Scotland

AUTUMN 1939

The Sisters of Notre Dame de Namur ran a school in an old castle overlooking the river Clyde. Their convent and school were situated north of Glasgow at the point where the Clyde widened out at Havoc. The swell and expanse of the river at that point meant that the nuns were the first to observe the daily flotilla of new carriers, ships, and barges for use in the impending war. The nuns were confident that the war could be won based upon the display of might they observed from their turret, but they said a daily rosary for victory to hedge their bets.

The flower gardens of Notre Dame were set like jewels in the rolling fields around the convent. They also planted corn, green beans, lettuce, cucumbers, and potatoes in the field behind the convent. There was a grove of fruit trees along the path to the river. Their simple dairy operation housed cows in a working barn, providing milk and cream on a daily basis and cured meats on a seasonal one.

The school year had begun as scheduled; by 5 September 1939, every room in the residence was filled. As staff, Domenica was given a room off the main hall. A curtain separated her small office from her living quarters—a cell with a window, a bed, and a wash basin. If Domenica had wanted to contemplate life as a nun, her current position would have been good practice. The only difference between the good nuns and her was her freedom on her days off. Instead of spending the day in cloistered prayer, Domenica went into Glasgow.

Domenica picked up her mail in the welcome house on Saturday morning. She smiled as she walked back to the main house, shuffling the envelopes with return addresses from Indiana, USA, to Paris, France. She recognized Mary Gay's scrawl on a blue envelope forwarded from Saint Joseph's. Her heart raced when she saw the sender's address typed in the corner. The letter itself was typed on pale blue stationery with the crest of the merchant navy at the top. Domenica's hand shook as she opened the envelope. It was postmarked 10 August 1939. She was lucky the letter had reached her at all.

Dear Domenica,

I hope this finds you in good health.

This letter is to inform you that I must put an end to our correspondence. I am on assignment, and it will be impossible for me to respond. It is best that I wish you well and thank you for your friendship.

Captain John Lawrie McVicars

Domenica folded the letter and placed it back in the envelope. She slipped on her coat, placed the letter in her pocket, and took the path down to the river. With every step she took, she became more furious. She was angry with herself for falling for a sailor, as their reputations preceded them. She had believed John McVicars was the exception, but she had been wrong.

Domenica cringed at the thought that the captain had dictated the letter to a purser to type, which meant there was a stranger in the world who knew that McVicars didn't love her before she received the news. The man she thought capable of great tenderness was also coldhearted. The captain wasn't brave after all; he hid behind the seal of his stationery. Domenica wondered how she could have been so misled.

Domenica reached the bank of the river Clyde where the nuns had built a platform at the water's edge. Domenica took the letter out of her pocket and fiddled with it; she folded it into a paper airplane. She squinted, aimed for the roll of the river where it undulated in waves to the sea, and threw it. The letter sailed through the air before landing on the surface, a tiny patch of blue that was quickly swallowed by the rapids. A cold sentiment deserved a frigid end. Domenica felt lighter as she hiked back to the convent. McVicars had given her an excuse to forget him. Now she could put him out of her heart for good.

When Domenica was a girl, her mother and aunt spoke of a woman who went abroad and married a good Polish fellow she met on the train. By all accounts, he was hardworking and prosperous, but he was not Italian. Eventually, their differences brought them unhappiness, her aunt explained. It was then that her mother confided, "When you marry a man from your own village, you know how he salts his food."

Domenica had spent the fall of 1939 acclimating to her new job at the school. The nuns celebrated every feast day from All Saints' Day in November through Advent to Christmas Day in December with decorations, special Masses, and novenas. Domenica didn't have time to be homesick or think about anything outside of her job because the nuns required full participation of the staff at all school functions; but she missed Saint Joseph's and the circle of friends that she had made in Marseille. By winter, she was the most lonesome she had ever been since leaving Italy.

The weather in Scotland had not helped her state of mind. Early winter had been brutal, forcing the students and teachers indoors. The students who boarded at Notre Dame de Namur could not go home for Christmas because a terrible blizzard had stopped all travel. The Sisters and staff did the best they could to keep the children amused. A flu went through the dormitory, which kept Domenica busy. She got a taste of what it must be like to mother many children. She decided there were women who were born to it, and she wasn't one of them.

Domenica poked the fire in the convent kitchen. She tossed a few lumps of shiny black coal onto the logs. The fire spit blue flames as tendrils of white smoke went up the flue.

Domenica re-created her mother's Christmas cake from memory. The gardener had provided her with butter and eggs. She used two cups of flour, two cups of sugar. She blended them together in a bowl with a tablespoon of water. The Sisters had put up cherries in liqueur last summer, the last jar of them would grace the batter. She fished them out of the jar and added them to the mix slowly, throwing in a half cup of cherry juice before stirring. She set the batter aside, sat by the warm fire, and cracked the walnuts, removing the meat and placing it in a bowl. She cracked enough walnuts to make a cup. The chore took longer because she ate some as she went. She folded the walnuts into the batter and then poured it into a pan and placed it in the oven.

There was a knock at the kitchen door. She figured it was the gardener dropping off lard to bake the Christmas goose. But

instead of the gardener, a small man, a stranger, greeted her, carrying a large bucket in one hand and a sack of bottles in the other. He
entered the kitchen, stomping the snow off his boots.

Domenica took a small whisk broom and removed the rest of
the snow from his coat. "Here, give me your coat. We'll dry it by
the fire."

"Perdona mi. I make work for you." The old man handed her
the coat.

"You're Italian."

"I'm a citizen of Scotland born in Italy. We're called Britalians.
Or Tallies, when they want their gelato. Arcangelo Antica is my
name."

"Where are you from in Italy?"

"Bardi."

"I know it. I'm from Viareggio."

"No!"

"And I miss it most at Christmastime. What did you bring?"

"Gelato and prosecco for the nuns' Christmas dinner. The gelato goes in the floor with the ice block," Antica instructed. "What
are you baking?"

"Christmas cake, Toscana style."

"Emilia-Romagna. My people. We make the cheesecake."

"With the sugared lemon?"

"That's it. Are you a postulant?"

"No, no. I'm the school nurse." She extended her hand. "Domenica Cabrelli."

"Bellissima." Instead of shaking her hand, he kissed it. "Cabrelli!
I know all about you. You know my friend Captain McVicars."

She nodded politely.

"Good man."

Domenica forced a smile. She hoped McVicars was a good man,
but she had little proof of it.

"Let me know if the Sisters need anything else from Glasgow."

"I will." Domenica helped the old man into his coat. "Buon Natale," she said.

Antica went outside into the snow. Domenica watched from the window as Antica followed the narrow plowed path covered with fresh snowfall to the road. The silver fields were lit by a full moon, which hung like a milky, pale blue cabochon in the dark sky. For a moment, she thought to grab her coat and follow him. She needed to be with an Italian family even if it wasn't her own. Instead, she wrapped two mopeens around her hands and lifted her mother's Christmas cake from the oven. She hoped her family was doing the same, wherever they were.

CHAPTER 27

𝔇umbarton

SPRING 1940

Spring in Scotland exploded in color. Black-and-white cows lolled in bright green pastures. The sheep that gathered on the hillsides were pink, their eyes deepest brown, and their horns gleamed like black patent leather. Out of their heavy coats and woolens, the women of Glasgow bloomed in pastel-colored dresses and flitted through the streets like butterflies.

Domenica took the trolley into Glasgow wearing her best summer dress.

She walked through the west end of the city, stopping to browse in shops along the way, making a day of it. There were ceramics from Deruta, fabrics from the looms in Prato, and olive oil from Calabria on display in the Italian-owned shops. Domenica had promised to bring an authentic Italian tomato pie home for the nuns' convent supper. By late afternoon, it was time to make good on her promise.

The Franzetti brothers on Byres Road made tomato pie, Toscana style, with a thin crust topped with slow-roasted tomatoes caramelized until they were sweet, with a light sprinkling of Parmigiano-Reggiano on the top. In season, a sheer layer of truffle slices was fanned over the pies and baked in the wood oven, and the scent of earthy mushrooms filled the entire west end. Slices of sweet garlic cloves were added as an extra, before the pies were drizzled with olive oil. Domenica's mouth watered at the thought of the pizza, which in turn made her long for her mother's kitchen in Italy. It would not be long until she could go home again.

Domenica placed her order. When the Franzetti boy laughed, a lock of his black hair fell forward, reminding her of an old friend. Domenica found a seat at a café table on the street as she waited for the pizza she ordered to bake in the wood oven. The restaurant was lively with customers; outside, the children ran up and down the street chasing a ball with a knotty stick. Their game reminded her of Viareggio, where the children also played in the streets. In her mind, it hadn't been that long since she was a girl. She picked up the rubber ball when it landed by her chair, tempted to join in the game. Instead, she tossed it back to the boys, who shouted, "Grazie," when they caught it in midair.

This Italian enclave was, like the afternoon she had spent in the west end, a balm to her. She hadn't realized how much she missed her language and her people. Her life before her banishment to Marseille seemed idyllic, whether it had been or not, and she desperately missed her home. Sometimes all it took was the scent of tomatoes and garlic roasting in an oven to remind her of the time wasted, away from her family.

Franzetti brought Domenica a glass of his father's homemade wine and a slice of pizza to eat while she waited. She closed her eyes and sipped the wine; the hardy grape burned her nose, just like her father's homemade table wine.

The boys in the street shrieked with laughter when a tall man stole the ball they were playing with and held it high over their heads. The boys jumped in the air around him, trying to reach the ball. The man made a game out of it and spun around, as though he were a gamekeeper in a booth at a carnival, ginning up the children to compete for a shilling in prize money.

The Franzetti women called to the children to stop bothering the customer who was making his way into the pizzeria. When the man turned in her direction, Domenica gasped.

Captain John Lawrie McVicars handed the ball to one of the boys.

"Do you know him?" Signora Franzetti asked.

Before she could answer, McVicars saw Domenica. It was too late to run; their eyes had met.

McVicars was surprised. What was Domenica doing in Scotland? Should he care? She had stopped writing to him. He did not agonize about women. Clearly, her feelings had changed. McVicars accepted it. It was easy to avoid any unpleasantness. McVicars shipped out and disappeared until enough time passed for the woman to forget him. He had hoped to see Domenica again, if only to surmise that she was in good health.

For her part, whenever Domenica thought about the captain, she imagined him far away at sea. It helped to banish him to parts unknown in her mind. She had been too hurt by his silence to fantasize running into him in Glasgow, but promised herself if she did, she would tell him what she thought of him.

The street boys encircled the captain as they begged him to play. One of the boys latched on to McVicars's forearms. He hoisted him like a barbell, up and down. "That's enough, Nunzio," McVicars said to the boy. "You're getting too heavy for the old dumbbell routine."

The Franzetti women apologized and wrangled the boys back out into the street to play with their ball and stick as McVicars made his way into the pizzeria.

The Franzetti boy brought Domenica the tomato pie she had ordered. She paid him and promised to return. She had turned to make her escape when the captain made his way over to her.

McVicars stood awkwardly before Domenica, not knowing what to say. She certainly had no idea what to say to him either. He rubbed his forearms, where the boys' grip had left a burn. She remembered how those arms felt around her, and blushed. She was ashamed of the mistakes she had made with him, under the assumption that he cared about her. The blush in her cheeks turned to anger.

McVicars wanted to confront Domenica for ignoring his letters. He figured she'd met someone else and didn't know how to tell him. After all, she was a beauty, and at a marriageable age. He felt his temperature rise, wondering if she had met another Scot she fancied more than him.

Domenica gave McVicars a nod and walked out into the street.

"Miss Cabrelli?" he called after her.

Not wanting to make a scene, she stopped. She decided to face him.

"It is you. What are you doing in Scotland?"

"Working," she replied.

"You look well. Did you join the order?"

"Am I wearing a veil?"

"I should say not. Unless they changed their habit altogether, and that wouldn't keep the order celibate."

Domenica did not laugh at his joke.

"That's a lovely dress," he said.

"I made it myself."

"You have talent as a seamstress."

"My mother believed every girl *and* boy needed to know how to sew. My brother can make his own shirts. Do you know how to sew, Captain?"

"Is this what we have come to? Small talk about your dreadful brother, Aldo?"

Domenica was sorry she had ever told him anything about

anybody in her family. "Excuse me, I must go." Domenica left him standing in the street.

It took McVicars a moment, but he decided to follow her.

"Che bella, no?" the Franzetti boy said as he lowered the awning over the entrance of the pizzeria.

McVicars did not answer him. Instead, he looked for Domenica, but she was gone. Another boy pointed to the corner. The captain thanked him and took the turn on the boulevard, to find Domenica walking across it. The skirt of her pale blue dress billowed out like a bell. McVicars wondered if he had ever seen anything so lovely.

"Miss Cabrelli!" he called out again. This time, he quickened his pace to catch up with her.

Domenica climbed the steps to the trolley station. She had not heard him. He broke into a run. The trolley arrived at the station. The doors opened; passengers disembarked. Domenica climbed into the crowded car and sat down. The doors were closing as McVicars attempted to enter the car. He pried them open and wriggled inside as the trolley pulled out of the station. He looked up and down the car for Domenica. He spied her shoes at the far end of the car and wove his way through the passengers to her.

"Do you know somebody in Dumbarton?" she asked without making eye contact.

"Only you."

The trolley shook over the tracks as it chugged toward the Dumbarton station. The clank of the wheels and the din of the crowded trolley car made it impossible for McVicars to talk to Domenica. It wouldn't have mattered if he could, because she looked straight ahead, holding the tomato pie in her lap.

McVicars followed Domenica when she got off the trolley.

"I want to talk to you," he said to her.

"You should go back to Glasgow," Domenica said over her shoulder, and quickened her pace. "There's nothing to say."

"Why are you angry with me?"

"I'm not angry with you. I thought we were friends, and I don't appreciate your behavior."

"*My* behavior?" McVicars was confused.

"The trolley will be along in a few minutes. There's a comfortable bench where you can wait for it. Goodbye, Captain."

"Is there someone else? Have you met someone else? Just tell me."

"Why would you care? You sent me a letter saying you wanted no further contact with me."

"Not true! Show me the letter."

"I threw it in the river Clyde." Domenica walked across the field to the kitchen door of the convent, with McVicars in pursuit.

"Wait. No. Listen to me. I didn't write the letter you threw in the river. *You* stopped writing to me."

"I sent you letters every week."

"I didn't receive them," McVicars insisted.

"I sent them to your home."

"Please. Write to me again."

"I won't."

"One more letter to Tulloch Street. Please. If I don't hear from you, I will understand that to mean you have no further interest in me."

Domenica entered the convent kitchen and closed the door behind her. She left the pizza on the kitchen worktable and called out to the cook, before going to her room. She parted the curtains, flipped the latch, and opened the window. She saw McVicars walk to the station as the rain began to fall.

CHAPTER 28

Each day, McVicars met the postman on the corner to sort through the mail before it was delivered to 28 Tulloch Street. The captain used the excuse that he was looking for his orders to ship out and wanted to intercept the letter before it arrived home and upset his mother. At the end of the week, a blue envelope with the return address of Dumbarton arrived addressed to him from Domenica. He was delighted. Instead of opening it, he instructed the postman to deliver the mail as usual, the letter from Domenica included. McVicars waited until he was certain his mother had gone through the mail to return home. He slipped through the front door and walked back to the kitchen. The mail was on the table. He sifted through it quickly. Domenica's letter was missing.

McVicars heard a strange sound coming from the garden behind the house. He peered out the kitchen window and observed his mother tapping a brick in the garden wall into place with a stone, until it was even with the others. McVicars left the house unannounced and walked the streets of Glasgow until tea.

The hours between tea and supper were the longest of McVicars's life. He felt cheated out of his own happiness, which was difficult to accept because it was his mother who had robbed him of it. He returned home with a heavy heart as night fell. He waited in his upstairs room until he heard her climb the steps to her bedroom. It was easy to avoid his mother because she did not seek his company, make his meals, or do his laundry. His childhood home was a place to lodge until his orders came through. He lit a cigarette and waited for his mother to fall asleep.

McVicars opened his bedroom door and peered out. He had done enough sneaking around in his youth; he knew how to pass the threshold of his parents' bedroom without making a sound or leaving a shadow. He tiptoed down the stairs and went through the kitchen to the garden. He lit another cigarette, and using the match for light, he found the stone his mother had left on the ground. He tapped the bricks with the stone until he found the loose one. The process took long enough that the ash from his cigarette, dangling from his mouth, burned close to his lips. He stomped out the cigarette before lifting the brick away. He found a stack of letters in a paper bag stuffed into the small tomb.

Once he returned to his room, McVicars placed the letters from Domenica on his desk. He lay down on the bed and began to read. He began with the last letter Domenica had sent to him from Marseille. It was dated 9 July 1939.

Dear Captain McVicars,

There is really little left to write. My thoughts are in the unanswered letters. I understand, or think I might, why you have not responded. I have written something that offended you. For that, I ask your forgiveness. It is possible another woman has crossed your path that is far more suitable for you than me. I hope this is the case and you have made a good friend of her.

With best wishes,

Domenica Cabrelli

His mother had sliced open the envelopes neatly with her hairpin. He stacked the sheets of stationery neatly, like pages of a book, before sitting down at the table by the window. He pulled the lamp close to the paper and read Domenica's letters slowly. The captain did not read them once, or even twice, but three times, to make sure he understood her intent. As he set aside the pages one by one for the last time, a lake of blue pooled on the table.

McVicars sat back, balancing on the back legs of the chair. He put his hands behind his head, looked out at the moon, and thought about the Italian girl. He understood Domenica now, having read the letters. He was ashamed that his mother had read them, not because of the content, but because he would have to explain this transgression to Domenica. What young woman, with a promising future, would want any part of such a family? If he knew one thing about Domenica, it was that family was the center of her life. Here he was, a man of nearly forty whose mother had managed to run one son off to New Zealand, the other to the sea. John McVicars was an itinerant sailor who managed to stay away more months of the year than he was home. His father, who perished at sea, was a disappointment to his wife, who complained that he died just to spite her. Grizelle felt cheated, which turned her bitter. She made it a point to make her family as miserable as she was. Grizelle's lack of respect for her son's privacy did not come from a place of concern; instead, it was her last attempt to keep her son John tethered to her after the other men in her life abandoned her.

The captain finished the last cigarette he had rolled that afternoon.

It was two o'clock in the morning. He stacked Domenica's letters in the order they were written on one side of the desk and cleared the other side. He retrieved his stationery, envelopes, and pen from the drawer.

He rubbed his eyes. He did not pick up the pen for a long time, but when he did, he did not stop writing until he finished a letter to Domenica Cabrelli. He doubted his words would matter, but that did not prevent him from writing them.

3 April 1940

Dear Domenica,

I have read the letters you sent. Thirteen in all. My mother had hidden them away, for reasons I do not understand. I cannot blame her entirely, however, for the distance between us. Letters or no letters, I should have returned to Marseille to see you and talk this through. The time wasted is my fault.

I have come to realize that the only time in my life that I found any happiness whatsoever was in your company. If this seems strange, imagine a man who preferred a life on the sea, who returned home to his mother's house only when furloughed. I would drop my kit and pass the hours at the local bar until I could return to the ship. Home does not fill me with pleasant memories as

Viareggio does for you. But I believe this is the only difference between us. We are simpatico, as your people say.

You see, before sleep, I picture the night we met. I sit in the chapel at Saint Joseph's with you. I remember every word you said to me. There was a scent of incense in the air, and I was transported to an exotic port where only the two of us existed. My hands were burning that night, and I did not feel the pain because I was interested in your thoughts about every subject in the world. We talked, and yet there was not enough time to properly discuss anything with the intensity I craved. Our conversation helped me sort things, and I was grateful to you for having taken the time with me. For the months that followed, I found peace when I went back to that conversation. I thought of it before I would go off to sleep, and the memory of it cleared my conscience. I had not experienced that serenity since I was a young boy.

You have choices in your life. Many suitors, I am sure. You deserve their best intentions for you, naturally. I would be the last candidate for your affections in that stellar lineup of men, I know. But I doubt wholeheartedly that any man could possibly ever love you as much as I love you. In my imperfect way, I understand you. And I pray that in your imperfect way, you might love me too.

John

"Here's another one of those blue envelopes from your captain." Sister Matelda joined Domenica in the garden. She handed her an envelope. "One a day. Two weeks of letters. The man must have an almighty cramp in his hand." Sister Matelda rubbed her hands together. "You'll either marry him or kill him the way this is going."

"Sister, what would you do?"

"With a man?" Sister Matelda was around Domenica's age. When a young woman neared thirty, she was in the waning months of her marriageability, though this did not seem to be an issue with Domenica. "I chose a different path, or rather, it chose me. So I am not one to give romantic advice."

"If you loved a man, and he had brought you nothing but aggravation, would you go back to him?"

"If we're talking about George Garrity of County Cork, I had to leave him behind when I took my novitiate. I left him a bereft man in Macroom. I was told he was useless like a chair with no legs after I broke his heart. But somehow and eventually, he found his footing. He married soon after I took my final vows five years later. A lovely girl. Mary Rose McMasters of Killarney. She had red hair like a sunset, I was told. They have six children now. Love finds its way; it clears all obstacles."

"You don't regret becoming a nun."

"There are days. I left my father's home in hopes of an adventure. There was none of that in Macroom. But as God would will it, I've had adventure here. I love to teach, and I have my calligraphy. I have my interests. The love of God makes me question my life, and that same love gives me the answers when I need them too."

"I want peace." Domenica stood and went to the window.

"Have you thought any more about becoming a novitiate?"

"When this is all over, and it will be, I want to go home. I'm an Italian and I belong there. I miss Viareggio and my family and my work in the clinic. If I were to become a nun, I would have to give that up. And I'm afraid I'm not selfless enough to do that."

Sister Matelda nodded. She understood. "Some of us can make our way in the world anywhere we happen to be. You have a place that you long for—that's not a selfish thing at all. It just means you know where you are best loved and the most useful."

Sister Matelda went back inside the convent. Domenica tucked the letter from John into her apron pocket and walked down to the river.

The curtains were drawn in the window of John McVicars's bedroom. A sliver of light rested on the sill under the rolling shade. He turned over in the bed away from the light and squeezed his eyes shut to finish the dream that was in full play as he slept. He found his way back to the scene where he had left it when the light stirred him.

"Where are you going?" he called to Domenica, who was in midair.

The wind fluttered her dress and lifted her body higher into the clouds. He could not reach her.

"Where are you going?" John hollered up to her again.

When McVicars woke up, he was feverish and his mouth was dry. He remembered the dream. Domenica was out of his reach. It was one of those dreams where you have a task and you cannot complete it because your feet are rooted in the earth.

Another chance, he thought to himself. Hastily he rose, dressed, and packed his duffel. He folded the letters on the desk and returned them to their envelopes before tying the stack together with a string. He tucked the letters into his uniform jacket before going down the stairs. He threw the duffel by the door before joining his mother in the kitchen.

"Do you want beans and toast? Bacon?" she asked.

"Nothing."

"How did you sleep?"

"Fitfully. Mother, I'm leaving this house."

"Where are you going?"

McVicars said nothing. He pulled the stack of letters from Domenica out of his pocket. "Mother, what did you do?"

The color left her face. She turned away and lifted the teakettle off the stove.

"You kept these letters from me. Why?"

"No son of mine is going to end up with a Tally."

"She's a nurse. And a good person."

"I know all about her." She snickered.

"Because you opened my mail and read my letters and then you hid them from me."

"They came to my house."

McVicars was furious, but he knew from years of experience that his rage would do nothing to move his mother to see his point of view. "I'm going to go to her, if she'll have me after what you've done."

"She won't," his mother assured him.

"Did you think for one moment pretending to be me, sending a letter I did not sign, typed on your old Underwood, would stop me from marrying the woman I love?"

McVicars grabbed his duffel and left.

Grizelle opened the *Daily Mail* newspaper on the kitchen table. She read the front page, then slowly turned to read the second. She adjusted the eyeglasses on her nose and peered down to read an article that caught her eye.

THE DAILY MIRROR

By John Boswell

There are more than 20,000 Italians in Great Britain. London alone shelters more than 11,000 of them. The London
Italian is an indigestible unit of population. He settles here
more or less temporarily, working until he has enough money
to buy himself a little land in Campania or Tuscany. He often
avoids employing British labour. It is much cheaper to bring a
few relations into England from the old hometown. And so
the boats unloaded all kinds of brown eyed Francescas and
Marias, beetle-browed Ginos, Titos and Marios . . . now every Italian colony in Great Britain and America is a seething
cauldron of smoking Italian politics. Black Fascism. Hot as
Hell. Even the peaceful, law abiding proprietor of the back-
street coffee shop bounces into a fine patriotic frenzy at the
sound of Mussolini's name . . . we are nicely honeycombed
with little cells of potential betrayal. A storm is brewing in
the Mediterranean. And we, in our droning, silly tolerance
are helping it to gather force.

Grizelle McVicars picked up a pencil and circled the word "betrayal." *He'll be back*, she said confidently to herself.

Amedeo Mattiuzzi the jeweler had received a wire from his cousin
in London dated 28 April 1940: *See you in Brighton. L.M.*

The wire was code and carried a dire warning. Mattiuzzi had to
move his important inventory out of the shop immediately. His
wife studied the newspapers upstairs and made notes in Italian

that she kept in an empty flour bin. She cut out articles about *Brit-alians* and *Tallies* who had been picked up in the streets of London for small crimes or on the suspicion of them. The articles mentioned gambling, illegal wine production, black market hard-liquor sales, and fenced jewelry. But the truth was, a man only needed his Italian surname to be implicated.

Mattiuzzi soon had proof that something dire had been planned. The equerry from Holyroodhouse showed up unannounced and asked for the ruby brooch and pin set that had been commissioned by the royal family. The previous plan had been for Mattiuzzi to keep the jewel until a ceremony the following spring. *They must know something*, Mattiuzzi figured. He gave them the jewelry, and they offered no excuse for the change of plan in return.

Trusting his cousin's urgent warning, slowly, over the course of two days, Mattiuzzi and his son removed pieces from the display cases, leaving identical paste copies behind, so as not to rouse suspicions.

When the enemy was invisible, you must be too.

Mattiuzzi wrapped the fine jewels in muslin, hid them in his coat, and went to morning Mass, where, instead of leaving out the front door, he stole down the steps of the sacristy, to the underground crypt, where he hid the inventory in the wall beneath Saint Andrew's Cathedral. Mattiuzzi walked back to his shop confident no one had seen him hide his valuable inventory.

The bells on the door of Mattiuzzi's shop jingled. Father and son were in the back sorting their tools. They looked at each other. Mattiuzzi motioned to his son to stay in the workroom. He removed his apron and went to the front room.

"How may I help you, sir?"

"Antica sent me to see you." The captain had shaved and was wearing his uniform. "Captain John McVicars. I'm looking to purchase a lady's watch."

Mattiuzzi pulled a velvet tray out of the display case. Two gold watches, one with a leather band, the other with a combination of leather and metal, were placed on the glass. They were the last two pieces of value in the shop. Mattiuzzi planned to put the watches on his arm in case of any emergency.

"She's a different sort of girl. I see these wristwatches on every other woman in Glasgow. Don't get me wrong, they're lovely. But I want something memorable."

"What sort of a gift is this?"

"A special one."

"Tell me about her."

"She's beautiful."

"Good for you."

"Yes. And she's a nurse."

"Your instinct to buy her a watch is a good one. She needs a watch fob. All the nurses wear them. I have one that I refurbished that's available for sale. But it's expensive. It's an antique. One of a kind. Would you like to see it?"

McVicars nodded. Mattiuzzi went to the back room and returned with the watch fob. His plan was to have a middleman sell the piece on commission, in case Mattiuzzi needed cash later.

"Why is the face upside down?" McVicars asked as he studied it.

"A nurse needs a timepiece she can read at a glance without having to move her wrist to check the time. There's a second hand. It's jeweled movement, which means it tells time exactly—it is never off by a second. Important when taking a pulse."

"I like the stone."

"You'll never see anything like it in all of Scotland, or the British Isles really."

"Would you engrave it?"

Mattiuzzi looked back at his son. The engraving pen and plate had already been packed. Piccolo shook his head no.

"I'm sorry, sir, we are not able to engrave it."

"It needs to be engraved. I would like it to say, *Domenica and John*. I came to you because she's Italian. I figured you would do your best for her."

"Is she in Italy now?"

"No, sir, she is thankfully working here in Scotland at the convent in Dumbarton."

Mattiuzzi thought to warn the man that his future fiancée could be in danger. An Italian national in Scotland was not safe from accusations of the fifth column. But Mattiuzzi couldn't be certain the captain wasn't on a fishing expedition to find out how much the Italian Scots knew about the potential roundup. As for the recommendation from Antica, the ice cream peddler knew everyone—that was hardly a ringing endorsement. Mattiuzzi kept quiet.

"You don't have to etch both our names—just our initials would be fine. *J and D*. Please. I'm going to ask her to marry me."

"In that case then . . ." Mattiuzzi brought the watch fob to his son.

Piccolo whispered, "Papa, I packed the tools."

"Unpack them. Do as the man asks."

The rolling hills and lawns on the grounds of Notre Dame de Namur glistened in soft folds of green. The red roses that surrounded the statuary of the Blessed Mother were in bloom. Fuchsia peony buds dangled from delicate branches along the walkways, ready to burst open at any moment.

The May Day garden was in bloom with pink azaleas and blue

hyacinths. The reflecting pool was dotted with lacy white lilies that floated on midnight blue water. The Sisters who prayed there called their pond a "mirror of heaven."

John McVicars paced back and forth in front of the convent.

Sister Matelda peeked out through the curtains on the main floor. "He's wearing a path on the lawn."

Domenica looked out the window. "There's something the matter with him."

"He's in love, that's all."

"You can tell from that far away, Sister?"

"You'd better go talk to him before he paces himself right into the ground and there's nothing left but his epaulets. Haven't you tortured him long enough?"

"Maybe." Domenica winked at Sister Matelda. She wrapped herself with the scarf McVicars had sent and walked outside to join him.

McVicars was regal in his navy blue uniform. He remembered a high-ranking officer in the merchant navy who once said to him, "Our uniforms are so sturdy, they will hold you up when you've lost your courage." McVicars was plenty scared that morning. As Domenica walked toward him, with every step she took, his heart beat faster. He believed his future was in her hands.

"The nuns are concerned about their lawn," Domenica said.

"Is it against the rules to walk here?" McVicars asked.

Domenica had compassion for McVicars. He wasn't his typical jocular self; ever ready with a joke or pointed remark, he seemed vulnerable. "Why are you here, John?"

He took a deep breath. "Domenica, I know I am not worthy of you."

"Did you come all the way from Glasgow to tell me that?"

"No, I came all the way from Glasgow to ask you to marry me."

Domenica buried her hands in her apron pockets. She hadn't

expected a proposal of marriage. She thought he had come to the convent to inquire if she would see him again. If she'd known that McVicars was going to propose that day, she would have put on her blue dress. Instead she was wearing her uniform and apron. It seemed she was never properly dressed when he had something important to say to her. Maybe that was the point. There wasn't time for artifice; their connection was the destination, not the dance that preceded it. She weighed the idea of life without him against the commitment to him for the rest of her life. Domenica was not an impulsive woman, but she found out in this moment that she could be. She wanted him; the decision had been made the night she met him.

"What's wrong?" he asked.

"This isn't how I pictured it."

He looked around. "There's no rain. It's warm. I got a haircut and wore my uniform. I splashed on some cologne."

"All that for me?" she teased him.

"If it's not enough, tell me what you want and I'll do it."

"It's enough, John. I'll be happy to marry you."

McVicars scooped Domenica up in his arms, held her close, and covered her face in tender kisses. She kissed him feverishly before sinking her face into his neck. The scent of the lemon water made her think of Italy, which made her feel torn. A marriage proposal was celebrated by the entire family in her tradition. McVicars swung her through the air, which made her laugh and forget that the circumstances of their engagement were not ideal. McVicars placed her gently on the ground and reached into his pocket. "This is for you." He gave her a velvet jewelry box from Mattiuzzi's.

She lifted the watch fob out of the box. It could not have been a better engagement gift. Domenica was practical. The watch was functional, but it was also elegant.

"So the jeweler told me about this stone. Aventurine, it's called.

It came from Mozambique; the gold is Argentine, he believes, and built with rubies from India. Small ones, but they're there."

"They sparkle. Small red tears."

"Or raindrops. There's a stone in this watch fob from each hemisphere. In a small way, it is bigger than the world. It's my intention to show you the world. There are places I can't wait to take you."

"I want to go."

"And it works." John held it up to her ear. "This will be closer to your heart than a ring. I rather like this. It's like a medal." McVicars pinned it on her apron. "May we never run out of time."

Domenica placed her hand over the green aventurine. "What did I do to deserve something so beautiful?"

"You said yes."

"I would have said yes sooner."

"Is that true? When did you fall in love with me?" he wanted to know.

"When I found you hiding in the chapel. When did you fall in love with me?"

"After breakfast," he admitted. "I make my best decisions on a full stomach."

Domenica put her arms around her fiancé and kissed him. When she closed her eyes and tasted his lips, she was no longer in Scotland. France had already faded from her memory. Instead she was home in Viareggio, where she knew the houses and streets, the exact number of steps it took to get from one end of the boardwalk to the other, the warmth of her mother's kitchen in winter and the first cool breeze of spring under the pergola in Boncourso's garden where, if you were lucky, you got kissed under the grapes as they ripened in the sun. John McVicars was part of all she held important; her old life and her new one came together in the gentleness of his kiss.

Domenica Cabrelli was happily betrothed to Captain McVicars, which was good news for the Sisters of Notre Dame because it meant McVicars the Glaswegian would be close by to do repairs when they needed him. Within a few days, McVicars plugged a leak in the convent kitchen, rewired the dining room chandelier, and even went to the trouble of filling in a large pothole on the stone drive to the convent entrance. The captain remembered the name of each nun, even though it was difficult to tell them apart in their habits. The Sisters laughed at his jokes and reveled in the energy he brought to the convent. It didn't hurt that McVicars was handsome, with eyes as blue as the robe of the statue of the Blessed Mother in the convent chapel. The Sisters appreciated beauty in all its forms, including the suave McVicars, because it was a gift from God.

Domenica and McVicars conducted a proper courtship, and not always by choice as they walked the garden paths of Notre Dame de Namur. The nuns roamed the same grounds as they prayed, keeping their eyes on the young lovers.

"When we marry, do the Sisters come with you?"

Domenica laughed. "There seem to be more of them around when you visit. They've grown fond of you."

John was leaning down to kiss Domenica when he saw the flutter of a black veil through the trees. He pulled away to a proper distance. "They're like locusts. We may have to make a run for it."

"My father and mother would be worse."

"I doubt it." McVicars offered his arm to her.

"When will you receive your assignment?"

"Merchant navy sailors are the last to be placed."

"So we have time?"

"It depends upon Italy."

Domenica winced. She loathed the Fascisti and the evil intentions of their leader. Mussolini had been appointed by the king—he was not elected—and yet his will would decide the fate of her people. She despised him for keeping her from returning to Viareggio.

"Will you take me back to Viareggio someday?"

"Of course."

"Not for a visit, to live there."

"I would be happy to live anywhere in the world you want to be."

"Sometimes I wish we could go somewhere and start over again. I like the idea of America."

"Do you, now?" McVicars smiled.

"We could discover a new country together. I've heard wonderful things about it. They say the brass rings on the carousels are made of gold."

He looked around for spying eyes before pulling her close. "You know what I love about you? You believe that claptrap. But if you want to see for yourself, I will take you. I have a cousin in New York. He works in the shipyard."

"Could you do that kind of work?"

"I'd do anything to provide for you. When we marry, your nursing days are behind you. No more washing soot off old men and bandaging their bloodied meat hooks and sewing up their wounds. That's over. I want you having my babies."

"The captain orders it and it's done?"

"Usually," he said sheepishly.

Domenica smiled. "Would you give up the sea for me?"

"You decide about your nursing," McVicars grumbled. "I won't ask you to give up anything you love."

"Nor will I," Domenica promised.

John McVicars watched as the procession in honor of the Feast of Corpus Christi passed by. The gold monstrance, swathed in a white satin talis, was held high in the air by the priest. The Mother Superior followed behind, carrying the pyx, a gold box that held the hosts to be served at Holy Communion. The girls of the school followed behind them, wearing white dresses, carrying small bouquets of red roses. Domenica, along with the teachers, followed the girls.

The groundskeeper let down the velvet rope separating the procession from the onlookers. The guests, including the captain, entered the church. The good Protestant had never set foot in a Catholic church. This was proof he would do anything for love, for Domenica Cabrelli.

John waited for Domenica when the service ended. In his pocket were the two gold wedding bands he had purchased at Mattiuzzi's that morning. Sister Matelda was to arrange a military wedding, Vatican-approved, with the priest for the next morning. Domenica had moved to the guest lodge of the convent. McVicars would join her there once they married.

John didn't like the look on his fiancée's face as she came toward him through the crowd after the service.

"He won't do it. The priest refuses to marry us."

"What do you mean? That's his job. There's four shillings in it for him. All right, I'll make it five."

"He's serious."

"Can the Sisters help change his mind?"

"Sister Matelda said we should go to Manchester."

"That's three hours by train."

"She called the priest there. If we leave now, we'll get there by nightfall. Don Fracassi is waiting for us."

Don Gaetano Fracassi closed the ledger on his desk. The priest looked around the vestry of Saint Alban's, Ancoats, with a heavy heart. No matter how hard he tried, he was in arrears on every bill owed by the poor church. The boiler was shot, the roof leaked, and the stone wall that hemmed the cemetery was crumbling from age and exposure to the elements.

The church needed funds. The bishop left it to the local priests to raise the money through tithing and events. In desperation, last fall, Fracassi thought to rent out the church hall for civic meetings. His best customer had been the local brotherhood of the Fascisti, whose membership was mostly comprised of English locals who followed Oswald Mosley, but there were also parishoners, English citizens of Italian descent, who attended, filling the church hall to capacity. Fracassi kept out of politics, but he did not keep the politicians out of his church hall if they were willing to pay.

The priest got up from his desk, accidentally kicking over the empty tin he had placed there earlier to catch the water that leaked through the hole in the roof. He grabbed the broom behind the door, tied a rag over the bristles, and swabbed the stone. He walked around the periphery of the wet floor and sat down next to the fire to wait for it to dry, reaching into the pocket of his cassock and peeling the orange he had saved from lunch. Fracassi savored the peel first, even though it was slightly bitter. He ate the sweet quarters slowly, releasing the nectar between his teeth. The fruit tasted of his native Italy, where oranges and lemons grew plentiful in the heat. The first thing he learned in England was that citrus fruit was hard to find and expensive. When he was done, he threw the seeds in the fire and rubbed his hands together. The oil on his hands from the orange peel released in the air like perfume on a beautiful woman. He sat back in his chair and placed his sore feet on the grate.

The poverty Fracassi endured in his Italian childhood influenced his decision to become a priest. He developed humility regarding his own ambitions and was determined to be useful. When he was assigned a position at the church in Manchester, he served a large Italian immigrant community. He often spoke Italian when delivering a sermon on a feast day, which comforted the Britalians. At sixty-four years old, Fracassi kept Italy alive in England for his flock as he himself longed for home.

The knock at the door startled him even though he expected the visitors. He wiped his hands on his cassock and shuffled to the door. The supplicants he had waited for had arrived. He opened it and smiled when the young woman began to speak in Italian, vehemently explaining the circumstances of their dilemma. She was followed into the room by her fiancé, an attractive, robust Scot in uniform.

Don Fracassi performed the wedding ceremony. He blessed the gold bands by the firelight. The bride knelt before his statue of the Blessed Mother for the benediction while her husband stood, his head bowed, his hand on her shoulder.

The good groom gave the priest a crown, a generous tithe for an intimate sacrament. The priest accepted the offering graciously. He wished them well. He opened the door and watched the newlyweds make a run for it in the rain.

Domenica and John were soaked from a downpour when they took their room in the inn outside of Manchester. John made a fire as Domenica hung their coats to dry on the mantel. She opened a basket filled with food. She had made tarelles to eat with the hard cheese and olives. There was a fresh loaf of bread. There was a jar of peppers with alige and two cans of sardines. There was a bottle of wine and cherries canned in syrup from the nuns' reserves. She placed the cotton napkins she had pressed beside two small wine-glasses on the table.

She shivered as John poked the fire. Soon the wood was burn-ing, throwing orange flames up the flue. She stood and watched as her husband stoked the fire. She finally felt warm after a day of being wet and cold.

"What's this?" he asked.

"Your wedding feast."

John scooped his new wife up in his arms. "I'm not hungry. Not yet."

John kissed Domenica as he had intended to kiss her when Don Fracassi blessed them, but somehow it had not seemed proper in the presence of the old priest. He meant to kiss her on the way to the train, but they had to run through a downpour in order to board in time. And he most resisted kissing his wife on the train. She was a modest girl, he believed, and what they were together was not something for others to see, but for the two of them to pursue with feeling in private. But now they were alone. It was simple suddenly. Any apprehension either of them had was washed away with the rain. It was just Domenica and John, the roaring fire, and a feather bed.

John carried Domenica to the bed and placed her gently on the coverlet, as if she were made of crystal so delicate, the glass would break if held too tightly. She put her hands on his face and guided his lips to hers. The moment filled her heart, which filled the room and would fill her life. There was only John Lawrie McVicars and the warmth of the fire he had built for her.

As his lips found her neck, his gentle kisses made up for the loneliness she had felt since she left Italy. Nothing, no matter how wonderful, had been able to fill her up until now. She was no longer alone in the world. She had a partner, a man she trusted, believed in, and admired. His love made up for all she had lost. Someday she would see her family again, and he would become part of them.

John loved Domenica more than his heart could hold. He had lived a rootless life until now. His mother's home on Tulloch Street had never been his. Now he wanted a home worthy of Domenica. He was ready to build a new life and offer himself in faith to her. His past washed away like the letter Domenica had thrown into the river Clyde. All the hurt dissolved, like the ink on the paper in the undertow. Love, it turned out, could shelter the banished and lift the broken spirit, but he had no idea that it was one woman's love that could do both.

Sister Matelda had left a letter in the guest lodge for Domenica. Her hands shook as she opened the envelope. She sat under the window and unfolded the letter.

6 June 1940

My dear Domenica,

The Sisters of the Sacred Heart in Lucca promised me that this letter would reach you. I do not want you to worry. Papa and I are in good health. We are leaving to go up the mountain where we will be safe. The Gregorios and Mamacis are going with us. We have sent word to the Speranzas to join us. Their situation is difficult, but Papa believes Speranza's good friendship with the church will help. We have hope. Your brother, Aldo, remains in Africa. Reggimento Puglia. His last letter was brief, but he is also in good health. We trust the good Sisters will take care of you un-

til we can be together again. Pray. We will pray too. Your mother

and father and brother love you. This is the last letter I will write

until the conflict is over. The Sisters cannot deliver any further

mail.

Mama

The captain entered the lodge, sat on the step stool by the door, and removed his work boots. "How was your day?" He called out, "Mrs. McVicars?" When she didn't answer, he went to look for her. He saw the letter from Domenica's mother on the table. He read it.

Domenica stood in the doorway. "I will never see them again," she said.

CHAPTER 29

Venezia, Italy

Summer 1940

The bruting wheel sustained a high-pitched screech as Romeo Speranza gently polished the ruby. Filaments of red dust fell through the air and into the work tray as the gem cutter pumped the pedal underneath the table. One carat. Peruzzi cut. Following a few final spins of the wheel, he held the stone up to the afternoon light through the street-level window. The ruby held the saturated color of burgundy wine, so red it was practically purple. He buffed the jewel in a cotton cloth between his thumb and forefinger.

Agnese collected the polished ruby and knelt to return it to the lockbox inside the safe in the floor. "Romeo, your shoes."

Speranza looked down at his shoes with a critical eye. The oxblood leather was covered in dust from the wheel. He wiped his hands on a rag tucked in the back pocket of his work trousers.

"There's a shoeblack on Calle Sant'Antonio."

"Should I go now?"

"They won't get polished by themselves." Agnese's lips almost curled into a smile. "Come back as soon as you can. No stopping at

Bar Maj. I would go with you, but I have to make the challah for Shabbos."

"Va bene." Speranza grabbed his hat.

He buttoned his vest as he walked along the canal to the piazza. Overhead, the sky matched the dull blue surface of the canal. He passed the mesh baskets filled with fresh silverfish, clamped to the wooden bumpers in the ice-cold water of the canal. Soon the air would fill with the scent of a woodsy smoke, as the smelts and sardines were grilled for Friday dinner.

The heavy-lidded black Madonna carved from marble looked down from her perch on the roof of Santa Filippa. Beneath her alcove, a soldier in the uniform of the Blackshirts stood guard, his hand resting on the butt of the rifle perched on his shoulder. Speranza remembered when there were no guards or guns in Venezia. Now it was overrun with soldiers in makeshift uniforms. There were more of them than pigeons.

The piazza was filled with traders from the four corners of the world. Their voices ricocheted off the walls as they haggled. The buyers wove in and out among the tables, on the hunt for particular treasures. The sellers, in contrast, modeled their wares—silver, fine fabrics, leather goods, and ceramics—with flair, hoping to close a final deal by sunset. Speranza walked past the display racks of textiles. Nuns, swathed in their navy habits and crisp white wimples, compared the quality of the wool as they bargained with the Scottish merchant. The haggling was spirited. Speranza could barely hear himself think.

Where is this guy? Romeo wondered as he walked along Calle Sant'Antonio. As usual, his wife was right. The shoeblack was waiting for him. The boy was thin, his skin the color of mahogany. He beckoned and bowed from the waist as his customer made his way to the chair.

"Polish and wax?" the boy offered. "Six lire."

"Grazie." Romeo sank into the chair. The boy loosened the laces and went to work. "My wife does not like a dirty work shoe, even though that's their purpose."

"Your wife is a beautiful woman."

"You say that about all the Venetian wives? Where are you from?"

"Ethiopia."

"The land of the white sand and the sapphire ocean."

"You know it!"

"There's an aventurine mine there. I went to North Africa to buy the green stones and spinel. After that, I went south to a diamond mine."

"The Cape of Good Hope. There's no good and no hope there. Pirates. More rock is stolen than mined."

"How is that possible?"

"My father and brother work in the mine there. The conditions are terrible. And there are days the owners do not distribute the purse. They steal from the workers. That's why I came here. I can shine shoes for more than my father's day wage. I can take the money home someday to help my family. I would like to farm. I know how to farm."

"You'll have to go north."

"Your wife said there are farms outside Treviso to the north. Fields of corn and wheat." The boy looked up at Speranza.

"Yes. Green fields. Blue sky. And in the far distance, the white peaks of the Dolomites. I live on a farm outside Treviso with my wife in the summer."

"Do your children work the farm?"

"We don't have children." Speranza smiled, but in truth, the mention of children was a sore point with him. He couldn't give Agnese a child, her highest dream.

"Signora is strong."

"Yes, she is. She is a mother to all."

The boy smiled. "I have a strong mother." The boy stood back with his rag. "There."

Romeo looked down at his shoes. "I can see the oxblood. More importantly, Signora Speranza will be able to see the oxblood."

"Fine leather."

"Florentine. The best leather." Speranza dug in his pocket. "Shoes should be comfortable. You get more work out of yourself that way."

The shoeblack's feet were bare.

"I'm in a shop on Calle Soranzo. A jewelry shop. Come by in the morning, and we'll see what we can do about your dreams of working on a farm." Speranza handed the boy seven lire.

"Mille grazie, Signore. Mille grazie."

"You may change your mind when you meet my cow."

"I will work hard."

"You'll have to. The cow is ornery, the pig is stupid, and the donkey has a bad foot."

"I understand."

"Where do you sleep?"

"Under the bridge." The boy pointed.

"What's your name?"

"Emos."

"Come and see me tomorrow, Emos."

"I will, Signore."

Speranza walked back to the shop. He stopped in the street when he realized what had transpired with the shoeblack. He hadn't been sent to Calle Sant'Antonio for a shoeshine. Agnese had sent him to the boy to size him up, so the hire would look like his idea. She had probably already made a deal with him to work the farm. He grinned. That would be just like his wife.

The clang of the church bells accompanied the sun as it began its descent. The blue shade of night was slowly pulled over the city. Venezia turned silver in the light. One by one the palazzi that graced the canals fell into shadow, like saints in their alcoves in a dark church when the candles were extinguished.

The island of Murano twinkled in the distance, lit from within as the flames danced in the glass kilns. The furnaces raged, throwing a glow overhead, forming a white halo in the purple sky. *Every place is holy when the sun goes down*, Speranza thought as he moved quickly through the coming darkness, home to Agnese and Shabbos.

LIVERPOOL

June 9, 1940

The ocean liner docked in the harbor was so tall it blocked the moon. The moan of the moorings sounded like the wail of ghosts. Glamour took a holiday on the docks of Liverpool even when the ships were grand. A crew of men worked around the clock repurposing the *Arandora Star* to join the wartime fleet.

At first, the *Arandora* transported Allied troops as they evacuated Norway and France. A plan to flip the *Arandora* was devised quickly by the Royal Navy and executed by the working men of Devenport. The requisitioned ship would join the merchant navy fleet in Liverpool to transport Axis nationals and prisoners of war.

Their docks of Liverpool were soon shored up by the Irish, who poured into the city looking for work. The requisitions were only part of the mandate to prepare for war; the Welsh had been building ships as well. The production lines operated twenty-four hours a day as shipbuilders, technicians, and laborers finished a new fleet of submarines and military cruisers for battle. The slips along the harbor were occupied, packed with a clutter of boats of all sizes enlisted or built by the Crown.

Britain had declared war in September 1939. Germany had attacked the Low Countries and France by May 1940. The men working the shipyards experienced an escalation in their workload and an urgency to finish the jobs quickly. All seaworthy boats from skiffs to ocean liners were requisitioned to defend the island. The Brits had already suffered losses in France and been humiliated at Dunkirk and were prepared to do whatever they must to win. They were determined to show the world the best ships were built in Liverpool.

The pubs overflowed with men between shifts. Dockworkers showed up for a pint covered in gray and white paint, proof that the final coat applied to the *Arandora* meant war was imminent. The Second World War would soon erupt over their island like a volcano, burning them with firebombs and heat from the Luftwaffe.

Liverpool was an important military hub on the northwestern coast of England. If you weren't feeding sailors, sewing their uniforms, or housing them, you were not considered a loyal subject. Liverpool was no longer a city of working people going about their business; instead, it had become a hub for the business of war.

There were efforts made to preserve the grandeur of the *Arandora Star* and her ilk, while using her size and power to serve the Allied cause. Hand-carved mahogany trim and William Morris wallpaper had been covered with thick cotton batting. The extravagant crystal chandeliers, which once graced the staterooms like jewels, hung from the ceilings carefully preserved in muslin beehives. Removal would have meant a rewiring of the ship's electrical grid, and there was not time for it. The remainder of architectural and decorative splendor was removed, with the exception of the captain's private dining room, which remained intact.

Three boys from Liverpool, around the age of twelve, slipped along the pier in the darkness carrying their BB guns. They moved swiftly, crouching behind the piles, motioning to one another to lie low until they agreed to leapfrog forward to the next hiding spot, with the goal of reaching the *Arandora Star*.

The boys spied as several men hammered the spiked border of the final sheet of barbed-wire fencing on the lower deck. The boys peered up and saw the upper decks swathed in similar barbed-wire fencing. The wide decks, once open and filled with chaise longues, where passengers had played cards and taken the sun, were now empty cages. Soon the posh ocean liner would be completely encased in mesh as though she, too, were a prisoner.

The boys heard the murmurs of the workers as they left the ship and departed for the pub. The ruffians waited until the only sound they heard was the *Arandora Star* herself as she heaved and creaked, trapped in the tight slip like a gray whale.

One boy whispered to his pals, "The grandest one of all."

"Gonna fill it with dirty Tallies 'n' send them all back to It-lee where they belong."

"How do you know?"

"My ole dad told us that they're gonna round them up and ship them out. They stole our jobs. Thieves."

"Is your dad working?"

The boy shook his head that he was not.

"There's your trouble."

The boys hid behind the gate on the dock and took in the changes on the exterior of the *Arandora*.

"They wrapped 'er in wire so the Tallies can't jump."

One of the boys took aim at the first row of lifeboats pressed against the side of the ship with his BB gun. "This is for my uncle, who ain't had a job in a year. Tallies took his place on the assembly line at Evermeade." He aimed and pulled the trigger. A ping could be heard as the BB bounced off the fence of the deck.

"Blighter," the red-haired boy teased his friend. "You're a bad shot."

"Take yours, then," the boy said defensively.

The red-haired boy took his time. He squinted over the barrel of the gun and followed the red line along the ballast of the lifeboat suspended off the stern. The boy steadied his shot and took aim. He fired. The BB hit the inflated rubber ballast dead center. The rubber lifeboat began to deflate. "That's for your uncle."

The boys popped off several lifeboats, taking aim at one all at once. The BBs hit the rubber simultaneously as the boys coordinated their shots.

When the boys heard the sound the rubber lifeboat made as it deflated, they laughed. They lowered their weapons. They forgot about deflating the lifeboats and rendering them useless. The red-haired boy became giddy; he lost his balance, tripped, and tumbled down the embankment between the dock and the landing. The other two boys shinnied down the hill after him, laughing all the way.

CHAPTER 30

Glasgow

June 10, 1940

John and Domenica had been staying as newlyweds in the guest lodge on the grounds of the convent of Notre Dame de Namur at the invitation of the Sisters since they returned from their wedding. Domenica continued her work as school nurse while her husband made himself useful.

Sister Matelda waited as Domenica took care of a student who had cut her hand on the playground. Domenica looked up and knew instantly what the nun had come to tell her.

"He did it?"

Sister Matelda nodded. "Mussolini declared war on England and France in an alliance with Germany."

Domenica's heart sank. The news meant her husband would soon ship out. Her parents would remain in hiding. Families were splintered and friends were scattered, and no one was safe. The honeymoon was over, and there was no way to know what life would be on the other side.

June 11, 1940

Mattiuzzi looked around the apartment above his jewelry shop in the west end of Glasgow. His wife, Carolina, had left a teacup and saucer on the table and a hot kettle on the stove. He touched the kettle to make sure his wife had followed his instructions. She had. It was warm to the touch. He turned on the light by the window and lifted the shade by half before sprinting down the stairs to the shop.

Piccolo locked the display cases filled with replicas of the real jewelry his father had hidden weeks before. He cocked his head and looked up. "I hear them, Papa. Hurry."

"Go," Mattiuzzi whispered before turning off all the lights in the shop and lowering the shades. He had gone to the back room when he remembered the gold watches. He slipped back to the front of the shop in the dark and searched for the key. He remembered it was in his pocket. He trembled as he opened the drawer. He could hear the mob on the next block. He heard their chant and the smashing of glass. *They got the Franzettis.*

"Papa, *now*!" Piccolo said urgently from the doorway.

Mattiuzzi followed Piccolo to the back. He handed the gold watches to his son. As Piccolo went down the ladder, Mattiuzzi scattered worthless paperwork on the desk and tools on the work-table that he had planned to sell. He knelt and crawled under the worktable, following his son to the crawl space and basement below. Mattiuzzi placed his feet on the ladder. He took a final look around, making certain he had removed everything of value.

"Papa. Andiamo!" Piccolo whispered from below. Amedeo pulled the trapdoor shut over his head, locked it, and descended the ladder with his son's help.

Mattiuzzi had covered the trapdoor overhead with a piece of woven carpeting that matched the rug under the table. He'd rigged the pedal of the bruting wheel to snap into place over the carpeting so the trapdoor would hopefully go undetected. He prayed the ruse would work.

Carolina made the sign of the cross as her husband took a seat on the bench next to her in the dank hole. Piccolo snuffed out the tiny flicker of the oil lamp. Mattiuzzi's twelve-year-old daughter, Gloriana, was terrified in the void, but less so as her mother pulled her close.

The girl sat on the hamper of food covered with a blanket. There was a large flask of water, a lone tin cup dangling from its neck. There were more blankets and pillows stuffed underneath the bench. They brought the radio below and a spare can of oil for the lamp. Amedeo's wife had packed their dishes and crystal from Italy in crates, which cramped the basement room. He was too frightened to be angry with her. Their money and personal papers were stored on Mattiuzzi's person. Their cat, Nero, mewed.

"The cat?" Amedeo clucked. His daughter picked up the black cat and held her. The cat stopped mewing, as if she understood.

"What if they set a fire?" his wife whispered.

"They won't burn their own property." He pointed left and right to indicate the emporium and the bar, Scottish-owned.

Piccolo held his fingers to his lips and pointed above.

The Mattiuzzis heard the shatter of their glass storefront. They heard the repeated whack of an ax as it battered the front door down. They heard the voices. The chant of "Dirty Tallies" from the street was followed by the smashing of the display cases, one by one. Amedeo's wife closed her eyes and clung to their daughter. She silently prayed the rosary as their life's work was destroyed. Piccolo became enraged; his father had to restrain him from going up the ladder and confronting the looters.

"Matt-uh-zee," one of the men called out in a singsong fashion. "Matt-uh-zee?" The mispronunciation of their family name told the Mattiuzzis that the mob did not know them. The floor above them shook violently as the looters trampled through the work-room. Their footfalls were so loud the Mattiuzzis believed they might come through the warped floor.

The Mattiuzzis froze, barely able to breathe. They heard laughter, which sent a chill through them.

"Smash the wheel," one man said.

"Can't get it to move," another said.

"Take the papers."

The ordinary sounds of the workroom, the hum of the wheel and the tinker of the tools, were replaced by an ugly overture of violence, the swing of wooden bats destroying their worktable. The looters picked up the tools the jeweler had staged and destroyed Mattiuzzi's property with them too. Mattiuzzi felt the blows to his shop in his body as they smashed the window and shattered the glass in the picture frames and mirrors. They even swung at the lightbulbs overhead until nothing was left but wire.

"Go upstairs!" a man barked. "Make work of it!"

The apartment was his wife's domain. She took her husband's hand and gripped it as she imagined their feather beds ripped at the seams and the destruction of the wooden rocker her husband had made for her before Piccolo was born. She pictured the hand-carved spokes of the chair ripped from their sockets and the tongue-and-groove skis that curved the supports snapped in half. Ruined. Carolina thought of Gloriana's room and her dollhouse. She had made her daughter a rag doll when she was little. "I have Fissay," she whispered to her mother. Too old to play with dolls, Gloriana treasured her childhood toy because her mother had made it especially for her. The girl was not about to allow a group of thugs to destroy her mother's handiwork.

More men poured into Mattiuzzi's building, tramped up the stairs, only to return to the shop moments later, once again shaking the floor overhead. The family heard the footfalls cross from the back of the store to the front. They heard the tinkle of the bells over the front door as the mob left through the open frame. Mattiuzzi put his head in his hands. The front door of the shop had been a work of art, inlaid with the finest Scottish lead glass made in the mills of Edinburgh. *They are destroying their own creations*, Mattiuzzi thought.

After a few minutes of silence, certain they were gone, Piccolo whispered, "Let's go up, Papa," as he lit the oil lamp.

Mattiuzzi shook his head no, blew out the lamp, and looked up when the workroom floor creaked over their heads. Someone figured out where they were hiding.

More footsteps clomped through overhead as several men joined the man in the workroom.

In the basement, the Mattiuzzis dared not move. Soon the lingering footsteps crossed the workroom and followed the rest out the front door. They heard the jingle of the bells again as the door shook and the looters climbed through it.

"They're gone," his wife whispered.

"I'll go look," Piccolo said.

"We will not go upstairs until the sun comes up."

"I'm afraid, Papa," Gloriana whispered.

"Don't worry. They're cowards. They won't show their faces in the light."

"But, Papa . . ." Piccolo began.

"McTavish is coming for us at daybreak. If he says it's safe, we go up. Not until then."

The Mattiuzzi family settled in their hiding place.

Mattiuzzi's father had been an immigrant who married a fellow Italian upon his arrival in Glasgow. Mattiuzzi felt indebted to Great Britain for the good life he enjoyed with his wife and children. The family had flourished in Glasgow. Proud Scots, Mattiuzzi had joined the British Army to serve in the Great War in France, fighting in the Battle of the Somme. They were active in community life. Carolina led the Thistle Sewing Circle, one of the oldest Scottish women's clubs in town. His daughter had won an essay competition at her school, titled "Scotland for One and All." His son, Piccolo, was in love with Margaret Mary McTavish, a family with a plaid whose father owned the emporium next door. It was Lester McTavish himself who had warned Mattiuzzi about the night of sticks and stones planned against the Italian Scots. He had heard about it after church in a gathering of Glaswegians. The merchant had hustled home that morning to warn his friend. There was not enough time to flee; instead, they quickly hatched a scheme. Now, they were living it.

Mattiuzzi lit the oil lamp. He thought of home. But it wasn't the green hills of Bardi, Italy, covered in sunflowers that he pictured; it was the Highlands of Scotland, where he'd taken Piccolo to hike during the summer since he was a boy. Mattiuzzi had taught his son to fish in the same river where he had learned to fish as a boy. They camped in the open air and ate wild raspberries in the sun. The heather graced the hills, drenching them in blue. The air in the Highlands was the sweetest Mattiuzzi had ever breathed. But those mountains and the fruits of that river no longer belonged to him. The Scot in him wanted to fight back, while the Italian in him hoped to endure. Mattiuzzi was a man without a country, even though he had been willing to die for it. It was pure luck that he hadn't died in combat, because the loyalty only went one way.

June 15, 1940

While Mattiuzzi considered Scotland his country, Domenica remained loyal to Italy. Her intention had always been to return to

Viareggio, but fate had led her far from home. She was married to the captain now, which made her a Scot. But in her heart, if she put politics and the hubris of powerful men to the side, she remained an Italian and would die one. Her brother would be fighting against her husband. Her parents were hiding in the hills, and if family was her life, it meant that part of her was hiding too.

Domenica had begun to fall in love with Scotland despite her occasional bouts of homesickness. At first, she couldn't see its beauty. She had traded, against her will, the warm waves of the Italian coast for the cold, green waters of the River Clyde. Eventually, she began to make her peace with it. Love had changed her point of view, and reminded her of her upbringing and duties. In her tradition, she had learned that her husband came first, so she placed him there. Domenica took care of John. She cooked for him, kept the cottage, and worked in the school to save her salary so they might be able to buy a home of their own someday. She would do her part. That morning, she had packed John's duffel. His uniform was laid out on the bed. She had one more task to perform before he departed.

"Let's get to it, Domenica," her husband said.

He followed Domenica to the garden wearing his undershirt and trousers. She tied a bedsheet around him up to his neck, like a barber's apron. Domenica combed his hair. She lifted a lock of hair and snipped it short.

"Careful of the ear, darling," he said to her. "I need it to hear the enemy."

"It's the curves that are difficult. Sit still."

"I'm certain you're doing a fine job," he joked.

"My best."

"That's all I can ask for. Let's agree to a game of pretend this morning. I don't ship out and we stay in this cottage for the rest of our days."

"They'd come for you."

"I said this was a game of pretend. For once, don't be practical."

"I have to be. I'm a problem. An Italian in Scotland."

"You married a Scot, which makes you a Scot. Besides, I don't think the Germans could get past the nuns. They haven't for centuries. Even in Germany."

Domenica removed the bedsheet from John's shoulders and shook it out in the bushes.

"I like it," John said, looking in the hand mirror at the haircut Domenica had given him. "It will suffice. But you must retire the scissors. You have no skill for it. Our children will look like numpties when you're finished with them."

Domenica put her arms around her husband and held him close. She kissed his neck.

"Mrs. McVicars." The captain wanted to make love to his wife. He kissed her. "There will be none of that."

"Not for a long time." She ruffled his freshly cropped hair.

He checked his watch. "We do have the morning."

"Do we now?" Domenica laughed and ran into the lodge. John followed her inside, closed the door, and locked it.

🌀

Grizelle McVicars stood at the window and watched her son John open the gate for his wife at the house on Tulloch Street. She groaned at the sight of the couple. She could not believe her son had the temerity to bring his Tally bride to her home.

"What did she say when you called?" Domenica asked as he let her inside the gate.

"Not much. This was your idea. Too late to turn back now."

The front yard of his mother's house was overgrown with long-necked lilies poking through gnarls of boxwood. Yellow paint peeled off the old clapboard, and the porch sagged where the wood had buckled from the storms that winter.

"You should've painted your mother's house."

John shot his new bride a look as he knocked on the door.

Grizelle McVicars met her son at the door. She opened it and extended her cheek as a greeting. She wore a modest black dress and brown shoes. Her white hair was pulled back in a plait.

"Mother, I'd like to introduce you to my wife, Domenica," John said.

Domenica extended her hand. Grizelle did not extend her own in return. "Well, come inside then," she said before looking both ways to see if her neighbors had observed them.

John looked at Domenica and rolled his eyes.

The couple followed her to the kitchen, where she had put out biscuits. The teakettle whistled on the stove. Domenica and John sat down at the table.

"Mother, I've received my orders."

"I see you're in your uniform. Where are you going?"

"I've been asked not to share that information."

"But I'm your mother."

"They ask us not to share details. This way, none are shared."

"I see. Does she know?" she said, without looking at Domenica.

"Yes, Mum."

"But you can't tell your mother?"

"No, Mum."

"What will she do?"

"I will continue to work as a nurse," Domenica offered.

"Mother, are you going to offer us tea?"

"There's the pot," Grizelle said, and left the room.

"Did I say something?" Domenica looked worried.

John stood and turned to his wife. "Stay here."

John went into the living room. His mother was not there. He looked through the screen door to the front porch. She wasn't there either. He climbed the steps to her bedroom. He rapped gently on the door. "Mother?"

She didn't answer.

John tried the door and pushed it open. His mother stood at the window. "Mother?"

"Get out of my house and never come back."

"But, Mother." John could see that she was pulling at her handkerchief nervously, with such resolve he was certain she would shred it.

"I told you not to come back to this house. You married behind my back. A Catholic. A Tally. You don't bring her around to meet me before you run off, but you bring her here now when there's nothing I can do to stop it? You expect me to accept this thing?"

"You did all you could to prevent this marriage. I came here to give you the opportunity to apologize."

"Do you realize they are rounding them up? They are sending the Tallies away because they are involved in all sorts of treachery. They cannot be trusted. They're dirty. They gamble, they sell liquor, they take jobs from our young men because in Scotland, swarthy is exotic. Well, you see how exotic they are as they are shipped out to sea as common criminals. Churchill didn't move fast enough, in my opinion."

"Mother."

"Their women are whores. Surely you know that."

"I will not have you speak against my wife. Glasgow is no longer safe for good people. It's you and your kind that are responsible for the violence."

"There are more people like me than you know."

"I don't doubt it. But I know for sure my father would be ashamed of you."

"Do you think that concerns me? He was a sneak. Who saw him? He was always at sea. And when he was home, he drank."

"He had good reason. He had a conniving wife. He would never open anyone's mail but his own. How could you do that? Do you know how much time we lost because of you?"

"I wish I would have burned them. But I couldn't destroy them knowing that someday, those letters might be all I had of you. But now I don't care. I am glad you found them! What the war does with you, it does with you. I lost you for good when you married her."

Domenica was waiting for her husband by the front door when he came back down the steps. He followed her out onto the porch.

"Let's go," he said, taking a look at the house for the last time. "I will never return to this house."

"She'll come around," his wife assured him. Domenica Cabrelli McVicars would see to it.

John held Domenica's hand as they took the trolley to the convent. She was stoic because she didn't want to upset her husband after his mother's rejection, and besides, what good would a display of emotion do now? Decisions were made by men who hadn't considered women like her. The trolley bell clanged as they disembarked. The expressions on the faces of the passengers on the platform waiting to board were as somber as the overcast sky.

"It's going to rain," Domenica said.

"Yup," he replied. "Miserable day."

"Your boots and rain gear are in the duffel. I ironed your shirts, and I tightened the buttons on your uniform. They were loose."

"I noticed." He tapped the buttons on his jacket. "Thank you."

They approached the entrance of the convent. She did not want to go inside the gate, and he did not want to leave her there. So, they stood and looked at each other, holding each moment like a jewel.

Domenica had held a rare six-carat star sapphire when she was girl. A middleman had brought it through her father's shop and allowed her to hold it. She remembered holding the rare gem so long, the gentleman had to ask her to return it to the lockbox. Domenica had not seen the color of that sapphire again until she met the captain, whose eyes were the same deep blue-green.

Domenica put her arms around her husband. He leaned into her embrace.

There was a place between Domenica's ear and shoulder, in the crook of her neck, that McVicars cherished. The scent of her lived there, roses and vanilla. He had found himself in that place every night since they married. When he woke in the morning, he was surprised that he had slept through the night in her arms. Before Domenica, he had been a fitful sleeper. He wondered if he would get a wink of sleep at all until they were together again.

"I don't want to go to sea," he said. "And it's the first time in my life I've dreaded it."

"You were afraid I'd take you from it."

"Now I wish you could."

"But you love the sea."

"Not as much as you."

"You know what, Captain McVicars? I almost believe you." Domenica stood back from him and examined his uniform. "Take your rest when you can."

"I will."

"And eat an orange whenever they offer them."

"I will."

"Be a peacemaker. Please stay safe." She made him promise. "And pray." Domenica reached into her pocket. "This will remind you." She showed John a gold medal on a chain. "This is Our Lady of Fatima. She will protect you." She reached up and clasped the medal around his neck. "Don't take it off."

John took his wife in his arms and kissed her goodbye. "The next time you see me, this horrible haircut will have grown out."

She laughed and waved him off.

As he walked down the drive to return to the trolley, which would take him into Glasgow to catch the train to Liverpool, which would deposit him on the pier where he would join the ranks and crew on the deck of the *Arandora Star*, John McVicars felt a pain in his heart. The last thing he heard was Domenica's laugh, which sounded like a bell.

CHAPTER 31

―――――――

Liverpool, England

June 15, 1940

McVicars stood on the gangway of the *Arandora Star* and looked up. He had witnessed the savage world and the cruelty of men as a sailor. He shuddered at the harpooning of a whale in the Aleutians and had nightmares about a brutal fight between two sailors, whereby one was thrown overboard to his death. He had experienced all manner of despair on the open sea, but he had never seen a ship desecrated in this fashion. The *Arandora Star* was wrapped in barbed wire. Shame washed over him as he reported for duty. Anger fueled his steps as he climbed to his cabin, located on the bridge at the top of the ship, where he had been assigned as first mate to assist the captain in the navigation of the *Arandora Star*.

McVicars unpacked his dress uniform and hung it in the closet of his cabin. He placed his shoes in the bin on the floor before closing the hatch. He looked out the porthole and saw nothing but blue. The waterway of Liverpool was clear. Fleets of ships were docked in the harbor, awaiting their assignments. One by one, they would eventually set sail on the open sea to fulfill their duty. McVic-

ars tapped the thick glass of the porthole before opening it. The
sash around the porthole was cherrywood. The details of the bindings and latch were elegant, polished brass, nothing but the finest
for the ocean liners of the Blue Star Line. It was obvious to McVicars that this was a deluxe ocean liner requisitioned by the government because of its size and capacity, but there was no hiding the
luxurious details of this tub. He imagined his honeymoon on a luxury liner. He was eager to find out where the ship was going because
when he knew that, he would know exactly how many days it would
be before he could return home to his wife. He had vague information. He had heard chatter that it was heading for Canada, but he did
not know the purpose of the crossing. As first mate, he had two
weeks to prepare the ship and organize the crew. He pulled the port
closed and went to find his superior on the deck outside.

As McVicars walked through the passageways of the ship, he
observed that tarps had been placed over the hand-painted murals
and the floor was covered in rubber mats, obscuring the polished
walnut parquet. The paint was so fresh, the scent of it filled the
ship. Dull military gray and bright white pigment replaced the
opulent silver and gold trim from the days when the *Arandora Star*
had sailed for pleasure.

"Reporting for duty, Captain Moulton." McVicars saluted the
captain. Moulton was an older gentleman with white hair, mutton-
chop sideburns, and a bit of egg on the chest placket of his uniform. *He had a traditional English breakfast*, McVicars thought to
himself, *because he's wearing it like the Legion of Honor medal.*

Moulton saluted McVicars. "I'm too old for this job." He smiled.
"Ten years ago I was too old for it."

"Sir, you look to be in excellent shape," McVicars fibbed.

"I'm in decent enough shape to steer this tub. They give the
exciting assignments to the younger men, as it should be. Explains
why you and I were assigned to the *Arandora*." Moulton laughed.

"Perhaps they need our wisdom, sir."

"For what? Hauling prisoners? When did the British government become prison wardens? I would not have accepted this assignment given a choice."

"Who are these prisoners?" McVicars asked.

"There are a few legitimate Nazis, and of course the German intellectuals and professors. Around five hundred of them altogether. Neither group supports England. The largest group will be composed of Italian Scots, and a few Italians from other provinces."

"Italian Scots?" McVicars blanched.

"Yes, boys to men age eighty. Around seven hundred thirty Tallies in total. The authorities are rounding them up, arresting them."

"What did they do?"

"There are concerns about the fifth column. We can't have spies among us. We're dropping them in St. John's, Newfoundland. They've got prison camps set up there."

"Why Canada? What about Orkney Island?"

"There's a boat for Orkney too," Moulton said.

McVicars had known many Britalians in his life before he met Domenica. Hadn't he just bought their wedding rings at Mattiuzzi's? "These enemy aliens are citizens. Just because they have an Italian surname doesn't mean they're loyal to Italy."

"The authorities can't tell a good Tally from a bad one, so they all have to go," Moulton explained. He looked over his reading glasses and peered at his first mate. "Why do you care, McVicars?"

"My wife is an Italian expat. Will she be forced to leave Scotland?"

"She should stay put for the duration. You want her to be safe."

McVicars decided he would send a ship's telegram to his wife as soon as the plans for the crossing were clear. This was not the merchant navy he loved, nor was it the Scotland he knew, but he would not agonize about the changes. McVicars's goal was to return home to his wife. Domenica loved him, that's all that mattered now.

LONDON

June 17, 1940

Ettore Savattini, the dapper maître d', sat down in the kitchen of the Savoy Hotel for a light breakfast before his workday began. He picked up a pan of steamed milk that foamed on the burner using a mopeen wrapped around the handle. He was pouring the creamy foam into the demitasse of espresso when a drop hit his patent leather loafer. He cursed, placed the pan on the stove, and swatted his shoe with the dish towel. He finished pouring the steamed milk into the cup, then returned the pan to the stove, turned up the flame under the burner, and threw a dollop of butter into the frypan before cracking two eggs into it. The whites of the eggs sizzled in the pan. Savattini cranked the pepper mill over the eggs as they cooked.

Savattini threw a fresh mopeen over his shoulder. He leaned against the counter, folded his arms over his chest, and took stock of his life. He had a wife back in Italy with a new baby. His mother was well. Savattini had sent enough money back to Italy to build a house in the hills outside of Firenze. The Savoy Hotel had just given him a raise. He was in a good place. Savattini slid the eggs out of the pan and placed them on a plate. He had set out a linen napkin and silver on the chef's table. The newspaper lay near the place setting. There was a loud knock at the hotel kitchen door. The milkman rarely pounded it with such ferocity. Savattini threw open the door.

Two policemen friends followed him into the kitchen. Chapman and Walker were regulars for dinner in the kitchen after their double shifts on Saturday evenings. The hotel had a good relation-ship with local law enforcement.

"Gentlemen. You're a bit early for your after-shift dinner."

"We apologize, Sav," Chapman began, and looked at his partner.

Savattini smiled. "For what?" Savattini knew well, through his contacts, that they were coming for him, but he wanted to hear the charges firsthand, a right surely still in place for all subjects of the king in England.

"All enemy aliens are to be deported immediately," Chapman explained.

Savattini lit a cigarette. He had been working in England for seventeen years. He lived in a small room at the hotel, worked seven days a week, and served the elite of London with distinc-tion. He was neither enemy nor alien but servant.

"Well, er, that's what they say you are," Walker explained. "We don't believe it."

"Of course you don't. Because it's not true." Savattini smiled. The maître d' had been in enough tight spots in his life to know there was no point in panicking now. He kept his emotions tucked neatly away, like his pocket squares. "Shall I call my barrister to meet me at the precinct?"

"Afraid not. We are putting you on a train to Liverpool."

"I'm not a shipbuilder, gentlemen."

"From there you will be dispatched to a prisoner of war camp. The prime minister wants all Italians off the island immediately."

Savattini nodded. There was no way out of this one. His moth-erland had shown loyalty to the wrong side, and now he would personally pay the marker.

"Forgive us," Walker said quietly. "We saw your name on the list and made sure it was friends who came to collect you, to make this as dignified as possible."

Savattini exhaled. "Before we go, may I finish my breakfast?"

Walker and Chapman sat down at the table. Savattini handed each man a linen napkin before pouring two cups of coffee. He served them and placed the sugar and creamer on the table when Savattini remembered an American guest he had served in the hotel years before. The American spoke of his own misfortune when he shared, *"The haves are the haves until they have not."* Now, Savattini understood the riddle. The maître d' sat down, snapped the linen napkin open, placed it on his lap, and ate the cold eggs.

MANCHESTER

Don Gaetano Fracassi looked up from the Communion railing as two policemen entered the back of Saint Alban's Church in Ancoats. They removed their hats and stood beside the holy water font, one on each side, resolute like the statues of Saint Peter and Saint Paul on the altar.

The priest continued to distribute Holy Communion to the communicants kneeling along the rail. An elderly parishioner served as altar boy. He was holding the paten when he looked up and saw the police. The gold paten held under the chin of a communicant began to tremble in his grasp.

After receiving the host, the communicants blessed themselves and returned to their pews. Fracassi brought the extra Communion wafers back to the altar. He placed the lid on the gold pyx and set it aside. He drank the remaining wine in the chalice and buffed it with the altar cloth. He folded the cloths neatly before placing the pyx filled with the consecrated hosts into the tabernacle.

Fracassi sat for the reflection, his back to the pews. After a while, he rose to give the final benediction. He blessed the parishioners, making the sign of the cross over them.

Fracassi usually led the recessional to the back of the church and greeted his flock as they dispersed. Instead he said, "My friends, I would like you to leave the church before me this morning."

The parishioners looked at one another, confused. They turned and saw the policemen in the back of the church.

"Do not be alarmed," the priest said kindly. "The gentlemen are only following orders."

Instead of exiting the church, the small group of parishioners lined up at the foot of the altar to express their gratitude. The priest blessed each one and advised them to be instruments of peace and leave the church without trouble. When the church was empty except for the priest and the policemen, Fracassi joined them.

"Don Fracassi, you are under arrest."

The priest nodded. He turned and genuflected to the altar. In his haste, he had left the tabernacle door open. The good Sisters would close it when they came for the altar linens.

GLASGOW

Amedeo and Piccolo Mattiuzzi were waiting on the sidewalk outside their shop to be collected by the police. They had packed one suitcase each, per the law. They wore their Sunday suits and shoes. Mattiuzzi wore the Borsalino hat his wife had given him on his last birthday. His son wore his father's old brown fedora, which was still in good shape.

Lester McTavish, their stout Scot neighbor who owned the emporium next door, joined them outside. "Best to be agreeable with these folks. You'll be back in no time. I'm talking to the authorities. Don't worry."

"Do you know where they're taking us?" Mattiuzzi asked.

"Isle of Man or one of the Orkney Islands."

"And for how long?" Piccolo asked.

"May be a week or two until they process the good Tallies from the bad."

"Two weeks," Mattiuzzi grumbled. "I don't have time for this nonsense. My business will suffer."

"I will help your wife however I can. She'll keep the place open, take orders until you return. Look at your arrest like a glitch. You'll take some sun, get some good rest, and the war will be over in no time," McTavish assured them. "At least it's summer."

Mattiuzzi's wife and daughter watched from the upstairs window. Mattiuzzi had been fearful that if the women waited with the men on the sidewalk, the police might have a second thought and take the women too.

Margaret Mary McTavish wrapped a proper shawl around herself as she closed the door of her father's shop and joined the men on the sidewalk.

"Hurry up, Margaret Mary," her father said as he surveyed the street from side to side. "They'll be here soon."

"Yes, Papa."

Piccolo followed Margaret Mary into Mattiuzzi's shop. "I wanted to say goodbye." She smiled.

Piccolo pulled her close and buried his face in the waves of her russet hair. He inhaled the familiar scent of jasmine. He kissed her tenderly. "When I come home, I'll talk to your father."

"You'd better." Margaret Mary gave his arm a playful slap before she covered her lover's face in kisses. When she saw her father turn toward the storefront out of the corner of her eye, she pushed Piccolo away. "Go on," she said.

"You cannot take your telescope, Arcangelo. There's no room," his wife, Angela, said as she arranged his suitcase for the last time.

"It will fit."

"No it won't. Cheese or a telescope? Eat or dream? Those are your choices. You can give up looking at the stars, but you can't starve. You're taking the cheese. I want to know you're eating. There's a long baguette."

"I'll be back in a day or two. That's too much bread and cheese."

"There'll be others who packed nonsense and forgot their cheese. You will see. You'll need extra. You'll thank me."

Antica stood across the bed he had shared with his wife for forty-seven years. "Yes, Angela. I will share the cheese. And the sausage."

"And the grappa."

"And even the grappa."

"There are three pair of socks. Three underpants—"

"Please. I understand, after all these years, how to dress in the morning."

"I want you to know what I've packed." She snapped the suitcase shut.

His wife left the bedroom. Antica held up the telescope he had made. He had fashioned the optical tube out of birch wood, which was soft enough to bend into a cylinder. The eyepiece and lens were made at the jeweler's. Mattiuzzi cut the glass and beveled the sides with a file. It had taken several tries to get it just right. Antica attached the lens, along with the focusing knob and the cradle. He mounted the telescope on the tripod he had built. Any night without rain would find him on the roof of his home in Glasgow, looking at the stars overhead.

He cocked his ear and listened for his wife. He removed the extra shirt and a pair of underpants to make room for the telescope. He placed the telescope next to the cheese and his socks and closed the suitcase.

"Arcangelo," she called out. "They're here." Angela's voice

broke. She waited at the bottom of the stairs for her husband. When he reached her, Angela put her arms around him and kissed him repeatedly.

"That's enough." He took his wife's face into his hands. "I'm coming back."

BURY

Savattini sat next to the window on the crowded train as it sailed through the English countryside. The morning had begun as a lark, but the situation had turned. Savattini had waited in a long line with his fellow Britalians before enough train cars showed up to transport them. He listened to the conversation of the British soldiers to glean information but was disturbed when he realized they knew less about this roundup than he did.

The train passed the horse track, familiar to Savattini, that had been converted into the base of prisoner operations. The train blew by the circus grounds; the elephants and tigers were long gone, and now, underneath the tent of orange stripes, German prisoners of war were housed until they could be shipped out to internment camps. The train buzzed with banter as the British Italians were quietly outraged at being compared to Nazis.

Don't they understand? Savattini thought to himself. *There are only two sides in a war. And just my luck, Italy is on the wrong side.* Savattini generally stayed away from the topic of politics, but like any other reasonable working man in Great Britain, he observed the fixed class system and had his opinions. You either served or were being served, not much in between.

Clothing factories had been converted to make military uniforms instead of skirts and blouses. Private homes had become recruitment centers, and public buildings were outfitted to create military hospitals. Where there had once been the production of wool and crystal and porcelain, now stood empty factories stripped of all equipment, waiting to be filled with enemy aliens. It wasn't only the government that wanted the Italian men and boys shipped out of the country; public opinion supported it. Where there had been children at their school desks, there were now prisoners locked in classrooms until arrangements could be made. Germans. Austrians. Italians. Nazis. Fascisti. Intellectuals. Suspects all, classified as enemy aliens.

Word spread quickly among the Italian Scots in their shops and restaurants about the pending arrests and subsequent deportation, tipped off mostly by their Scottish neighbors and friends. Most were so eager to show the English government how agreeable they could be, they packed ahead of time and waited on the curb to be taken away. There were a few who hid from the police but they would soon be found and join the rest.

The spiderweb of train tracks from points north and south converged outside Manchester. The tracks that ran along the river Irwell had not seen such a steady flow of locomotives pulling cars into the platforms outside Manchester since the mill had been in operation. When the men and boys arrived by train in Bury, they disembarked and found hundreds more men on the platform waiting to be processed.

The Italian prisoners of war had been rounded up from one end of England to the other. Herded into groups, the Britalians did not resist. They listened carefully and followed instructions issued by the guards, whose guns were held at the ready should there be trouble.

The abandoned fields by Warth Mills were an ideal location for a prison camp, according to the men who designed such things. The prisoners would be processed outdoors in cordoned-off stalls, herded single file like cattle for the slaughter. Once their names and personal information were recorded, they were admitted indoors to the mill. Two thousand men would fit in the makeshift barracks, though the number swelled to three thousand that day, and all still managed to squeeze into the abandoned cotton mill. Barbed wire fences surrounded the lot and building. Armed guards stood at the entrance.

As the prisoners filed inside, they found no chairs, benches, or beds, just a massive, filthy factory two acres deep. In the far distance, across the floor, was a group of prisoners who had arrived first and finished the task of sweeping the floor clean for the incoming. Word soon spread that they were professors and teachers from Oxford, men of the Jewish faith with roots in Germany and Austria who might be spies. The Britalians did not believe that these teachers were any more a threat to the English government than they were. But it didn't matter. They were the side without weapons.

The mill was dreary. The air was thick with the filaments from the cotton looms. There was grease on the floor, left behind from the machines, no doubt. Overhead, the glass panels of the skylights were so filthy you could not see through them. The glass was broken and cracked, allowing the elements inside. The walls crawled with black mold.

The prisoners were issued canvas sacks to fill with straw for their beds. Once they stuffed the sacks, the prisoners stood around and wondered what would come next. Boys sat on their duffels. Some men turned their suitcases upright and propped themselves upon them. The incoming prisoners circulated, looking for familiar faces in the crowd.

Confusion was the mother of fear, and the lack of information given to the prisoners fed their anxiety. No one had explained exactly why they had been brought to Warth Mills and where they were going.

Antica joined the line to pick up a canvas sack and straw to make a bed.

Mattiuzzi and his son, Piccolo, picked up their mess kits: a tin plate, bowl and cup, knife and fork. No food was offered with the empty plate.

Savattini entered the mill, having disembarked with the last load of men from the train station. Savattini tried to assess the situation as he looked at the behemoth mill, filled to capacity with men. He wondered where the kitchen was located.

Fracassi entered the mill several men behind Savattini. He had been brought to Warth Mills in an army truck with thirty other men, outfitted with benches that could seat only ten comfortably.

As Fracassi joined his fellow prisoners, he moved through the crowd dressed in his long black cassock and Roman collar. The internees stood out of respect, creating a path for the priest to pass. They bowed their heads and murmured greetings to the old priest. Fracassi nodded, acknowledging the men until he made it through the crowd to the far end of the mill.

Savattini walked through the mill, searching for familiar faces, knowing that the most important aspect of a maître d's duties was to make connections. His eyes fell upon a group under a window, three men who had formed a circle. This looked like the group for him. He needed a drink and they were sipping grappa. Savattini reached into his pocket to count his cigarettes. He had exactly thirteen left, which would get him through to the morning.

"Gentlemen," Savattini said as he joined Antica, Mattiuzzi, and Piccolo. "Where are you from?"

"Glasgow." Piccolo extended his hand, introduced himself and the others.

"No, I meant in Italy. Where are your people from?"

Antica lit up. "Bardi. Do you know it?"

"I'm from Emilia-Romagna too. From the hills."

Antica made room on his suitcase. "Sit, sit."

Savattini sat. "What do you make of this?" He drew a circle in the air with his cigarette.

"I served in the Great War," Mattiuzzi offered, "and there's nothing about this that makes any sense at all."

"They arrested me in the hotel kitchen. I was starting my day as I always do."

"I never met a cook who wore patent leather shoes." Mattiuzzi offered the men taralles, savory biscuits his wife had made.

Savattini laughed and helped himself to a tarelle. "I'm the maître d' at the Savoy. I live in the hotel. I observed plenty in my time there, and I figured they arrested me because I knew a thing or two about the gambling that goes on in the salon there. Half of Churchill's cabinet sits in on the games."

"Write to him," Antica said. "If you know the man, write to him and tell him this is a terrible mistake."

"Let them play their games. This is a message for Mussolini and nothing more. Churchill cannot tolerate spies and sacrificed the Italians to make a point."

"But we are not the enemy. We are loyalists!" Mattiuzzi insisted.

"It's almost impossible to prove one's loyalty. It's a lot like love, it can only be proved in reciprocity," Savattini explained.

Antica poured Savattini a cup of grappa. The tin cup was regulation, issued by the British navy. Savattini thanked him and swirled the liquor inside the cup. He sipped the grappa. It burned his throat before the warmth spread through his body.

"A man used to drinking from crystal won't like the taste of the metal cup," Antica said.

"It doesn't matter what I like now, gentlemen, or what I'm used to; it's about what I can endure." Savattini looked around the mill. "What *we* can endure. I'm happy to make new friends."

Fracassi had spent the evening comforting the prisoners. The following morning, he found a corner and set up a makeshift altar on his suitcase. The altar cloth, chalice, paten, and pyx were placed on the suitcase as they would be on the marble altar at Saint Alban's in Ancoats. The police had been kind enough to let him pack the essentials of his trade in the rectory before putting him on a train to Warth Mills. Fracassi opened his prayer book and made the sign of the cross. A few men removed their hats and joined him.

Word spread through the mill that the priest was saying Mass. "Let's pray," Mattiuzzi said, and turned to the altar. Savattini was skeptical. He whispered to Antica, "My faith is in the farmer who churns the butter for my scampi." Savattini believed it until the chatter in the mill fell away, until a reverent silence set in and the only voice that could be heard inside the mill was Fracassi's.

"Gentleman, it may appear, in the situation that we're in, that we are helpless. But I assure you, God is listening."

Antica leaned in to hear the message. Piccolo Mattiuzzi put his hands on his father's shoulders. Savattini pulled a cigarette out of his case. He looked to the altar and sheepishly returned it to the case. He, too, listened to the priest.

Fracassi continued. "He will not forsake you. He will not abandon you. But you must pray. God knows your heart. Saint Bernard of Clairvaux was the wise doctor of the faith. He encouraged us to reflect on the past. Make peace with it. You cannot control the evil done to you. You cannot turn back and right the good left undone. You cannot make up for the time wasted. But you can earn your salvation. Open your heart to His love. All is forgiven. We find strength in our confession. And we need it, gentlemen. We need it."

Antica shivered when he heard Fracassi's words. Did the priest know something?

"Forgive me, my brothers, I don't have enough wafers to give each of you Holy Communion. When I was collected at the church yesterday, I brought only the essentials."

It did not matter to the men. They knelt for the consecration.

Antica opened his suitcase. He smiled at the thought of his wife, who had insisted he take the bread for his journey. Even in this instance, she was right. Antica tapped the man kneeling in front of him and handed him the bread. The man nodded and tapped the man in front of him, giving him the bread to pass forward, and so it went, until it was passed through the crowd and made it to Fracassi's altar. Fracassi thanked the men for the bread and proceeded with the Mass. He prayed over Antica's donation and consecrated it. Fracassi broke the bread and invited the men to take Communion. A prisoner in the front row stood to serve as altar boy. Others became ushers and helped organize the rows of communicants in an orderly fashion, so Fracassi might serve every man in Warth.

Fracassi began to distribute Communion to the men closest to the altar. He broke a few crumbs, placed one on the tongue of the first prisoner, then another and another. Each communicant made the sign of the cross before returning to his knees. By the time the priest reached Antica in the back, there was a small piece of the consecrated bread left.

"You provided the bread?"

Antica nodded.

"Thank you."

Antica kept his head down. He hadn't been to church since the incident that ruined his hand. "I'm not worthy, Father."

"You are worthy, my brother."

Fracassi waited. He placed the consecrated host, a crumb of bread so small the priest had to pinch it between his thumb and forefinger, on Antica's tongue. Antica tasted the bread of life and felt redeemed.

At night, the mill heaved with a sound reminiscent of the breath of a whale as the men slept on their straw sacks. Moonlight streamed through the broken skylights. Antica sat against the wall on his straw bed. He couldn't sleep. He looked out over the vast factory floor. The round contours of the men's bodies in repose in the dark reminded him of the harvest season on his father's farm outside Bardi, Italy, when he was a boy. Antica would watch his father from the farmhouse window as he walked the field in the moonlight. His father would caress the wheat and whistle. For anything to grow in this world, you had to first love it. Antica wondered if he would ever see anything grow again. He would have to survive this, but deep in his soul, Antica was not sure it was possible.

CHAPTER 32

JULY 1, 1940

After a two-week stay, the internees of Warth Mills were ordered to pack. Savattini decided to shave before the transfer. He used the basin the four men had shared, foamed up the brush, and carefully shaved his beard. He cleaned the implements and packed them away in a leather travel case. He put on his cleanest shirt and tie. He snapped the cuff links into place. The jewels shimmered in the light.

"Are those rubies or garnets?" Mattiuzzi asked.

"You're the jeweler, you tell me."

"I need a loupe. My eyes aren't so good anymore."

"You'll have to take my word for it, then. They're rubies."

"Do you know where they're from?"

Savattini shrugged. "Does it matter?"

"Only if you want to sell them someday. The best rubies are from India."

"Didn't I tell you? These rubies are from India."

They shared a laugh.

As the prisoners lined up to be taken to the train that would deposit them at their final destination, they found out that they were going on foot.

The polished shoes, pressed shirts, and well-cut suits they'd worn upon arrival were shabby. Their suitcases were lighter, after they had consumed the wine, cured meats, and cheese their wives and mothers had packed for them. They were two weeks into their internment, and three days into being hungry again. Mattiuzzi turned to his son, Antica, and Savattini and whispered, "Stick together."

The single-file line of rumpled men snaked out of the mill and into the street, extending all the way to the railway station in Bury.

"They're putting us on a train," Piccolo whispered quietly.

The Britalians were loaded into train cars, which would transport them to Liverpool. The prisoners said little on the trip that lasted less than an hour. When they arrived in Liverpool, they disembarked the train in silence. The men and the boys were herded into two lines that led them to the gangplank of the *Arandora Star*.

They stood in the shadow of the ship's enormous hull. Her dual smokestacks, now painted gray, appeared to be the size of two cuff links.

Savattini surveyed the grandeur, which lifted his spirits. "Boys, this is a luxury liner."

"At least it will be safe," Mattiuzzi exhaled.

"The Blue Star Line," Savattini confirmed, knowledgeable of its previous reputation and splendor. "The food will be better on this ship," he said to them, half joking. "I will see to it."

"I was sick of Warth. I don't care where they take us," Piccolo said.

"You should care. We aren't the only prisoners on this ship," Savattini said as he climbed the gangway. "Non guardare in alto. Tedeschi." Looming overhead on the second tier above the waterline, behind barbed wire, were German prisoners of war. They glared at the Italians as they boarded. The word soon spread down the line that the Italian Scots, loyal British subjects, were considered as dangerous as the Nazis.

"We don't even get our own bloody ship." Mattiuzzi sighed. "We are forced to sail with the German riffraff."

"This is an awfully large rig to transport us to the British Isles," Piccolo noted.

"The old girl, she was a beauty in her time," Savattini marveled as he stepped onto the deck and into the ship. The vestiges of the ship's previous life as a luxury liner could not be completely obscured. Her wide decks and corridors were stately. The lines of her hull and mast were architectural and sleek.

"She's not so handsome wrapped in barbed wire," Mattiuzzi said.

British soldiers were lined up on either side of the entrance hall, holding their rifles close. The prisoners formed a single-file line between the soldiers and proceeded aft, to the stairs that led them down to their quarters.

"Tallies to the bottom," the purser barked. "Padre, step aside and wait."

Fracassi did as instructed.

"Italians in steerage. Naturally," Antica joked as they descended the narrow stairs into the bottom of the ship that held the boiler room, the coal carriage, and the crew cabins. The temperature rose as the men went deeper into the ship. The smell of oil and coal burning in the furnace wafted through the passageway.

Savattini led the men into the first cabin at the foot of the stairs, farthest from the boiler room. They were housed below the waterline, so there would be no light or fresh air. The portholes were sealed shut. They placed their luggage on the cots and began to remove their jackets and ties against the heat.

"Four men in a room built for two."

"That's about right." Piccolo reclined on a cot.

The men had grown close at Warth. They shared information, bread, and shaving soap. The unlikely quartet had spent time discussing their options, even though as prisoners, they had none. The men's trepidation about the transfer had exhausted them. The tight quarters and the heat made them drowsy. They lay on their cots, barely an inch between them. It was not yet evening but sleep was their only reprieve from their suffering. But *too* much sleep made a man soft, Savattini reminded them. They woke to the sound of a sentry shouting.

"Captain has given permission for prisoners to go up on the deck."

Savattini stood in the doorway and peered down the passageway. Every cabin was filled with prisoners. If the men stepped out into the hallway at the same time, there would be gridlock. Savattini called out, "Gentlemen, let's begin with the cabin closest to the boiler. Latrine is at the end of the companionway. Stairs take you up to the deck. Let's do this in an orderly fashion."

"Aye, aye, Captain," one of the Britalians shouted out. The men laughed and followed Savattini's suggestion. As the cabins emptied out, Savattini saw boys as young as sixteen and men as old as seventy file past.

"Now we're dead last to get up to the deck," Piccolo complained.

"We are building goodwill. Trust me. We'll need it later," Savattini told them.

"What I'd give for a cuppa Mazawattee tea," Antica said. "Hot. Proper tea in a Lady Carlyle cup and saucer."

"I'd rather have a beer." Piccolo swabbed the sweat off his face.

"My mother taught me, when it's hot, don't think cool, think hotter and then you'll cool off," Antica offered.

"Go on," Savattini said. "Dream."

"I've got my tea. A sweet trolley arrives with a tower of biscuits, sandwiches, and chocolates. I pick up the little silver tongs and help myself to a sugar-dusted brioche. Pot of fresh butter churned that morning to dress it. I close my eyes and inhale the steam from the teacup. Madagascar. Sri Lanka. The islands," Antica mulled.

McVicars entered their cabin. "Well, well, well. The west end Glaswegians!"

"McVicars! You old dog!" Antica stood to greet his old friend.

"How did you find us?"

"I saw you on the list," McVicars said cheerily, but when he took in the cramped berth, his heart sank. He could not stand fully upright in the cabin; he slouched as he spoke to them. This was no way to treat human beings, no way to treat his friends.

"Ettore Savattini." A man McVicars didn't recognize extended his hand toward him.

"He's our new friend," Antica explained. "Maître d' at the Savoy Hotel."

"I wish we could offer you better accommodations here." McVicars shook his hand.

"They are acceptable. And we thank you for checking on us."

"Look how handsome you are in your merchant navy uniform, Captain," Antica exclaimed.

"I'm first mate this go-round. Captain in memory only, I'm afraid."

McVicars poked his head out into the hallway, checking right to left. The line to the latrine and up to the deck flowed steadily. He closed the door.

McVicars opened his jacket and from the interior pockets produced a sleeve of biscuits, a hunk of cheddar cheese, and two pasties—half-moon-shaped meat pies stuffed with potato and onion, baked in a crust, and wrapped in cloth. The men passed the food around. McVicars reached behind and produced a flask of whiskey from his back pocket. He put his finger to his lips.

"You're a saint!" Antica whispered. "I don't have the constitution for the sea any longer. A shot of whiskey will help settle my stomach."

"When you take that shot later, toast your old friend. I'm a married man now," McVicars told him. "Married the Cabrelli girl."

"Auguri! I met her at the convent at Christmas. Bellissima."

"She told me about it." McVicars had the notion that feeding the Italians would please Domenica. He rummaged through his pockets and produced a stick of butter. "For your bread in the morning. Don't let anyone know that you have it. I've seen mutinies for less. They serve coffee and plain rolls for breakfast. The coffee is strong but there's plenty of cream to cut it. The butter helps on the rolls. I will get you moved above the waterline. Give me time."

Savattini clapped his hands together and rubbed them as he schemed. "Will you tell them I can cook?"

"What's your best dish?"

"All of them. Eggs. Potatoes. Roasts. Spaghetti! I just need a little water and flour."

"I will alert the galley crew, sir." McVicars looked out into the corridor. "I must go."

"John, can you tell us where they're taking us?" Antica gripped McVicars's arm.

McVicars patted Antica's hand to reassure him. "Canada. Seven to ten days in the crossing. Sometimes these tubs take longer, so don't hold me to it."

The Italian faces fell into despair.

"Now, now. Don't fret. I'm on board." McVicars smiled. "There will be more biscuits! And I will get you out of here." John McVicars left the men better than he found them.

"I will sleep well tonight," Mattiuzzi admitted as he savored his last bite of the meat pie. "The pasty is the pride of Scotland."

"They are quite good," Savattini admitted. "I wish I would have visited the Highlands. I worked seven days a week. I never left London."

The men passed the small whiskey bottle around. Antica took a swig. "How could something this perfect not be Italian?"

"Because the Scots invented hard liquor. Give them their due. It might help us. Right now, you can do no worse than to be an Italian or a descendant of one," Mattiuzzi concluded. "The Nazis over our heads are treated better. They get the light and the air."

"No charges have been made against us. They arrested us without cause." Piccolo was determined to seek justice. "This is a mistake and they will realize it."

"They may not. Churchill takes lunch at the Savoy occasionally. Pleasant gentleman. One of his cabinet members, a mediocre gambler, never missed Blackjack Wednesdays or the free refills on the table. He told me that the threat of the fifth column was real. From the start, there was a plan to lock up the Italians in England for the duration of the war. Well, they couldn't bloody well do that, so they rounded us up to ship us off the island entirely. It does not matter to them if we are innocent; if you are from Italy, you are not to be trusted. I gently suggested that if Churchill banished us, there would be no ice cream or pizza for the duration of the war. I was joking of course, but he wasn't. Churchill made the order. He said, 'Collar the lot of them.' We are those men. We're the lot. Right or wrong, we've been collared."

"If we keep a good attitude, we'll be all right," Mattiuzzi assured them. "We'll follow their orders and we'll be home soon enough."

"If we stay close to your friend McVicars, we'll be even better," Savattini promised.

🌀

A man could sleep when he had hope.

Mattiuzzi, Piccolo, and Savattini slept soundly on their cots in their undershorts and undershirts, certain the worst was behind them. As the *Arandora* followed Moulton's route, she sailed north past the Isle of Man, through the North Channel between the Mull of Kintyre and Northern Ireland, and past Malin Head due west. By morning, the ship would be on the Atlantic Ocean heading for Canada, where they would be interned until the conflict was resolved.

Antica turned over on his cot. The room beneath the waterline suffocated the peddler. He slipped off the cot, and without making a sound, he dressed. He grabbed his telescope and tiptoed out the open door of the cabin. He gulped fresh sea air as he climbed the steps to the deck. As soon as he felt the cold ocean breeze, all apprehension left him. Fellow prisoners propped against the wall snored blissfully as they slept. Antica stood at the railing behind the barbed wire and breathed deeply.

There was a space between the barbed wire thorns and the deck overhead. It might have been just a foot or so, but it was enough space for Antica to angle the telescope lens through the mesh to observe the dark sky unobstructed. He counted the prongs of Orion and moved the lens across to find Venus and Jupiter, a pair of twinkling agates in a peacock-blue sky. His despair left him in the presence of such majesty.

Antica took the configuration of the stars as a sign that all would be well. There was a certain amount of relief, especially after McVicars promised them he would take care of them. He knew the

Scot was trustworthy. Antica yawned and lay down on the deck, cradling the telescope in his arms. The barbed wire fencing was a few inches from his nose, but it didn't bother him. He had made his peace with being imprisoned. In time, it would be proved that the hundreds of men with roots in Italy were decent, hardworking men with good families to support. The truth was as bright as the moon, and soon everyone would know it. Antica yawned again. The air off the coast of Ireland was clean and sweet. Antica went to sleep.

The *Arandora Star* was heavy with men, from the hull to the bridge. She sailed peacefully. The surface of the sea barely rippled as she passed the northwest coast of Ireland at dawn. The rocky cliffs of the Emerald Isle turned golden as morning broke. John McVicars stood at the top of the ship, on the bridge, and lit a cigarette.

DONEGAL

July 2, 1940

At the bottom of the sea, U-47, a German U-boat, kicked up fins of sand as it rose off the ocean floor along the coast of northern England. The U-boat was the pride of the German fleet, with its modern equipment and expertly trained naval crew. The U-boat had the ability to creep low and dive deep in seconds, its movement undetected in the depths.

Kapitänleutnant Günther Prien pursed his thin lips as he studied the route back to the Black Sea. He checked the numbers on the navigation panel when he spied an ocean liner crossing his path. He took a sip of bitter black coffee and spit it back into the cup before setting it aside. He checked his navigation wheel and discerned that the *Arandora Star* was unaccompanied, sailing in the open sea like the *Queen Mary* on Christmas holiday. He couldn't quite believe his luck, but the English were idiots, by his calculation, so he wasn't surprised that the ship sailed alone. Over 1,700 men, most of them prisoners of war, were defenseless against any enemy. He knew that there were fellow German nationals, loyal Nazis, on board and he didn't care. The Jewish intellectuals on board meant nothing to him. There were 719 Scots of Italian descent, British citizens, and Prien was eager to take them down because he *could*.

Prien had one torpedo left in his arsenal on his return trip to the Black Sea from a practice round of deadly attacks in the North Atlantic. It would be personally gratifying to blow up a pretty ocean liner. He also wanted to make a point to the enemies of Germany: *You will not know the day, you will not know the hour. But* I *will*, Prien thought with a sneer.

Prien took his time targeting the *Arandora*. The Nazi did his calculations several times.

When he ordered the move to fire, he was only half certain he could hit the ship at all.

One torpedo. One unaccompanied 15,500-ton ship in the open sea. One shot.

Prien issued the command to fire. The lone torpedo was packed with powdered aluminum and hexanite set in beeswax, which held the explosives in the chamber. The massive steel cylinder, once fired, propelled through the water toward its mark. The torpedo drilled into the hull of the *Arandora Star*, splitting it open as it blasted into the boiler and ruptured, shattering the electrics and the mechanical grid.

Prien grinned, his dark smirk smeared like an ink stain across his face. The German crew erupted in applause as the *Arandora Star* expelled clouds of black oil into the ocean, until the ship was obscured in the pitch.

Prien ordered the U-boat to change course, before his deed was discovered. His U-boat slithered down to the ocean floor like a snake and headed south. He shouted to his men to run U-47 deep, slip around Portugal, and glide through the Italian channels, which were friendly to him.

McVicars had thrown his cigarette overboard and was on his way to the galley for his morning coffee when he heard a rumble followed by a loud blast. The ship rocked from side to side. He lost his footing and grabbed the railing. McVicars was uncertain why a ship with full ballast tanks would pitch from side to side. He slid to the companionway to make his way down to the electrics to assess the problem.

The attack triggered the emergency sirens, shattering the serenity of the early morning. The Italian prisoners poured out of their tiny cabins and stuffed themselves into the narrow passageways in the belly of the ship. The ship was so overloaded with passengers, there was no room for them to move. Soon the men mobilized, and in a reasonable fashion, one by one, they took their turns climbing the stairs to the third deck. Those who had spent the night on the deck instinctively reached for the life jackets on the wall and began to hand them out to the bewildered men who joined them from below.

Above them, on the second tier, comfortably above the waterline, some of the Nazi prisoners reacted quickly and broke through the hatches to climb up to the top tier, the bridge, where the decks were not encased in barbed wire. They loaded into the lifeboats quickly and efficiently. The Nazis who were trapped on the second tier stomped on the fingers of the Italians who attempted to climb up to the second tier to board the boats. On the top tier, the Nazis made fast work of dropping lifeboats to the surface. They paddled off with the lifeboats half empty.

McVicars climbed down the emergency ladders all the way to the hull to coordinate the lifeboats for the Italians. The prisoners had gathered on the deck, with more men trapped in the companionway and the passageway below. Some were fully dressed; others were in their undershirts and shorts. Most were barefoot. McVicars directed them to the lifeboats. The sentries arrived and began to hand out life jackets. McVicars scanned the deck for his friends, but there was no sign of them.

Through the barbed wire mesh, the Italians could see the Nazi prisoners launching lifeboats off the side of the upper tier. The lifeboats lowered past them to the surface of the water, guided by the German puppeteers overhead. Whoever controlled those ropes determined who would be saved. The Italians began to grab at the lifeboats as they went past, as though their rubber handles were brass rings that could change their luck. They cut themselves as they reached through the barbed wire thorns, lacerating their hands, arms, and faces as they fought to escape. Others took the stairs and followed the Germans to the top tier.

"Son of a bitch," Savattini muttered as he slipped a life jacket over his dress shirt and pants and pulled the waist cord tightly. Mattiuzzi and Piccolo pulled on their life jackets. The sentries funneled the Italians through the holes they had hacked in the barbed wire to clear the way for prisoners to jump and save themselves, but clearly there was no guarantee of that. The irony that the soldiers ordered to transport the prisoners to their Canadian prison camp were now authorized to set them free was not lost on Savattini.

"Where's Antica?" Mattiuzzi shouted over the mayhem.

"He wasn't below," Piccolo hollered.

"I'll look for him."

Piccolo turned around and grabbed the chest straps of his father's life jacket. "You can't, Papa. You can't go back! You can only move up."

"I will find him," Savattini shouted. "Secure a lifeboat!"

The ship shook as the boiler and furnace imploded, knocking the men on the decks over. The storage hull caught fire. Smoke from the burning carcasses of beef stored in the refrigerated vaults made it nearly impossible to breathe. Mattiuzzi looked back as the smoke billowed up the stairs of the companionway and engulfed the lower deck. Filaments of orange, burning embers from the fire below, sizzled in the thick air. If Antica was below, he would not survive the fire.

Savattini hurled himself into the smoke and called for Antica. He circled around the deck, grabbing the barbed wire because he could not see. He pierced his hands and cursed. The sentry shouted, directing the men to go up the stairs. Savattini made the sign of the cross for his friend and looked for a way to save himself. He climbed the stairs to the second deck.

"Move!" the sentries shouted as they pushed the Italians wearing life jackets through the wire. The recitation of the rosary could be heard as the Italians jumped. They remembered the miracle at Fatima and called on the Blessed Mother to save them. When no miracle was revealed, the men called to their own mothers as they jumped. Many would break their necks and backs as they hit the water before sinking into their cold tombs.

The fire in the boiler raged and was soon followed by the flood. Black oil leached from the boiler, feeding the flames, which set the remaining ballast tanks loose. Fire ignited on the surface of the seawater that surged in the passageways. The smoke blew off the decks and out over the ocean in charcoal clouds so thick they blocked the sun.

In the darkness that blanketed the *Arandora*, the prisoners and crew who remained on the ship froze in terror. The rumble of explosions deep in the hull were followed by the crash of steel beams ripping apart. As the smoke lifted on the outer decks, prisoners ran to the edge of the ship as the *Arandora* lumbered onto its side. For any man who hadn't made it to the lifeboats or escaped into the sea, the glug of seawater as the *Arandora* slowly capsized was the sound of time running out.

Antica stood against the railing on the far end of the lower deck as the last of the men scrambled up the stairs through the hatch. He had already made his decision. He reacted to the chaos in a state of calm. A man who has reached three score and ten has lived a full life and fulfilled the biblical promise. Let the others save themselves.

"There are holes in this one," an Italian prisoner shouted, unable to inflate a lifeboat. "È inutile! Accidenti ai Tedeschi!" A lifeboat full of Nazis paddled away from the ship. An Italian threw a chair at them through a hole in the barbed wire. "Die!" he shouted as he climbed the companionway to try to find another way to save himself. Antica, a few prisoners, and the sentries guiding them to jump were the only men left on the lower deck. Antica slipped away from them and found a spot where he could be alone.

Antica had dreamt that night of the accident in the marble quarry that had maimed him for life. When he was jolted awake by the explosion of the Nazi torpedo, it had sounded eerily like the quarry blast that disfigured his hand. At twenty years old, Antica took the job of setting off the dynamite because it paid the highest wage in the marble quarry. Young Antica was fearless. *Hunger gives you cour-*

age, Antica believed. Earlier in the morning on the day of the accident, Antica had prepared the explosives. He measured and loaded the cylinder with powder, placed the capsule inside, and inserted the long wick, careful to pintuck the paper tube closed around the rim of the tube as though he were pinching the edge of a piecrust. It was all so routine. Antica was placed in a rig and lowered down the sleek rock wall of black marble to place the cylinder and light it.

Antica methodically stuffed the explosives in a shell hole dug out of the wall by a fellow quarrier, who had cut the nesting holes from the bottom to the top of the quarry wall.

The crew overhead watched in horror as the explosives blew before Antica had a chance to light it. The blast took two fingers off his right hand. He temporarily lost hearing in both ears. Antica never found out why the explosive went off before he lit it. He surmised it might have been a piece of ash from a cigarette from the workers on the ledge overhead, where the men were planing marble. Or, it was a dangerous methane level in the quarry that triggered spontaneous combustion. He would never know.

Antica's mother had been waiting for him when he returned home. Attempting to lift his spirits, she said, "Be grateful to God. You still have three fingers. They will remind you of the Holy Trinity." Antica would understand when he became a father that his mother's reaction, which hurt him at the time, was for his own good. She did not want her son to wallow in self-pity for all he had lost. When his mother died, he found out she had wept about the accident every night for the rest of her life.

Antica had believed that no woman would ever love him, damaged as he was. Later he found great love in the arms of Angela Palermo, who couldn't have cared less about the injury and agreed to marry him. They had six children—five daughters and one son—who gratefully had gone to America to work with his cousin and avoided the roundup. The thought of his children made him smile. He was slipping his right hand into his pocket when the strangest sensation occurred. He felt the phantom fingers and their touch return. His hand felt whole as it had when he was young, before the accident.

Antica understood explosives. A torpedo was a steel version of the dynamite tube he created to blast the rock in the quarry. He could only guess the power of the military bomb, but he was certain the torpedo that hit the ship would sink it.

Antica calculated that the *Arandora* had a few minutes left before it sank into the ocean. He was not the only man on board with that notion, as the prisoners jockeyed to jump now that the lifeboats were filled. A few prisoners who had not made it to the upper decks were scrambling around him, desperately looking for a way off the ship. At his age, Antica could not help them. The burden of the decision to jump was not to be made by an old man, but by the men who had something to live for.

It was odd to surrender when he had done nothing but fight his whole life. Antica would never see his family again. He would never see Scotland again. He would never take that last trip home to Bardi. How strange to know that those long-held dreams would, for certain, never come true. Soon Antica felt emancipated from the craving for something he could never have. The struggles of life were no longer his problems. Antica observed the grand finale of the horrible attack, as the young men dove off the side of the ship one by one, like acrobats into the water. A teenage boy did a swan dive, which in itself was a work of art as he broke the surface of the water without creating a ripple. A white ring of foam appeared, followed by his head through it, as though it had been a stunt, the curtain call of a seaside circus act. The boy opened his mouth wide and gulped air. Antica whispered, "Breathe."

Antica looked up at the morning sky. Free of the barbed wire walls, he could take in the expanse of it. He did not see a single cloud. The sky was an odd color, the patina of slate. The sky did not appear bright as in a Bellini or Tiepolo painting but fractured like a mosaic, made of tesserae, shards of glass, pieces of ceramics, and smashed bits of stone, shattered elements that find beauty anew even in their broken state. He wondered if this particular sky was the blue portal of purgatory. He closed his eyes and recited the Hail Mary. He made the sign of the cross slowly. His mother had said in times of trouble, pray to the Blessed Lady; like any mother, she would hear your plea. The men who had saved themselves by diving into the ocean and the men who had found a seat on the lifeboats called for their mothers as they jumped. So, what his mother had told Antica as a boy was true. He whispered to his mother to meet him in the sky when his moment came.

"Come on, old man." A sentry, his face covered in the oil from the boiler, carried a spare life jacket covered in sludge in his hand and attempted to put Antica into it. "She's going under," he said matter-of-factly, as though ships of this grandeur sank every day.

"I'm all right." Antica wriggled his arm loose. "They need you." He pointed overhead to the second tier. The sentry left the life jacket with Antica and climbed the stairs.

An Italian boy ran past Antica to take the stairs. He stopped. "Andiamo!"

Antica smiled. He handed the boy the life jacket the sentry had given to him.

"Put it on," Antica suggested.

The boy slipped on the life jacket. "Come with me," the boy said. "I will help you!"

"You go!" Antica pointed to the hole in the barbed wire. "Don't worry about me. I'll meet you in the water." The boy jumped into the sea.

Antica looked over the railing. The boy bobbed in the water. He had made it! He had his whole life before him.

Antica searched the surface of the sea for his friends. There were so many men in the water, he could not discern faces. A man was only as lucky as the friends he had made. Their fate, your fate. In this regard, Antica, even in the hour of his death, felt blessed. He had not been chained or beaten as a prisoner. He had not starved to death. The ice cream peddler had gone to sleep the night before having enjoyed a meat pie followed by a shot of whiskey with his friends. Antica had even managed the rare feat of grown men and made a new friend in Savattini. Even the burden of his salvation had been lifted. Don Fracassi had given him absolution. His soul was as pristine as an altar cloth of white linen.

Who was Antica to complain? He was slightly befuddled at the odd turn his life had taken and so quickly, but it was all right. There was nothing to fear because Antica knew how his life would end. There was nothing left but surrender, and there was no pain in that. Antica, the Italian-born immigrant, had thrived in Scotland. The streets of Glasgow had crackled with life: his life. He knew the names of the children on his route and took delight when he rang the bell and they came running for a dish of ice cream. He made a living, enough to provide for his family. His children were hard workers and his wife had been a faithful and loving partner. It had been a good life. Gratitude filled his heart like warm honey.

"You deaf, old man? Jump!" the sentry cried from his perch on the landing above Antica.

The old man pretended to be deaf. Antica tucked the homemade telescope under his arm like a spare umbrella on a cloudy day.

He gripped the railing and waited for the *Arandora Star* to capsize. "You will not know the day, you will not know the hour," the Scripture taught. Antica smiled, because in fact he knew the day and the hour, because he was living inside of it. That too was a gift at the end.

Antica looked down at his feet. The deck, painted white, was now black and roiling with a sludge that had bubbled up from the bilge. The stench, similar to the pungent smell of a blacksmith's barn when the horses were shoed with iron, made him dizzy. Fire would have engulfed the ship if it were not sinking quickly into the water. It was either the *Titanic*'s fate or the destruction of the temple on Good Friday—Antica believed the tragedy of the *Arandora Star* was both.

Sound fell away.

The men's cries for their mothers became muffled as the survivors paddled farther away from the sinking ship.

Antica was alone on the lower deck. The boilers rumbled, shaking the deck floor beneath him. The thick red arrows painted on the walls to indicate the upward direction of the stairs disappeared as the black sludge crept up the wall.

The last of the lifeboats careened in the distance over the waves, so tightly packed with men, only a few could loosen their arms to paddle the boat away from the capsizing ship. The small rafts made zigzags in the water as the waves carried them off. The men for whom there had been no room in the lifeboats clung to any object made of wood that had snapped off the ship's décor or slid off the deck into the ocean as the ship tilted. Antica could see a long wooden banister, a tabletop, and the back of a cane chair—all had human life attached to them in some fashion. The survivors, their desperate faces lifted to the light, looked like a field of sunflowers following the sun.

The seawater was up to Antica's knees.

Antica sat down on the deck, placing his hands by his sides to steady himself. The cacophony of the ship's contents crashing as the boat tipped over made Antica's heart pound faster.

The water crept up to Antica's chest and neck. As the *Arandora Star* sank into the Atlantic, Arcangelo Antica did not hold his breath, nor did he call for help or panic; instead, he let the ocean take his life from him. The water was cold, but Antica did not feel it. He let go.

McVicars and the crew stood behind Captain Moulton. Don Fracassi emerged from the hatch to join them. His black cassock dragged on the floorboards, soaked with oil from the lower decks. He had blessed the men before they jumped to save themselves. For the Italians, the last words many heard before dying were a prayer in their native language. The priest managed a smile for McVicars, who made his hand into a fist in solidarity with the priest. "Coraggio," Fracassi said to McVicars as he took his place with the crew on the bridge. Moulton moved to look over the side of the ship.

"Jump!" Moulton shouted to a boy who clung in fear to the nets on the side of the ship, tears covering his face.

The captain reassured the boy: "Don't be afraid, son! You can do it! Jump!"

The boy jumped into the sea. Moulton returned to his position with the men.

John McVicars stood tall as the *Arandora Star* sank into the ocean. The crow's nest was swallowed by the depths. John took the last moments of his life looking not out to sea but up, to the sky. His last thoughts were of Domenica Cabrelli, the Italian girl he had been lucky enough to love and marry. A smile crossed his lips when he pictured her, the delicate woman with the will of a general and the heart of a healer. She was the best person he had ever known. His heart was full of so much love, he imagined that her love might save him. He kept his face to the sky. The sea was no longer his world, and he had seen enough of it. He embraced the morning sky and the clouds that had moved in. The clouds were so low, he could touch them. He said a prayer of his own. McVicars would find his way back to God, and in so doing, he was certain that he would see his wife again. He reached into his uniform jacket and pulled the holy medal Domenica had given him to his lips. He kissed the medal.

Domenica woke in the bed she had shared with her husband as thunder shook the windows in the stone cottage in the convent garden. The front door blew open in the wind, banging against the wall behind it. Heavy rain began to beat on the ground as lightning seared through the black clouds. Domenica sprung out of bed and stumbled to the door. A fierce gale-force wind blew her back inside and off her feet. She got up, pushed the door closed, and bolted it.

She had locked the door the night before. She had closed all the windows. Something was wrong. She feared the house would crumble. Domenica was not usually a fearful woman. A terror seized her, and she was unable to move. The world seemed to be ending. She would wait until the storm subsided and run to the convent over the hill, where she knew she would be safe.

Piccolo clung to a wooden baluster from the grand staircase of the *Arandora Star* that had been thrown into the water by a desperate sentry who had run out of life preservers. Piccolo was a good swimmer, and he wore a life jacket, but he saw good swimmers slip out of the life preservers and drown all around him.

When the ship *Ettrick* arrived to rescue the survivors, Piccolo was pulled from the wreckage on the surface of the water. He set out to find his father aboard the rescue ship sailing back to the port at Liverpool. He called out his father's name so many times, he lost his voice. He found a man who had last seen Mattiuzzi on the first tier. He went from man to man, asking if any of them had seen his father. His worst fear would become his lifelong grief. Amedeo Mattiuzzi was gone.

Piccolo did not learn the fate of Antica, though he knew that a man of his age would not have survived jumping into the ocean. Savattini was not among the survivors on the rescue ship either, but Piccolo figured if anyone could survive the bombing of a mighty ocean liner, it would be the stylish maître d' from London. Savattini was a gold lariat of a man; he slipped through trouble with ease, any knot in the chain that bound him was easily undone.

Piccolo wrote a letter as he wept and explained the circumstances of his father's death to his mother and sister. He wrote a second letter to Margaret Mary McTavish and included it in the envelope to his mother. Piccolo explained that he had survived the bombing of the *Arandora Star*, but fate was not through with him. The *Ettrick* was due to set sail for Australia, from Liverpool immediately taking survivors of the *Arandora Star* with it. There would be no reprieve for the Italian Scots.

DUNMORE STRAND, IRELAND

July 8, 1940

Eleanor King took a walk along the beach at Dunmore Strand every morning after Mass at Saint Patrick's Church. She walked over slivers of black and gray shells that covered the beach and crunched under her feet. Her posture was upright for a woman of seventy-seven. She moved along the shore at a brisk pace as she said her rosary. She was praying, keeping one hand in her pocket on the beads, when she looked down the beach.

"Not another one," she muttered as she approached a corpse that had washed ashore, the eleventh body that week.

Eleanor knelt next to him. She was startled that his eyes were open; they were as blue as thistle. He was handsome too. Eleanor King liked a tall man. His skin was bloated and waxy and tinged with green from the drowning, but his color didn't trouble her. He looked like a painting. The stranger's hand was glassy, and his gold wedding band, lodged on his finger, was intact. His uniform hung in tatters on his body, the gold bars of his naval rank having survived.

"A Catholic. God bless him," she said aloud. She peered down at the medal around his neck. *Our Lady of Fatima*. Eleanor closed her eyes and said a prayer to the Blessed Lady. She stood and looked around. She spotted a couple on the peak above the dunes. She waved to them. They acknowledged her. "Police!" she shouted. They went for help.

Eleanor King would stay with the body on the beach at Dunmore Strand until the coroner arrived. She planned a proper Catholic funeral for the stranger. Only she; her husband, Michael; the priest; and the organist were in attendance when the Mass of Christian Burial was said for the unidentified victim of the *Arandora Star*.

Somewhere, high in heaven, John Lawrie McVicars was laughing at the irony of a lifelong Protestant ending up in an unmarked grave in a Catholic cemetery in Ireland. That was the luck of McVicars.

CHAPTER 33

Viareggio

Now

Anina blew her nose into the tissue. She pulled several more out of the box, drying her tears. "My great-grandparents had a tragic love affair."

"Are you crying for them or for yourself?"

"Nonna, I've been thinking a lot about my life. I don't make good decisions."

"Because you haven't had to make them. Enjoy your youth. If you're lucky, and you're like me, you'll be old much longer than you are young, and you will enjoy the wisdom that comes from experience. But you have to plan for that. That's why it's important to find something you love to do. I loved numbers so I became a bookkeeper. The truth was, I wasn't an artist so I couldn't create the jewelry, but I could find a way to participate that made me feel like I was part of the business. Do you like filling in for Orsola?"

"I do. And nobody's more surprised than I am. I don't mind the customers when they're picky. I put myself in their place and understand that when they're making an investment, every detail has to be perfect. I'm on their side."

"How do you like working with Nonno?"

"He never forgets to give me my lunch hour."

"An artist never stops, not even to eat. You can learn a lot from your grandfather."

"I'm sorry it took me so long to figure that out."

"You have time. Take advantage of the opportunity and build on it."

Anina pulled the cushions off the chair, forming a cot.

"What are you doing?" Matelda asked her.

"I can sleep in the chair. It folds out, see?"

"Fold it back. Go home and sleep in a proper bed."

The nurse brought Matelda her medication. "Nurse, tell my granddaughter to go home. One of us should be getting a good night's sleep. This hospital is a circus after midnight. Tell her."

"Go home," the nurse said as she left.

"Do you need anything else?" Anina asked her grandmother.

"Giancarlo Giannini."

"I'll see you tomorrow." She kissed Matelda. Anina dimmed the lights before leaving the room. "We have all the time in the world," Anina assured her.

Sure, Matelda thought to herself. All the time in the world might only be a matter of minutes. She relaxed under the covers. The sounds of the machines that monitored her breath marked time with their ticks and whistles, lulling her into a deep sleep.

Matelda dreamt of her mother, who came to her as clearly as she had been in life.

Diaphanous clouds floated over the beach like loose wedding veils.

"What did you find?" Domenica called out to her daughter, who ran along the water's edge. She reached her hand out for her daughter, and Matelda ran to her. The girl was five years old. She opened her hands, revealing a collection of delicate seashells the color of the water.

"Did you leave any shells for the other children?"

"There are lots more. I didn't take them all," her daughter said as she loaded the shells into the pocket of her mother's apron.

Matelda's hair was a nest of brown curls that turned gold under the summer sun. Her mother pushed a curl from her daughter's eyes.

"The ocean brings more when the tide rolls in," the child reminded her mother.

"You have an answer for everything."

"Sister Maria Magdalena said you have to seek answers," Matelda said.

Domenica watched as her daughter ran into the surf. "Don't go out too far!" she shouted after her. "Stay close to the shore!" She sounded like her mother when Netta Cabrelli had taken her children to the beach. Everything had changed and yet it resembled the past she remembered. Her parents were back in Villa Cabrelli. She knew how much joy it brought them to have her and Matelda living in their home; it was almost as if things were as they had been. Aldo had died in Tunisia in the war, and her mother decided to pretend that he was in the army permanently instead of coping with the grief of the loss of him. Her mother wasn't the only one in a state of pretend after the war. No one in the village referred to her as Signora McVicars; in their minds, she had returned to Viareggio redeemed. The priest who had banished her had also died. The only evidence that Domenica had ever left Viareggio was her daughter, Matelda.

Domenica was resigned when she looked down the beach, no longer the pristine playground of her youth. The white sand she remembered was now ashen with flecks of hardened black char where the tanks had rolled over it, leaking oil.

There were monuments to destruction up and down the shore. The rusting shard of a blasted gangplank was marooned in the sand. There were deep pits where fires had been built by the enemy to signal their bomber jets. The sandbags of the abandoned dugouts where German soldiers had sheltered, in their futile last stand against the Allies, remained stacked by the pier, at the ready for nothing. The seawall had been blown apart. Hunks of ancient stone that anchored the pier were shattered by the shells. The smooth wooden planks on the boardwalk were splintered and missing where the soldiers had sliced them open to create entries for soldiers who entrenched beneath them. The steps to the boardwalk were loose and missing, like a prizefighter's teeth after a brutal battle. In the end, it was all stagecraft, as flimsy as a magician's handkerchief. As if the greatest general could keep anyone or anything off an open beach! By the end of the war, the Italians had no bullets, not even a kitchen knife to use in self-defense. Mussolini had stripped them of everything they had and would need to save themselves in order to save himself. He had been a failure at that too. What a waste. Poor Viareggio. The war had stolen her beauty for an enemy who did not value it. The time wasted was incalculable.

Viareggio was home, but every corner was filled with disappointment, when it wasn't filled with hunger and despair.

Matelda ran to her mother.

"Look." Matelda went up on her toes and held a seashell close to her mother's face. "Scungilli!" she said proudly. The white conch was streaked with pale blue like an opal. "Bella!"

"Bella, bella," her mother agreed. "Let's go up to the boardwalk." Domenica took her daughter's hand once more. "Someday you'll see this beach as I remember it. When I was a girl, I played on the white sand. It was smooth, like a silk coverlet. There were red-and-white-striped umbrellas, as far as you could see. The beach looked like a field of peppermint candy. When I stood on the water's edge in the shallow ripples during low tide, little pink fish would swim around my feet in the blue water and tickle me."

"I haven't seen any pink fish," Matelda admitted before she ran ahead to the steps to climb up to the boardwalk. Luckily, the little girl was still young enough to see magic in the world. The rusted equipment that had been abandoned on the beach became kingdoms in Matelda's imagination, while they were shapes of grief for her mother. As Matelda climbed the rickety steps, she knelt down and picked up a small, thick piece of glass wedged between the slats. "Mama! A clock!" Matelda shouted.

Domenica ran to her daughter. "What did you find?" Domenica held her hand out. Matelda dropped the thick shard of glass into her mother's hand. "Matelda, you cannot pick up anything on the beach but seashells. You have to be careful when you walk."

"It was sticking up," the child said defiantly.

"Walk around it from now on."

"Yes, Mama." Matelda climbed up the rest of the steps.

Domenica turned the glass over in her hand. It appeared to be a timepiece from the equipment panel of a fallen airplane—or was it a small clock of some sort? She couldn't tell. There were numbers and a small shank of metal protruding from the thick glass. She pulled her handkerchief from the strap of her camisole and wrapped the glass in it. She would ask her father the origins of the clock that no longer told time.

There had been too much death and dying in Matelda's storytelling but there was no way around it. Anina couldn't let go of Matelda and dreamt about her at night. Her dreams, unlike Matelda's, were not about the past, but set in the future. New faces drifted in and out announcing themselves. There were flying dreams as

Anina sailed over rooftops and oceans. She was looking for something in the dreams and woke up before she found it. Mostly, Anina wanted to reach into the years ahead and bring her children into the present so her grandmother would know them. She wanted them to hear the family stories from the source. After all, her grandmother didn't just tell the family stories; she *was* the story. Matelda had lived a rich life that should not be lost or forgotten. Her life was the treasure—all she had learned and experienced—not the objects of beauty she had collected. At long last Anina was paying attention to that life and learning from it. She would not dismiss an elder's wisdom ever again. Going forward, Anina would pay attention. This life lesson was more important than how much salt her grandmother put in the tomato sauce. Anina felt the family history begin to slip through her hands like a satin rope. She had to find a way to hold on. Anina dressed quickly that morning to go to the hospital.

She skipped putting on makeup and fussing with her hair. There wasn't a moment to waste.

Matelda woke with her fists clenched. She released her fingers and rubbed her knuckles. The dream of her mother floated through her consciousness as she tried to retrieve her mother's words and their conversation. It was still dark outside. She never knew what time it was in the hospital.

Matelda hadn't had a good night's rest since she'd entered the hospital. She would have liked to have slept, but there was perpetual drama on the third floor once the sun went down. Patients would yell for nurses. Some were in pain, God bless them, but others didn't know how to operate their phones or the television remote. It wasn't worth it to try to rest on this particularly noisy night on the third floor, so Matelda raised her bed to the sitting position.

Matelda's phone was charging on the nightstand. She reached for it. She scrolled through the apps and tapped on *Classic Movies*. The titles of the movies of her youth in 1950s Italy were listed. There were star ratings next to their titles. She paid no mind to the reviews. Instead, she scrolled through, looking for the first movie she had ever seen in a theater. She remembered her father taking her to Lucca for a treat.

She became giddy when she found *Sciuscià* on the queue. She tapped on it, slipped in her earbuds, and lay back on the pillow. *Shoeshine*. She had thought about the film through the years but could never find it. Matelda could not believe how many of the scenes she remembered. The boys shining shoes to buy a horse, the boys riding on the horse, the juvenile prison. The bad boy who got the good ones in trouble. As the scenes played out, her thoughts took her back to her childhood in Viareggio. Her mother and father had tried to make her feel safe in the world. Matelda naturally felt dread so much more easily than courage, as if fear was her primary emotion.

Matelda turned the movie off. She felt her chest tighten. She thought of her doctor's conversation with her. Who knew the heart was the cause of memory loss? It seemed to Matelda that the heart should hold every experience, making the muscle stronger. Instead it was revealed that the heart, like any good machine, could only take the stress of age, use, and disappointment until it no longer could. Eventually, the parts would wear out. She lay still and listened to her own heartbeat as she drifted off to sleep. When she woke, the breakfast tray was untouched and her doctor was looking at her.

"Oh, Dottore, it's you. What time is it?"

"Nine a.m. How are you feeling, Matelda?"

"Better. I'd like to go home."

"I don't advise that."

"I knew you wouldn't. But I'm not trying to get well, because I can't get well. You and I both know I'm at the end."

"We don't know that, Matelda."

"It's harder for me to breathe. I can't walk. Sometimes I can hear my heartbeat in my ear, and I know that's not good. So let's make a deal. I'll wear my oxygen tank and I'll do my exercises and anything else you ask of me at home. Please let me go. I have lots of help, meals, and so forth. Dottore, I have a terrace that looks out over the sea. It's so blue this time of year—there's no jewel plucked from the earth as spectacular. I don't want the last thing I taste to be your broth, the last thing I see to be this pressboard ceiling, and the last thing I hear to be the beeps of these machines. I want to see the waves and the sky. I want to hear the birds and feel the breeze from the ocean, and I want to take a shot of whiskey whenever I please."

"How are you doing today?" Olimpio said from the doorway. Anina followed him into the room.

"I feel grand. Tell him the good news, Dottore." Matelda looked up at the doctor.

"Matelda can go home." He smiled down at his patient, took her hand, and gave it an affectionate squeeze.

"Aren't you glad I put the elevator in?" Olimpio wheeled Matelda off the lift into their apartment.

"I'm so happy." The sun split the apartment with stripes of white light illuminating the place and things she loved most. "But I'm thrilled you convinced me to take the penthouse. I love the light."

Anina emerged from the kitchen. "I juiced some kale for you, Nonna."

"Oh, bella, you enjoy. Pour Nonna a Campari and soda."

"Coming up." Anina brought Matelda's bag to her room.

"I'd better call Nicolina and tell her we're home," Olimpio said.

"Before you do, leave me outside in the sun."

Anina brought Matelda's cocktail and an oil pretzel on the terrace. She pulled a chair over to sit next to her grandmother. "It's early for alcohol."

"Not when you're over eighty. It's never too late," Matelda said.

Anina tore the oil pretzel in two. The spongy center was buttery and fresh, while the outer shell was glossy and hard. She handed half to her grandmother.

"I'm going to miss oil pretzels." Matelda dunked a piece into her drink to soften it. She tasted it. "The nuns in Dumbarton used to make the Scottish version. They called them popovers. I miss those too."

"We could try to make them for you," Anina offered.

"Sometimes the memory is sweeter," Matelda said. "At least for me."

"Italians never forget what they eat if it's good."

Matelda nodded. Her granddaughter had just summarized her entire life in an oil pretzel.

PART THREE

LET WHOEVER LONGS TO ATTAIN ETERNAL LIFE
IN HEAVEN HEED THESE WARNINGS:

When considering the future, contemplate these things:

Death, than which nothing is more certain

Judgment, than which nothing is more strict

Hell, than which nothing is more terrible

Paradise, than which nothing is more delightful

CHAPTER 34

𝕲𝖑𝖆𝖘𝖌𝖔𝖜

July 3, 1940

D omenica moved quickly through the crowded streets before
stopping at a newsstand. She bought the morning newspaper
and unfurled it, searching for a mention of her husband. The news
of the fate of the prisoners and crew on the *Arandora Star* had
spread through Ireland and Scotland, though few facts were available. Sister Matelda had shared the news that McVicars died with
the captain and most of the crew, but Domenica refused to believe
it. Her husband would have found a way to return to her.

Her search for McVicars had become more desperate as the
hours passed. Finally, the newspaper printed a list (though incom-
plete) of the passengers and crew. The photographs were not clear:
she did not find her husband's face among the survivors. She
winced as she read the spotty details of the attack. The story as
reported seemed fanciful; the facts were vague. Domenica turned
the page. *Victims of Attack*. She traced her finger down the list. She
found her husband's name. She felt her heart shatter inside her
body as all hope was lost. Droplets fell onto the newspaper. She

looked up, but it wasn't raining. She put her hand to her face. Domenica was drenched in a feverish sweat.

Domenica stood at the screen door of the McVicars homestead and took a deep breath before knocking.

Grizelle appeared at the door. "I know why you're here."

Domenica followed her inside to the kitchen. The house held a dank smell even though the windows were open and the hawthorn tree outside the window was in full bloom with white blossoms.

"I'm so sorry, Mrs. McVicars."

Grizelle kept her back to Domenica and gripped the counter. "I went into town this morning. I saw the paper and I didn't buy one. I didn't have to. I knew. I walked by the list of the dead at the post. I knew his name was there and I did not want to see it in ink, on a wall, with all those people standing around. But I looked. He was on the list."

"He was a devoted son. The funeral—" Domenica began.

"There will be no funeral," she said without emotion. "He died at sea."

"The merchant navy would like to—"

"I don't care about the merchant navy. I told him to join the British navy. Better assignments. Did he listen? Not once."

"But, Mrs. McVicars—"

"They took my son and now he's dead. There is no medal or certificate etched in gold that will bring him back to me. They can keep their trinkets."

"He died a hero."

Grizelle spun around and faced Domenica. "To whom? To the Tallies? Your people? Bunch of crooks. The Germans? You watch. They'll own us in short order. They have bombs. They will flatten us from the air with the Luftwaffe. The Austrians? Who cares about them? Do they care about me?"

"This is about your son. He should be remembered."

"I have my memories."

Domenica thought it odd that her Victorian mother-in-law possessed the same demeanor in tragedy that she displayed under ordinary circumstances. Grizelle didn't appear to grieve but to sulk, as if it were an inconvenience that her son had gone off and gotten himself killed in service to his country.

Grizelle poured hot water from the kettle into the teapot. She did not offer a cup to Domenica. She covered the pot in a tea cozy shaped like a cottage sewn from bits of velvet and felt. The cottage had windows and a door. Tiny felt lilacs spilled out of the corduroy window boxes. The whimsical tea cozy was a touch of warmth in a house with none, and an indication that there was a time when Grizelle imagined a happy home.

Domenica tried to picture Grizelle McVicars in her youth as a loving mother, but it was impossible. Grizelle clung to disappointment like the morning glories on the roof with their twisted arabesque stems that gripped the copper gutters like fingers. A lifetime of disappointment had hobbled her good nature. Grizelle was on an emotional crawl that dug her deeper into the pit of her own unhappiness. There was no way to comfort her. Nurses called these patients "malcontents."

There was no common courtesy either. There was not to be an offer of a cup of tea, or a biscuit, or a memory to share with her daughter-in-law.

"Mrs. McVicars, I know you are heartbroken, and I am too."

Grizelle did not respond.

Domenica continued. "I must ask you for something, because you're the only person in the world who could help me going forward."

Grizelle spun around. "There is no money. You are entitled to nothing. If I had an extra quid, I wouldn't give it to you. You were barely in his life."

"You misunderstand. Let me finish. I don't want money. You're his mother and you should keep all reminders of him, including any change you find in his pockets. But if you could spare a photograph of him, I would be grateful."

Grizelle's eyes were wild with fury. "If I had a photograph, I would rip it into pieces before I would ever give it to you. You are the reason I lost my son."

Domenica was ushered out of the house. Grizelle slammed, then locked the front door behind her. The gray clouds that had gathered over Glasgow dropped low in the sky like a clutter of pots. The rhythmic tings of rain on the roof made a sound that reminded Domenica of the inn in Manchester on their wedding night. There hadn't been a radio with music, so they danced by the fire to the sound of the falling rain.

John had chided her because the Italian girl never remembered her umbrella in bonny Scotland. His wife was not one to think of rain when the sun was shining. Domenica waited for the storm to pass, but it soon became clear that the downpour was the beginning of something far worse. She ran out into the rain and did not look back.

VIAREGGIO

Now

Anina placed the sleek strands of fresh linguini on the drying rack in Matelda's kitchen. "How did I do?" She stood back and wiped her hands, dusted in flour, on the apron.

"More flour will prevent them from clumping." Matelda pointed at the intersecting strands of linguini on the board. "Try it. Dust the board and pull them out, one strand at a time."

Anina separated the strands and hung them one by one on the wooden dowel. "The extra egg made the difference. The consistency is just right."

"Good." Matelda's arms felt heavy that morning. She rested them on the handles of her wheelchair. She couldn't help Anina cut the pasta dough, but she was still strong enough to bark a few orders.

Anina handed her grandmother a glass of fresh juice.

"I really don't want it," Matelda said.

"You need the vitamins. Drink it."

"You people and your healthy drinks." Matelda took a sip. "They are a medical miracle for no one."

"Just trying to help you get better, Nonna." Anina sat down on the stool. "Mama gave me some good advice."

"To put Campari in the juice?" Matelda winked.

"No. She said I should make a list of all the questions that I never asked you but meant to."

"I must be on my way out." Matelda took another sip. "If that's true, do you really think disgusting green juice can save me?"

"It might, if you ever finished a glass. Nonna, I just want to clarify a few things. Where were you born?"

"At the convent in Dumbarton, Scotland."

"And your mother named you for a nun there, right?"

Matelda nodded. "I lived there with my mother for almost five years of my life. My mother spent every day of those five years trying to get home to Viareggio. But as long as the war was on, it was impossible. But in spite of all the obstacles, Mama continued to try. There was always some scheme brewing. Maybe Mama and I could go to Sicily and wait, or some priest promised to write a letter on our behalf to get us extradited through Switzerland. But nothing ever came through. The truth was, we were safer in Scotland with the nuns than we would have been in Viareggio, so we stayed." Matelda brushed away a tear. "Here's the sad part. When the time came to return to Italy, I wanted to stay in Scotland. It was the only home I had ever known. The stories my mother told me about my Italian grandparents and all my cousins seemed like fairy tales to me. They weren't people in my life; they were characters in a story for which no book had been written. So, the night before we left, I got out of bed and went to the convent and told the Sisters that I was running away. I didn't want to go to Italy. I wanted to stay with them."

"What did your mother do?"

"It was the only time in my life she spanked me. She said, 'I am your mother. You belong with me.' I never ran away again, I assure you."

"You were all she had, Nonna."

"When my mother died many years later, I called Sister Matelda. She had to be ninety when we spoke, but her mind was sharp. She remembered my father. She said a more gallant man never lived. He was tall and blue-eyed and had thick, shiny brown hair. He was funny. When he wasn't smiling, he was whistling. Do you know that's the only image I have of my father, an old nun's memory? That's it."

"Why didn't you ask your mother what your father looked like?"

"I did ask for a picture once, but she got so upset, I never asked her again. Later on, my mother felt bad about the way she reacted and she told me about my grandmother Grizelle McVicars. Mama said to me, 'Matelda, don't ever turn bitter like your Scottish grandmother.' But I have a little of her mean streak in me, don't I?"

"You have your reasons."

"And I suppose my grandmother did too. There were many

people that had it worse than I had it, but somehow I managed to be bitter for all of them."

Anina laughed.

"I'm still angry about the Speranzas. No person should ever go through what they endured. That's when the Italians turned on the Italians."

VENEZIA

October 1943

"La bella famiglia," Speranza said as he examined the photograph from America. "Aggie, how did you get this letter delivered?"

"I paid Goffredo."

"He didn't offer to give you the mail you have a right to receive?"

She waved her hand. "We are long past civility. Doesn't my brother look happy?"

"Yes. His wife? Not so much."

"She's begging us to come to America." Agnese stood over her husband as he read.

"She makes New York City sound wonderful."

"Maybe we should think about it. I could help Freda with the girls and the new baby. Venezia is not what it used to be. I don't want to live in a place where we're not welcome. You could work with Ezechiele. He says there is more cutting to do than he can manage. They have shop after shop of cutters in the diamond district. Can you imagine? Streets of cutters."

"I'll think about it."

"You'd better think fast." Agnese placed dinner on the table.

"I don't need to think because you've already made your decision." Speranza tasted the artichoke.

"You make it sound like I'm the padrone when I'm your obedient wife. Wherever you go, I will go. Just like Ruth and Naomi. You don't go? I stay too." She patted him on the shoulder.

Agnese had made Speranza's favorite meal. She had one artichoke, which she split open and roasted in the fire. She made cannoli stuffed with chicken roasted with garlic and onions, bathed in a butter and lemon sauce. She made the shells out of the last bit of flour she had in the bin. Goffredo had brought her a chicken he found on the piazza. She wrung its neck, plucked, washed, and roasted it, just as she had when times were good.

When night fell, they ate by the light of the traditional Shabbos candles. Before Speranza closed the shutters to the brisk night air, he leaned out and looked up and down the canal. The torches flickered, reflecting light on the surface of the pale blue-green water, which formed a path of light to the sea.

"Do you see something?" Agnese asked.

"A way out," he replied before pulling his head back.

"You know, we don't have to go all the way to America immediately. Cabrelli invited us to stay with them. They're in the mountains above Viareggio."

"What's the difference between Venezia and the other coast of Italy? Both are crawling with Fascisti. No, the only place we can go is America."

"Va bene. I will make a plan," Agnese offered.

"I've been soldering medals for the Fascisti. They know where we live. The government needs the jewelers to make the claptrap. Medals and pins. Regalia. All of it."

"Good. Let them think you approve of them." There was a knock at the door.

Agnese quickly blew out the Shabbos candles and moved the small candelabra to the windowsill. The last thing they needed was a stranger observing them as they practiced their faith. Agnese nodded. Speranza answered the door.

"Goffredo!" Speranza was relieved to see his friend in the doorway. "Come in."

Goffredo's eyes followed the tendrils of smoke that remained in the air from the Shabbos candles. Agnese waved her hand through the air to clear it. "Thank you for the chicken. Won't you join us?"

"Grazie, but I can't. I came here to tell you that your paperwork at the passport office was kicked upstairs."

"This is good news!" Agnese clasped her hands together in gratitude.

"No, it means they won't let you travel. I tried to pull your paperwork, saying it was a mistake, but they caught it and flagged you."

"But they're issuing passports!" Speranza insisted.

"Not anymore."

"What do you recommend we do?"

"You could go to your farm."

"I believe the city is safer," Speranza said.

"But it isn't."

"How much time do we have?"

"The morning. I wanted you to know what I heard. What I saw. They don't follow the law. You're good people, but the world has gone mad."

"But the good people haven't gone mad, have they?"

"Forgive me; I tried. I am not in charge."

Speranza opened the door so Goffredo could leave. He looked left and right before slipping down the dark street. Speranza closed the door behind him. "What do you think that was all about?"

"He had papers in his coat pocket. He's just the messenger."

"What do you want to do, Agnese?"

She didn't answer her husband. She needed to think.

Agnese spent the night packing her most precious possessions away. She hid the silver under the floorboards and placed her china in a basket hidden deep in her closet. She packed a bag for her husband and one for herself. She bathed, washed her hair, and put on her best dress as the sun came up. She made breakfast. Agnese lifted the pan of steamed milk off the stove and poured it into the bowl with the espresso. She put out the heels of the challah bread to dunk into it. Speranza sat down at the table.

"We're going to take the car and drive to the mountains," Agnese announced.

"But, Aggie, they won't let us buy gas. If they stop us, we'll be put in jail."

"The trains are too risky. I have plenty of money. We will bribe our way across Italy until we get to the Cabrellis'," she schemed.

Speranza did not argue with her. They drank their hot milk and espresso and ate the day-old bread in silence. When they were finished, Agnese asked, "Are you ready?"

They went through their home a final time. Agnese quickly straightened the bathroom and bedroom. Speranza carried their suitcases to the door. Agnese joined him in the kitchen.

"Why are you locking the cupboard, my love?" Speranza asked his wife.

"Because I always do."

Speranza closed the shutters on the window overlooking the canal and swung the latch, locking them shut.

"Why are you closing the shutters on the windows?"

"Because I always do." Speranza took his wife into his arms and held her close. "Maybe we'll be lucky. Maybe when we return, everything will be in place, including the mice. Where is your ring?" He kissed her hand.

"I gave it to Signora Potenza."

"She'll hold it for you until we return."

"She said she would."

There was a loud pounding on the door. "Ebrei" was followed by more pounding. "Ebrei!" the men shouted.

Agnese looked at the locked window to escape. Speranza thought about climbing to the roof, where he and Aggie could jump from one rooftop to the next until they reached the aqueduct. Instead he did the thing he had done since he was a boy in school. Speranza faced the bully head-on and opened the door.

Two young Blackshirts stood on the stoop of their home, facing the Speranzas through the sights of their gun barrels. They were teenagers, sixteen, seventeen years old at the most. Speranza did not recognize the boys as Venetians. When they spoke, Speranza detected a Bari dialect from the south. *They're recruiting from afar*, he thought to himself. *They're already short of troops. That's a good sign.*

The Blackshirts yanked Speranza out into the street, even though he offered no resistance. Agnese said nothing and followed her husband with their suitcases, one for each of them. She looked up and saw the familiar faces of her neighbors in the windows on the street where they had lived for thirty years. They had shared sugar and flour and their lives, but now they did not acknowledge Agnese. She did not expect them to; she did not acknowledge them either.

Agnese and Speranza were herded onto a transport truck, a military vehicle, with a tarp roof. There was no place to sit. The bench around the perimeter of the cargo bed was also overflowing with people. There was not enough room for two more passengers, but the group shifted to accommodate them anyway.

The Blackshirts lifted and slammed the rear gate shut and locked it, trapping the Speranzas inside with the others. The soldiers jumped on the sideboards of the truck as it moved through the piazza to collect more of their fellow citizens.

The House of David was burning in Venezia, but there was neither smoke nor fire.

The train on the first leg of their journey had seats, but upon transfer in Germany, the prisoners were loaded onto cattle cars. Agnese observed a passenger train moving slowly in the opposite direction, back to Venezia. Just three years earlier she and her husband had been on that train, after a holiday in Germany. Agnese could see the pressed white table linens through the windows of the dining car. There were silver flutes with a single pink rose in each window. On their side of the tracks, there was no music or fine dining; there was only fear, muffled weeping, whispered conversations, and hushed prayers. Speranza held his wife's hand, which soothed him. He closed his eyes because the expressions of terror on the prisoners' faces were too much for him to bear.

When the train pulled into Berlin, Nazi soldiers separated the women from the men. Agnese was stoic and pushed her husband's hand away when he tried to hold it. She knew if the Nazis saw they were together, they would separate them to be cruel. They might have a chance to come out on the other side of this if they showed no connection to each other.

Speranza was called off the line by an officer, not a high-ranking one, but he had enough seniority to have acquired new boots. Speranza would not have noticed the boots, but Agnese did. Agnese's mother had taught her to pay attention to a man's shoes. *A man's shoes tell you everything about the person wearing them.*

When Speranza looked at Agnese, she looked away, but she placed her hand on her heart so her husband knew that it belonged to him.

The Nazis shoved Speranza and four other men from the line into a car too small to accommodate them, throwing the men's suitcases onto the back of another truck as though they were trash. The herding of her people into small spaces was not a function of a lack of planning on the part of the Fascisti and the Nazis, but a belief that the Speranzas and their fellow Juden were animals.

The Nazis pulled one more man off the line. He held on to his hat as they shoved the additional prisoner into the car with Speranza and the others. Agnese recognized him as an engineer from Firenze. He had wanted to understand the jewel movement of timepieces, and Speranza had shared all he knew while Agnese made them supper.

Agnese Speranza was relieved as she saw her husband drive away with the other men. He had a skill. They needed him. Romeo would live, and they would have to feed him so he could work. The thought brought her joy. She was happy for him. The nature of her love for her husband was to seek his happiness above her own. Agnese didn't feel the prod of the baton to her ribs when she was shoved onto the next train, which would take her to Buchenwald.

CHAPTER 35

𝕳𝖔𝖒𝖊

Domenica yanked her daughter's hair when she brushed it on the train from Lucca to Viareggio.

"Mama!" Matelda rubbed her scalp. "Too hard."

"There was a knot." Domenica gently rubbed the sore spot on her daughter's scalp. "I'm sorry."

Matelda McVicars was almost five years old. She thought, *You should be sorry. You took me from the garden house I loved for a train ride where I threw up twice and couldn't sleep.*

"You're going to love Viareggio. Wait until Carnevale. There are giant puppets and parades and bomboloni."

Matelda didn't want to hear about bomboloni when her stomach was weak. She wanted to call them doughnuts like they did in Glasgow. She didn't want anything Italian, not even something sweet. She wanted the train to sprout wings like a bird and fly her back to Scotland.

Domenica took her daughter's hands into her own. "What's the matter, bella?"

"I don't speak Italian very well, Mama. I'm not going to understand anybody. I want to speak English. I had good friends at Notre Dame. I miss Marnie and Hazel. Why couldn't we stay there?"

"My family is here. Your family. Families have to stay together to be strong."

The train pulled into the station at Viareggio. Matelda watched her mother kneel on the seat and look out the window. Her mother began to wave and smile; soon she was crying, but they weren't sad tears. Matelda decided that anything that made her mother happy was more important than anything that made Matelda sad. She knelt on the seat across from her mother and looked out the window, hoping to find the wondrous village her mother saw, but there were no puppets or parades or gelato makers. It was raining harder than she had ever seen it pour in Scotland. Viareggio wasn't pretty at all. It was dark and gray like a wet winter sock. How could her mother have left a place as green as the convent for a place so drab?

"What do you think, Matelda?"

"It's beautiful, Mama. Che bella," the girl lied.

Domenica pulled her daughter close. "You will use your Italian, and you'll be surprised at how much you already know."

Matelda rested her face in Domenica's neck, where she found the familiar scent of vetiver and peaches. Her mother's cheek was soft and her kisses reassured Matelda.

The porter helped her mother with their luggage. He looked at Domenica as men would do. It was always the same. The man was cowed by her mother's beauty and wanted to be near it, so he would speak too loudly and make broad gestures to impress her. He would offer to do anything she needed. Her mother would endure the attention politely but not encourage it. Instead, she elevated them with her proper behavior. To that end, Domenica placed her gloved hand on top of the porter's and disembarked the train in a ladylike fashion. The reaction of the crowd that had gathered to welcome them confirmed that her mother was someone special in this seaside town.

A group of women ran to Domenica to greet her. *They must be cousins*, Matelda thought, because her mother had told her so many stories about the children on Via Firenze. Domenica's family formed a whirlpool around her, welcoming her home.

An old man knelt before Matelda and extended his hand. "I'm your grandfather." He reached into his pocket and gave her a peppermint.

"Really, Pietro? Candy?" Netta, Matelda's grandmother, admonished him. "You must be Matelda." Netta, thin and strong, wearing a green velvet bonnet, stood before the four-year-old and looked her over. "Sei carina e bellissima. We are so happy you're home. I'm your grandmother." Netta embraced her granddaughter and kissed her.

Matelda thanked her grandparents for their hospitality. They seemed nice. There was something very familiar about them. Domenica had told her daughter stories about their family, Carnevale, and their neighbors in Viareggio. They were the last colorful thoughts Matelda had before sleep, so they sat like jewels in gold in her subconscious. Matelda would add details to the stories, creating her own world from bits of her mother's.

There were tales of hidden treasures, stolen maps, and bullies on the beach. Matelda learned about Cabrelli's jewelry shop. The child understood soldering, grinding, sawing, lapping, sanding, and polishing of the gems. She knew about the bruting wheel and cobbing rough stones before measuring them. Matelda learned the shapes of the finished gems: briolette, baguette, marquise, and round brilliant. She understood that her grandmother could make anything delicious out of chestnuts. Her grandparents, whom she had never met before, had been as real to her as her own mother because of Domenica's bedtime stories.

"I want to see the ocean, Mama." Matelda pulled on her mother's sleeve. "You promised."

Domenica leaned down. "Wait until you see it. When the clouds go, you'll see it's as blue as your sash."

"We will take her to the promenade." Her grandfather extended his hand. "It's true. When the rain stops, the sea turns blue again," Nonno confirmed.

Netta took Matelda's other hand. "We made a feast to welcome you home, Piccianina!" And just as it went in every small Italian village, Matelda was given a nickname. Going forward, the white-haired Viareggians would call her *Picci*.

It was only her father, John McVicars, and his people, the Scots, who would fade away in time. Eventually, Scotland became a fragment of her past, like a gold thread dangling from an ancient tapestry that would be neither knotted nor pulled for fear of destroying it altogether. The story of their years in Scotland and her father's demise would remain untold for the next seventy-seven years of her life because there would be no looking back. The story had taken a turn. Matelda was an Italian.

Christmas Eve 1945

Dottore Pretucci opened the brown paper box tied with a ribbon. Netta Cabrelli's chestnut candy glistened in the box like whiskey diamonds. "My favorite!" Pretucci helped himself to a sugar-drenched chestnut and offered the box to Domenica. "Your mother is so kind to us—even during the years you were away. She'd drop off a cake or a loaf of fresh bread."

"That was her way of keeping my position open."

"It worked." Pretucci handed her an envelope. "For the holiday."

The envelope jingled when Domenica placed it in her pocket.

"Thank you, but I wish you wouldn't. You made the arrangements to bring my daughter and me home, and we will never be able to repay you for all the trouble."

"It is not a debt to be paid. You've done your penance. I'm happy to have you back in the clinic."

Domenica pulled on her coat. She followed Pretucci out the door. "I don't know how you did it."

"It was about timing, as most things in life," Pretucci began. "Once the war was over, the new priest was happy to help. Evidently the clerics are, as advertised, in the redemption business. The redemption of their own reputations, of course. I believe they were embarrassed at the way you were treated."

Pretucci tucked the box of candy under his arm and walked home. Domenica locked the door of the clinic. It wasn't helpful to hear that her banishment had been a mistake. Domenica liked to believe that there was order in the universe. Her punishment had been strict and unfair. She sipped the cold air and shivered. It felt like it might snow, even though it rarely did in Toscana. She hoped it would for Matelda. Her daughter longed for the snowstorms at Dumbarton and the sunny winter days that followed when the Lowlands were covered in white diamond dust.

Viareggio was also enchanted in winter. Candles twinkled in the windows of the houses on the hillsides above the beach. The doors on the shops along the boulevard jingled as customers went in and out. Their storefront windows would fog, framing the glass in ice crystals.

Domenica held the door to her father's shop open. A woman emerged with a parcel. She wore a stylish wool coat with balloon sleeves and mohair cuffs with brass buttons.

"Signorina Cabrelli?"

"Signora McVicars," she corrected the lady politely. "I'm sorry, I don't think I know you."

"Monica Mironi."

Monica was elegantly turned out. Her leather boots were polished. This was not the put-upon mother of three Domenica remembered.

Monica continued. "We have something in common. I'm not Monica Mironi any longer. My first husband died in France during the war. I remarried a wonderful man. Maybe you know him? Antonio Montaquila?"

"Yes, I do. He owns a shop in Pietrasanta."

"That's him. He sent me to pick up a gift for his mother. He said your father would have something appropriate, and he did. A beautiful brooch."

"I'm glad." Domenica took Monica's hands in hers. "I'm happy to see you so well."

"I didn't know where to turn when Guido died. The children were bereft. But God had a plan for me. I'm almost ashamed that I found happiness again when there's so much suffering in the world."

"You had your share, Monica. You deserve happiness."

Domenica watched Signora Montaquila walk down the boulevard. Fate had spared her a long life with a horrible husband and given her a second chance. If she could forgive Guido Mironi, Domenica could too.

Domenica entered Cabrelli's and greeted Isabella, the seasoned clerk who was waiting on a customer. The display cases were practically empty. Before the war, this would have been a good sign for the family purse. But following the war, most items from Cabrelli's were purchased on credit. It would be years before her father would be made whole. Credit had replaced profit in postwar Italy.

"We have company, bella," Cabrelli said as Domenica walked past him to the back room to hang her coat on a hook.

Silvio Birtolini stood up from his seat on the bench under the window. He wore his best suit and tie. Silvio pushed a stubborn curl off his forehead before giving Domenica a kiss on both cheeks. "How are you, old friend?"

"Old." She laughed.

"I don't want to hear it! You're still a baby," her father said. "Look at that face." Cabrelli pinched his daughter's cheek before going to the front room.

Silvio, like all Italian men, was thin after the war. His black hair remained unruly. His face had matured, bringing out the angles of his cheekbones. "I'm happy to see you made it through the war," Silvio said.

"I'm happy you did too." Domenica felt something she had never felt in Silvio's presence: awkward. She attempted small talk. "Do you need a gift? I don't know what's left." She pulled an apron on over her nursing uniform. "Choose something and I'll wrap it for you."

Silvio put his hands in his pockets. He looked down at his polished shoes. "I'm not here to buy a gift."

Cabrelli returned to the workroom with a gift that needed to be wrapped. He gave it to Domenica. "I just hired Silvio to cut for me. Would you wrap this for me, Nica?" Cabrelli went back into the showroom.

Domenica opened the box. She pinned the delicate gold chain to the cotton batting. "You finished your apprenticeship?"

"I did. I worked in Firenze until I was drafted into the army. At first, I was a guard at the prison camp in Friuli. Horrible place."

"Where did they send you after the camp?"

"They didn't. I left the army because my country left me. I was in the mountains north of Bergamo in the resistance."

Domenica thought of John McVicars, who would not have left active service regardless of his own beliefs. She wrapped the box in gold paper and twine.

"There were many Italians who believed there were some good qualities at play with the Fascisti, but I'm not one of them."

"I'm not either," Domenica agreed.

Silvio smiled. "So you don't judge me."

"No, I don't." Domenica patted his hand. "I can't judge anyone who fought for the good. It was a terrible time, but in the midst of it, there was some joy. I was married to a Scotsman, a very proud one. He was killed on the *Arandora Star* five years ago. We have a daughter."

"That's wonderful. She must be a comfort to you."

"She is. She's my heartbeat. She's almost six years old. Do you have a child close in age?"

"I don't have children."

"I'm sorry. Maybe now that the war is over, you and your wife will have them."

"I'm not married."

Isabella poked her head into the workroom. "Signore? Maria Pipino called to say dinner is on the table."

"Thank you," Silvio said as he reached for his hat and coat. "I took a room at Signora Pipino's."

"On the Via Fiume? Go, go. Signora Pipino is a good cook. We'll chat another time."

"I hope so." Silvio kissed Domenica on both cheeks. "I'll see you soon." He placed his hat on his head. "Your father is a wise man, but he's wrong about one thing. You're not a baby anymore. Sei una donna magnifica."

Before she could thank him for the compliment, Silvio was in the front room shaking Cabrelli's hand. Wait until she told Amelia LeDonne about the Birtolini boy. Surely, she would remember him.

Domenica buried her hands in the pockets of her coat as she walked home. Instead of taking the shortcut, she climbed up to the boardwalk. The moon lit a path on the surface of the sea, rip-pling the waves like ruffles of black satin. She strolled along the pier guided by the blue lights installed by the Italian navy. From the roof of Villa Cabrelli, the boardwalk below sparkled like a sap-phire bracelet. Besides Matelda, the blue lights were the only good thing that came out of the war.

Christmas Eve felt like a new start, even though she and Matelda had been back for a few months. Holidays and the feast days of the saints helped Domenica fold back into family life as if she had never left. Matelda was slowly making friends—it helped that she was surrounded by cousins who welcomed her and did not tease her about her funny accent.

When Domenica lived at the convent in Dumbarton, she had brought the custom of La Passeggiata with her from Italy. She took nightly walks after supper on the river Clyde and imagined the At-lantic Ocean as it heaved in the far distance, miles away, with its whitecaps and dark green surf, a reminder of what had been taken from her off the coast of Ireland. Domenica talked to John McVicars on those walks, hopeful he was listening on the other side. She shared stories about Matelda and her work. But mostly she longed for him. Over time, those walks gave her perspective. She learned how to walk with her grief.

The one-sided conversations she had with her husband stopped when she returned to Viareggio. Occasionally she still called his name, or he came to mind when Matelda said something funny, but she could no longer feel him listening. When McVicars died, his love covered her like the heat of the sun; years later, that warm connection had all but faded. She was more alone than she had ever been. "Love changes over time, but so does grief," the old widows in the village promised her.

As she climbed the front steps of Villa Cabrelli, she had a strange feeling. Domenica stopped on the landing and looked into the window where her sleeping cot had been placed when she was a girl. She remembered the night Silvio Birtolini came to see her before leaving the village for good. Domenica shivered at the thought of his kiss but blamed it on the cold night air. She went inside and called out for her daughter.

"Add a plate for Christmas dinner," Cabrelli said to his wife as he threw a log into the fire and stoked it.

"There's plenty to eat." Netta crumbled fresh sage over the loin of pork that browned in the pan. "What straggler did you pick up this time?"

"I think you'll remember him. He went to school with Domenica."

"Stop right there! You didn't invite il bastardo did you? I heard he was around. I saw Signora Pipino at the fish market."

"Signora is correct. Silvio Birtolini has returned to Viareggio and is lodging in her hotel. In a few short years, he'll be forty years old. I think we can stop calling him il bastardo."

"Fine, but that doesn't mean he isn't one."

"He grew up, got his training, and he's excellent. I hired him."

"In our shop? You can't be serious."

"He's presentable. Silvio has better manners than that fancy cousin of yours from La Spezia who came to apprentice and lasted a few months until he crapped out entirely. You know who I mean, the one with the airs. He did more loafing than cutting in my shop."

"Ignazio Senci comes about his airs honestly. He multiplied a good inheritance. He did not squander it. Let him have airs because he has the cash. Some families came out of the war with less, and some with more."

"Nobody was better for having endured it," Cabrelli countered.

"We have to make up for the time wasted. We lost our savings, and we earned nothing in those years. And what do you do? Hire a horrible boy with an awful reputation in a town that forgives no one."

"I need Silvio. I can take in more commissions. He's a fine cutter."

"Va bene. Don't overpay him. We have a household to run here."

"Netta, you have become enamored of money."

"Try to live without it. I will not be beholden to others for my supper ever again. I have nightmares about that war. Hiding and foraging and begging for scraps in the forest like the animals."

"We never begged. We survived. Where's your gratitude? Our house was still standing when we came home. Others were not so lucky."

"I do not want Silvio Birtolini at my Christmas table."

"Well, I do."

"Have you asked your daughter how she feels about this?"

"I'm going to surprise her."

"You'll surprise her right out of this house. She will not be pleased."

"They're old friends."

"Pietro, you are such an innocent. I'm ashamed for you."

"I don't want my new employee to spend Christmas alone."

"Did you invite Isabella? She's your employee too."

"She has a family."

"That she comes by honestly."

"Netta. Enough." Cabrelli did not raise his voice, but his tone was firm. "Silvio has paid his penance in full for a mistake that he did not make. This is a good and honest man. We have no room in this house for your prejudice. It's Christmas. Humble yourself like the poor shepherd."

Matelda ran into her grandmother's kitchen, followed by Domenica. Matelda peeled off her mittens and hat. "Nonna, Signore Birtolini drove the carriage on the sand."

"On the beach?" Netta forced a smile.

"All the way to Spiaggia della Lecciona and back," Domenica confirmed as she collected Matelda's coat and mittens.

"Yes, and it was so much fun." Matelda jumped up and down. "He had bells on the bridle, and he let me shake them when he brought the horse back to Signore Giacometti. I told Signore Birtolini that we had snow in Scotland, so he said to pretend the sand was snow, and I did."

"Let's go, Matelda. Out of these wet clothes." Domenica followed Matelda up the stairs.

"Hang the coat on the rod in the bathroom, please," Netta called off to them.

Silvio stood in the doorway in his coat and hat. "Next time I hope you'll join us on the carriage ride, Signora Cabrelli."

Netta sniffed. "If I have the time, maybe. Thank you for taking Matelda. Children love a carriage ride at Christmas."

"May I help with dinner?"

"The fire in the dining room is going out. The wood is stacked under the house."

"I'll take care of it." Silvio closed the front door behind him.

"Good thing he didn't take his coat off," Cabrelli commented as he entered the kitchen. "You put him to work."

"He's on his best behavior. All men are models of civility at first. We'll see how long it lasts."

"He is a good friend to your daughter. And now your grand-daughter."

"As long as he stays that way and as long as that's all he is to them, I am fine with it."

"Netta, you are such a romantic." Cabrelli took his wife in his arms, pulled her close, and smothered her with kisses. She beat off his advances with her spatula. "Let me go, old man."

Cabrelli released her.

"My daughter didn't lose her first husband, a decorated sea captain, to wind up with an apprentice." Netta straightened her apron.

"He won't be an apprentice for long."

Silvio dried the last of the dinner dishes and placed it on the shelf with the others. Netta Cabrelli's kitchen was pristine and orderly once more. Silvio made sure to put every platter and plate away where they belonged.

Domenica joined him in the kitchen.

"That was fast," Silvio said.

"Matelda couldn't stop talking about the carriage ride. All that fresh air was good for her. She went right to sleep."

"Or was it your mother's Christmas cake?"

"Maybe a little of both." Domenica laughed.

"What did you think?"

She whispered, "The cake was a little dry."

"I meant the carriage ride."

"When my daughter's happy, so am I."

"You've done a good job with Matelda. She's very sweet and polite."

"Thank you." Domenica picked up the mopeen and placed it on the hook to dry. "Why did you do the dishes?"

"To impress your mother."

"Let me know if you're successful."

"Signora has a long memory. She thinks of me as the fat little boy that went around town stealing maps. Now she'll think of me as the dinner guest who washed the dishes, I hope. Do you feel like a walk?"

Domenica and Silvio tiptoed past Netta, who had fallen asleep in her chair by the fire. Cabrelli, reading a book, looked up at them and smiled. They pulled on their coats and went outside.

"The cold air feels good," Silvio said.

"After you were up to your elbows in hot water. Let me see your hands."

Silvio placed his hands in hers; Domenica turned them over. "Put on your gloves."

He held onto her hands. "You're bossy."

"Part of being a mother." She reached into his coat pocket, removed the gloves, and helped him into them.

"Don't blame Matelda. You were born that way. When we were children, I knew what you would become when we grew up."

"How did I do?"

"You're not a general. Yet."

"I thought of you a lot." Domenica slipped her arm through his. "The last time I saw you, you were engaged. Why didn't you get married?"

"Barbara was a good girl, but she was not from an understanding family. I know disappointment, and I ended up being one to her. After I saw you at Carnevale, I went back to Parma and decided I needed to be honest with her. You never treated me poorly because of my family situation, and it gave me the courage to tell Barbara the truth. Everybody in Viareggio knew I was il bastardo, but no one in Parma did. She was going to be my wife, and there shouldn't be any surprises about her family or mine. In order to tell her the truth, I had to find it."

"Did you ever meet your father?"

"Yes. He's a good man who did a stupid thing. He has regrets. Well, he had them. He died last year."

"I'm sorry."

"My mother met my father and fell in love with him when she was nineteen and he was thirty-three. After she found out she was having me, he told her that he was married. It was an impossible situation for my mother."

"She must have been scared."

"She decided not to go to her family for help. That's how she came to Viareggio. She heard of a job through the church and moved here."

"The ladies at San Paolino still complain that the church is not as nice now as it was when Signora Vietro kept it."

"My mother made wonderful friends, until they found out about me. It wouldn't take long. They disappeared. But even Barbara liked my mother and stepfather. Barbara decided not to tell her parents about my status, and I didn't think it was my place to tell them. When her father went through the proper channels to find out about me, as parents will do when their daughter is in love with a young man without means, he was furious. Her father had gone to the priest to look for the Birtolinis of Parma, and he could not, in any of the church records, find me. This led to an exhaustive hunt for the fanciful tribe of one that I belonged to—which unearthed the truth, which ended the engagement. Signore Bevilacqua told me that he could not give the dowry for his daughter to a bastard, so he forbade our marriage. Barbara begged him to reconsider but he refused. The rich man looks after his money first, before his heart, his children, and your interests."

"My husband had a philosophy about the rich too. John would say, 'No matter how grand, every boat stinks of seawater and piss.'"

Silvio laughed. "I would have liked your husband."

"You would have. Very much. But you know, it's been nearly six years, and it's almost like our marriage happened to someone else. I prayed when he died that I would never forget him, but he has left me. I don't feel his spirit any longer."

"I'm sorry."

"I don't mean to make it sound so sad. There's more joy in my life than grief. I loved being John's wife. When I look back, there is nothing like the feeling of being responsible for someone else's heart. It was one of the great gifts of my life."

They walked through the dark winter night hand in hand. Neither would remember how many times they walked up and down the stretch of the boardwalk lit by pools of blue light. They found themselves at the end of the pier that reached out into the ocean like a black evening glove. Silvio reached for her. She put her arms around his neck.

"I don't mind that you loved him first," Silvio said.

"I loved John McVicars," Domenica said quietly, "but I didn't love him *first*."

"There was someone else?" Silvio's voice caught.

"I knew a boy in school. I used to boss him around."

"Is that all you remember about him?"

"He was funny. He was strong. He needed me."

Silvio held Domenica tightly until her feet left the ground as he lifted her to kiss her ear, her neck, and her cheek. The warmth of his touch in the cold night air made her feel that she belonged, something she hadn't felt since John died. Domenica rested her face on Silvio's shoulder; his neck had the scent of sweet pine, like the forest above the village at the end of summer. When they were children, they hiked those trails, drank from the stream, and sat under the shade of the trees, eating bread and butter. Silvio Birto-lini was an important part of her childhood. His friendship was the beginning of a lifelong love that would heal her.

Silvio had spent years hoping Domenica Cabrelli would wait for him. The daydream took on different aspects as he grew older, but the end of the story was always the same. She would love him as he loved her. When Silvio's lips found hers again, the sweetness remembered from a night long ago filled him with desire. He had not forgotten her; in fact, he had spent his life holding on to the feelings of that first kiss goodbye. As he kissed her face, he tasted her tears, which reminded him of the salty waves of the sea. Domenica had returned to him from the same sea that had kept them apart.

"I have a secret," he whispered as he took her face into his hands. "I came back because of you."

"How did you know I would be here?"

"I didn't." His eyes scanned the beach behind them. "This is the place of my deepest pain and highest dream. Both live in me, but I've learned that the love is greater than any hurt."

Domenica sat in the dark in her bedroom. Matelda and her parents were asleep. She couldn't rest—her mind was on fire after walking with Silvio. His kiss still made her tremble. She wasn't sure if she was afraid or jubilant. Domenica's heart raced with the revelation that she had found love again. How could this have happened? Two great loves in a lifetime when one love is not guaranteed.

Domenica pulled her jewelry case from the dresser drawer and carried it downstairs to the parlor. The fire was dying, orange embers twinkling in the grate above the powdery ash. She turned on the reading lamp. She sat for a while with the velvet box on her lap before opening it. She lifted the watch John had given her for their engagement. She hadn't worn it or wound it since he died. She held the cool green stone in her hand, turned it over, and ran her finger over the engraved initials. She was five years older now and had taken to wearing a wristwatch after the war. The watch fob had become too heavy to wear on her nurse's uniform. It was of another time.

Domenica sorted through the religious medals that represented the sacraments she had taken in her youth. Her wedding band from Mattiuzzi's Jewelers lay at the bottom of the box. She twisted the gold band between her thumb and forefinger. The gold was smooth and held the same shine it had when it was first placed on her hand. There were no nicks, scratches, or dents on the gold because the metal had never been tested.

Domenica put the ring back in the box. She would save it for Matelda.

Domenica wanted Matelda to know the father she had never met, but she didn't know how to keep his memory alive without the pain. As a nurse, she trusted the power of healing, but as a woman, she wasn't so sure.

CHAPTER 36

Viareggio

Now

O pen the windows, Anina." Matelda was propped up in her bed.

"I don't think the night air is good for you, Nonna."

"Do you want me to sleep? I can't sleep without fresh air."

Anina did as she was told. She slipped her shoes off and sat at the bottom of Matelda's bed.

"What's the matter, Anina?"

"I'm thinking about the Mattiuzzi family."

"It wasn't all tragic. Piccolo married Margaret Mary. My mother stayed in touch with them. They were the last link to that time in her life. And then there was Savattini the maître d'."

"Did he die on the ship?"

"He survived. By clinging to a tabletop from a stateroom. He broke his leg when he jumped, but he didn't know it until he was rescued. He was placed in a hospital in Liverpool, where he hatched a scheme to escape back to London instead of getting onboard another ship as a prisoner. The plot worked. They hid him in the kitchen at the Savoy until the war ended. When the

Mattiuzzis went to London on their honeymoon, they had tea at the Savoy. Piccolo thought he saw a ghost when he saw Savattini cross the dining room in his tuxedo. They had quite a reunion."

"What happened to the Franzetti boys? The family that had the pizza parlor?"

"They were interned in Australia. They ended up staying there after the war ended. I understand the grandsons are still there operating a chain of pizzerias." Matelda threw the coverlet across Anina. "You're really interested in the Scottish side of the family, aren't you?"

"It explains some things." Anina pulled the coverlet around her. "When you talk about Scotland, I feel like I've been there."

"I hope you will visit someday."

"You'll go with me."

"We'll see." Matelda smiled. "I've never gone back to Scotland. When I was a little girl, I promised myself that when I grew up, I would live there again. But it remained a childhood dream, which was for the best. You see, I couldn't hurt my mother. Scotland had caused my mother pain. She had endured enough of the ugly aspects of life, and I vowed not to make things worse or remind her of them. As time went on, living anywhere but here felt like a betrayal. Whenever I traveled with your grandfather, about three days in, I'd get antsy and start badgering him to come home. I missed my family, this house, and the ocean. I traveled a lot with your grandfather, and a few times we were close to the Lowlands. He'd say, *Let's go.* I was tempted but didn't follow through. Too many ghosts."

"I wish I had a hundred years with you, Nonna. Ghosts and all. I like how you lived in the old days. All the families together in one house."

"And we didn't kill each other. That's the miracle." Matelda chuckled. "After my uncle Aldo died in the war, and we returned to Viareggio, we lived with my grandparents. My mother decided to stay with her parents after she married Silvio, and he was happy to do so. And I was happy too. I had a father."

"Even though Netta didn't like Silvio?"

"They figured out a nice way to get along with each other. I think she grew to love him eventually. It might have occurred to Nonna on her deathbed. My nonna wasn't working with my father day-to-day. My grandfather was. I never heard the men argue about the business. They went to and from work together."

"You and Nonno had your fights."

"Most married couples fight about money, but I was the book-keeper and knew the numbers. I had the facts on my side, you see. Your grandfather learned to be a businessman, but it took years. He's an artist, and they're dreamers. Never trust an artist to hold the purse, because it will be returned to you empty. Olimpio and I were good for each other. We worked together. We held each other accountable. You need that in a good marriage."

"Paolo and I did fine with money. It was the intangibles we had trouble with—Don Vincenzo told me that the recipe for a happy marriage was Forgive. Forget. Repeat. I wrestle with *forget*."

"I do too. I hope I've been forgiven for my shortcomings," Matelda said quietly. "I hope you can forgive me, Anina. I know I've been difficult."

"We're good, Nonna."

"I'm glad. When I was young, my nonna Netta was impossible. And I couldn't understand why old ladies were so mean."

"I wonder about that too." Anina rolled her eyes.

"When you see an old lady who's on the wrong side of a good mood, now you know why. She has a past that you can't understand because you didn't live it. As she ages, her feet hurt, her back aches, her knees click, she cooks, she cleans, she worries, she waits, and then she gets sick and dies. Be kind, Anina. Someday you'll be the old lady."

CARNEVALE

February 1946

Domenica followed the screech of the bruting wheel when she entered the shop. She found Silvio in the back room working. "Busy day at the clinic," Domenica shouted over the sound before Silvio turned off the wheel. "One broken arm and two migraine headaches—the migraines are from the limoncello at Carnevale. Pretucci hates Carnevale. He says it's an excuse for drunkards and daredevils to act like fools and drink like fish."

"I'm almost done." Silvio tapped diamond dust in the tray into a box.

When he was finished with his work, Domenica put her arms around him. Silvio pulled her close and kissed her. "What would you say if I told you I didn't want to renew my agreement with Signora Pipino?"

"Where would you live?"

"I'd like to move closer to the shop."

"There are lots of rentals."

"I don't want to rent another room. I don't want to be in another room if you're not in it. Would you—" Silvio stammered.

"Yes."

"How do you know what I was going to ask?"

"I'm a strega," Domenica joked before placing her head on Silvio's chest. His heart was beating fast, which meant that she mattered to him. When Domenica had returned to Viareggio last fall with her daughter, it appeared that everything was broken, from the pier to the roads to her heart. She found herself tiptoeing around the pieces when she rediscovered the only thing that could make her whole. "I have to know if you love Matelda too. She is a good child, but the day will come when she will understand what she lost—and she may take it out on you."

"I can't be him. But I will love her as my own daughter. I will listen when she wants to talk about her father."

"We won't be the young couple who builds a family together," Domenica said wistfully. "I'm sorry I can't give you that."

"You gave me a family. There is nothing else I want. And now that I have it, I will protect it for the rest of my life." Silvio reached into his pocket and handed her a small box.

Domenica opened it and lifted out a ring. Silvio placed it on her finger.

"This ring is the symbol of our new life," Silvio began. "The blue sapphire for Il Tirreno, the purple amethyst for the thistle of Scotland, the yellow citrine represents the Italian sunflower, and the diamond is the clean slate. We have one, you know, as we begin again. We can choose to be happy together. Will you marry me?"

"Yes." She kissed him.

"I cut the stones just for you."

"I will never take it off," Domenica promised. "What can I give you?"

"It's not customary for the bride to gift the groom. But there is something you can give me. Our family needs a real name, not one my mother chose from a list. A barrister in Firenze made up the surname Birtolini for a boy without a father to claim him. We will be a family when we're married, and our family deserves a name worthy of it. I want to be a Cabrelli, if you'll have me."

Domenica was elated. She kissed him again. "We shall be Cabrelli."

The newly engaged couple walked home arm in arm to share the news with Netta, Pietro, and Matelda. They were waiting with cold champagne and cake because Silvio had already sought their permission before he proposed. All that was left for Domenica Cabrelli to do was to be happy.

Matelda slept in her bed in the alcove. Domenica gently brushed powdered sugar off her daughter's cheek before kissing her. Domenica hoped that Matelda was happy about the engagement and not just about having cake before bedtime.

Domenica reached into her closet and pulled out the hatbox where she kept important papers. She opened it and lifted out a stack of letters tied with a white satin ribbon. She tiptoed past her parents' room and down the stairs. She pulled on her coat, tucked the letters inside her pocket, and walked to the beach.

The firepits of Carnevale had died down; all that remained were circles of blue flames scattered along the beach. Domenica stood in front of the black ocean, holding John's letters. She held the only proof of their love. She had imagined, before Silvio came back into her life, that she would hold on to John's letters and read them when she needed reassurance that he had loved her, married her, and given her Matelda. Otherwise, what had happened between them would fade entirely like a dream.

John McVicars had been a squall that blew through Domenica Cabrelli's life. She learned that time could not be the measurement for the things that lasted. Sometimes what endured was that which changed us in a matter of moments, not years. John had not lived long enough to disappoint her, nor had they been married long enough for her to fail her husband. There had been no need for forgiveness; their time together had been brief.

John Lawrie McVicars had returned to the sea to live among the characters of myth, and the vagabonds, hustlers, and saints who found refuge in the deep. His spirit was protected by the granite waves that hemmed the rocky shores of northern Scotland. He no longer belonged to her.

Domenica threw his letters into one of the fires. A wind whipped up on the beach, igniting the paper. The letters soon burst into purple flames. The delicate paper formed tendrils of black ash, which floated out of the fire and into the air, where the wind carried them out to sea.

VIAREGGIO

Now

Matelda sat at the dining room table writing a letter. She folded it and placed it inside the stationery box.

"What are you writing?" Anina asked.

"Thank-you notes," Matelda said.

"I'm terrible about writing those."

"I know." Matelda shot her granddaughter a look.

"Mama, I brought you fruit," Nicolina said on the way to the kitchen.

"Enough. I'm going to turn into a papaya."

"It's on the list of foods the hospital recommended."

"Did you eat their food? They should not be handing out lists telling people what to eat," Matelda complained.

"Mama, Nonna is telling me the best stories." Anina straightened her grandmother's bedroom slippers on the footrests of the wheelchair. "I know the history of all of Nonna's jewelry."

"Good, because I don't," Nicolina teased them. "I kept meaning to sit with you and write the stories down. Now we have the time."

"Do we?" Matelda said softly.

"Don't be morbid, bella," Olimpio called out from the kitchen.

Anina sat down across from her grandmother. "I wonder what happened to Domenica's engagement band. The one with all the colors? I didn't see it in the box."

"That's because I don't have it. My mother was buried wearing it. It was her wish. I never told anyone about that ring until you, not even Nino. Of course, I was afraid he'd charge me for his half."

"He must have wondered where it went." Nicolina sat down with them.

"If he did, he never asked. A son might not come around much after he takes a wife, and he's not much help taking care of the elderly parents, but he rarely wants anything material when the parents pass away. Patrizia didn't ask for anything either."

"She wouldn't," Nicolina said. "She's not that kind of person."

"I wish he was more like Patrizia. My brother wanted more than jewelry, believe me," Matelda began. "Nino wanted the shop. But there were issues. My father wanted Olimpio to manage the shop and have Nino work for him. You see, Olimpio was a craftsman, and that was the tradition in the shop. It was about making things— it wasn't so much about selling them. Nino was a good salesman but a disaster at the wheel. When my brother saw what was happening, that's when he decided to move to America. That's when our Great Schism happened."

"Maybe it bothered Uncle Nino when you became Cabrellis."

"Don't think so. We were Cabrellis before he was born."

"I'm still a Roffo," Olimpio offered as he joined them at the table, "but I did promise Silvio that I would not change the name of the shop. He hoped his son would return to Viareggio someday. The family tried to mend things with Nino. I know I did."

"We all did. We went to visit them in America. What a trip that was. Nonna Netta, my mother, and me. We went to the shore in

New Jersey. It was pretty, but my grandmother Netta said, 'We have an ocean in Italy, and a beach too. We have to fly halfway around the world to sit in a different beach chair?' We saw Nino's factory. It was quite an operation. He was a successful manufacturer of—what would you call it, Olimpio?"

"Downscale costume jewelry. Known to the middlemen as a paste."

"That's it! Plated stuff. Not what we do here. He copied the fine jewelry we created here—Nino called them simulations. That's why Nino wasn't given the Speranza ruby. My father didn't trust him to make it into something of value," Matelda admitted.

"But he came around," Olimpio insisted. "After your parents died, Nino warmed up and would call from time to time and ask me things, and I did what I could to help."

"Did he still resent you for taking over the shop from Silvio?" Nicolina asked.

"He didn't seem to—by then, the old wound was scar tissue. Nino had made a success for himself in America, so the little shop in the village in the old country no longer mattered to him."

"The Cabrellis should have been united," Anina said.

"You would think so, after all they had been through," Olimpio agreed. "But the first thing that leaves in success is the memory of what it felt like to be poor. We shed that insecurity like an old pair of shoes the moment there's money in the bank. We slip into fine leather and forget how badly our feet used to hurt."

TREVISO

1947

Speranza spent two years working with the Americans in Berlin after the war. He provided them with the details of his work, the names of the men he had worked for, and the intelligence the Germans had hoped would die with him. When Speranza's work was done, he decided to return to Italy. As the train rolled through the countryside, he saw what the Nazis and Fascisti had done.

There were scorched-black fields where villages had been burned to the ground. The train would continue down the tracks ten miles or so, and the next village would be bustling with shops, people, and flowers in window boxes, gracious living intact, as though the whole pathetic mess had never happened.

Speranza had been too exhausted to sleep. The war had given him another gift: permanent insomnia. He stood up, gripping the train's luggage rack, and made his way to the sliding door. He opened it and stepped out onto the platform between the cars. He lit a final cigarette. The last miles of the journey home felt longer than the time he was away. Speranza barely felt the rumble of the train wheels as they sailed over the tracks. He was aware that most of the time he felt nothing. He had not wept much after the war, but the window boxes got to him. Life had gone on, but not his. Without Agnese, he walked the world like a ghost, and now he knew, they wept too.

Speranza had the clothes on his back and a rail pass back to Italy, a gift of the Americans. They had offered him a job in America. He politely declined. What good would that do him now? It was Agnese who had wanted to go to America. He would have followed her, of course, as was his habit. She made all the decisions; she was the architect of everything in his life that had worked.

Speranza's feet ached when he stepped off the train in Treviso. He was pleased to see the buildings still standing and the black gondolas floating in the canals. Returning to the Veneto meant he could breathe and move in the place where he had met Agnese and been happy. He didn't know what he would have done if they had leveled Treviso. It was the only proof he had that she had lived. Their romance began as they walked on the moss-covered streets of the city, along the pale blue canals. He would not return to the old shop or their apartment in Venezia. He knew it would break what was left of his heart.

As he walked through the streets of Treviso, Speranza did not recognize a single face and they did not know him. His world had the feeling of a graveyard now, nothing but stone markers and cold ground.

Speranza hitched a ride with a farmer to Godega.

The war had been a wily beast in Italy too; one side of the road, a house went untouched, and on the other side, for no reason other than bad luck, the Blackshirts had leveled the fences, barn, and farmhouse. It resembled the carnage of a tornado that blows through, there was no logic to the destruction. Speranza's stomach churned.

The men rode in silence until they passed the Acocella farm. Once prosperous, the dairy farm was leveled flat, the ground was covered in black char where the fields had been burned.

"It's been two years since the war ended. Why the smoke?" Speranza asked.

"That's the old farmhouse. Old Antonio made wine in the basement. He built tunnels underground to get between the barn and house during the winter. When the Nazis burned it, the alcohol fed the underground fire. When the spring rains came, I thought for sure it would put the fire out. They've tried, but it appears to be an eternal flame."

They chatted about the planting of the corn and wheat as though the German army hadn't occupied towns from Treviso to Friuli. The man didn't mention the prisoner of war camp, just forty miles north, which they could find if they kept driving.

"How is your farm?" Speranza asked the driver.

"We survived. For the first two years, we thought we were safe because somebody had to provide eggs and milk. The Germans had to eat."

Speranza nodded. He remembered how the Germans ate. Sausages. Ox. Fresh bread. Kreplach stuffed with a paste of ground chicken and beef. They ate with glee like gluttons while their prisoners of war rejoiced when they added potato to the broth.

"They took the Cistone farm. But first, they had Signora make them a fine meal. They ate well and drank their best wine. The next morning, before they departed, they burned it to the ground. They even took their horse. Where were you?"

"Berlin."

"In a factory?"

Speranza nodded.

"Lucky you survived."

"Am I?" Speranza said dryly.

Speranza was lucky until he went to the camp and learned of Agnese's fate. Up to that moment, he had been like his neighbor; he thought he had a chance.

The farmer stopped the truck. "Is this your farm?"

Romeo nodded. He offered the man money, but he wouldn't take it.

The truck drove off. Romeo began to walk the road shaded by a grove of cypress trees on either side. He looked down at the stone markers he had placed at the entrance. *Speranza 1924* was carved on the largest one, the year Romeo and Agnese Speranza purchased the property from the Perin family, who had picked up and sailed to America to do better and have more.

As Romeo walked down the familiar road, he noticed that from the bend to the house, flat fieldstones had been laid where there had only been dirt. He looked for his silo, the chicken loft, and the springhouse. All were intact. He wondered if his eyes deceived him. Was it a mirage?

The clapboard on the exterior was freshly whitewashed. The porch was swept. Was she here? Had Agnese escaped and made it home? His heart filled with anticipation. Speranza tried the door. It was unlocked. He pushed the door open.

The three-room house was as Agnese had left it. Speranza called out for her. He walked to the kitchen. He looked around before opening a drawer. He slid a long kitchen knife up his sleeve. He brushed his hand across the dining table—no dust. He went to the window. A soft breeze ruffled the paisley curtains Agnese had made from fabric she had purchased at the bazaar in Venezia. He walked through the house. The bed was made with a coverlet and feather pillows. The bathroom he had installed indoors as a gift to his wife was scrubbed clean.

Romeo went outside and walked to the back of the house. Across the green field, the breeze carried the sound of laughter and conversation from the one-room guesthouse beyond the spring-house. He walked in the direction of the sound.

Emos the shoeblack was chopping wood by the fence. He looked up. Romeo raised his hand to wave. Emos went into the house from the back.

"No! No! Emos, it's me," Speranza shouted.

Emos emerged from the front door with a woman who carried an infant in her arms. Soon a second child around age three followed them out.

Speranza watched them as they crossed the field. While he was busy wasting time in service to the enemy, life on the farm had gone on.

"Signore!" Emos ran to greet his padrone. "Welcome home! We've been waiting! Where have you been?"

"Berlin."

Speranza, who had not said a word or shed one tear when the

Americans brought him to Buchenwald to find his wife, began to weep.

"Oh no. No." Emos motioned to his wife. She took the children and went back inside.

Speranza removed the knife from his sleeve and handed it to Emos, who set it aside. Emos helped Speranza to the edge of the porch to sit.

"It's true what they did?" Emos asked.

"Signora did not make it out of the camp. She died there."

Emos's eyes filled. "She is safe now."

"I want to be with her," Speranza wept.

"But you cannot go because you want to," Emos told him. "Only God can call you."

Emos's wife emerged with a cup of water and handed it to Speranza.

"This is Eva. She worked as a servant for the Andamandre family until we married."

"Are you hungry?" she asked Speranza. "I will bring your dinner to your house. You may eat it there and rest."

"Thank you. I would like that," Speranza said to her. "Emos, how did you do it? How did you save the farm?"

"The Blackshirts never came up the road. Once, they looked at the place from the field, but for whatever reason, they turned back. Eva believes the farm is blessed."

"It's a small farm. That's all. My lack of ambition before the war kept them away. There wasn't enough here for them."

"They did terrible things to the Fontazza family. And that way, over the mountain, they murdered the people in the village. There was no plan. The evil drifted around us."

Emos led Speranza to the springhouse. The shallow, indoor pond was hemmed in fieldstone and filled with cold water from an outdoor spring. In the dark, the surface of the water appeared black. Emos removed a stone from the floor near the wall. He pulled a sack out of the hole and handed it to Speranza.

"There are dollars and lire and drachmas. And a pearl. I sell the eggs and save the money for you."

Speranza found the pearl among the coins. He rolled it between his fingers and held it up to the sliver of light from the half-open door.

"I was told it was valuable," Emos offered.

"It's not."

Emos smiled.

For the first time in a long time, Speranza smiled too. "It's all yours, Emos." Speranza gave Emos the sack.

"No, this is the rent. I have lived here for seven years."

"You took care of the farm."

"We have all we need. Food. A house. A garden. Our children."

"A man with children always needs money."

"I will hold it for you. The bank in the springhouse," Emos promised. "We will take care of you now."

"I can take care of myself."

"You must let us care for you."

"You are welcome to stay, Emos. I don't think I have the strength to farm the land any longer. I'll stay in the house, but you are not to take care of me."

"You don't understand, Signore. I promised Signora."

Speranza nodded. "You did? Va bene." Speranza was peace. Agnese was still the boss. They would do as she requested. They would follow her instructions.

Speranza sat down at his kitchen table for dinner. Eva had prepared a fine Venetian polenta with mushrooms and asparagus. The tomato gravy was tinged with cinnamon, as was the local custom. He cut a strip of the polenta and swirled his fork in the gravy. He took a bite, closed his eyes, and allowed the flavor of Agnese's recipe to flood his senses.

He did not remember a single meal he took in Berlin when he was a prisoner. He tasted nothing. Food was a way to survive and push through the workday, nothing more. Speranza was Jewish, but he was also an Italian. He did not know where one aspect of his identity started and the other ended, but the world no longer perceived him that way.

After he ate, Speranza went through the house, room by room. Every object he touched connected him to Agnese, and oddly, he was comforted. Speranza was an intelligent man. His wife, however, had been more curious than he; she had been an avid reader. As he perused her collection of books, he promised himself he would read them.

Speranza climbed into bed. He had dreaded going to sleep alone in the house they had built and the bed they had shared, but he shouldn't have. For the first time since the day they were deported from Italy, the country of their birth, Speranza slept deeply through the night, and he didn't wake until the sun rose the next morning.

VIAREGGIO

Now

Nicolina brought the bowl of paglia e fieno to the table. She tossed the fresh yellow and green noodles with parmesan and basil. Olimpio poured the wine. Anina placed salad on small plates. Matelda watched her family serve the meal as she used to do. "I feel useless," she said.

"Mama, enjoy it. Let us wait on you." Nicolina lifted the lid off a serving platter. "It's the season. Agnese's artichokes. I found the recipe in your box."

"Agnese taught my grandmother how to make them. I never met Agnese, but my mother loved her. They'd clear a floor of the house for them when they visited so they'd have plenty of space. The men worked in the shop, and my grandmother and Agnese would cook together."

Nicolina tasted the artichoke. "Pretty good."

Matelda was pleased that Nicolina knew how to make the dishes Agnese had taught Netta. Maybe she hadn't done such a terrible job of sharing the past with her daughter. "Speranza enjoyed his visits here after the war. My grandmother would make all his favorite dishes, as Agnese had taught her. He appreciated that his wife's cooking hadn't been forgotten after she was gone. It gave him back his ambition in a way."

"Nonna Domenica told me that Speranza was talented and good-looking. Evidently many women in the Veneto set their caps for him, but he didn't want another woman after Agnese."

"She told you that?" Matelda asked.

Nicolina nodded. "Bisnonna Netta told Nonna everything and she told me."

"I'm glad you talked." Matelda was pleased that her daughter had felt close to her mother. "Around 1949, Speranza began cutting gems again. He and my grandfather even collaborated on some projects for the church. Speranza was like family. I remember when we went to see him in Venezia too."

"What was he like then?"

"I was a teenager, and I wasn't paying close attention. In the mid-1950s, our little country was suddenly popular around the world. Italy had the Ferragamos, the movie stars, the Agnellis, and the cropped haircuts. All I wanted to be when I was sixteen was *older*. I wanted to sit at an outdoor café and drink espresso and smoke a cigarette. Of course, I couldn't smoke—my father would have had a fit—but I did have the espresso and the attitude."

VENEZIA

1956

Silvio Cabrelli drove over the Ponte della Libertà into Venezia. The city seemed wrapped in silver lamé, so bright under the sun Matelda squinted and could only see the shapes of the palazzi on the canal as she leaned out the window. The water in the canals was so still, it seemed to be made of green marble.

The cars stopped on the bridge. Silvio checked the rearview mirror. His black hair was showing the first signs of gray at age forty-seven. "Your papa is getting old, Matelda."

Matelda had just turned sixteen. Anyone over the age of thirty was old to her. "Papa, can I go for an espresso?" Matelda was slim and tall. She had cropped her hair short like the movie star Gina Lollobrigida, who had introduced the new "Italian cut" to the world.

The traffic moved. Silvio took the side streets until he found a parking spot in front of the bank. "Business first. You wait. And then I'll take you for your coffee."

"But you don't need me, Papa."

He smiled. "Go ahead." Silvio knew better than to attempt to negotiate with a teenage girl.

Matelda crossed the street and took a seat at a café table under a canopy. She slid her dark sunglasses from the top of her head over her eyes.

The young want to be old and the old want to die, Silvio thought to himself.

Emos drove the old Fiat up to the bank. He got out and helped Speranza out of the car. "I will wait for you here," Emos said.

"Silvio?" Speranza made his way up the steps of the bank to greet Cabrelli's son-in-law. They embraced. "How's my friend Cabrelli?"

"He drove my mother-in-law to see her sister in Sestri Levante." Silvio bit his hand in the Italian style. "He said to tell you he'd rather be here."

"He's a patient man." Speranza laughed.

Silvio followed Speranza into the bank. Speranza spoke with the manager. The manager brought the men into the vault room, where he unlocked a safety deposit box. Speranza lifted the velvet gem roll out of the box, placing it carefully on the table. He gently unwrapped the Peruzzi-cut ruby. The light in the room was dim, but the ruby caught all aspects of it in the facets of the shimmering stone.

"The best there is. Pigeon blood ruby from Karur." Speranza examined the ruby through the loupe. He handed the loupe to Silvio, who peered at the stone. "Your father-in-law was with me in India. This was the last stone I cut before the war."

Silvio gave Speranza an envelope with the payment for the ruby.

"Thank you," Speranza said, placing the ruby back into the velvet sleeve. "I thought about this stone, and I couldn't figure out what to do with it. It turns out it was my pension." He gave the ruby to Silvio.

"My father-in-law thanks you for the purchase of the stone. He has big plans for it."

"Cabrelli always has big plans. But unlike other dreamers I have known, he sees his vision through. He finishes what he starts. He's a true artist."

"That's what he says about you, Signore. What are your plans?"

"Now that I'm rich? I'm going to make a future for my family. Agnese was close to her brother in America, who had four daughters. I'd like to leave them something." Speranza smiled. "Agnese would like that."

On the drive back to the farm in Godega, Speranza was quiet. Emos looked over at his boss, who had drifted off to sleep. Speranza seemed to have pleasant dreams. Sometimes he would utter a word in Italian; other times he had a look of contentment on his face. Emos took these as signs that his boss was ready to be with Agnese once again.

"Life is a list, Emos. One by one, you check off the things you want to do and have to do, and soon you come to the end of the list. There's nothing more to do, you're finished, and it's time to die."

"You're tired today, Signore. That's all."

The sun set as Emos drove toward home. He pulled on the headlights in the old Fiat as he drove through twisting lanes of the Venetian countryside. The fields fell away in rolling blue folds from the road.

"Slow down, Emos. These farm roads are terrible."

"Forgive me, Signore."

"We've no reason to rush. The news won't get there before we will."

"I'm not going to let you do what you want to do."

"It's my money, Emos."

"But we're not your family."

"But you treat me as family," Speranza insisted.

"There must be a cousin, or a relative somewhere."

"I wired money to Agnese's nieces from the bank this afternoon. The rest is going to you and Eva. I deeded the farm and its contents to you. There is a copy at the barrister's office in Treviso, and one in the drawer of the nightstand in my bedroom."

"I can't accept your gifts. You have already done too much. You gave me a job and a place to live. My family is thriving. We have enough. You could sell the farm with me as the caretaker."

"Agnese wanted you to have the farm. You must honor her wishes."

"Thank you, Signore. It's so beautiful here that I have almost forgotten my home in Ethiopia."

"That means you love your new country. When an immigrant loves their new country, it changes the country for the better." Speranza leaned back in the seat. "Maybe you'll bring your family here when I'm gone."

"Eva would like that. Is there any place you'd like to go on holiday? Anyplace I can take you?" Emos asked. "The beach at Rimini? I can drive you to Viareggio."

"There's no place I want to go, but there are places I don't ever want to see again."

"Venezia?" Emos asked.

"Berlin. There were four of us in a small office. An architect, a professor, a mathematician, and me, the stonecutter. We slept in that office, worked there, and took our meals there. We made timepieces. Jewel movement."

"For whom? The consorts of the generals? The wives?"

"For the bombs. I try not to think about where the bombs with my timers landed, how many people they killed, and how many homes were destroyed. But knowing the Nazis, they hit their targets more often than not. So, as I cut the stones, I justified the job by telling myself I was building time itself, which would bring me one second closer to seeing Agnese again. Of course, like any of the promises made in Germany at that time, it was nothing but a con. You cannot buy time when it has been stolen from you."

The rooster crowed the next morning at dawn as it sat aloft the coop on Speranza's farm. Emos had already milked the cow, skimmed the cream, and set the clean bucket in the cool stream of the springhouse. He walked toward his house and the breakfast Eva was preparing for him when he felt an ache in his chest and stopped. He placed his hand on his heart and meditated. Soon the pain lifted. He looked over to the main house and was surprised to see that all the lights were on inside. Speranza was good about saving electricity, so the sight of the house ablaze with light from every window concerned Emos.

He walked to the main house and pushed the front door open. He stepped inside and found Speranza slumped over in his chair, over a book that rested in his lap. Emos rushed to his side. "Signore, Signore." Emos tried to wake him, but it was no use. Speranza was gone.

Emos gently lifted the book out of Speranza's lap and left it on the side table open to the page he had been reading. Emos went into the bedroom and grabbed the blanket off the bed. He lifted Speranza onto the sofa and laid him out straight on the cushions. He gently covered the finest man he had ever known with the blanket, now a shroud.

The shoeblack, now a keen and successful farmer who sold milk, butter, and cream in Treviso, sat down next to the body. He lifted the book off the table. On the endpaper was a book plate that read, *Return to Agnese Speranza*. Emos's eyes fell on the last words Speranza had read before he died.

I want you to realize that this whole thing is just a grand adventure.

    A fine show. The trick is to play in it and look at it at the same time.

    . . . The more kinds of people you see, the more things you do, and the more things that happen to you, the richer you are. Even if they're not pleasant things. That's living . . .

Emos moved the bookmark so he would not forget the passage from Edna Ferber's novel *So Big.* He had not been present for Speranza's final breath and last words, but at least he had the comfort of knowing the words his friend had been reading when the moment came. It was then that Emos knelt before Speranza's body and called on God in His heaven to welcome the good man home.

Eva appeared in the door. She joined her husband and knelt beside him in prayer.

Emos dug a grave in the field above the farm within twenty-four hours of Speranza's death, as was the Jewish custom. Eva and the children covered the soft black earth with branches of fresh cypress, until there was nothing but green.

Emos set the stone he had cut himself and looked up to the sky. "Signore, I am no artisan, but I hope this pleases you."

ROMEO SPERANZA

Husband of Agnese

Stonecutter of Venezia

1889–1956

CHAPTER 37

Home

Now

Anina pushed Matelda's wheelchair on the boardwalk; it creaked over the slats. Olimpio walked beside them. The ocean breeze wafted over them as the sun warmed the village in tangerine light.

"I don't think that the sky and the sea have ever looked the same twice in my lifetime," Matelda commented. "There's always something new."

"Are you warm enough?" Olimpio asked.

"I have more blankets on me than my mama used on the tubs to raise the Easter bread." The memory of kneading the dough, placing it in tubs, and covering it with baker's paper followed by layers of blankets, where it would rest in a sunny window until the dough rose, was inseparable in Matelda's mind from the memories of her mother, Domenica. "I still miss my mother. Isn't it funny? You forget plenty, but never your mother."

"Maybe that's all you need to remember," Olimpio said quietly, remembering his own mother, Marianna.

"Did your mother like me? You can tell me now. They're all gone," Matelda teased her husband.

"My mother thought you were a fine girl." Olimpio caressed Matelda's hair. "She thought you were blunt, but she appreciated your honesty. Most of the time."

"I'll bet she did."

"Nonna, do you want some water?"

"Please, Anina. I am up to my gills with water."

Anina's face fell. Matelda changed her tone. "But there's something to all the guzzling. I'm improving."

"Do you think you're ready to take that trip around the world?" Anina asked.

"Maybe." Matelda winked. "Where do you want to go?"

"Everywhere."

"You'll have to work hard."

"I'm working hard, aren't I, Nonno?"

"You're doing well. You could apprentice anywhere you wanted."

"Better she does well at Cabrelli's," Matelda said. "I hope my family keeps the business going after we're gone."

"I'm the fourth generation in the shop. Don't worry about the future, Nonna," Anina assured her.

"I will always worry."

"And there's good reason for that. The family business is forever in peril, a delicate operation," Olimpio offered. "There's a danger of going under every morning when you turn the key in the lock. The success of the family business lies in the ring of the cash register: how many times a day it rings, and how many times a day it doesn't. But I don't want you to think about it, my love. I want you to relax." Olimpio kissed Matelda.

"I want to learn the wheel." Anina looked at her grandfather.

"You want to cut stone?"

"Yes, Nonno, I do. Do you think I can do it?"

"Of course you can," Matelda interrupted. "Haven't I been telling you that for years?"

"It takes seven years to master the wheel," Olimpio reminded Anina.

"That's seven years I'd like to give to Cabrelli's."

Olimpio placed his hand on Anina's. He reached down and held Matelda's with the other. "You have a deal, Anina."

"Yoo-hoo? Matelda?" Ida Casciacarro stepped off the elevator and into Matelda's apartment. Ida looked all around, giving the apartment the once-over. The room was so bright, Ida did not remove her sunglasses.

"She's on the terrace, Signora," Anina called out.

Ida poked her head into the kitchen. "How is she?"

"She's getting stronger."

"Thank God!" She handed Anina a bag. "Sesame cookies. I made them myself. They're still warm. Whatever you don't eat today, freeze."

Ida joined Matelda on the terrace. "You look good, Matelda."

"No, I don't."

"You've lost weight."

"A little. Big deal. Everybody is thin in the end. And what good is it then?"

"Exactly." Ida laughed. "The sun is helping, isn't it? The healer in the sky."

Matelda whispered, "Where's my family?"

"They can't hear you."

"I'm going down the pipe, Ida. The end is coming soon."

"How do you know?"

"I don't have the breath to get those balls in that plastic box to jump."

"The breath machine." Ida clucked.

"Whatever the hell they call it. Those balls lie in the bottom of that cup like they're made of lead."

"I hate gizmos." Ida sat down. "Who wants to play breathing games at our age?"

"How's your grandson?"

"Lorenzo got another tattoo to celebrate his six months of sobriety. He's running out of limbs to cover. Do you remember, when we were kids, ever seeing anyone drunk in Viareggio? Never! What is wrong with my family? Thank God the Metriones are dead because the Casciacarros have hit the skids."

"Don't worry about him, Ida. He got sober. He's a strong person. You're a good family."

"Not good enough." Ida gestured with her hand.

Matelda laughed, but it caused her to cough. "Your family has seen worse."

"I know. That's where it comes from—they see worse, and therefore they do worse. What's the difference to them?"

"Anina canceled her wedding."

"I heard. She's a smart girl. A seer! She can see the future. Maybe she should be cutting tarot cards instead of rock. She is doing the right thing. Take a hard stand with that nonsense when they're young, because when men hit forty, it's over. It only gets worse."

"We push men through the midlife crisis, and ten years later they need a pill to get the train moving."

"You can keep the train. I jumped off that train and didn't even get a bruise," Ida confirmed.

The old friends laughed.

"I want you to get better, Picci."

"It's out of my hands. God's will be done."

"God's will," Ida said, echoing her friend's prayer. "My mother told me that she was grateful to have the time to sit and think before she died."

"Your mother was right. A little time is a big gift. All my life I worried about death. Not my own, but, you know, the kids, my parents. Friends. There's no way to prepare for death unless you're the one dying."

"Are you sure you're dying?" Ida looked into Matelda's eyes. "You don't have the look of death. You don't have the rattle. I don't see any signs."

"I don't know when, Ida. But it's getting closer."

Ida leaned in. "Is there anything you want? Anything I can get you?"

"I have what I need. I'm home. I have a nice wheelchair. Better than a Maserati. Keeps me right here, where I belong. That ocean is my salvation. It's been my constant companion, you know. My mental health. I come out here and talk to God. I've been doing it all my life. How lucky I am. I grew up in this house, I raised my family here, and I will die here."

"You Cabrellis with the villa. How many houses did Hitler bomb in Viareggio, and this one made it! Do you ever think about that?"

"That Nazi bastard got me good in other ways, so let's not get too excited about what we didn't lose."

"Did you hear about Bim? He dropped dead last night. You remember Bim? He was in our class. He was a looker. I always thought Bim looked like Robert Redford when he was young."

"How does he look now?"

"Robert Redford? Better than Bim. He looks like *The Way He Was*." Ida laughed at her own joke.

"It's awful to get old." Matelda sighed. "They're fussing over me."

"Let them. At a certain point, you get to be our age and look around the room and you realize that you've changed the diapers of every person that is taking care of you. So if they want to get you a cookie, or help you take a bath, let them. As long as they don't drop you." She checked her watch. "I have to go. I have a doctor's appointment."

"What's wrong with you?"

"My feet. My toes are so bad—when I'm barefoot, they look like I'm wearing the shoebox instead of the shoe."

"Are they that bad?"

"You will never know." Ida stood. "My feet are the only thing that's wrong with me, but feet are a big one. You need them to get around." Ida gave her a hug. "Do your exercises. Lungs are a big one too. You need them to breathe. I'll be back tomorrow."

"So soon?"

"What else have I got to do?"

Matelda heard Ida chatting with Anina inside. She sipped a short breath and another. She coughed. She tucked her hands under the blanket and raised her face to the sun. Ida Metrione Casciacarro was a good friend. Time spent with her was never wasted. They had kept busy at church. They volunteered as tour guides at the Villa Puccini. They went out to lunch, and when Ida was in the mood, she'd join Matelda on a walk through the village. They kept each other in the loop, but mostly Ida helped her remember. There are many gifts a friend brings to a woman's life. History. Empathy. Honesty. Lucky was the woman who kept a childhood friend because that friend remembered what you looked like, who you were, and your people. Lucky was the woman who had a friend from the age of ten, when girls were brave, gutsy, and full of questions and had the time and pep to seek the answers. That friend knew who you really were. That friend had seen your soul.

Nicolina joined her mother in her bedroom. She carried a tray with a cup of chamomile tea and a few of Ida's cookies on a plate. She set it on the dresser before going to her mother's bedside. "I gave Anina the night off."

"Do you think she's seeing Paolo?"

"I'm afraid to ask."

"Don't worry about her."

"All I do is worry," Nicolina admitted.

"Don't. It gives you wrinkles. Besides, Anina will do what she wants. She follows her heart and has a good sense of direction, from what I can see. When she realizes that she has the answers she won't look to Paolo to make her happy. She will commit to being an artist."

"Is that how it works?" Nicolina smiled.

"Yes. Until the end of time."

Nicolina pulled the table close to the bed and placed the tray from the dresser on it.

"So, it's your shift?"

"Yes, Mama. How am I doing? I'm not a nurse, you know." Nicolina straightened the blanket and fluffed the pillows. She handed her mother the cup of tea.

"It's in the genes. A life in medicine skipped my generation, but I thought it would get yours. Remember that doll hospital you used to run?"

"They were just dolls, Ma. There was no blood. Do you want me to raise the headboard?"

"It's fine. I don't want you to wait on me."

"I like it. Mama, you took care of me all my life; this is the least I can do."

"You have been a wonderful daughter. You have been a good mother too, Nicolina."

Nicolina turned away. She wiped the tears from her eyes on her sleeve before turning back to her mother. "Thank you."

"Don't cry," Matelda said.

"Too late," Nicolina said. "I waited twenty-five years for you to tell me that, Mama."

"You should've asked. Who waits around for a compliment? Ask for it. Then take it. And when you do, you realize you knew the truth all along and you didn't need anybody else's opinion in the first place. No one has to tell you that you did a good job."

Nicolina laughed through her tears. "You know what? You're right."

"Is there anything you wanted that you didn't get?"

"Nothing. Mama, I was thinking how rich we are. Not the shop and the business, but the important things. We had your parents live with us. And I had my great-grandparents too for a time."

"Wasn't it fun? When I was a girl, Nonna Vera came to visit during the summers. She took Nino and me to the beach a lot. She packed sandwiches made with ham and butter. They were so delicate and delicious, and she cut them up in shapes. Circles, triangles, and fish. She kept the sodas cold by wrapping them in a black cotton scarf."

"Nonna Domenica taught me how to sew."

"That's right. You should get the machine out and make something!"

"I might." Nicolina smiled.

"I hope all these stories don't get lost. Women like Vera. My mother loved Vera, so I loved her too. She was my prize. My extra grandmother. Vera Vietro Salerno. Silvio's mother. My mother's wonderful mother-in-law. Nobody talks about her anymore. It's so sad. The names get lost eventually, then forgotten. Great women gone and lost in our family history. Vera was a few years younger than my grandmother Netta. Vera had a lot of pep. But you know what I loved about her? She had been mistreated most of her life, and it did not turn her bitter. She was always looking to help people, to be of use. Always smiling." Matelda placed the teacup and saucer on the table.

"I will remember her, Mama. I will tell her story. And Bisnonna Netta's. And Nonna Domenica's. And even yours. Do you need a friend?"

"I'd like that."

Nicolina climbed into the bed and held her mother. "Mama, let's remember all your best meals."

"I was a good cook."

"No one better."

"Don't tell Ida. She's a little competitive."

"I remember your pastina. It's the first food I remember eating. The hard biscotti you made for Matteo and me when we were teething, and then you kept making them because we loved the taste. The tortellini. The manicotti with your crepes. The roasted chicken with sage, and the potatoes that went with them."

"You didn't like my ravioli?"

"I loved it."

"I thought so. It's so hard to make your children happy. The only way is through food."

"Just having you as my mother made me happy. You know I love you, Mama."

"I love you, Piccianina." It had been years since Matelda had called her daughter by her childhood nickname, which had also been her own.

"I wouldn't have wanted to be any other woman's daughter."

"You may have had a day or two." Matelda smiled before she closed her eyes. "And it would have been completely understandable. I'm not easy."

Anina lit the overhead work lamp with a single bright beam. She was alone inside Cabrelli's Jewelers on the main boulevard in Lucca. Night had fallen but she didn't notice it. She didn't check the time because she didn't care how long it would take. She could hear the laughter and conversations coming from the street as the young set in town headed out to the clubs. She looked up and smiled to herself. That used to be her routine. Soon, the sound of the car horns and their voices fell away as she concentrated on the task before her.

Anina slid the work goggles over her eyes. She flipped the switch to turn on the bruting wheel. She tapped her foot on the pedal, gently pumping the machine wheel. She cocked her head to listen for the sound it made when it was operating at the proper speed.

The apprentice picked up a sliver of peach quartz and held it against the rough edge of the wheel. It jumped between her fingers and out of her hands. She turned the machine off. Anina got down on her knees and looked for the stone. When she found it in a crack in the floorboard, she stood and held it under the light.

She heard her grandfather's voice in her head. She examined the quartz, turning it over to find the stone's point of strength. She adjusted the light and started the machine again. She hoped the stone would not shatter in her hand and tumble into the catch tray below the table. The stone felt substantial as she tilted it against the wheel, slowly grazing the quartz against the abrasive rim of the wheel. She held on to the stone, gently guiding it, shifting it slightly to create an edge on the cut. She heard the music of the cutting as the wheel spun faster, the notes climbing an octave. Anina stopped breathing as the quartz squared in her hand. The stone, cut by her own hands, had a top, smooth, without cracks or fissures. Anina stopped the wheel. She looked at the stone. The quartz grabbed the light. Cutting was all about the light. *Yes,* Anina said to herself, *yes.*

Anina sat with her grandmother on the terrace. "This is the best view in the village," she decided.

"I think so. But it's the only one I've ever known. Maybe the Figliolos have a better one."

"Maybe." Anina pulled the chair closer to her grandmother.

"I'm afraid, Anina."

"Are you in pain?"

"I'm all right if I don't move." Matelda grinned.

"So don't. Are you afraid of death?"

"No. Not at all. We're promised that the afterlife will be beyond our imaginations. I'm looking forward to seeing what that could possibly be. But I am afraid I won't recognize John McVicars when I meet him in heaven."

"Maybe you won't recognize him, but he'll know you."

"That's actually wise." Matelda nodded. "You with the tattoo knows about the afterlife?"

"Nonna, a jab? Really?" Anina took her grandmother's hand and squeezed it affectionately. "I'm trying to help."

"I'm sorry. I say whatever I'm thinking and half the time it's just rot."

"It's your sense of humor. Don't apologize for it now."

"My humor is so dry, it could be the bread crumbs in your meatballs. Well, that's what happens as you get older. You lose your patience, and it's replaced with sarcasm. I can't help it. I look around and what I see is stupid. You will find out for yourself when you're my age. It's the sign that it's time to go." Matelda took sips of air. "Have you heard from Paolo?"

"He wants me back."

"Do you think you'll take him back?"

"The Ulianas are good people. A little overbearing. His mother texts me to see how I am. She says she doesn't care whether I go back with her son or not. She says she loves me."

"Who cares what she thinks?"

"You told me, 'You marry the family.' I should have it tattooed prominently."

"No tattoos! I didn't mean what I said. You marry the man. It was my attempt to get you to think with your head and not your heart. Can I take it back?"

"You can do whatever you want, Nonna."

"If Paolo makes you feel that everything is possible, marry him. If you think you have to make everything possible for him, don't marry him. A woman appreciates support; a man needs to believe he did it all on his own. It's ridiculous but accurate." Matelda shielded her eyes from the setting sun. "Is there still a bottle of prosecco in the refrigerator?"

"Would you like some?"

Matelda nodded. Anina went into the kitchen and opened the bottle of prosecco and poured two glasses. She had made her decision about Paolo. It wasn't anything he had done; it was what he had left undone. He had not taken an interest in her dreams. It was never a bad idea to listen to her grandmother.

Anina gave Matelda a glass of prosecco and toasted her.

"No, no, let's toast you," Matelda said, holding up her glass. "Screw Paolo Uliana."

"Nonna."

"Listen to me. Love yourself. That's the greatest adventure. When you love yourself, you want to find your purpose, something only you can do in the way only *you* can do it. Make things. Create. And if a man comes along—and believe me, he will—the relationship is already off to a good start because both of you love the same person. *You.* Lucky him."

The church bells rang in the distance. Matelda hummed along to the melody of the chimes.

Nicolina prepared her mother's breakfast in the kitchen. She placed it on a tray and brought it out to the terrace. "I don't miss those bells in Lucca. Every hour on the hour is too much," Nicolina said as she placed the tray on the table next to her mother. "Mama, Matteo is coming today."

"Again?"

"Yes. He wants to see as much of you as he can."

Olimpio carried the moka pot to the terrace and poured a cup of espresso for his wife.

"You eat," Matelda said to her husband, pushing the tray of food toward him.

"I had my breakfast." Olimpio gently pushed the tray back toward her.

"I don't feel like it."

"I can make you an egg, Mama. Would you like an egg?" Nicolina asked.

Olimpio held Matelda's hand. "She's cold as ice. Get a blanket, please."

"I don't feel cold." Matelda watched the seagulls circle in the distance over the beach.

Matelda was calm. The priest had brought her Holy Communion. She had given her confession, and as a bonus, he offered her the Anointing of the Sick. She happily accepted the sacrament. In her mind, it was insurance. She did not want to do anything between this moment and the hour of her death that might prevent her from seeing the face of God. Her conscience felt buoyant in her body. For any evil she had done, she had asked for forgiveness.

She had not wasted time. Women rarely did. They squeezed each moment out of the day serving others. But the good left undone? Had she been enough? Done enough? No answer came, but it wasn't her problem anymore. Her final desire was to leave this world in a state of grace. *His will be done* would be her redemption. The only thing left for her soul to do was the business of her salvation. Matelda took a deep breath and did not cough. Her lungs opened to the sea air like a bellows.

Nicolina returned with the blanket and Anina.

"Isn't it beautiful?" Matelda looked at the tourmaline-blue sea. She had waited for spring and the color to return, and miracle of miracles, it had. Even though she hadn't put her feet in the sand, she felt herself sink into the powdery bliss as the sea water filled in between her toes, making clay from the tide, then puddles cooling the soles of her feet. Little pink fish gathered around her feet and nibbled at her toes. Far away on the horizon, billows of coral clouds settled in the light, making a path to the sun. Matelda squinted down the hemline of the white shore, when she saw her mother on the beach. Matelda sat up in her chair. She saw a little girl run toward her mother. She recognized the girl. *"Domenica! My Domenica,"* she whispered.

It was then that she heard the braying of an elephant, or was it the trumpet voluntary of the angels, or Puccini's revelry? Whatever it was, the sound was sweet.

Nicolina followed her mother's gaze and surveyed the beach. "Do you see something, Mama?"

"She said *Domenica.* Nonna, what do you mean?" Anina asked her.

But Matelda did not hear her. As she began to leave the world, their voices and words became a language she did not know. Each aspect of her person began to fold, one into the other, until her soul rose from her body. She felt herself become faceted light, rays of the brightest white sun set in the deepest blue.

Matteo sprinted out onto the terrace. "Mama!" He leaned down and kissed his mother. "You look good, Mama."

Matelda did not hear him.

"It's me. Your Matteo," he said loudly before looking desperately at his father, sister, and niece. "Something's wrong with her. Call the doctor!" When his father didn't move quickly enough to his liking, Matteo, frustrated, stood and felt his pockets to find his phone.

Anina knelt before Matelda. The perfume she had spritzed on her grandmother that morning filled the air with the scent of gardenia. Anina buried her face in Matelda's neck. She whispered, "It's all right, Nonna. Go to your mother."

Matelda took three short breaths and bowed her head. Anina stood.

Olimpio knelt before his wife, placing his hands on hers. He made the sign of the cross.

"What happened? Do something!" Matteo took her wrist. "Don't go, Mama." But there was no pulse. Matteo cried and turned away.

Nicolina stood behind Matelda with her hands placed gently on her mother's shoulders, protecting her like an archangel. Tears silently flowed down her cheeks. In the bright sun, Nicolina's face appeared to be made of varnished plaster like the saints in the courtyard at San Paolino.

Even though the ocean had called Matelda all her life, it had just been a lure to catch her eye. In fact, it was the sky overhead that would become the gateway to the eternal. It was the sky Matelda would reach. Her soul would ascend through a portal of clouds to a brocade of stars where she would find her mother and daughter, the father who raised her, and the father she never knew again.

"Fly." Olimpio wiped his eyes with his handkerchief. "Fly." He kissed his wife goodbye. Anina turned away and wept until the sea her grandmother had loved became a blur of blue.

The bells of Chiesa San Paolino rang as Matelda McVicars Cabrelli Roffo was carried out of the church and into the morning light fractured by the cypress trees. Olimpio stood behind the casket with Matelda's brother, Nino, and his wife, Patrizia, followed by Matelda's children and grandchildren. The spring day was neither warm nor cold, but suitable for one of Matelda's beloved walks through the village.

Ida Casciacarro nodded to Giusto Figliolo, who took her arm as they processed behind the casket and family out of the church and into the piazza. Row by row, the ushers directed the standing-room-only crowd to recess.

"I can't believe she's gone," Ida whispered. "She kept telling me she was going to die; I just didn't want to believe her."

"She knew, Ida." Figliolo remembered the day Matelda had given him a golden apple. "If we pay attention, we will recognize the day and the hour."

"It's that bird. That fat seagull! The bastard nipped her and marked her for death. If the superstition hadn't killed her, the germs would've."

"You talked to a strega?"

Ida shook her head that she hadn't. "I have a little strega in me, you know. The Metriones could be seers when none were available. When that bird attacked her, I thought, *The end is near.*" Ida dabbed her eyes with her handkerchief. "I don't like being right."

Anina turned to look at the crowd of mourners who had gathered on the church steps behind the family. Paolo Uliana smiled at Anina and formed two fists with his hands. He mouthed, *Coraggio.* She nodded her head in gratitude. Paolo's parents stood behind their son.

The procession followed Olimpio and the family to the cemetery for the burial. The priest said the final prayer. Matelda's family and friends covered the casket in flowers.

The family led the mourners down the street to Ennico Bakery. Umberto had made fresh trays of cornetti glazed in apricot, and plenty of coffee with cream to serve with the pastry. He had blocked off the street with tables and chairs dressed in white cloths and festooned with vases of peonies and roses. Matelda's funeral and reception went as she had planned.

The terrace doors at Olimpio and Matelda's apartment were open. Beppe slept in the sun. Argento, the cat, rolled on the terrazzo underneath the dog's chair. The turquoise sea was calm. Inside, Matelda's grandchildren helped set up the luncheon. Nicolina handed them her mother's best china and silver. The pressed-linen napkins were placed next to the luncheon plates. Anina rearranged the pink peonies in a vase before setting them in the center of the table.

Olimpio sat at the head of the table as the designated mourners milled around the apartment, taking in the details of the everyday life of the woman they gathered to mourn. Their home was as it had always been, except Matelda was no longer there.

Nicolina placed her hand on her father's shoulder. "Eat something, Papa."

"I will."

"Shall we get started?"

Olimpio nodded. Nicolina called the guests to the table and seated them.

"This is a Matelda move if there ever was one," Ida whispered to Giusto as he held out her chair to sit. "We're the only people here who aren't blood family." She sniffed and snapped the stiff napkin open and placed it on her lap.

"I'm honored to be here," Giusto said softly.

The light conversation that underscored the luncheon soon subsided as the guests finished a delicious meal. Anina and Nicolina made sure the guests had their fill.

"Matelda had my tortellini on occasion, but I never tasted hers," Ida shared. "Not bad."

"I have all the recipes." Nicolina smiled as she refilled Ida's water glass. "My mother loved you and your cooking."

Ida burst into tears, weeping into her napkin. "I loved her too."

The silver urn began to chug as the coffee percolated. Anina and Nicolina cleared the dishes and placed cookie trays down the center of the table. They served the guests coffee with the help of Nicolina's sister-in-law, Rosa, and her daughter, Serena. Once all the guests were served, Nicolina took her place at the head of the table and stood next to Olimpio.

"My mother asked me to invite you here today, into her home. She lived in this house since she was four years old. She was born in Dumbarton, Scotland. Her parents married in Manchester, England, on June 3, 1940. Mama was born eight months after her father, Captain John Lawrie McVicars, died on the *Arandora Star* on July 2, 1940. My mama and her mother, Domenica Cabrelli McVicars, waited in Scotland at the convent for five years for the war to end, and when it was over, they returned home to Viareggio. The only father my mother knew was Silvio Cabrelli, who was wonderful to her. Silvio was Domenica's first love and they married when he returned to the village to work for Pietro Cabrelli. My grandfather Silvio took the name Cabrelli to carry on the tradition of our family business. Mama loved her only brother, Nino. They lived happily in this house with her parents, Netta and Pietro, and Silvio's mother, Vera, visited during the summer."

"That was a lot of fun," Nino remembered. "Vera was a pistol."

"You know our mother. She chose the menu, the flowers, and the guest list. My brother and I don't know the details of what happens next, so forgive us in advance. We will be as surprised as you are, as we follow her instructions."

Nicolina went to the safe and opened it. She lifted the velvet box out of the safe. There was an envelope resting on top of it. "There's a letter—" Her voice broke. She brought the box and the envelope back to the table and read the letter aloud to the guests.

My beloved family and friends,

In this box: history. My history and now yours because you will own a piece of it. There is something for each of you. You may not like what I chose for you, but in time, you will come to appreciate that it was more important for me to have selected something for you than it was for you to like it.

A laugh rolled through the gathering. Nicolina continued to read:

Before Nicolina disburses the gifts herein, I want to thank her and my son, Matteo. I thank their spouses, Giorgio and Rosa. I thank my grandchildren, Anina and Giacomo, Serena and Arturo.

I thank my brother, Nino, and his wife, Patrizia, and their daughter, Anna. And most of all, I thank my lover and husband, Olimpio, who had to put up with my nonsense but always did so with such grace. You made a good life for us, and you were a great steward to my grandfather and my father's family business.

My friends, I want to thank you all for being polite as I got older. I forgot facts, stories, and numbers. Day-to-day, a slip of the memory doesn't matter much, but when you add them up over time, they're a landslide called old age. Remember me in the rubble.

These jewels made me think of you. So think of me when you wear them.

And a big kiss,

Matelda (Mama, Nonna, and, to the old-timers, Picci)

Ida nudged Giusto. "Class," she whispered.

The box was filled with a series of small envelopes with a handwritten note on each parcel from Matelda to the person receiving the gift. Nicolina went around the table and handed out the envelopes.

"This is like Christmas," Ida said as she opened her envelope.

Dear Ida,

I wore a string of pearls that my mother gave me every day of my life until my mother died and I stopped wearing them. I never liked them. I'm not a pearl person. But you are, Ida. You admired

them often. I hope you weren't humoring me, because if you were,
too bad, Ida, you're getting the pearls.

                                        Your friend,

                                        Picci

"She didn't have to do this," Nino said.

"She wanted to, Zio Nino." Nicolina gave her uncle the Santa
Lucia medal that Vera Vietro and Silvio gave to Domenica when
they were children. "For you, Zia Patrizia—" Nicolina gave her
aunt the ruby cluster ring.

Patrizia cried, "Look what she wrote to me." She showed Nino
the note, which read, For my long-suffering and most excellent sister-
in-law.

"Kept her sense of humor to the end. Dry and droll." Nino
shrugged.

As the relatives opened their gifts, their sadness was replaced
with giddy joy as they shared the notes Matelda had left behind.

The platinum brooch with sapphires went to her daughter-in-
law, Rosa.

The gold earrings from Domenica's childhood went to her
granddaughter Serena.

"Help me with the clasp, Giusto." Ida leaned over as Giusto
snapped Matelda's pearls around her neck.

The ruby cuff links made and worn by Silvio went to her grandson Giacomo.

The gold pocket watch that Pietro gave to Domenica when she
was banished to Marseille went to Giusto Figliolo. The note read,
Dear Giusto, I hope you live to be one hundred.

Matelda's wedding band, which had belonged to her mother,

Domenica, from John McVicars, the diamond from Olimpio, and the aquamarine bracelet and earrings went to Nicolina.

The Vatican medal bestowed upon Olimpio and Matelda by Pope John Paul II for their service went to Matteo.

Silvio's San Antonio medal went to Arturo.

Silvio's watch went to Giorgio—For my wonderful son-in-law.

Netta's wedding band went to Nino's daughter, Anna.

The aventurine watch fob that was given to Domenica on her engagement to the captain went to Anina.

The Speranza ruby went to Olimpio—Please, Olimpio, do something with this ruby. It's time. When I see Speranza and Agnese in heaven, I am certain they will ask.

"Anina, this is also for you," Nicolina said.

"But I already have Bisnonna's watch fob." Anina opened the second envelope and looked inside.

"What is it?" Ida said gently.

Anina read the note aloud.

When you marry someday, offer this wedding band to your husband. It belonged to my father Silvio, who you know now was my stepfather. I never knew my father, John McVicars, and Silvio Birtolini Cabrelli spent his life trying to make up for that loss. My papa Silvio kept his own counsel all his life when he had no reason to believe in himself. Born poor, without a father to claim him, he could have taken the wrong path. But his mother, Vera Vietro, taught her son to love no matter how poorly he was treated. I was not of his bloodline like my good brother, Nino, but Papa never made me feel that I wasn't, nor did Nino, for that matter. When you choose a husband someday, choose wisely. This gold band was worn by the man who chose to be a Cabrelli.

Nicolina stood in her stocking feet in her mother's kitchen, rinsing the final platter from Matelda's funeral luncheon. "That was the longest day of my life."

"It just feels like that, Mama"—Anina took the platter and dried it—"because you had to talk to so many people. You had to read Nonna's letter. No one knew how hard it was for you to speak in public. You did a good job."

"Grazie. When I die, please don't tell anyone I still had social anxiety when I was fifty."

"It will be the first line in your obituary." Anina climbed the step stool. Nicolina handed her the stack of clean dishes. "I can't believe how many people turned out for Nonna today."

"Mama was loved in this village. Seventy-seven years is a long time to live in one place."

"I wish you would've named me Matelda. It's such a pretty name."

"I gave you a family name. I named you for Uncle Nino. Sort of. We were close when I was little, and I always said I'd name a child after him. But Mama and her brother were feuding when Giacomo was born, so I named him after the Tizzi side. When you were born, I thought if I named you after Uncle Nino, it would heal the rift between my mother and uncle once and for all. That's where I got the name Anina. But even that didn't work. Mama and Uncle Nino put each other on the island through the years as though they bought a time-share on it."

"The island?"

"That's what we called the place Mama sent her brother when she wasn't speaking to him. I never told you about it because I didn't want you to pull that nonsense with your brother."

Anina laughed. "We get along just fine. The only island we go to is Ischia for the annual clam festival."

"Keep it that way."

"You could have named me Domenica."

"Do you want to change your name?"

"No, I just think it's odd that we don't have a Domenica in my generation."

"There's a good reason for that. When I was seven or so, and Matteo was ten, Mama got pregnant. She told me that if the baby was a girl, she was mine, and if it was a boy, it was Matteo's. We were always competitive, but this was ridiculous. We both wanted another sibling, and we waited for that baby like it was Easter Sunday. Anyhow, Mama went to the hospital, and when she came home, she didn't have a baby. We found out later that she had a little girl, but she was stillborn. Mama had named her Domenica."

"Poor Nonna."

"And here's the crazy part. I loved my baby sister, Domenica, and I never met her. Now, how can that be? How can you love someone that you don't know and never will, but they are as real to you as anyone in your family?"

"Nonna loved her father the sea captain, and she never met him. She cried when she told me about him. So I guess you can love someone you've never met."

"She cried?"

"She did."

"I can count on one hand how many times I saw my mother cry. When she came home from the hospital, she cried when she dismantled the bassinet. It was white wicker and she had covered it in tiny yellow bows. It took her days to make the bassinet."

"You remember it in detail, Mama."

"Because the baby mattered to me. I longed for my sister my whole life. Mama was a different person after the baby."

"Mama, why didn't you tell me about your sister?"

"I didn't want you to be afraid to have your own child someday."

"It doesn't scare me, Mama." Anina embraced her mother. "Now it makes sense. When Nonna was dying she said, *Domenica.* She saw her daughter."

"Do you think so?"

As Anina held Nicolina, Anina promised herself she would name her daughter Domenica someday. Domenica Cabrelli.

Anina sat in her grandmother's chair on the terrace when she heard Beppe bark and the glass door slide open behind her. "Do you need something, Nonno?" she asked, keeping her eyes on the sea.

"Ciao, Anina."

Anina turned and faced Paolo. She wore an apron over the dress she had worn to the funeral. Her feet were bare, and the mascara she had cried off formed two black shadows under her eyes.

Paolo pulled up a chair. "I'm sorry about your grandmother. She was a great lady. My parents said it was the biggest funeral they ever attended at San Paolino."

"Thank you. I was glad to see you there. Please thank your parents for coming."

"I will. We didn't think it was appropriate to go to the coffee afterward."

Anina managed to smile and took his hand and squeezed it before letting it go. One of the things that attracted her to Paolo when they met were his manners. "You and your family are always welcome."

"It's funny." He smiled. "I feel that."

"How have you been?"

"All right. I moved back in with my parents, but not for long.

I'm going to Barcelona. A couple of friends invited me to come and work at their start-up."

"Congratulations. That's great news! I didn't know."

"How would you know? We don't talk anymore." Paolo looked down at his hands.

"We will. I spent the last few weeks with Nonna."

"I didn't have a problem with you spending time with your grandmother."

"I know. I said some things I shouldn't have. And I probably did some things I shouldn't have. But I learned a lot from her in the past several weeks. I'm going to try to do better. I'm going to try really hard not to control everything in my life. That includes the people I love."

"I didn't want you to let go of me."

"But look what happened when I did. You got a job! I wanted things to go well for you so much I prevented them from happening."

"No, Anina. You encouraged me."

"I tried. But I also held you back with my own fear about things. I wanted you to be happy in a job you loved, but I didn't take time to find out what it was you loved to do. I was an obstacle, and now you have a good position. It's all connected."

"If you say so."

"I'm sorry I got caught up in getting married. Who cares about the parties. The dress. A diamond ring."

"Your family is in the jewelry business."

Anina laughed. "Right. But it shouldn't just be about the accessories that go with a commitment; it should be about the marriage."

"You're working with your grandfather?"

She nodded. "I'm learning the wheel."

Paolo sat with Anina until the sun, the color of a pat of butter, began to melt into the sea. Every once in a while, he would turn to her in the light, and she'd forget why she had let him go. Her heart still leapt at the sight of him, but she couldn't admit it. Not to him, anyway.

If Paolo knew that she still had feelings for him, he might have given up the job in Barcelona. But he no longer felt he had the right to ask her about her heart. He lost her trust and believed there was no building it back.

"I should go." Paolo stood.

Anina walked him to the elevator. He got in.

"Paolo?"

She held the button that kept the doors open.

"Yes?" he said.

"Life is long."

"Are you giving me hope?" He smiled.

"There's always hope." Anina let go of the button. The doors closed. Anina placed her hand on the watch fob. She unpinned it from her dress and held it up to her ear. She heard the gentle ticking of the gears. "Nonna!" she whispered. "It works!"

Nicolina offered to stay after she straightened the apartment and prepped the moka pot for breakfast the next morning, but Olimpio insisted she go home to Giorgio. Anina was already asleep in the guest room. For the first time since Matelda died, Olimpio was alone. He sat in his pajamas and reread the note Matelda had left for him along with the Speranza ruby.

Olimpio,

This is Papa's manifesto. He wrote it the night he took the name Cabrelli. Will you print it up and give it to our children and the grandchildren? I forgot I had this and meant to share it. Papa was right. A family is only as strong as their stories.

Love you,

M.

MANIFESTO DE LA FAMIGLIA

Family. We are the barnyard, the circus and the stage, the forum, the playing field and the track. We are the structure, the architecture, and the stronghold. We are the comfort, the solace, and the dream. Our connection is our sustenance and hope. If the survival of the family is left to whim or chance, consider it neglect and the family dies at the root. We must put the family above work, play, and ambition. There must be a plan to grow and prosper. Life is less without family, it becomes a series of events, a bore, a litany of miseries and a slog toward loneliness. Without a common goal, productivity and industry are replaced with a slow decay followed by want. When the family fails, so goes the world.

Silvio Cabrelli
1947

Olimpio went on to read Silvio's coda.

I have told my grandchildren the story of the elephant, which was told to me by Pietro Cabrelli, my father-in-law. He heard it from a man he met in India many years ago. The elephant died at the end of the story, but through the years, I changed the ending because it seemed to scare the children, so I let the elephant live. Dear family, you are the author of your destiny. In your hands is the ending of your story and the start of a new one each time a baby is born. God knows what He's doing.

Olimpio folded the document and placed it back in the envelope.

Olimpio filled Argento's kibble bowl and gave Beppe a snack bone. He grabbed one of Ida Casciacarro's sesame cookies off a tray in the kitchen and nibbled on it as he went through the apartment and turned out the lights. He made his way up the stairs to their bedroom. He sat on the edge of the bed and finished the cookie. He went into the bathroom and brushed his teeth. He performed the ritual without looking at himself in the mirror.

Olimpio returned to the bedroom. He folded the coverlet down to the end of the bed. He slipped out of his bedroom slippers and climbed into his side of the bed. He reached his hand over to Matelda's side. He had kissed the same woman good night for fifty-four years, and now she was gone. All his life he had wondered what a broken heart felt like because he had never known its pain. Now he knew. He began to weep uncontrollably. After a while, he sat up and wiped the tears on the sleeves of his nightshirt. He heard Beppe scratching outside the door. He turned on the light. He got up and let the dog in, but strangely, Argento was behind him. The cat and dog had never slept in their bedroom. The dog had a bed under the stairs, and the cat, for all he knew, wandered through the house at night until she found a bookshelf to her liking.

Olimpio looked down at the dog and cat. "What are we to do, my friends?" he said aloud. Olimpio turned to go back to bed, but instead of going to his side, he went to Matelda's. He slid under the covers. He turned off the light. He put his hands behind his head and looked up at the dark ceiling as if it were a bare stage in a theater. Young Matelda appeared on the stage. He joined her in the moment that they first met. He watched their love story as it unfolded. He remembered what she wore, how she moved, her scent and her smile. She had been the only woman in his life he could talk to; believing this might be the key to a happy marriage, he kept the conversation going. He loved one woman, and what a woman she had been.

Beppe jumped up on the bed and rested his head on Olimpio's chest. His master was gently petting the dog when he felt four cat feet walk up his leg to his chest. Argento proceeded to take a spot on the pillow between Olimpio and the headboard. The three mourners soon fell asleep and remained together until the sun rose.

CHAPTER 38

————

Glasgow

Now

"Here, Nonno." Anina unlatched the seat-back tray table on the airplane in front of her grandfather.

"Don't baby me, Anina."

"You should baby *me*. Check your ticket. It's August twenty-eighth. I was supposed to marry Paolo Uliana today."

"Should we turn back?"

"Not anytime soon, Nonno."

Olimpio smiled. "Did you read the contracts that I left for you?"

"Yes. I have some questions."

"I hope I have the answers."

"If you don't, the lawyers will. You're easy to work with, Nonno. You say what you mean."

"Do I? Your grandmother called me a mule. And I can be. My people were farmers in the Lombardia. When I came to Toscana to work, your great-grandfather Silvio gave me a job. He trained me. I started out just like you."

"When did he retire?"

"He didn't. But I taught him something too. Silvio would cut stone seven days a week. If he didn't have a commission, he would take in work from other jewelers to stay busy when the shop was fallow. I tried to explain that the fallow time was the gold. Fallow is when an artist dreams. Thinks. Imagines. The constant grind of the wheel wears down the gemstone and the artist along with it. You'll never know how hard it was for me to convince him to turn off the wheel."

"Did he ever do it?"

"By the end, my father-in-law understood what I was talking about. I'd catch him strolling on the boardwalk, stopping to drink from the fountains. He'd play cards in Boncourso's garden with the other old men. He learned that if you keep your head down at the wheel, you don't see what's up. You miss life."

By the time Olimpio and Anina picked up their luggage and made it through customs at the airport in Glasgow, Scotland, it was early afternoon. Their first appointment with a new buyer wasn't until the next morning. They dropped their luggage at the hotel and set out on foot to explore the city for the first time.

The sun peeked in and out of periwinkle clouds that floated over the city in patches of blue. Glasgow's neighborhood along the north end of the river Clyde was a mix of charming brick buildings, rambling factories, and new shops. High-rises with mirrored windows were set in the background reflecting the cityscape.

Olimpio and Anina entered the bronze doors of Saint Andrew's Cathedral. The nave was bathed in golden light that poured into the church from the windows along the vaulted ceiling. The pale walls, light marble floors, and oak pews conjured a field of wheat in bright sun.

"It's like being on the inside of a wedding ring," Anina said to her grandfather. "A lot of gold." They blessed themselves and genuflected at the main altar. Anina made her way to the alcove that held a statue of the Blessed Lady. She looked up at the serene Mother, hands extended, gown flowing as her foot crushed a plaster snake curled around a blue globe. Anina fished in her purse for change. Olimpio stood back as Anina deposited the coins into the box and lit a candle on the votive tray. She knelt, closed her eyes, and folded her hands in prayer. A few moments later, she stood and blessed herself. She turned to her grandfather. "Nonno, do you want to light a candle?"

"Did you light one for your grandmother?"

"I did."

"We're covered," Olimpio said, but changed his mind as a particular thought caused his brow to furrow. He reached into his pocket, retrieved a coin, dropped it into the box, and lit a candle. He knelt to pray.

"Nonna will appreciate it." Anina patted her grandfather on the back.

"It wasn't for her." Olimpio stood. "It was for Domenica. Your grandmother was never the same after we lost the baby. It was a sadness that she carried with her until the end."

Anina followed her grandfather outside.

The Italian Cloister Garden was placed inside a stone wall next to the cathedral. The iron gate to the garden was propped open.

Olimpio stood at the entrance and read aloud from his phone. "The garden was designed by a Roman architect. Giulia Chiarini." He put the phone in his pocket, clasped his hands behind his back, and walked among the mirrored glass sculptures in the center of the outdoor space. "We've come all the way to Scotland to see the work of an Italian."

A stream of rushing crystal water ran through a silver trough that cut through the tall shards of glass etched with wisdom from philosophers and poets and saints. Anina explored the space until she found the plinth of names of the Italians and crew who died on the *Arandora Star*.

"Nonno, come over here."

Olimpio joined her at the wall and peered up at the names. "That's him." Olimpio was emotional. "That was Matelda's father." It would have meant the world to his wife to have seen proof that John Lawrie McVicars had lived and died, and had been honored for his service, in this Italian garden in Scotland. "I should have brought her here," Olimpio said with regret.

"You can't do everything you want to do in one lifetime," Anina said, sounding a lot like Matelda. She unrolled the tracing paper and placed it on the plaque. She pulled a pencil from behind her ear and rubbed over the letters. Soon, her Scottish great-grandfather's name emerged in blocks of gray on the field of white paper, as though McVicars himself was coming through the gray clouds to greet them.

"Anina Tizzi!"

"Yes, Nonno?" Anina continued to stencil her great-grandfather's name.

"Is that a tattoo on your arm?"

Anina's sleeve had revealed the new tattoo as she stretched to stencil the McVicars name. "Don't look."

"Your grandmother hated them."

"She might have liked this one."

Anina slipped the pencil behind her ear, rolled up her sleeve, and showed her grandfather the tasteful tattoo. *Matelda* was drawn in a delicate swirl of India ink on the underside of her arm between her elbow and her hand.

"How did they do that?" Olimpio was intrigued.

"They're artists. I had them copy Nonna's signature from a

check she sent me on my last birthday. I never cashed it. I had a plan all along, I guess. Do you like it?"

"I think I do." Olimpio was surprised at his reaction.

"I'm glad. I'm a wee bit Scottish after all, you know. A bit of a rebel."

The sky opened up without warning, as it did in Scotland. Rain poured down from the heavens above on the Italian tourists with a particular intention.

Anina shoved the tracing paper under her jacket to protect it.

Olimpio buttoned his coat and looked up.

"Come on, Nonno. Run!"

EPILOGUE

***

𝕶𝖆𝖗𝖚𝖗, 𝕴𝖓𝖉𝖎𝖆

Now

A slender boy of eleven kneels in a pit in the red earth. He digs in the dirt, going deeper with his hands, where he has made a trench over the course of a few months. It's his trench—he dug it alone. It's about two feet wide and five feet deep. His T-shirt is tied around his head because he hasn't got a hat to wear in the hot sun. He gets some relief when the pink clouds cover the sun in the lapis sky. He is barefoot and shirtless, and his shorts, which are too large, are knotted at the waist to hold them up. Embroidered in large letters around the leg of the shorts, it reads, Nike.

An empty basket rests on the ground in the hole next to him. He picks up a stone shaped like an arrowhead and taps against a vein of rock in the open hole. He lowers his head to the ground. About twenty feet away, his brother digs in a similar fashion. He is ten feet below ground, but he is older and more experienced in aboveground mining, so he's faster.

Scattered across the immense field are more boys from their village, doing the same work, using the rock-on-rock technique, seeking the same result. They are listening for a hollow sound, where rock has turned to ruby.

The boy softens the earth around the rock. The ground is wet, which means snakes, or an underground stream. The Amaravati River is close by. After the spring rains, there is mud as the water retrenches underground, with fingers of streams that reach for miles. There's an ancient story about an elephant that died on the banks of the river, after saving a haul from a mine in a mountain, and now, centuries later, lush greens grow where she perished. They're called elephant's ears in her honor.

The boy taps the arrowhead rock against the embedded stone, loosening it. He pulls the rock free. It's about the size of a large man's shoe. He taps the rock against the side wall of the hole. He removes the T-shirt from his head.

The rock is heavier than a fieldstone of similar size. His hands tell him that this rock is different. It feels spongy, but there are also dense grooves and pits in it. He grazes his fingers over the raised columns of hard rock, running through the fissures. There are cool rivulets of stone that feel like glass. He buffs the rock with his shirt. One side is striated in gray and black like any ordinary stone. His heart sinks. But a gut instinct tells him not to give up.

The boy turns the rock over and buffs the underside with his T-shirt. The fabric snags on something. There are points on the underside. He grabs the ends of the T-shirt and rubs it across the points; clumps of red earth dislodge and fall away. The boy begins to sweat because he is excited about the rock's prospects, but he's tentative because he is not accustomed to good news, nor does he trust his own eyes. He finds glints of gold and streaks of blood red in the striae of the rock so dark it appears to be purple. Pigeon blood ruby. He knows it because the dealers let him hold a similar stone once. He retained a picture of that ruby and sees it in his mind every night before he goes to sleep, visualizing that one day he will find one just like it. And now, he has. His heart swells and feels as though it might explode inside his small body.

He wraps the rock in his shirt and climbs out of the hole. He surveys the muddy field speckled with boys as far as he can see. He calls to his brother. "Aaie!" he shouts. His brother runs; he knows by the urgency in his younger brother's voice that he has found the treasure.

The boys working in the field drop their tools and climb out of their trenches. "Aaie!" they shout. Soon a small army of boys runs to the one holding the rock. They encircle him.

If one boy finds a ruby, they share the yield equally. When they share the yield, they eat. They are family connected by something much deeper than one name. There is one table and all are welcome to the feast.

The boys jump and holler and dance in celebration of their good fortune. The boy holds the ruby high in the air for all to see. The lucky one lifts his face to the sun and shouts, "Life!"

ACKNOWLEDGMENTS

This novel is about how we live and what we leave behind after we go. Of course, you, beloved reader, will tell me that it's about a lot of other things too—and always, at the center of everything, or at least the stories I attempt to tell, is the family. I dedicate this book to our daughter, Lucia. Her arrival in this wonderful and weary world has made our lives worth living. Named for my maternal grandmother, Lucia Bonicelli, our daughter inherited her good heart, empathy, and eye for detail.

When Lucia was five years old, I asked her what she wanted to be when she grew up. I expected her to say teacher or artist or astronaut, instead she said, "Nice." She understands the moral obligation of kindness. Nobody taught her that—it's just *in* her. I hope, in addition to God's gifts, that she has been presented with a set of values that will sustain her long after we are gone—and of course, the greatest of these is love.

I am honored to be published by the great folks at Dutton and Penguin Random House. I return to the fold under the magnificent leadership of Ivan Held, a trusted, longtime friend who embraced this novel with enthusiasm and support. Maya Ziv is a glittering star in the pantheon of young editors, and I am lucky to work with her again. Sometimes fate throws a rose your way, and I will cling to Maya as long as she allows it. My deepest gratitude to Dutton's spectacular team: Christine Ball, John Parsley, Lexy Cassola, Amanda Walker, Stephanie Cooper, Katie Taylor, Jamie Knapp, Hannah Poole, Caroline Payne, LeeAnn Pemberton, Mary Beth Constant, Katy Riegel, Chris Lin, Julia Mehoke, Susan Schwartz, Ryan Richardson, Dora Mak, and Tiffany Estreicher. More gratitude to the PRH Sales team, who puts the books in your hands. Kim Hovey is a gem. Vi-An Nguyen created a cover that tells the story inside in glorious color and detail. The interior design is as beautiful as I have ever seen in any novel. Pat Stango is the great technical wiz at PRH.

At PRH UK, I am grateful to Clio Cornish, Lucy Upton, Gaby Young, Madeleine Woodfield, Deidre O'Connell, Kate Elliot, Hannah Padgham, Louise Moore, and Maxine Hitchcock, and the irreplaceable Eugenie Furniss, and Emily MacDonald of 42. I am grateful to Tara Weikum, Danielle Kolodkin, and my old friends at Harper's, and to Suzanne Baboneau and Ian Chapman of S&S UK.

At *WME*, thank you to the petite dynamo and my longtime champion Suzanne Gluck, thank you to the beloved Nancy Josephson, Jill Gillett, Andrea Blatt, Nina Iandolo, Ellen Sushko, Wesley Patt, Caitlin Mahony, Oma Naraine, Tracy Fisher, Sam Birmingham, and Alicia Everett.

At *Sugar23*, I am thrilled to work with the high-octane team of Katrina Escudero, Sukee Chew, Michael Sugar, Esmé Brachmann, and Viola Yuan. At Sunshine Sachs, the great Brooke Blumberg drives the bus. My gratitude to the producers, Laurie Pozmantier, Larry Sanitsky, and Katherine Drew. Richard Thompson of Breechen Feldman Breimer Silver & Thompson, LLP, is the best attorney in the business.

My evermore thanks and love to Bill Persky, mentor, dad, friend, and pal, whose creative genius on the page and stage has made all of our lives richer, better, and more fun.

Gail Berman is the sister I call to solve problems and point me in the right direction. My gratitude for your wisdom and loving heart.

Michael Patrick King, whether it's the morning call or the panic at midnight, you are there; I thank you for all you are and all you do.

The Glory of Everything Company is led by Alexa Casavecchia, smart, tireless, and focused. Thank you to Alexa and our team: Emily Metcalfe and Maxwell Seiler, who bring you *Adriana Ink*, along with Andrea Rillo, the brilliant artist behind our social media campaigns. Our interns are the future stars of tomorrow. Thank you: Jacob Cerdena, Jaden Daher, Emma Freund, Ashley Futterman, Paige Michels, Steffi Napoli, Annika Salamone, Maddie Smith, and Lauren Taglienti.

Cynthia Olson conducted meticulous research and worked tirelessly to bring veracity and historical context to the events in the novel. In Italy, thank you to my family, Andrea Spolti, Paolo Grassi, and Andrea Pizio. My great uncle and journalist, the late Monsignor Don Andrea Spada, was the longtime editor of the *L'Eco di Bergamo*. The great newspaper and its superb articles informed the contemporary arc of this story.

I took a class at Christie's Auction House in New York about the jewels of the Maharajas & Mughals in India at the invitation of Kristin Dornig, which provided the core knowledge that became the bedrock of this novel. The Montaquila family, longtime jewelers in Connecticut, gave me insight into the mechanics of jewelry design. Thank you, Madeline.

If you are interested in the expulsion of men and boys of Italian descent in Scotland during World War II, I recommend Peter Gillman and Leni Gillman's *'Collar the Lot!' How Britain Interned and Expelled its Wartime Refugees* for further reading. *Inside Europe* and *Inside Latin America* by John Gunther provided insight into the political, economic, and moral state of the countries of Europe before and during World War II.

Among the reading for broader historical context to the events in this novel, I read books by H. G. Wells, Erik Larson, Philip Paris, Donatella Tombaccini, and Oswald Mosley. Benito Mussolini's *Es-*

says on Fascism is a primer on the diabolical cunning of dictators. For truth and beauty, please consider reading Helen Barolini's *Crossing the Alps*, Kinta Beevor's *A Tuscan Childhood*, Franco Zeffirelli's autobiography *Zeffirelli*, and *Giuliano Bugialli's Foods of Tuscany*.

We owe a great debt to our nurses, without whom there would be no healing. I am humbled to honor their work and the stories they shared with me on these pages: Thank you to the good nurses of Saint Vincent's Hospital emeritus, New York City, and the Poor Servants of the Mother of God at St. Mary's Hospital, Norton, Virginia. Catherine Shaughnessy Brennan provided insight into geriatric nursing. My sister-in-law Brandy Trigiani, an oncology nurse, inspired the relationships of the young nurses in Saint Joseph's Hospital in Marseille. The late Irene Halmi served as a nurse in World War II, her stories of that time were treasures. Ralph Stampone, honorably discharged from the U.S. Navy in 1946, provided knowledge into medical procedures during the war.

The story of the Italian immigrant in Scotland could not have been told without the story of Nina Passarelli, who boarded at the Notre Dame de Namur Convent School at Dumbarton during the war. Nina's daughter Anna shared the stories passed down to her in detail. Sadly, Nina passed away as I was writing the novel. I am grateful to the entire Casavecchia/Passarelli bella famiglia for sharing Nina's life with me. Thank you, Anna, Joe, Erica, and Joseph Casavecchia, and Joseph Casavecchia Sr.

The cast and crew of *Then Came You* 2020 made me fall in love with Scotland and her people. The majesty of the countryside reminded me of my Appalachian home. Thank you, Kathie Lee Gifford, for trusting me to direct your movie/baby. Andy Harris, our set designer, showed me the timeless beauty of his country, which Reynaldo Villalobos, the great cinematographer, captured expertly. Megan and Craig Ferguson, my favorite castle keepers, made sure Scotland would remain in my soul long after leaving it.

Thank you to the powerhouse Italian Americans: Louisa Ermelino, Mary Pipino, Joe Ciancaglini, Robin and Dan Napoli, Mario Cantone and Jerry Dixon (IBM), Gina Casella of AT Escapes, Angelo and Denise Vivolo, Anthony and Maria Tamburri, Aileen Sirey, Eileen Condon, Pat Tinto, Rossella Rago Pesce and Nick Pesce, Brenda Vaccaro, Lorraine Bracco, John Melfi and Andrew Egan (IBM), Joanne LaMarca, Caroline Giovannini, Mary A. Vetri, Ed and Chris (Pipino) Muransky, Gina Vechiarelli, Beth Vechiarelli Cooper, Dominic and Carol Vechiarelli, Denise Spatafora, Lora Minichillo, Dolores Alfieri Taranto, Dominic Candeloro, Marolyn Ferragamo Senay, Theresa Guarnieri, Carla Simonini, Donna DeSanctis, Marisa Acocella, Violetta Acocella, Susan Paolercio, Regina Ciarleglio, Josephine Pellegrino, Florence Marchi, Anthony Giordano, Lisa Ackerman, Christine Freglette, Miles Fisher, the women of NOIAW, the Sons and Daughters of Italy, and the Columbus Citizens Foundation. The incomparable author David Baldacci is my honorary brother and coach—there is no one better.

In this era of loss and suffering, so many magnificent family and friends have passed to the next life, and we mourn them in this one. My family mourns our cousins Bobby Ferris, Ignatius Farino, Eva Palermo, Constance Ciliberti Bath, Constance Rose Ruggiero, Connie Butler, and Catherine "Kitty" Calzetti. We also mourn Great Aunt Lavinia Perin Spadoni and Aunt Peggy McBain.

The Virginians: From Big Stone Gap to the capitol, we remember Senator John Warner, Carolyn Bloomer, Dr. Henry David Patterson, Ginny Patterson, Ben Allen, Midge Hall, Paula Sue Gillespie Isaac, David Isaac Jr., Morris Burchette, Johnny Cubine, Butch Lyke, and N. Brent Kennedy. *The Miss Americas*: Phyllis George and Leanza Cornett. They were beauties inside and out, and loving mothers. *Glenmary priest/pastor/writer/rabble rouser*: Father John Rausch was my spiritual counselor since I was a girl. I was blessed to know him.

Beloved actors/artists/writers/designers (and not just by me): James

Hampton, Leila Meacham, Ed Stern, Mary Pat Gleason, Walter Hicklin, Jay Sandrich, Lynn Cohen, Robert Hogan, Alice Spivak, Rebecca Luker, Monty and Marilyn Hall, Dorothea Benton Frank, and Willie Garson. *Angels*: Melissa Smith's son and Susan Sanders's grandson; Logan Smith, Shannon DeHart, Patricia Lynn McMahon Vogelsang, Aunt Pauline "Polly" Harold, and James Natel Gomes de Oliveira Filho.

The New Yorkers: Bunny Grossinger, the great Charlie Weiner (Lynn's husband, generous and kind), Sonny Grosso (half of *The French Connection* and full stop Italian American), Dorothy Tota of Long Island and Cartier's, and Dr. Emil Pascarelli (Dee's husband and as fine a man as ever lived).

The Fathers, good and kind men: Victor Peccioli, Dr. Vincent De-Franco, Marvin Gilliam, Vincent Festa, Joseph V. Trigiani, Jordan Barnette, Bruce Kerner, Jack Carrao, Alfred Shelton, Dennis Richard Myers, Joseph B. Rienzi, Eddie Mugavero, Gregory Piontek, Robert E. Isaac, Sr., Joe Toney, Ronnie Coughlin, L. C. Coughlin, Steven Goffredo, Jack Hurd, and Bernard Passarelli.

We will hold these beautiful mothers in our hearts forever: Doris Emmerson, Betty Joyce Ball, Patti Webb Cornett, Marie Castellano, Barbara Ann Festa, Nellie Millet Williams, Esther D. Wing, Jean Hendrick, Evadean Church, Carlotta Browder, Janet Salerno Bellanca, Nancy Cline Toney, Eleanor "Fitz" King, Ardeth Fissé, Dolores "Dee" Losapio, Marie Trigiani, Rita Joan Holwager, Susan Cooperman Tannenbaum, Theresa Joan Winiecki, Portia McClenny, Marie Salerno, Cheryl Scarelli, Rosalyn Mugavero, Nina Coughlin, Martha Bolling Wren Ford, Billie Louise Peters Gabriele, Norma A. Siemen, Jean DeVault Hendrich, Rosalia Helen LaValley Pentecost, and Marie Casavecchia.

The loss of Shirley Cavallo, visionary/chef/designer and owner of La Locanda Del Cavallo in Easton, Pennsylvania, is enormous. I learned a great deal from her sumptuous and gorgeous largesse at the table, in the garden, and in her home. Her beloved son Brondo, my honorary brother, carries on her spectacular work.

James Huber Varner drove the Wise County Bookmobile. When I was a girl and he stopped in Big Stone Gap, it was always an event. He was never without a smile or a recommendation for this young reader. I adored him.

The wonderful educators changed the world and live on in the keen intellects of the students they taught: Dorothy Ruggiero, Dr. George Vaughn, Peggy Vaughn, Connie Clark, and Anthony Baratta will be missed.

The Origin Project serves over 2,500 students in grades 1 through 12 in my home state, Virginia. The program's Appalachian roots have grown a garden of talented young, published writers. The in-school writing program would not exist without executive director and co-founder Nancy Bolmeier Fisher's vision and pluck. Our deepest gratitude to Ian Fisher and Ryan Fisher. Linda Woodward keeps the wheels on the bus, and Rhonda Carper rotates the tires when we need it most.

Thank you to *The House of Love* team at Viking, who brought joy during the process of writing this novel, while my first children's book was illustrated by the incomparable Amy June Bates. Thank you to my brilliant editor Tamar Brazis and her team: Olivia Russo, Ken Wright, Denise Cronin, Lucia Baez, Jed Bennett, Leah Schiano, Alex Garber, Lauren Festa, Carmela Iaria, Summer Ogata, and Shanta Newlin.

Thank you, Ernestine Roller and Billie Jean Scott, the librarians who welcomed me into their school libraries in Big Stone Gap with open hearts. I owe a great a debt to them.

My evermore thanks to: Jean and Jake Morrissey (the only two friends in the world who would actually pick up the phone at 2 a.m.), Tony Krantz and Kristin Dornig, George Dvorsky, Bruce Feiler, Mary Ellen Fedeli, Ron Block, Dorothy Isaac, Dianne and Andy Lerner, Spencer Salley, Jayne Muir, Nigel Stoneman and Charles Fotheringham, Kim Isaac DeHart, Liza (Brian) and Jamie (Mark) Persky, Ali Feldon, Alan and Robin Zweibel, Lou and Berta Pitt, Doris Gluck, Tom Dyja, Wiley Hausam, Dagmara Domincyzk and Patrick Wilson, Philip Grenz, Christina and Willie Geist, Joyce Sharkey, Jody and Bill Geist, Jackie and Paul Wilson, Sister Robbie Pentecost, Karen Johnson, Roland LeBreton, Steven Williams and Michael Stillman, Heather and Peter Rooney, Aaron Hill and Susan Fales-Hill, Mary K and John Wilson, Jim and Kate Benton Doughan, Joanna Patton, Polly Flanigan, Michael Morrison, Angelina Fiordellisi and Matt Williams, Michael La Hart and F. Todd Johnson, Richard and Dana Kirshenbaum, Karen and Gary Hall, Michael and Rosemarie Filingo, Nancy and Jimmie Kilgore, and Kenny Sarfin.

I am honored to be published so elegantly in the country of my roots. Thank you to the team at Tre60 in Milan: Stefano Res, Cristina Prasso, Chiara Ferrari, Valentina Russo, Barbara Trianni, and Giulia Tonelli.

Thank you to the glorious women whose friendship I treasure: the great *attriche* Mary Testa, Ruth Pomerance, Elena Nachmanoff, Dianne Festa, Wendy Luck, Jasmine Guy, Jane Cline Higgins, Helene Bapis, Monique Gibson, Liz Travis, Cate Magennis Wyatt, Sharon Ewing, Kathy McElyea, Mary Deese Hampton, Sharon Gauvin, Dori Grafft, Dana Chidekel, Mary Murphy, Nelle Fortenberry, Dee Emmerson, Norma Born, Christina Avis Krauss, Rebecca Pepin, Jueine D'Alessandro, Barbara Benson, Eleanor Jones, Veronica Kilcullen, Andrea Lapsley, Mary Ellinger, Iva Lou Johnson, Betty Fleenor, Nancy Ringham Smith, Michelle Baldacci, Sheila Mara, Hoda Kotb, Kathy Ryan, Jenna Elfman, Janet Leahy, Courtney Flavin, Susie Essman, Aimee Bell, Constance Marks, Becky Browder Neustadt, Connie Shulman, Sharon Watroba Burns, Sister Karol Jackowski, Elaine Martinelli, Karen Fink, Sarah Choi, Robie Scott, Pamela Stallsmith,

Candyce Williams, Margo Shein, Robyn Lee, Carol Fitzgerald, Robin Homonoff, Zibby Owens, and Kathy Schneider. Thank you, Betty Cline, my honorary mother.

More gratitude and love to: Emma and Tony Cowell, Hugh and Jody Friedman O'Neill, Whoopi Goldberg, Tom Leonardis, Dolores Pascarelli, Eileen, Ellen, and Patti King, Sharon Hall and Todd Kessler, Charles Randolph Wright, Judy Rutledge, Greg and Tracy Kress, Mary Ellen Keating, Lorenzo Carcaterra, Max and Robyn Westler, Tom and Barbara Sullivan, Brownie and Connie Polly, Beáta and Steven Baker, Todd Doughty and Randy Losapio, Craig Fissé, Steve and Anemone Kaplan.

When they say you never stop grieving the loss of your mother, they are right. I thought about my mom, Ida Bonicelli Trigiani, a great deal during the process of writing this book. My grandmothers were with me during the process. Somehow, my grandmother Viola Perin Trigiani found her way into the subconscious of Matelda Roffo and stayed there. My dad, Anthony, is never far from my thoughts when I write about the creative life and/or dictators. (He would find that hilarious. Maybe.)

I thank my brothers and sisters, their husbands, wives, and families. Dave and Carol Stephenson are about the best in-laws you could hope for—their son, my husband Tim, can fix anything, including broken spirits. He's stuck with me and that's that.

I am grateful to two priests. Reverend Joseph M. McShane, the great Jesuit, has given his life and heart to Fordham University, among others. He leaves a long shadow. And secondly, to the priest at Saint Andrew's Cathedral in Glasgow, who invited me to visit the garden in honor of the Italian Scots who perished on the *Arandora Star*. A chance encounter sparked this novel and a true story was revealed that changed the way I look at the world. Father, though I don't know your name, I will never forget you. Mille grazie.